I0716552

Pasola

Maria Matildis Banda
Translation from the Indonesian by
Yuni Utami Asih

Dalang Publishing
San Mateo, California

Dalang Publishing LLC

San Mateo, California

www.dalangpublishing.com

dalangpublishing@gmail.com

Names: Banda, Maria Matildis, author. | Asih, Yuni Utami, translator.
Title: Pasola / Maria Matildis Banda ; translated from the Indonesian by Yuni Utami Asih.
Description: San Mateo, California : Dalang Publishing, [2024] | Originally published
             in Indonesian as Pasola. Indonesia : Penerbit Nusa Indah, 2022.
Identifiers: ISBN: 978-1-7357210-8-8 (print) | 978-1-7357210-9-5 (ebook)
Subjects: LCSH: Horsemanship–Indonesia–Sumba Island–Fiction. | Weaving–Indonesia–Sumba
             Island–Fiction. | Friendship–Fiction. | Interpersonal relations–Fiction. | Sumba Island
             (Indonesia)–Social life and customs–Fiction. | BISAC: FICTION / World Literature /
             Asia (General)
Classification: LCC: PL5089.B29 P3713 2024 | DDC: 899.22133–dc23

ISBN: 978-1-7357210-8-8

Ebook: 978-1-7357210-9-5

Pasola

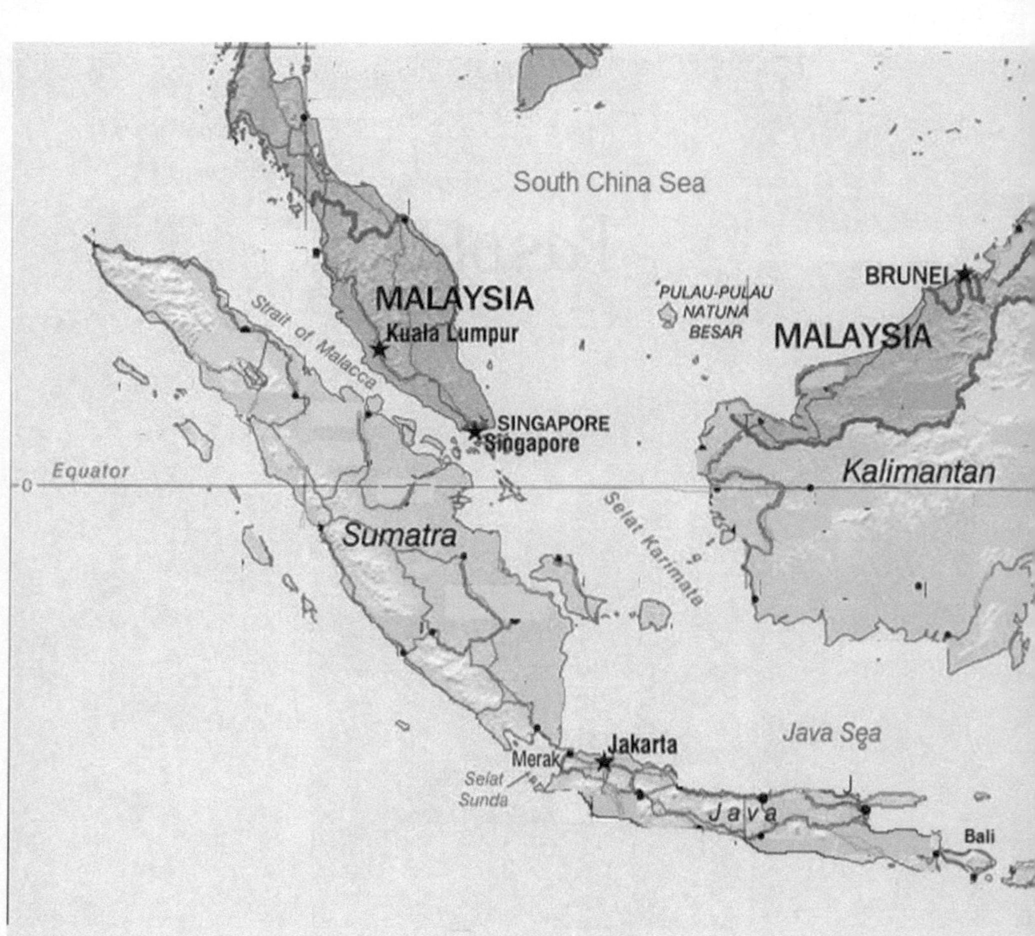

South China Sea
MALAYSIA
Kuala Lumpur
Strait of Malacca
PULAU-PULAU
NATUNA
BESAR
BRUNEI
MALAYSIA
SINGAPORE
Singapore
Kalimantan
Equator
0
Sumatra
Selat Karimata
Jakarta
Merak
Selat
Sunda
Java
Java Sea
Bali
INDIAN OCEAN

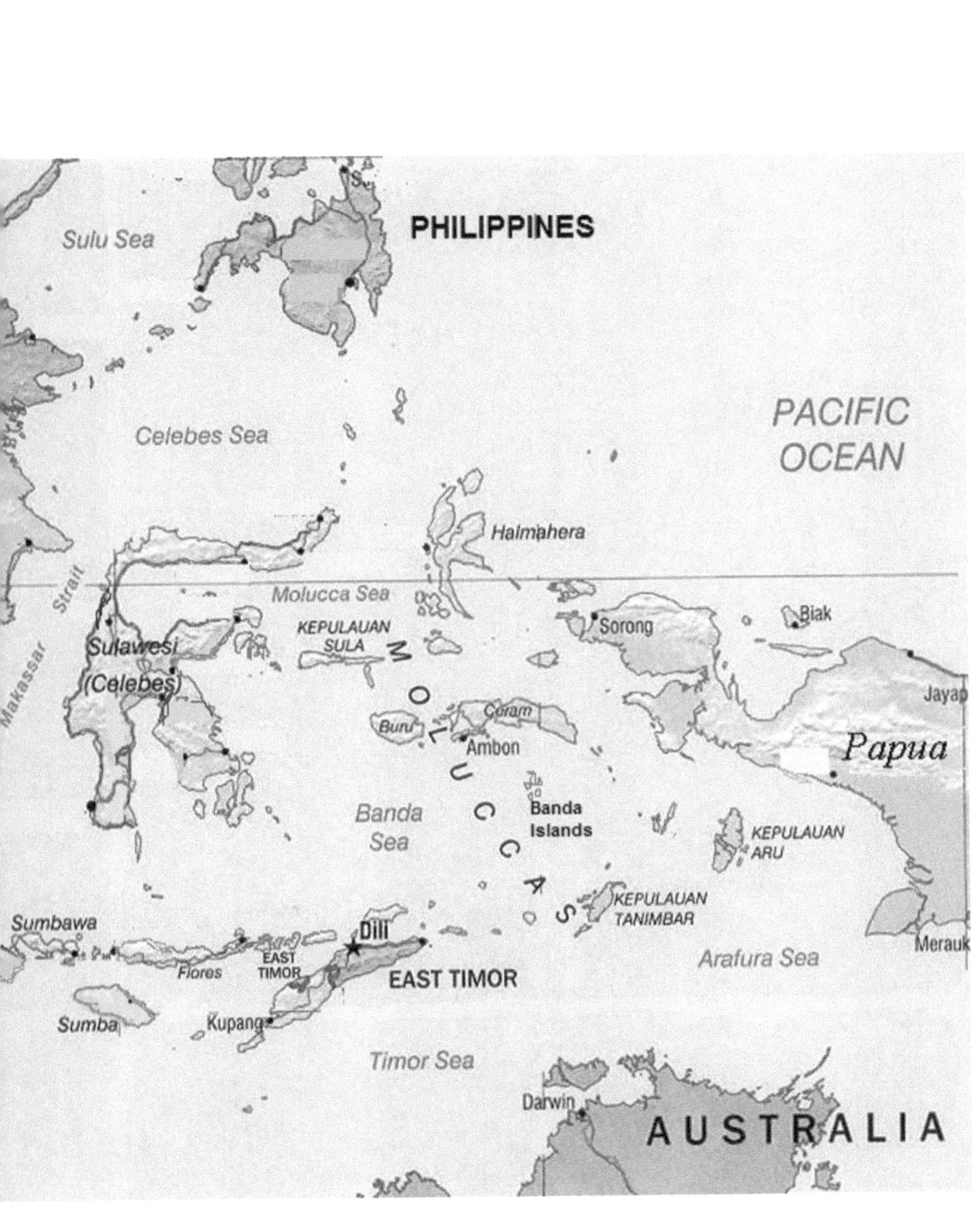

Sulu Sea
PHILIPPINES
PACIFIC OCEAN
Celebes Sea
Halmahera
Molucca Sea
Biak
KEPULAUAN SULA
Sorong
Makassar Strait
Sulawesi (Celebes)
MOLUCCAS
Ceram
Jayap
Papua
Buru
Ambon
Banda Sea
Banda Islands
KEPULAUAN ARU
Sumbawa
KEPULAUAN TANIMBAR
Dili
Flores
EAST TIMOR
EAST TIMOR
Arafura Sea
Merauk
Sumba
Kupang
Timor Sea
Darwin
AUSTRALIA

Nusa Tenggara Timur

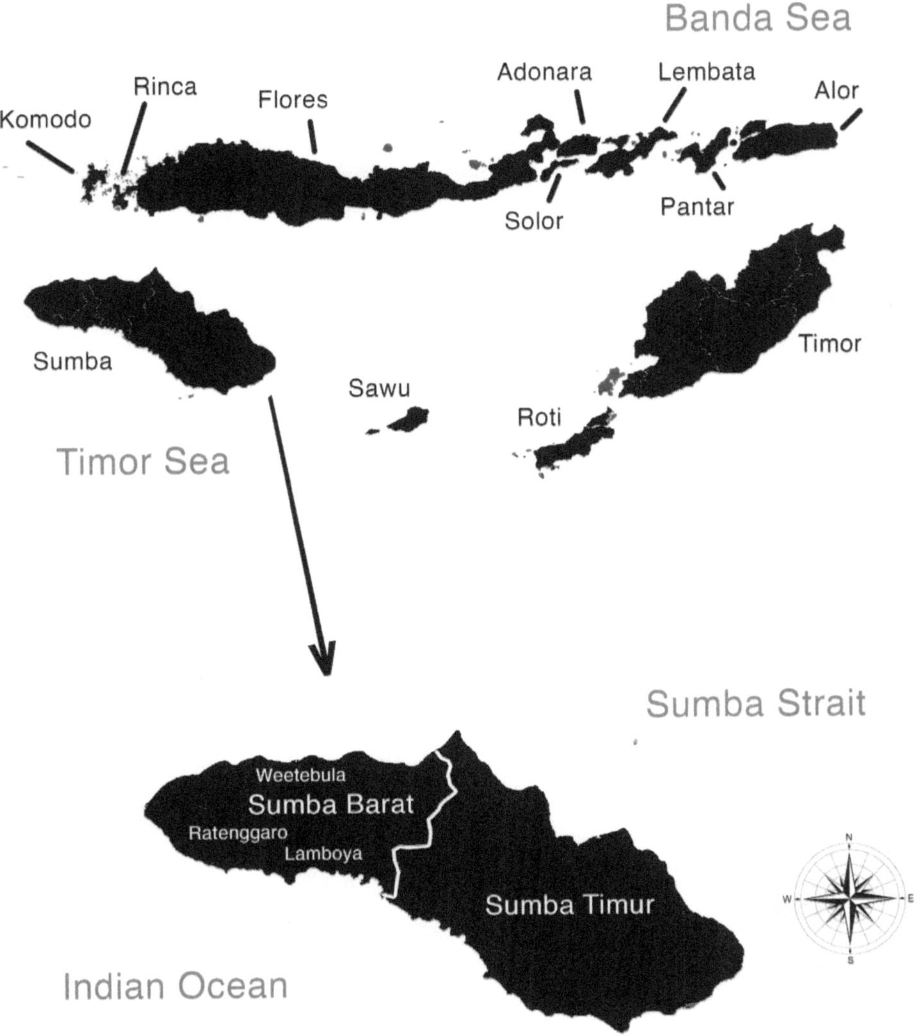

TRANSLATOR'S NOTE

It is an honor to translate *Pasola*, Maria Matildis Banda's latest novel. *Pasola* is based on East Nusa Tenggara tradition. It illustrates the annual sea worm harvest followed by the Sumba equestrian competition and, more importantly, it portrays the strength of Sumba women amid the dominance of patriarchy.

Mother and daughter, Koni and Wula, demonstrate loyalty, resilience, obedience, and respect for tradition in their own ways. *Pasola* stirred up my feelings during the scenes where females were treated as male property. Polygamized wives had to accept whatever their husbands decided, and daughters had to resign themselves to being sold by their fathers to be a friend's wife.

Although *Pasola* addressed village life of more than 70 years ago, the problems and conflicts are still relevant today. Domestic violence, poverty, low levels of education, and health care are still issues the average islander struggles with.

Translating this novel offered me a new adventure. It was like a journey to a world I previously had only heard about from others. I was lucky and blessed to meet Lian Gouw, who allowed me to start my experience in translating literature. Terre Gorham's comprehensive insight on the translation work and the content of the novel were a tremendous help. I thank Maria Matildis Banda for allowing me to translate her captivating work. A thorough discussion with the Dalang Publishing team has helped me grow and improve the quality of my translation skills. Translating a work from one language into another is an art as much as a craft.

In the interest of clarity for the English-speaking reader, I had to make a few adjustments in the translation. However, none of the deviations altered the story's content in any way.

January, 2024, Yuni Utami Asih

FOREWORD

Pasola is one of the traditional customs still kept alive by the four major tribes in west and southwest Sumba, namely Lamboya, Wanukaka, Gaura, and Kodi. In accordance with their Marapu religion, the ceremony represents an expression of gratitude to the Creator for everything, both joy and sorrow, that humans receive in life. The members of the four tribes ask for forgiveness and abundant prosperity in the form of crops and livestock. This custom is celebrated once a year and begins with the ceremony of harvesting *nyale*, sea worms, followed by Pasola.

In this face-to-face equestrian competition, men from two different tribes gallop head-to-head while throwing blunted javelins. The assessment of winning or losing in the Pasola is determined by how agile the participating equestrians are and how many competitors — and horses — are hit by the javelin throwers. The outcome is not announced publicly, but rather is left to the spectators to judge for themselves.

The followers of the Marapu faith believe that the blood spilled on the Pasola field fertilizes the soil and produces abundant crops and livestock. The more blood shed, the better. Blood on the ground, whether it is from riders and horses in the Pasola or from the chickens and pigs sacrificed at the ceremony, is believed to create *syalom*, harmony, between people. New life begins with a relationship in harmony with the universe and especially with the Creator. Therefore, for the four tribes, and others who practice this custom, Pasola is considered a new year's celebration.

Dr. Maria Matildis Banda wrote *Pasola*, a novel set in Ratenggaro, a village facing the Indian Ocean. The work begins in 1934 and portrays the customs and culture that the village residents live by, while exploring the inner messages of life that transcend space and time.

The author conveys the scheming that occurs in the implementation of the traditional Pasola ceremony. Among the Pasola figures are humans with negative qualities, such as arrogance and deviousness. These cunning and deceptive characteristics are passed down from generation to generation in an endless, vicious circle. Revenge occurs not just on the Pasola field, but also in everyday life.

The figure of the Bapa Tua represents the generation of elders who uphold honesty, loyalty, and responsibility on and off the Pasola field. As a representative of the older generation, Bapa Tua becomes an ideal figure and role model for his descendants. He has fought for and lived up to the Pasola's original noble values.

Waleka, Bapa Tua's son, and Ndalo, Waleka's neighbor, are two characters who deviate from ancestral traditions as outlined and adhered to by Bapa Tua. They are controlled by jealousy, arrogance, and the passion to defeat each other, even through underhanded ways. Waleka and Ndalo represent the current tribal generation who live the Pasola tradition in very different ways from how Bapa Tua lived it.

As the novel's characters continue to evolve, the meaning of Pasola also shifts. Banda's *Pasola* explores how many of today's competitors no longer understand the original meaning of the Pasola ceremony, how many of them join merely to participate in a trend. At times, Pasola even becomes a place to prove their competence as an equestrian without understanding the true meaning of Pasola's ancestral tradition.

However, for some Sumbanese, Pasola as a religious custom will never die. It is impossible to have a conversation about Sumba culture without mentioning Pasola.

I would like to congratulate Dr. Maria Matildis Banda on the publication of her novel, *Pasola*. I also want to express my deep gratitude for the dedication, interest, and attention she has devoted to writing novels with a Sumba background, especially *Pasola*. This novel is bound to become an important tool for research on Sumba.

I wish the readers happy reading. Sumba, with its various nicknames — Sandalwood Island, Island of a Thousand Horses, Savanna Island, and Island of a Million Yearnings — is cited by the German magazine, *Focus*, 2018, as one of the 33 most beautiful islands in the world. On this island, many aspects of life are specifically related to customs and culture, which should be recorded, along with the messages of life practiced by its inhabitants. The message of life is timeless — it will not be destroyed by time, nor will time annihilate it.

Happy reading!
Father Robert Ramone, CSsR
Founder of the Sumba Culture House
Weetebula, Southwest Sumba

Pasola

CHAPTER 1

Waleka grinned when he heard the horses' neighs break the calm sky over Maliti Bonto Ate, a *Pasola* field about one-third of a mile from Ratenggaro, his village in Southwest Sumba, Indonesia. He was just eighteen years old, but he already knew how to ride in a Pasola, Sumba's annual celebration. The traditional javelin fights on horseback between two villages heralded the beginning of the planting season. Sitting high in his saddle, Waleka wore a *henggul*, a triangular headband, handwoven by his mother. A *hanggi* was wrapped around his waist. The traditional hanggi, worn at a Pasola, had been passed down for generations. Waleka's father had inherited his hanggi from Waleka's grandfather, who had inherited it from his great-grandfather, and so on. Waleka had lost track of who had worn his hanggi for the first time.

Waleka rode his favorite stallion, Lenggu Lamura. Even though Lamura was surrounded by dozens of other horses, he remained calm. During the Pasola, Waleka would hold the reins in his left hand and grip a javelin in his right. The javelins used at a Pasola were blunted to avoid serious injuries. Breaking into a fast gallop, each *to- paholong*, Pasola rider, would raise his right hand, ready to throw his javelin at the opponents. Shouts would rip the air around the Maliti Bondo Ate field — one of the Pasola venues Waleka knew well.

Hooves thundered, riders screamed, spectators cheered — these were the memorable parts of a Pasola. When the winner emerged, the crowd erupted in admiration for the skilled to-paholong, whose equestrianism and marksmanship had defeated his opponent.

That was the spirit of the Pasola festival on the island of Sumba. It exemplified the qualities of chivalry and horsemanship in a competition where the winner always assisted his defeated opponent in exiting the Pasola field safely.

Ever since he started riding in Pasolas, Waleka had never been unhorsed. He always rode Lamura with valor.

The village of Ratenggaro sat on a high plateau near the sea. From the top of that cliff, Waleka could see the beach stretching along the Indian Ocean. Sumba's southern coast, with its raging waves, was a living testimony of the ever-present ocean. A row of *uma parona*, traditional Sumbanese stilt houses with thatched, high-hat roofs, overlooked the sea.

At the center of the village, a row of flat stones served as an altar, where the *Marapu*, followers of Sumba's indigenous religion, brought offerings to their ancestors and worshipped.

Waleka's uma parona was in the southern part of the village. His front yard was flat, and from his home's open façade, he could easily see the uma parona of Ndalo, his neighbor.

A large banyan tree threw shade against a low stone wall that lined the border of Waleka's property. Lenggu Lamura was usually tethered in the open area that also served as a gathering place for the villagers.

"Is that you, Lamura?" Waleka jumped off the porch of his stilt house and walked through the front of his property to see if the whinnying he heard came from Lenggu Lamura.

"You are impatient, aren't you?" Waleka patted Lamura's back and stroked the stallion's mane. He chuckled, knowing that Lamura understood him. In a few days, the Pasola festival would begin. Relatives would come from other villages, settlements outside the village, and outlying cities to celebrate. Not far from Lamura, several horses were already tethered. Waleka eyed them and concluded that Lamura looked far more handsome and healthy than any of the other horses — he always groomed Lamura himself.

"We will win, right?" Waleka said reassuringly. "Just stay calm and play it cool. Don't be restless. Don't make any noise. Your neighing doesn't just establish your presence; it might also imply that you are worried about winning. Understand? Just stay calm. Don't make any trouble." Waleka chuckled again as his thoughts turned to Limbu Koni, the woman he would soon bring into his uma parona as his wife.

Limbu Koni was the daughter of an elder from Lamboya, a village about a day's travel away on horseback. But although Lamboya was quite far, it felt close to Waleka because Koni would soon be his wife. Koni would not only grace his ancestral house, but she would, of course, also tend to his mother while he was away. As the only son of a village elder, Waleka was expected to travel from village to village to conduct various business and ceremonial matters.

"You stay here," Waleka told Lamura. "This year's Pasola is being held in our village. Limbu Koni will be here, too." Waleka looked forward to the Pasola festival impatiently. Not only did the traditional celebration herald the beginning of the planting season, but it also ended the longing of couples waiting to be married after the harvest.

"Who are you talking to, Leka?" Waleka's mother called from her seat on the front porch. The sun had just risen enough to peek over the cliff. Slowly, the radiant rays, firing new color into the surroundings, stretched to the foot of the stairs and the women who had gathered to gossip there.

"I'm boosting Lamura's morale, *Inya*," Waleka said, using the respectful term of endearment for a woman. "Just talking to make

Lamura happy." Waleka stroked his horse's forehead and smiled. "You don't think Lamura understands what I'm saying, do you, Inya? You think he's just listening."

"He understands; I'm sure he understands." Waleka's mother climbed down the ladder from the stilt house and joined her son. "A horse understands everything his master says to him," she told Waleka. "Therefore, a horse must always be treated as a close friend and part of the family — someone who is always present in happiness or sorrow. Do you remember what your father said?"

Waleka nodded. As the only son of a *tom mtuna parona*, a respected elder, Pasola was a part of his life. His five sisters had already married and moved to their husbands' villages.

Peke, his eldest sister, lived with her husband in Lamboya. She would travel home to Ratenggaro for the Pasola, accompanied by Limbu Koni and Koni's best friend, Biri. The three women would make the trip together for the 1934 Pasola festival.

After his marriage, Waleka would spend less time traveling. And when he did have to travel for an extended period, he would have his wife to take care of his parents at home while he was gone. Imagining his upcoming marriage, Waleka beamed.

All the houses in Ratenggaro were filling with arriving relatives. Peke arrived with Limbu Koni, Biri, and a few family members. Koni and Biri joined other young folks on the village square, who were chanting *kawoking*, a mantra to attract the *nyale*, sea worms, for the nyale harvest that night.

> *Nyale ayam wo wo wu*
> The mother of nyale, Mother Nyale
> Spawn abundantly
> Lay as many eggs as a snail
> As many as a grasshopper

Cut up the many egg clusters
Nyale ayam wo wo wu, chicken nyale *wo wo wu*
The mother of nyale, Mother Nyale
Lay as many eggs as a snail.

While chanting the kawoking, Waleka kept his eyes on Limbu Koni. She and Biri sat among the other women. His heart pounded when their eyes met.

Waleka's neighbor, Ndalo, sat among the elders. He followed Waleka's gaze and fastened his eyes on Limbu Koni. *What a beautiful woman*, he thought.

"*Nale manu wo wo wu. Inya nyu nyale. Talu pinja namloro.* Mother of Nyale, spawn abundantly." Ndalo joined the kawoking while stealing another glance at Limbu Koni. Ndalo's shrill voice made everyone laugh. He rose, walked over to Limbu Koni, and pulled her hand. "You'll make me a perfect wife," he said arrogantly.

"Ndalo! Shame on you!" shouted a man near Limbu Koni. "You already have two wives and three children! Your eldest son Zoga is almost three! Shame on you!"

Waleka jumped up. "Hey! Ndalo!" Waleka motioned for Limbu Koni and Biri to go home as he faced Ndalo. The elders quickly quelled the scuffle, and Waleka followed the two young women home.

CHAPTER 2

The night was pitch dark. A village elder had calculated the moon journey and declared that the sea worms were to appear at the Ratenggaro Beach on the seventh night of March 1934. Earlier that afternoon, every family in the Ratenggaro village on Sumba Island had cleaned the ancestral graves and their surroundings. Through the evening, women and men danced and chanted on the village square while waiting for the arrival of the nyale.

After Waleka left the village square to follow Limbu Koni and Biri home, people continued to party. But around four in the morning, most of the villagers headed to the dark beach. The annual *Bau Nyale*, the traditional ritual of catching sea worms, was about to begin.

On their way to the beach, not far from their uma parona, Waleka led the procession of his sister, Peke, her son Banu, Limbu Koni, Biri, his parents, and other family members. Koni held Banu by the arm as they walked.

"Why do nyale come when the moon is dark?" asked Banu.

"The nyale are afraid of the moon and sun!" Koni replied. "Hopefully, there will be a lot of fat, colorful nyale."

"Is it 'nale' or 'nyale,' Inya?" Banu asked.

7

"Nale and nyale mean the same," Biri replied. "Both words refer to sea worms. I believe there will be an abundance of sea worms this time."

The wind gently caressed their hopeful faces as they walked to the Ratenggaro Beach. "You should be living here, near a beach," Koni told Biri. "During the time you've been here visiting, you haven't had a single asthma attack."

Biri replied by chanting the kawoking mantra call for the nyale, then whispered, "The man who pulled your hand — is his name Ndalo? Such a shameless man!"

"Don't worry about him," Limbu Koni replied. "Just leave it alone."

"We're going to have a party today!" shouted Peke. "We'll celebrate the nyale catch and then the sacred Sumbanese Pasola. Waleka will be dashingly handsome!"

"I want to be a to-paholong like *Bapa* Waleka," Banu said, using the respectful endearment for a man. He pulled at his mother's hand.

"That's good!" Peke replied. "You can be like your Uncle Waleka, a javelin fighter who sits high in his saddle. He's as handsome as —"

"Banu!" Banu replied, laughing.

They walked happily through the *binya bakolo*, the main gate between gravestones, and entered the footpath to the beach. The sound of rolling waves told them they were almost there. Starlight, hope, and need led the eager villagers to the Ratenggaro Beach in search of nyale.

Waleka again chanted the kawoking,

> *Nyale ayam wo wo wu*
> The mother of nyale, Mother Nyale
> Spawn abundantly
> Lay as many eggs as a snail
> As many as a grasshopper
> Cut up the many egg clusters
> *Nyale ayam wo wo wu*, chicken nyale *wo wo wu*
> The mother of nyale, Mother Nyale
> Lay as many eggs as a snail.

People took turns chanting the mantra as they walked. They hoped the sea worms would be as prolific as grasshoppers and snails. Everyone waded into the receding sea. The chilly water stung their bare legs. Their feet moved across the slippery pebbles while they groped for sea worms. Voices called out in turns: "I caught some!" "They are slippery!" "Wow! There are a lot!" "It tickles!" "Wo wo wu, wo wo wuuu!" The smell of the seaworm catch filled the air.

Waleka jumped around, fingering rocks and bed gravel for the sea worms. He held on tightly to the worms he caught.

Peke and Banu followed him, carrying baskets. Limbu Koni and Biri were nearby. Biri, experiencing her first Bau Nyale, kept dipping her hands in the water, trying to catch the evasive, slippery worms.

Limbu Koni steeled herself when the worms touched her feet. She looked down while exploring the rocks. So did Waleka. Both laughed when their hands touched as they caught worms around the same rocks. They proudly added their catch to the growing number of nyale in the baskets Banu and Peke carried.

"A nyale ball!" Waleka shouted as he yanked up a nyale nest. The clump of worms formed a large squirming ball, slightly larger than a soccer ball. He immediately returned to the beach with everyone on his heels.

"Let's find some more!" Banu shouted excitedly. He wanted more worms because he only had a few in the small basket hanging from his neck.

"We have enough," Waleka whispered to his nephew. "This is already a lot. We must share with other people."

The Bau Nyale came to an end as the rising sun reached the hollow of the small headland below the cliffs of Ratenggaro. Everyone left the shore with their catch and walked cheerfully back to the village. Waleka was the only one who had found a nyale nest.

Though Limbu Koni had not said anything, Waleka knew she was proud of him and admired his successful nyale harvest.

"The nyale ball is a sign that you are here for Waleka," Peke teased Limbu Koni. "You are meant for each other. Everything will go smoothly."

"My fiancé, Wuri Wona, and I, too, will soon have a celebration!" Biri added.

"Just like you, your Wuri Wona can't wait!" Limbu Koni and Biri burst out laughing.

Back in the village, the nyale nest was unraveled beside the wood stove, sitting in the center of the stilt house being used as a communal kitchen. The ball was divided into thirds. Limbu Koni, Peke, and Biri each took a third. The slippery masses wriggled from their hands several times. As the worms were loosened from the ball, they writhed and crawled, searching for sea water. Banu picked up the escaped worms and put them back into the basket. There were so many fat, bright, colorful, tantalizing worms!

"Red, green, yellow, white, black — wow, we have every color!" Banu shouted happily. Waleka's parents and all the other villagers were happy too. "The worms are fat!" Banu shouted again. "They are bright! What does it mean, Mother?"

"It's a sign of fertile land, abundant harvests, and a better life," Peke replied. Biri and Limbu Koni nodded, as they skillfully helped Peke and Waleka's extended family prepare a variety of nyale dishes.

Together with her future sister-in-law and Biri, Limbu Koni prepared nyale *palowor*, a stew of nyale, thick coconut milk, and various spices. It smelled fragrant and tasted delicious. They also made a peppery sauce with green chilies and fat, bright, colorful worms. "Are we going to make *bodho*, too, Inya?" Biri asked.

"Yes, we'll store the nyale jerky here." Waleka's mother handed over an earthen pot. "Wow, we have plenty!" she exclaimed proudly. "This will be enough for several months!"

Waleka was pleased to see Limbu Koni and Biri help with all the kitchen activities. He was especially taken with Limbu Koni. He and his future bride stole furtive glances at each other, then immediately looked away after being caught by the other. But Waleka knew that later that day, on the Pasola field, everything would change. Everything would become more beautiful, more intimate.

Finally, breakfast was served. Before everyone started to eat, Waleka's father, Bapa *Tua*, respected elderly one, gave a speech in the Sumbanese dialect.

In front of the villagers and relatives who had come from afar, the old man underlined several things to the gathering in their stilt house.

"Waleka, you caught a nyale nest during the Bau Nyale on the beach," he said. "Take care of that fortune throughout life. To find a big nyale nest with colorful, fat, luminous worms is special, very special indeed! Not all nyale seekers find one. This is a sign for a lifetime of fortune. You're the only one who caught a nyale nest. That is remarkable. You've been given much. Take good care of the gift. If you ever fail to appreciate how much you've been given in the form of a nyale nest, you will lose everything."

"Yes, Bapa," Waleka answered solemnly.

Bapa Tua continued imparting life's wisdoms that had been passed down for generations. "Live a life that's faithful and honest," he continued. "Be grateful for everything you have. Don't take more than you need. Whatever the challenge might be, never take more — let alone things that don't belong to you."

Waleka listened carefully to his father.

"You will be the best to-paholong throughout your life," Bapa Tua said, "and faithfulness and honesty are the keys — but not just in your equestrian marksmanship and your ability to become one with your horse, Lenggu Lamura. When the javelin is thrown, you must also be faithful and honest to the horse you are riding. On the Pasola field, you and Lamura are one." Bapa Tua looked meaningfully at Waleka before repeating, "You and Lamura are one. Remember that."

"Yes, Bapa!" Waleka agreed wholeheartedly.

"Keep faithfulness and honesty, not only in the victory and satisfaction of defeating an opponent, but also in your humanity in embracing and helping your defeated opponent." Bapa Tua spoke each word carefully. Everyone present listened attentively, including Limbu Koni.

Waleka's bride-to-be studied the face of her future father-in-law: calm eyes beneath thick eyebrows, high cheekbones, and a strong jaw. Waleka looked very much like his father.

"You must believe that every drop of sweat and every drop of blood that falls on the field falls honestly and faithfully and will not dry up there. Not just for the harvest, but more than that, for real life. Loyalty and honesty are the keys!"

Limbu Koni was moved by Bapa Tua's words. He was a true *kabani pa ate,* a worldly and wise man. In his youth, Bapa Tua had traveled to Flores, Timor, Alor, even as far as Maluku and Sulawesi, to trade livestock. His children, grandchildren, and extended family believed that Bapa Tua's experience enlightened him in his old age. This was especially true for Waleka, the only son in the family.

"Bapa Tua is an extraordinary kabani pa ate," Biri whispered to Limbu Koni. "Hopefully, Waleka can live up to Bapa Tua's words for as long as he lives. Hopefully."

"Yes," Limbu Koni replied. She felt that Bapa Tua's words were not only directed at Waleka as a to-paholong, but also at her, accepting her as a part of Waleka's extended family.

Waleka felt the same. He realized, as a Ratenggaro man, that he must be a faithful and honest man. His heart fluttered when he met Bapa Tua's intent look.

"By being faithful and honest, you will most certainly be able to take care of family pride, uma parona, Ratenggaro, *kabisu* — your tribe, and yourself." Bapa Tua smiled. The look in his eyes lighted Waleka with hope.

Silently, Limbu Koni memorized all Bapa Tua's words in her mind and heart. She lifted her head for a moment to watch the old man's face again. When Limbu Koni shifted her gaze to Mama Tua, Waleka's mother smiled warmly.

"Do you understand, Waleka?" Bapa Tua asked his son.

"Yes, Bapa." Waleka said with confidence.

CHAPTER 3

At noon that day, after the nyale feast, the Pasola proceeded with great enthusiasm. Waleka, along with Ndalo and other Pasola riders, was among the team on the left side of Maliti Bondo Ate field. Ndalo kept silent, embarrassed by Limbu Koni's rebuff the night before, and jealous of Waleka's winning her. Moreover, the warnings from several elders added to his shame and hatred. *I should be the one marrying Limbu Koni, not you,* Ndalo thought as he glanced at Waleka. *And I should have been the one who found the nyale nest, not you.*

The elders of Ratenggaro had invited a team from Lamboya to face off against the Ratenggaro team. In the middle of the Pasola field, Waleka stroked Lenggu Lamura's neck and smiled. The match was about to begin.

Throngs of people lined the playing area, which stretched three times the size of a football field. Up on the viewing stand stood Koni, Biri, Peke, Banu, and all of Waleka's extended family. From that height, they had a much better view of the competition.

"Peke," said Biri, smiling happily, "Limbu Koni is already familiar with Ratenggaro and the Maliti Bondo Ate Pasola."

13

Peke smiled, too, happy that Koni would be her sister-in-law and live in Ratenggaro. "Look over there!" Peke pointed to the field. "The Pasola is about to start!"

"Yes, look over there, Koni!" Biri laughed. "Look closely for the best to-paholong, both on the field and in your heart!" The three young women giggled.

A traditional ceremony opened the Pasola. In view of all participants, a *rato,* chairman of the board of elders, introduced the rules of the Pasola to ensure that the festive event ran smoothly. He welcomed a happy new year and gave thanks for a bountiful nyale harvest. The abundance of sea worms caught earlier that morning signaled a successful Pasola, and a successful nyale and a successful Pasola signaled a successful harvest and bright future. The best time to catch sea worms was determined by the *ndara* nyale, the leader on the Pasola field. In this way, nothing stood on its own; everything was interrelated. One event connected to another to form a long series of events that affected the lives of each Ratenggaro resident and those of the surrounding villages.

Nearly a hundred horses circled the field prior to each competing team taking its place — one on the west side of the Maliti Bondo Ate Pasola field and one on the east side.

This year's Pasola was not a typical Pasola for Waleka. This year's Pasola would be the last one of his bachelorhood. He turned his head to catch a glimpse of his future wife. Wherever he turned, he felt her presence. "This will be an unforgettable day for the rest of my life," Waleka murmured to himself as the Pasola began.

Warming up was done in two cycles. Waleka was at the front, with Ndalo and dozens of horses behind him, as they circled the field in thunderous majesty to the cheers of the crowd. The opposing team followed in equal grandeur. The thunder of pounding hooves exploded through the sky and across the earth of Ratenggaro, triumphant under the blue sky. The vast fields, the bawling cattle, and the breezes blowing in from the sea carried hope for the abundant harvest to come.

Waleka faced the leader of the opposing Lamboya team, centering himself and becoming one with Lenggu Lamura. Drawing himself upright, Waleka urged Lamura into a gallop. Waleka's left hand controlled the reins while his right launched the blunted javelin. Cheers erupted, followed by applause and *kayiliking* from the women standing at the edge of the field.

"Ririri, ririri, riri, riri, riririiiii!" the women's voices ululated, filling the air with the sounds of neighing horses.

In the next round, the Lamboya team took control of the battle. A javelin flew toward Waleka's head. He dodged it skillfully, and the opponent's javelin shot into a tree trunk and fell.

The match continued, as the sounds of clattering hooves and kayiliking women filled the sky. "Ririri, ririri, riri, riri, riririiiii!"

A javelin shot toward Waleka's chest. The spectators gasped. Again, Waleka dodged quickly then sank his own javelin into the opponent's arm. The opponent toppled off his horse, amid the cheers and kayiliking of women from both sides.

Waleka quickly jumped off his horse and, surrounded by his teammates, helped his injured opponent to the back side of the Pasola field.

Ndalo was among Waleka's teammates. He feigned concern for the injured opponent, but he had wanted Waleka to fall, not his opponent.

The Pasola proceeded well and ended late in the afternoon. Everyone left for Ratenggaro and other surrounding villages. Food was served in every house. People were glad that the Pasola's festivities had run smoothly. It was a common belief that every drop of sweat and every drop of blood that had fallen on the Pasola field would fertilize the land of the ancestors and bring prosperity to all.

The elders and the youth, including Waleka and Ndalo, were the center of the post-Pasola celebration. They greeted every family member and every member of the competing teams from Lamboya and other villages. Although some of the wounded competitors had been escorted home to Lamboya earlier, everyone was happy and joyous.

They felt sure the ancestors' presence had blessed the hereditary cultural event. Waleka felt as bright as the glare of the sea on a sunny day. *Soon,* he thought, *Limbu Koni will live in my house.*

This Pasola especially touched Waleka's and Koni's hearts. Peke saw it. She was thankful and hoped for Waleka's happiness. She planned on returning to Lamboya the day after the Pasola with Banu, Koni, and Biri, but she wanted to talk to Waleka before leaving Ratenggaro.

It was drizzling at dusk. Peke joined Waleka in the *kambu luna,* the place underneath the stilt house, where Lamura was stabled. "You must be proud because Limbu Koni chose you," she said. "Many men want to marry her."

"Really?" Waleka asked proudly.

"Do you know what the name Koni means?" Peke asked. "Remember the story Bapa Tua told us when we were children? He always repeated it on the night before the Nyale."

"Yes, the story of sisters Koni and Biri!" Waleka laughed.

"Correct!" Peke replied. "Limbu Koni's name originated from the fairy tale of Koni Wuka Nika, whose body was cut into pieces. Her blood and flesh turned into rice, corn, and other crops. Her sister, Inya Biri Nyale, grieved deeply for her dead sister, so she went to sea every year and returned in the form of nyale, sea worms." Waleka and Peke laughed, recalling the story of the two sisters their father had told them during their childhood in Ratenggaro.

"That story makes Nyale and Pasola happen each year," Waleka added, "in memory of Biri and Koni." Waleka and his sister laughed again. "Nyale and Pasola continue to exist today and will continue to exist forever, because our ancestors, Biri and Koni, sacrificed for us."

"You must be proud to get Limbu Koni as a wife," Peke repeated. She looked at her brother intently and continued, "You too have a great name. The word Waleka originates from *Woleka,* a traditional ceremony where everyone sacrifices together to give the best of themselves for the sake of *one* family, *one* uma parona, *one* kabisu, even *one* province."

Waleka sensed that his eldest sister wanted to remind him of the spirit that united their people. "If you had finished your schooling, you would have been an educator now, Inya," Waleka teased his sister. "You would have been a brilliant teacher."

"The most important thing is that you stay faithful and honest, just as Bapa Tua told you," Peke said.

"Of course!"

"Being faithful and honest to Koni, Limbu Koni." Peke looked meaningfully at her brother.

"Well, of course!" Waleka repeated, with even more confidence.

The wedding of Waleka and Koni was planned for July 1934, after the harvest. Biri and Wona would marry earlier. Ndalo knew that Waleka would travel to Lamboya to attend Biri's wedding, but also, and more importantly, Waleka would travel to Lamboya to meet Koni. Ndalo kept his jealousy to himself. He decided to cozy up to Waleka. He found the opportunity to do so one day after bathing their horses in the river.

Waleka let his horse graze; Ndalo did the same. He sat beside Waleka. "Let's go to Lamboya together," Ndalo suggested. "I'd like to attend Wona and Biri's wedding, too."

Waleka was suspicious of Ndalo's contrived friendliness. "After Wona and Biri's wedding, I will bring Limbu Koni here," he replied cautiously.

"That is so complicated!" Ndalo lit a cigarette. "When Koni came for the Pasola, you should have made her your wife then. You were stupid! Limbu Koni is the type of woman fit only for a man like me."

"So you are also going to Lamboya?" Waleka asked, ignoring Ndalo's harsh words. Ever since Ndalo had pulled Limbu Koni's hand on the kawoking night before the Nyale and Pasola, Waleka had tried hard to keep being respectful to Ndalo.

"Yes, I'm going to Lamboya," Ndalo answered. "You're moving too slowly. It has been three months since the Pasola last March. Stupid! You should just kidnap Koni!"

"We are leaving tomorrow morning," Waleka said evenly, his patience fading.

Ndalo grinned and blurted out, "Kidnap Koni after Biri and Wona's party! Grab her and lock her up!"

Waleka, now irritated, looked away and said, "I am traveling with several family members to Lamboya tomorrow morning. If you want to come along, you may."

The next morning, Waleka spurred his horse through open fields, up hills, and onto the paths to Lamboya. He led many families from Ratenggaro who were traveling with him to attend Wuri Wona and Biri's wedding. This was a perfect opportunity for Waleka's family to meet Limbu Koni's parents and family to discuss their wedding plans.

Waleka's family was welcomed into Limbu Koni's ancestral house with a firm handshake, a meal, and stories of horses, Nyale, and the recent Pasola. Wedding plans would be discussed later.

Limbu Koni felt very proud because, in addition to coming to discuss the wedding, Waleka had also come to attend Biri and Wuri Wona's wedding. Wuri Wona and Waleka were both to-paholongs. For Koni, Waleka's visit proved that they would marry as planned, as well as tighten their friendship with Biri and Wuri Wona. "Waleka and Wona are best friends," Limbu Koni told Biri, "both on the Pasola field and off."

"It has been arranged by *Bo Kalo Mata Mbe Leko Roka Tilu*, the Big-eyed and Wide-eared One god who watches over us!" Biri laughed.

"Best friends on the Pasola field, at home, in the village, everywhere!" Limbu Koni laughed happily.

"After Wona and I are married, you should not wait too long for your marriage." Biri added. "We will see each other at every Nyale and Pasola."

"I hope you are happy because someone is taking care of you," Limbu Koni said to her friend. "If you have an asthma attack, Wona will be the one to help you." They both remained silent for a moment.

"If I did not have asthma, I would prefer living in Wanokaka," Biri whispered. "I would study and become a teacher."

"The fact is, we cheered on the Pasola fighters with the loudest kayiliking," Limbu Koni continued. "Both of our men won, so we won. When they lose, we lose." They both smiled, realizing they were each marrying famous Pasola riders. Waleka and Wona had a good reputation on all Pasola fields. They had never been unhorsed, and they always helped injured opponents from all teams.

"Waleka and Wona are best friends on the Pasola field, as well as in the village," Limbu Koni said proudly. "Pasola, Ratenggaro, and Lamboya!"

As such, the Pasola always held a special place in the hearts and minds of Wona and Waleka. There were no grudges between the two, no animosity from either side, even when a team member was unhorsed. In fact, the unhorsed riders brought happiness, because the tears, sweat, and blood that fell on the Pasola field brought fertility and success. The finding of a nyale nest had ensured it, as the skills of a to-paholong had proven it.

Nyale and Pasola became the connecting factor that unified Ratenggaro and Lamboya with a strong foundation and a definite goal. The tradition existed and remained part of Waleka's and Wona's lives as to-paholongs. Waleka and Wona believed in the connection between land and sea; among the moon, the stars, and the sun; between the wind of the land and the wind of the sea; and between the high and low tides during Nyale and Pasola in their harmonious world.

With the support of both families, Waleka and Limbu Koni's wedding ran smoothly. Koni's family joyfully accepted Waleka and his big family, who had come to Lamboya with dozens of buffaloes and horses.

In return, Koni's family had gifted several original fabrics woven by Koni and her other family members. The party was organized merrily. "We accept Waleka," one of Koni's family elders said.

Led by a *rato marapu*, a traditional religious leader, Waleka promised to be faithful and honest. He gave Koni a *mamuli* — pair of earrings, and a *marangga* — necklace.

Koni gave him a henggul.

After the exchange of gifts, Waleka was allowed to enter Koni's room. The newlyweds stayed three days in Lamboya before Waleka took Koni to Ratenggaro. As a sign of blessing and support from both families, a big party for Waleka and Limbu Koni was also held in the village uma parona in Ratenggaro.

Chapter 4

Waleka's marriage improved his life but increased Ndalo's jealousy, especially because Waleka continued to show him respect and treat him kindly.

Ndalo was still disgruntled because the village men kept teasing him about his attempt to approach Limbu Koni on the kawoking night of the Pasola. His envy flared whenever he saw Waleka's wife. She was tall and fair, with thick hair. During her daily activities, she walked calmly and confidently. From behind the lattice of his house, Ndalo spied on Koni whenever she sat outside her home, or in the shade of the banyan tree, leaning over her loom to weave effortlessly. Ndalo's eyes followed Koni when she walked out the village gate toward the spring, and again when she returned carrying a container of water in each hand.

Inya Tua, Ndalo's first wife, took note of his spying, but she was pregnant with her second child and did not dare say anything.

Waleka and Limbu Koni had been married for two years when, one day, Inya Tua, sitting and weaving beside Ndalo on their terrace, exclaimed, "It is embarrassing for them to be married for two years and still not have any children! Koni is the daughter of traditional elders. Waleka should find a new wife so he will have descendants."

Ndalo, leaning back sleepily, bolted upright. His mind immediately filled with plans.

Waleka had, over the two years of marriage, willingly made sacrifices in accordance with his family's expectations. He had remained a faithful and honest man, just as Bapa Tua had instructed him to be when welcoming the Nyale and Pasola before his marriage. The nyale nest he had found had applied its meaning well.

But Waleka now found himself sinking under the influence of Ndalo's constant lecturing on the importance of having children and the endless questions as to why Waleka didn't have any. At first, Ndalo's badgering simply moved Waleka's father's message a bit farther from his heart. But in time, Ndalo's words erased it.

Ndalo had already taken a third wife. She was not a descendant of elders, but she was almost as beautiful as Koni.

Slowly but surely, Waleka began to feel the need to find a second wife, like Ndalo suggested. He was the family's only son, and it was up to him to produce the male heir to continue the lineage. Reluctantly, Waleka's parents and sisters convinced Koni to accept her husband's plans to take another wife, one who could give him a child. At harvest time, in 1937, Waleka married Inya Duyo. Like Limbu Koni, she came from Lamboya.

"Please, don't be angry with me," Duyo said to Koni on her first day in Ratenggaro. "You are still the first."

Koni chose to stay quiet, in painful acceptance, while doing her housework. She spent more time with her mother-in-law, spinning yarn and weaving.

"You will have a child soon," her mother-in-law said carefully. "Although the child will come from Inya Duyo's belly, it will be your child too."

Koni kept weaving.

"If Inya Duyo gives birth to a daughter, she will be as nice as you," her mother-in-law added. "And if it is a boy, he will also be as good as you, and the family will have an heir."

A few months later, Duyo gave birth to a son, Raga.

"I am truly a grandmother now," Koni's mother-in-law said, as she and Koni sat weaving together on the porch. "My husband and I have become grandparents, and our family has an heir."

"Yes, *Nenek*," Koni replied, using the endearing term for grandmother. But then the crushing sadness that she had not borne the family's male heir washed over her. *Why can't I bear a child?* she grieved. *What had caused this unfortunate fate to befall me?*

Koni diligently passed her loom's shuttle back and forth, back and forth. *Shush-click, shush-click, shush-click.* The rhythm of wood meeting wood, the shuttle moving in cadence between the yarn threads, strand by strand, slowly creating something of use, soothed her wounded and lonely heart. She vowed to remain steadfast in her efforts to heal her pain in silence.

One day, when Raga had just turned two years old, Duyo approached Koni. "I am going home to Lamboya," she announced. Waleka had taken a third wife, Inya Telu — a woman he'd eyed for some time — by kidnapping her. The bride kidnapping was an old tradition still practiced by wealthy and influential men. The shame it cast on a bride's family was easily placated with generous gifts of buffaloes, horses, and acres of land.

"I must go home. I am so embarrassed!" Duyo cried. She and Koni had grown closer over time, due in large part to Duyo's humble nature that respected Koni's place as "first wife."

Koni glanced at Duyo standing before her. "Raga is your son," she said patiently. "You must take good care of him."

"Because Waleka took a second wife, he thinks he can take a third one!" Duyo cried. "I am leaving!"

"Don't go. You have a son, Raga," Koni repeated. "Stay here."

Duyo looked down. "My pain is probably nothing compared to yours — when I came."

Picking up Raga, Koni said, "Let's weave." She nodded toward the back door and repeated, "Let's weave." The two wives stepped outside, hearing their in-laws — *Kakek*, grandpa, and Nenek — weeping softly in their bedroom. They heard Waleka and his third wife, Telu, in another bedroom.

"I must go," Duyo said, standing on the porch stairs.

"You can go after you finish weaving the cloth for Raga," Koni said.

Duyo quickly set up her loom, tidied the threads, took a seat on one of the sides with a backrest, and began to weave. She moved her loom's shuttle back and forth, back and forth. *Shush-click. Shush-click. Shush-click.*

Koni's understanding and kindness persuaded Duyo to stay in Ratenggaro. In the days that followed, Limbu Koni and Duyo worked in tandem. They wove, fetched water from the spring, gathered wood in the garden, picked corn, cooked by the fire, and tried to look after Kakek and Nenek. Koni helped Duyo raise Raga and the siblings who followed.

What they could not do was stop Waleka from taking more wives. He kidnapped his fourth wife not long after kidnapping the third. Again, he paid hush money in the form of dozens of buffaloes and horses, as well as several acres of land. Waleka no longer cared about his first two wives or his parents, and Koni and Duyo could not ease Kakek and Nenek's shame and sadness. In time, Waleka's parents fell ill.

The life Koni had dreamed of took a completely different turn. Koni returned to Lamboya often to visit the home of her happy childhood and teenage years. Her best friend, Biri, still lived there, providing a patient ear to all Koni's stories about Waleka, his wives, and his children. Duyo, too busy raising her family, rarely went home to Lamboya.

"I will definitely come," Koni promised when she heard that Biri, at the age of thirty-four, was finally pregnant. After sixteen years of marriage, this pregnancy was an incredible gift for Biri and Wuri Wona. Their faithfulness to one another had paid off. Honesty found the eyes of love in a birth that was patiently and steadfastly awaited. Wuri Wona planned to celebrate the pregnancy with a special event. He and Biri hoped that a child would help Biri's asthma and his flagging stamina.

"Nyale and Pasola have given the sign," Biri told Koni. "The nyale ball Waleka found so long ago had the best bright and colorful worms! If now he kidnaps woman after woman, he will surely suffer the consequences of his actions."

"Don't think about him," Koni said calmly. "*Pitu Ndani Awung*, the One on Seven Layers Above God, is taking care of you by giving you and Wona this child."

"That Pasola was truly amazing," Biri reminisced dreamily. Her pregnancy coincided with the harvest season, and the midwife predicted Biri would give birth after the upcoming nyale and Pasola.

"So, in April or May?" Koni was heartened to see how content Biri still was with Wona. He was always loyal and honest as a Bau Nyale and Pasola to-paholong. Biri's happiness raised Koni's spirits. Moreover, Koni was touched by Wona's patience in waiting sixteen years for Biri to become pregnant. "If only Waleka had waited for me like Wona waited for you," Koni whispered.

"Even though he was given a nyale ball, he is ungrateful," Biri said. "I am so sad for you, Koni!"

Koni dabbed her eyes and smiled at her friend. The reality of her life was bitter now, but she was determined to carry on.

After taking his fourth wife, Waleka built several houses in the large fields that had been owned by his parents and ancestors for generations. These field houses, however, were not part of the traditional ancestral home in the Ratenggaro village. Inya Telu and Inya Potoh, his third and fourth wives, lived in one of the field houses.

When Raga was nine years old, Waleka took a fifth wife. "Don't count the number of his children," Duyo said to Koni while spinning yarn. "Don't count." A single tear fell on the lump of cotton she spun.

"Waleka does not count either," Koni replied.

"I still have not gone home," Duyo said. "Home to Lamboya."

"There is another cloth to weave," Koni said. "Please stay here." Koni knew Raga was now old enough to hear the quarrels and feel the tension in the ever-growing family. The uncomfortable situation Waleka caused drove Raga away from his half-brothers and distanced him from his father — especially when Waleka left Ratenggaro for months at a time. Raga grew closer to Duyo and Koni.

After Raga finished elementary school, Koni and Duyo agreed to take him to Weetebula, in Southwest Sumba, to continue his education. "Let him go," Koni urged Duyo. "He will be fine. He will return home after studying there. Weetebula is not far from Ratenggaro, less than a day and night's trip."

Koni knew the real reason Raga wanted to go to junior high in Weetebula: He was embarrassed. One time, Koni had found little Raga crying in a corner of the ancestral house after his father overtly visited with his new wife for just a few hours to fulfill the requirement that his new wife enter the traditional house and meet his parents. Raga was crying from shame.

"You are as great as this country," Ndalo chuckled. "Your fifth wife arrived on the same day as Indonesia's fifth Independence Day. Do you remember listening to the news on Father Bili's radio in Weetebula?"

"Yes, yes, yes!" Waleka joined in the laughter, remembering Bapa Bili, the priest who taught agriculture and livestock skills at a convent in Weetebula. The two neighbors were enjoying a cup of coffee in the shade of a banyan tree.

"It has only been five years since the country's independence, and you're already bringing a sixth wife," Ndalo's voice boomed.

He deliberately spoke loudly so Koni could hear him from inside Waleka's house.

"The spell of the nyale nest you found sixteen years ago has apparently worn off," Ndalo continued in an even louder voice. Watching Waleka's stilt house, he saw Koni descending from the home's terrace behind Duyo. Ndalo had noticed that despite being betrayed many times, Waleka's first wife never looked broken or hurt. Her posture remained straight, and her eyes remained level and calm. The way she sat at her loom, passing the shuttle back and forth, back and forth, never changed. The sight of her still thrilled Ndalo. "Yes, the spell of the nyale nest of sixteen years ago has worn off," Ndalo repeated, laughing even louder.

In April, Limbu Koni traveled to Lamboya for the birth of Biri's child. She also looked forward to seeing Waleka's sister Peke and Peke's son, Banu. Wona had waited faithfully for sixteen years, and the time had come. He had calculated the delivery date well. He knew from Bapa Bili that this year, 1950, Indonesia was celebrating its fifth Independence Day. Bapa Bili had heard it from the radio in town. Limbu Koni had been thrilled. She wanted the same thing to happen to her. It drove her to wish that Waleka would go with her to see Biri.

But this trip to Lamboya would be different than planned. Wuri Wona would not be there. When Biri was six months pregnant, Wona had been unhorsed on the Pasola field in a neighboring village and stopped breathing. After waiting for a child for sixteen years, Wuri Wona was not alive to see it born.

When Koni arrived in Lamboya, Biri wasn't there. "Inya Biri went to the farmhouse for the smoking ritual," her family explained to Koni. "She is going to deliver the baby and stay there."

Koni was shocked. "Why would she take part in the smoking ritual?"

"Everyone does the smoking ritual!" one of the neighbor women replied. "I also did it. The roasting sauna is warm and healthy for Biri and her child."

"But —" Limbu Koni stopped. There was no point in arguing. The smoking ritual following childbirth, a custom passed down from generation to generation, was believed to be healthy for mother and baby. Duyo and other new mothers had done the same. Koni had never questioned it. But now, she worried. Biri had asthma. Being in the farmhouse hut with the fire's heat and smoke could kill her.

"Oh, *Yang Bermata Besar dan Bertelinga Lebar* — the Big-eyed and Wide-eared One," she prayed.

"The farmhouse is too far for you to travel, Inya," said Banu. "You should not go there. You have traveled a long way from Ratenggaro to Lamboya, and the farmouse is even farther. There's no way you could make it in time for the birth."

Koni's heart beat wildly. Biri was her best friend. They'd spent their childhood together. They'd both dropped out after elementary school because the nearest junior high school was too far from Lamboya. The road to the junior high school was dusty in the summer and muddy in the rainy season, and with the strong winds and hot sun, it would be too difficult for Biri. So for the next two years, the two lived at Father Bili's convent in Weetebula, learning various agricultural and livestock skills. Under Bapa Bili's guidance, they learned how to conduct themselves better.

If only Wona were still alive, Limbu Koni thought. *He would never have allowed Biri to give birth in a smoke hut out in the field just because it was a local belief and custom. But Wona is not here, and I must go.*

"Biri!" Limbu Koni broke into the smoke hut. A midwife and two assistants had just helped Biri deliver her baby. Smoke billowed into the room from the fire burning beneath.

"Biri suffers from asthma!" Koni shouted. "She won't be able to breathe!"

"Women who are delivering have to be smoked," the midwife replied.

"Take the baby out of here!" Biri wheezed. She coughed. "Take him! Take him with you!"

Limbu Koni grabbed the baby and hurried out of the hut and down the stairs. She then raced back up to Biri. "You're getting out of here, too!" The midwife watched them impassively.

"Mada Wolli!" Biri gasped hoarsely. "Call him Mada Wolli! Take him with you — take care of him!" Biri collapsed.

Limbu Koni shrieked. The two assistants left to extinguish the fire under the hut while Koni pulled Biri into the fresh air. Biri coughed and fought for air as another spasm attacked her lungs. Lying at the foot of the hut, she kept struggling to talk to Limbu Koni. "Take Mada Wolli ..." Biri panted. "Take care of my son!" Then Biri was quietly freed from the shortness of breath she had suffered all her life and said no more.

After passing through various traditional ceremonies to send Mada Wolli away from his family in Lamboya, Koni took the baby boy to Ratenggaro. Waleka immediately agreed to adopt the infant into his home. "Wona and Biri must be happy," was all Waleka said.

For Koni, after sixteen years of marriage without having her own child, Mada Wolli's existence was fate's expression of gratitude, which Limbu Koni celebrated throughout the years.

That same year, in 1950, Koni and Duyo escorted Raga to Weetebula to start junior high school. Raga rode the horse, and Koni and Duyo took turns sitting behind him in the saddle and leading a buffalo on the long journey from Ratenggaro. The buffalo was payment for Raga's education. Koni and Duyo came specifically to ask Father Bili's permission to allow Raga to study agriculture while continuing junior high school.

Father Bili agreed because it would expedite the farm and livestock trading knowledge that Raga would need to conduct Waleka's family business. "The most important thing is that Raga works hard and finishes studying," he said. "I have eight children who are working while studying. Raga can join them."

Koni understood the importance of education. She agreed to everything Father Bili asked for. "Thank God your child wants to study!" he exclaimed. "But where is Waleka? He hasn't been here in a long time."

"Yes, Bapa Bili, Waleka is busy selling livestock to other islands," Koni said excitedly. "This buffalo is to cover Raga's expenses while he is here."

"Good!" Father Bili beamed. "Indonesia has been independent for five years! Children should be independent too. Please make sure all of your children learn and understand the importance of education."

Koni nodded and happily accepted the task.

When Koni first brought Wolli to Ratenggaro as a newborn, Ndalo's family had a newborn, too. Koda was Ndalo's first grandson from Zoga, his eldest son. Ndalo had always felt luckier than Waleka, and he felt the need to build power by hiring strong mercenaries that he could use for his nefarious purposes.

As time went by, whenever Raga visited Ratenggaro, he took Wolli to the beach on horseback. Wherever Raga went, Wolli was always with him. Soon, Koda had joined the two of them. Koda's deepening friendship with Raga and Wolli was something new that spurred Ndalo's jealousy.

"He's only an adopted child," Ndalo sneered to everyone who talked about Wolli. "What is the use of an adopted child?" Ndalo was sure his words would reach Koni.

Koni's maternal attention to Wolli seem to calm Waleka for a time. He started to care again about his first two wives, his parents, and especially Wolli. Waleka started staying home more and more.

But it was not Wolli's presence that brought Waleka to his senses, but rather Raga's departure to the junior high school in Weetebula without telling him goodbye.

"When did Raga leave?" Waleka asked Duyo.

"Two weeks ago," Koni replied.

"Oh!" Waleka swallowed hard.

"He told his grandparents," Koni continued, "so I assumed he had also told his father."

Waleka stared at his first two wives. "Why did he go to school in Weetebula?" he asked. Koni and Duyo both sensed that Waleka's question was heartfelt.

"You were gone so long, and when you came home, you brought your sixth wife, Inya Nomo, to the field house," Koni said. "Raga couldn't take the shame anymore and asked to be sent off somewhere else to attend junior high. So Duyo and I took him to Bapa Bili, to work and go to school."

Waleka was silent for a while. "Zoga is gone, too. Did Zoga go with Raga?"

"What? Zoga? Isn't he six years older than Raga?" Koni's tone was curt. "Take care of your own children; don't worry about others!"

Waleka jumped off the porch and stalked back to his field house.

Watching him go, Duyo and Koni whispered to each other. Both knew why Zoga had disappeared. Zoga had left because he was angry with Ndalo for stealing the girl he wanted to make his new wife. Zoga's father never stopped taking new wives, either.

Every six months, Raga visited his home in Ratenggaro. By the time he turned eighteen, he was taller than Waleka.

Waleka tried to rebuild a relationship with his eldest son and arranged Raga's marriage to Hamoli, a girl Raga met in Weetebula. But Raga remained aloof from his father and maintained the distance between them.

"He is only eighteen," Duyo said to Waleka when the topic of arrangements for Raga's marriage came up. "Did he talk to you about this plan?"

"Yes, yes, yes! Don't ask so many questions! Just take care of everything needed for my son Raga's wedding!" Waleka's rapid-fire answers came from his embarrassment that Raga never asked for his consideration in anything, unless he talked through Koni and Duyo.

"Hamoli, my future daughter-in-law, is educated," Waleka boasted. "She graduated from junior high school and learned agricultural and housekeeping skills in Weetebula." He was sure that when Raga eventually became the head of the family, he would save his family's face. To garner Raga and Hamoli's affections, Waleka started paying more attention to his family and parents. He wanted to show that he was always there for his family and that he wasn't as bad as everyone said he was.

"Raga is going to be just like you — having many wives," Ndalo said mockingly. "That's why you need to marry again, Waleka! What's so great about your first wife? Barren Limbu Koni can't give you anything."

Waleka didn't know what to say. In the turmoil of his feelings, he wondered if Raga's wedding might be a sign for him to stop taking wives. "I will stop," Waleka told himself, and placed his hope in Raga. Raga would give him a grandson soon. Waleka smiled imagining that.

It thus came as a big surprise to everyone, that when Hamoli announced she was pregnant, Koni, after 23 years of marriage, announced she was pregnant too.

The big news spread like wildfire through Ratenggaro, Lamboya, and the surrounding villages. It never once crossed Waleka's mind that Koni could be pregnant.

When Wolli started first grade under the full moon in March 1957, Koni gave birth to Tila Wula. Koni was forty-one years old. Something that had seemed impossible for her had finally happened.

Koni never tried to figure out which number of Waleka's children Tila Wula was. At that time, Waleka had six wives.

"Tila Wula will grow up together with Raga and Hamoli's daughter, Lara — our granddaughter," Duyo said. "Wula will be loved by Raga, his wife, and his children because Inya Koni is also their mother." As usual, Duyo opened her heart just as she had done since first arriving at the ancestral house.

"And Wula will be a best friend for Lara." Hamoli gently stroked her newborn baby.

Chapter 5

Waleka's ancestral house stood at the end of the village, about thirty feet from the edge of the high cliff overlooking the sea. From the side of his house, the waves could not be seen. Their presence was known only by the crashing sound as they broke and pushed the water to the foot of the cliff. The wind carried the sounds of high tide. The beach was clearly visible from the cliffside.

One day, in early 1974, the arrival of relatives who lived away from the village began to crowd Ratenggaro. They had come home to celebrate the imminent Bau Nyale and Pasola. The number of children and grandchildren had increased so rapidly over the years, that it became difficult for a parent like Waleka, now fifty-seven years old, to keep track of everything.

Lara, Wula, and Ida, Ndalo's granddaughter, were among the crowd. The sixteen-year-old teenagers had just started their first year at a vocational school for teachers, in Anakalang — a city quite far from Ratenggaro. Meanwhile, Wolli was finishing up his degree in teaching at a university in Kupang, on Timor Island.

Lara, Wula, and Ida sat together in the garden, waiting for Galuh, their friend from elementary and junior high school.

Wolli had just returned from grooming Lamura and tethered the horse to the banyan tree.

"*Gha* Wolli!" Wula, Lara, and Ida all called Wolli "older brother."

"It's good to see three best friends!" exclaimed Wolli. "Where is Galuh? Isn't she coming?"

"She is definitely coming," Wula answered.

"I thought she went to the vocational school with the three of you," Wolli said.

"Poor Galuh, she could only finish junior high, then dropped out." Lara explained and shrugged, "If you don't go to school, you get married."

"Sixteen is too young to get married!" Wula exclaimed.

"Going to school is much better," said Ida.

"Yeah! Galuh couldn't possibly want to marry," Lara said. "Let's persuade her to go back to school." Lara pulled out a white hairpin and showed it to the group. "This is a gift for her. Did you bring her a gift too?"

"I brought her a small wallet," Ida said.

"I brought a storybook," Wula said. "Galuh can read it, but I want it back when she's finished."

The three girls missed Galuh. She had always been with them on their commute to school on horseback, when they were younger.

"Koda will be here, too!" Wolli said.

"Ida's older brother is coming?" Wula asked in disbelief.

"Yes, Gha Koda is coming too!" Wolli grinned.

The village children gathered happily around them. Whenever Lara, Ida, and Wula came home from Weetebula, they always brought souvenirs of sweets and shared them with children and adults alike.

"Lara!" Wula called, laughing as Lara passed out some candy.

"Yes, Aunt Wula can have one too!" Lara chuckled.

"Lara!" Wolli called. "Do I also get a piece of candy?"

"Yes, Uncle Wolli," Everyone laughed. Lara then carefully explained to the children the importance of knowing and respecting each other.

Starting with grandfather, father, uncle, aunt, brother, and sister, everyone should know their place on the family tree, because they had a large family. "Very large," Lara ended.

"How do you know that, Lara?" Ndalo sat next to Waleka, watching the teens.

"School!" Lara answered, smiling.

"You're smart!" Waleka said proudly.

"I'm as smart as you, *Ambu*," Lara laughed.

"Correct!" Waleka beamed as he praised his granddaughter's intelligence.

"Sure, it's great that all of you go to school and learn a lot," Ndalo continued in a mocking tone, "but don't forget to come home to join in all the traditional ceremonies!"

Lara stared silently at Ndalo. Then she and Wula gathered all the children and grandchildren and headed to the cemetery at the village entrance, where they would clean the graves in preparation for the Bau Nyale. Ndalo and Waleka followed.

Under the scrutiny of Ndalo's watchful eyes, the youngsters cleaned. Ndalo surveyed the group with hands on his hips, huffing importantly.

Waleka glared at Ndalo. He wasn't just observing the youths, he was staring at them as if he wanted to devour them one by one.

Waleka looked away, offshore, in the distant horizon. A few seconds later, the two men glared at each other and then looked away again.

Ndalo took a long drag from his cigarette and exhaled quickly. "Are you sure you'll be able to kidnap Galuh?" he asked Waleka.

"Why do you care?" Waleka answered. "What is it to you if she wants to be with me?" Waleka paused, then chuckled. "The time between my sixth and seventh has been too long!"

Ndalo's voice was flat. "Just don't forget your promise to me. Wula — you promised to take good care of her for me. If you don't keep your promise, you'll see what happens. You know I'll give you anything you ask for, for sure. So remember, she's mine!"

Ndalo took another deep drag on his cigarette and exhaled hard. "So you finally decided to take a seventh wife. After a long time of abstinence, you're indulging again." He chuckled. "You and me, Waleka, we are the same. Done! The important thing is you take good care of Wula."

"Wait for the right time!" Waleka snapped. "Soon! As we agreed, you'll have her after she graduates and receives a teaching assignment. That was the deal."

"Well, damn, Waleka!"

Waleka chuckled. "Defeat me on the Pasola field, and you can take Wula right then! Remember that!" Waleka knew Ndalo could never defeat an accomplished to-paholong like him. Waleka turned back to watch his grandchildren cleaning the graves. Ndalo kept his hungry eyes on Wula, Lara, and the group of children.

Waleka's habit of kidnapping women to marry was most embarrassing to Koni and Duyo. Waleka, however, took pride in it. Neither Koni nor Duyo wanted to know how much livestock and acreage Waleka had given away as dowries for all of his kidnapped wives.

Despite growing opposition, the bride-kidnapping tradition still occurred.

Koni had the worried feeling that something was about to happen again. Waleka was back at it. Her husband's new wife would soon enter this ancestral house. *The seventh woman!* Koni muttered with pain.

The village, with its towering traditional, ancestral houses, was becoming quieter through the years. Koni watched her children and grandchildren with pride and gratitude. The arrival of Lara, Wula, and Wolli always brought joy to Bapa and Mama Tua. Waleka's parents were now very old. They had become sad and quiet after Waleka brought his third wife to the ancestral house. The speech with life's generational wisdoms that Bapa Tua had given in 1934 to welcome the Nyale and prepare for the Pasola was no longer remembered.

On the morning of Bau Nyale in 1973, after kawoking the entire night before with the other villagers, Wula and her siblings walked home from the beach. They had just caught a large number of sea worms that the tide had washed onto the beach.

"Look how many there are, Inya!" Wula exclaimed to her mother. She sifted through the squirming worms, examining their colors. The slippery worms kept falling back into the container every time she picked them up. "Gha Wolli!" she called. "There are a lot of worms, but they are thin. Thin and pale."

"You're right." Wolli stirred the worms. "They *are* pale!" He turned to Koni. "Are you going to make chili sauce, Inya? It's delicious with boiled sweet potatoes." Koni did not reply.

Lara lifted the worms high and dropped them back into the container. "They are pale, thin worms! Why are they so thin? So thin and pale."

Wula caught some of the worms Lara dropped. "Yes! Please, Inya! Use them to make chili sauce!" When Koni remained silent, Wula asked, "Why are you so quiet, Inya? Are you sick?"

"I'm fine," Koni said slowly. "We'll make chili sauce. We'll make nyale palowor, too." Koni looked again at the worms her children kept turning and turning. *It is true. The worms are pale and thin.* Anxiety crept into Koni's heart.

Earlier that morning, on the beach, amid the crowd of villagers hunting nyale, she had not seen any unfamiliar young women, and she began to feel relieved that Waleka's seventh wife-to-be was not there. But then Duyo had grabbed her arm. "That's *her!*" she exclaimed, pointing. "That's the one Waleka will take back to the house."

"What?" Koni gasped. "But that is Galuh, Lara's classmate! Waleka's seventh wife is Galuh? Lara, Ida, and Wula's friend?"

"Galuh does not go to school anymore," Duyo replied. "She dropped out. There is going to be a big problem because Inya Telu's son, Logo, has already chosen her to be his next wife!"

"When will Waleka bring her to the house?" Koni didn't want to discuss Galuh's relationship with Logo, her stepson from Waleka's third wife.

"I heard the woman will be introduced today after the Pasola," Duyo whispered.

Koni did not see Galuh leave or with whom, but she knew exactly where Galuh came from and who her family was.

Now, standing in the kitchen surrounded by her children and the thin, pale sea worms, Koni wondered, *Does she want to be Waleka's wife?*

Ratenggaro village and its surroundings grew busier with the arrival of children, grandchildren, and extended family. Everyone gathered for lunch at the village chief's house before heading to the Pasola field. Eating together was one of the Pasola's traditions. The nyale dishes came from many of the ancestral houses. The men, together with all guests, ate the feast of nyale before heading out to the Pasola field. The kitchen of the village chief was open for everyone, and everyone could enjoy the dishes sent from each kitchen of the ancestral houses in the village.

The elders, including Koni's husband, would soon conduct the opening of the Bau Nyale communal meal at the village chief's house. Bau Nyale was a tradition Koni always put her faith in. She took comfort in knowing that the sea worms would always surface from the ocean floor and head for the beach to be easily picked up and brought home.

One of the assets of an elder was a new wife, a young wife. The number of wives showed his wealth, because having many wives meant he was rich enough to pay for many dowries. The dowry always reflected the wealth of the giver. What young woman would not want to be an elder's wife? What elder man would not want a young woman?

Koni took a long, deep breath and shook her head to erase the memory of time gone by. When she looked up, she saw Waleka sitting among the elders and other men, in the ancestral house's yard. Some of the guests who had come to watch the Pasola sat with them. Waleka and the elders sat on an elevated platorm, so they were visible above the crowd. For a man of his age, Waleka still looked buff and strong. His head was wrapped with a new *destar*, headband — one that Koni had never seen before. *Had Galuh given it to him?*

At that moment, Waleka turned his head toward Koni, and their eyes met. Koni did not blink or lower her gaze. It was Waleka who finally looked away.

"Will Bapa Waleka join the Pasola, Inya?" Wolli asked.

"Yes, he will participate in the Pasola."

"My father is great." Wolli could not hide his pride. He collected the nyale palowor that Koni had cooked to take to the communal meal at the village chief's house.

"Isn't the nyale palowor delicious, Inya?" Wolli sat beside his mother with a plate of sweet potato and nyale palowor accompanied by spicy chili sauce made from mashed nyale. When Koni didn't answer, Wolli continued, "Yes, it is delicious because my Inya cooked it. It is much better than the *opor*, chicken cooked with coconut milk, that I ate in a food stall in the city."

"It's not so good." Koni's voice was barely audible. "The worms were pale and thin ..." She took a deep breath. She knew the nyale always gave her signs. After the first five years of her marriage with Waleka, the nyale harvest had been similar: The worms had been thin and pale. *Was Waleka up to something in addition to taking a seventh wife?* Koni tried to ignore her feelings. "Where is Tila Wula?" she asked, looking around. She saw her beautiful daughter sitting on the platform with her father, near Ndalo.

Wolli immediately walked over to Tila Wula. "Come eat with us!"

Koni watched as Ndalo grabbed Wula's hand and said something to her. She saw Wula nod and exclaim, "Don't hold my hand so tight!" as she pulled her hand from Ndalo's grip. Koni looked at her daughter with pride as she followed Wolli back to the table.

"She is the first daughter of Waleka's family. Of course, she is the best." These words were voiced many times in various phrasings to emphasize that Wula was the first and primary daughter of their ancestral house. Koni was amused to see how her daughter handled her position with such poise. Wula had only just graduated from junior high school and had started her studies at the vocational school for teachers, but even though she was still very young, Wula already carried her future stature.

CHAPTER 6

Lara joined the table with Koni, Wula, and Wolli. Both girls had agreed to leave for the Maliti Bondo Ate Pasola field early to get a place on the stage.

"What did Ndalo talk about?" Koni asked Wolli.

Wolli looked disgusted. "He told me to take care of Wula." He did not tell his mother that Ndalo was always reminding him that he was not Wula's biological brother.

"Did he remind you again that you are not my biological son?" Koni asked, reading Wolli's face. "Biological means born from here," Koni said, patting her belly. "You were born from here." Koni pointed to her heart. "*That* is a biological child!" Everyone at the table laughed.

The elders left the village chief's house. Waleka mounted his horse with a single jump. Sitting upright in the saddle, he looked around. For a moment, his eyes rested on his ancestral house and swept over Koni's face.

Koni stared into the piercing eyes of the man she had been married to for more than half of her life. Her heart never failed to stir at the sight of him. Despite getting older, her love for him was still very much alive.

It was a love ignited at their first meeting, and kept burning by the ever-present fire of jealousy.

Waleka wore a new henggul and a sarong with an unusual color. Koni did not know which wife had woven the sarong with such a bright color. *Was it Inya Duyo, Inya Telu, Inya Potoh, Inya Lime, or Inya Nomo? Who wove that bright sarong for my husband?* It was not the usual shade, and it was not woven from the finest cotton and homemade coloring. This sarong was too bright — a cheap color easily bought in city stores. Clothes and their colors were a reflection of the person who wore them. *Which wife had made the sarong? What pattern did she use?* Koni took a deep breath while watching her husband ride out of the village with the other horsemen. She walked briskly to the end of the village and climbed onto a pile of rocks. From there, she could see the group of horsemen leave through the gate, turn, and descend onto the road that split the cemetery, heading for the main road to the Pasola field.

"Did you see Bapa, Inya?" Tila Wula appeared behind her mother with Wolli and Lara.

"Yes." Koni shifted so Wula could stand next to her.

"What are all of you looking at?" Lara asked.

"The most handsome and tallest father!" Wolli replied. "But he's wearing a bad sarong. The pattern is not a horse, chicken, or turtle — it's a snake! Why is Bapa wearing that kind of fabric?"

"That is Bapa!" Wula cried when she spotted Waleka's head above the heads of the other horsemen. Enthused, she continued, "The pattern of his fabric is so bright. Bapa looks tall!"

"Lamura is also tall," Wolli replied proudly.

"Yes, and he's clean and shiny," Koni added.

"Let's go to the field. Galuh is waiting for us there." Lara, Wolli, and Wula left Koni with her thoughts.

"Will you also ride in the Pasola, Gha Wolli?" Lara asked.

"Yes, I will alternate with Bapa. Let's hurry up!"

"The handsome Gha Wolli will ride the handsome Lamura," Wula said.

Koni watched Wolli as the children hurried to the field. He had asked what wearing the fabric's snake pattern meant. Koni knew exactly what it meant. The snake was a sign of cunning and deceit. Koni did not know where Waleka had obtained the sarong and she did not dare to ask which wife had woven it for her husband.

Almost every man and woman flocked to the Pasola field. This year's Pasola ceremony would be led by Waleka and Ndalo from Ratenggaro and several other elders. Everyone knew the old men would also be the ones to start the first round after the *Ndara Nyale, Ndara Wini,* and *Ndara Halato* had performed their duties. It was customary that the Pasola event was opened with a ceremony led by three horses and their riders. A team representing the sea worms, as the leader, another team that represented the fertile soil resulting in abundant crops, and lastly a team representing the spirit of the event — the honesty and cavalier attitude that was expected from the participants.

Waleka and Ndalo acted younger than fifty-seven-year-old men. They risked their reputation as elders who were accomplished to-paholongs, husbands of several wives, and fathers and grandfathers of several children and grandchildren.

After her husband, children, and grandchildren were out of sight, Koni turned around and slowly walked home.

"Aren't you going to the Pasola field?" asked an old woman, passing her house with several other women. "Oh! I see you are cooking some delicious dishes. Are you having guests?" The nosy women cleverly expressed their curiosity, without mentioning Galuh's name.

Koni had learned, through her very long life journey, which questions she had to answer and which she could ignore.

After Koni entered the kitchen of the ancestral house, Duyo shared the news that Waleka would bring the seventh wife into their Big House soon. "Everyone knows it." Duyo sat by the stone stove, helping Koni prepare food.

After fanning the cooking fire, smoke billowed, and the fire reignited. Koni stirred the food, while Duyo sliced chunks of meat and vegetables. Duyo's face was red from the heat and smoke. Wrinkles crisscrossed her forehead. Sharp cheekbones and the sunken flesh below made her look much older than Koni, even though they were only two years apart.

"Aren't you angry?" Duyo asked after a few seconds, almost cutting her finger.

Koni glanced at Duyo with a wry smile. *No,* she thought, *my anger ran out almost thirty-seven years ago when you were brought from Lamboya, just hours after the Pasola celebration was over. The nyale harvest that year was very bad. The worms were ugly, small, thin, and colorless.* Although unspoken, these words dwelled in Koni's heart. Koni stole another glance at Duyo, the second wife who had upstaged her a long time ago.

"Are you going to stay silent, Inya Koni?" Duyo asked again, fanning the fire. "You should be very angry! Waleka already has six wives, and now, he's going to have a seventh! He should be ashamed of himself and embarrassed in front of his children and grandchildren! Oh, my God, Inya, I am furious!"

Duyo continued to vent. She talked about the arrival of Waleka's wives and all the stories about them, their children, and grandchildren. "Only Logo and Uka are not ashamed to roam the village, perhaps because they are the eldest sons of Waleka's third and fourth wives. Some of the other children and grandchildren are ashamed; some don't know how to be ashamed. How should we tell them?"

Duyo's question was left unanswered.

"How many children have gone?" Duyo continued emotionally. "But Waleka keeps getting new wives. The horses, buffaloes, and land we own are decreasing. The children keep fighting over houses and land. But Waleka is not even aware of it!" Duyo wiped her face. But a few moments later, she laughed. "Raga despite being our eldest son and the eldest of all children, never says anything about it. He will not fight his father. I pray Raga does not become like his father,"

Raga was in his front yard, preparing to leave for the Pasola field, when he heard the thunder of horses filling the field. Breathlessly, Hamoli joined Raga. She had just returned from the Pasola field, where she'd gone to see if Galuh was there. "The woman is sitting on the highest part of the stage with Lara, Ida, and Wula. She is their friend. I saw her myself!"

"Hmmm," Raga replied, half-listening.

"She is their friend!" his wife repeated. "It's enough! Can't you please bring Bapa Leka to his senses?" When Raga continued to ignore her, Hamoli became worried. "Please don't follow in your father's footsteps!" she pleaded. "Think about your daughter Lara; think about her siblings! How would you explain things to them? Do you hear me?"

"Hmmm," Raga replied.

CHAPTER 7

Raga entered the Pasola field, confused. The Pasola of 1974 saddened him. Waleka, his father, was going to take a seventh wife. Raga tried not to look at the stage while he tied his horse near it. "Oh, Apu," Raga called out softly to his ancestors.

Lara called out to her father. Wula, Ida, and Galuh waved.

Raga nodded, smiling. Realizing what was about to happen, his heart pounded wildly. *Many relatives will come to the Big House after the Pasola. What will happen? Does Lara know?*

Raga quickly walked away, leaving his daughter on the stage, sitting with her future grandmother, Galuh, who wanted to look around the field but did not want to stand on the sidelines. Raga headed to the left corner of the field where his father and teammates convened. He squeezed in among the jostling spectators.

People from many villages crowded around the Maliti Bondo Ate Pasola field. Those who would test their skills in the field had also filled the sidelines. The center of the field was the place that would soon excite the entire audience. An elder advised all Pasola fighters to conduct themselves honestly and bravely during the event.

A few moments later, dozens of horses and their riders followed behind the valorous Waleka on Lamura's back. They trotted around the field, heads held high, javelins in their right hand and reins in their left hand. At the same time, fifteen horses and their riders left the right side of the field and galloped around the circumference. Grooms immediately helped hold the reins when each group returned to their places.

The first round would start soon. Waleka and Ndalo placed themselves on the left side of the field. The group on the right ran fast.

Waleka was in the front row, accompanied by cheers and flying javelins trying to hit and unhorse the opponent. A javelin would have hit his chest had the old man not dodged it quickly. The audience's screams broke out when Waleka raised his hands high.

"Ririri ririri, ririri, riri, riri, ririraiiii!" Kayiliking filled the Pasola field with a sense of satisfaction and gratitude for the first appearance. It promised joy.

Raga watched his father sitting high in his saddle amidst his teammates, galloping around the field once again. He knew exactly who the old man's eyes sought.

"You have a great father," some of the spectators on the sideline told him.

"He is so dashing!" another gushed. "He looks as if he is still a young man!"

"You lose!" another voice added. "You're still young, but you've only had one wife for a long time. Your father is going to have his seventh! Ndalo has six! Those two old men have several wives and a lot of children — even your younger brothers have more than one wife! Are you the only son who sticks to one?" The men on the sidelines laughed.

Raga moved away and began eavesdropping on the gossip circulating about his father's plan to add another wife.

He saw Waleka still riding Lamura around the back side of the field, where other equestrians waited their turn. Raga looked for Wolli, who was supposed to take the place of their father on the field. But Waleka remained seated in his saddle, focused on his own goals.

Raga saw his father lean forward and press his lithe body against the horse. He raised his head and turned to the stands filled with cheering spectators.

Raga had seen enough. He decided to leave before the Pasola ended. As he exited the field, he saw Lara, Ida, Wula, and Galuh, jumping up and down, adding to the joyful atmosphere which exceeded the usual.

The wind swept white clouds across a previously bright blue sky. Raga did not return to Ratenggaro. He did not join the post-Pasola celebration of the Pasola riders and the thanksgiving feast everyone shared with gratitude for the morning Nyale and the afternoon Pasola. Instead, he walked with his horse along the beach to sort out his feelings. He tried to overcome the disappointment he could not put into words, because he already knew with certainty that Waleka would do whatever he wanted and bring the seventh woman to the ancestral house — and there was nothing he could do to stop him.

Neither Galuh nor her older sisters had finished school. So, unlike Lara and Wula, Galuh was betrothed to Waleka who already had six wives. Lara and Wula, because they were educated, would be wed to unmarried men. Likewise with Ida, Ndalo's granddaughter. The difference was that Lara's, Ida's, and Wula's parents would receive their dowry after their daughters' suitors finished their education and were able to support their family. Galuh's parents would receive Waleka's dowry for their daughter much sooner.

"The *belis* will be expensive because the woman is very young," Raga's wife had told him earlier. Raga turned his horse towards the open fields and bit his lower lip. He was angry and disappointed, but he also feared his father. His horse's trot was as sluggish as Raga's spirit.

The wind blew harder. Raga stopped his horse in the middle of the field and looked far ahead. Shame covered his mind and heart.

"It's his right! Why should you worry?" The voices from his friends buzzed again in Raga's ears. "You should be proud to have an extraordinary father like him! You have to honor the pride of an elder like your father!"

Galuh had already visited his house several times because she was friends with Lara. Galuh had attended the Nyale ceremony that morning and participated in catching the sea worms. The rumor that she would be formally brought to the ancestral house after the Pasola squeezed Raga's heart. *What will Lara and Wula say?*

The strong wind created waves of rustling grass in the open field. Raga jumped off his horse and sat to the side while it grazed. The howling wind did not mask the sound of approaching hooves, but instead carried them to Raga's ears. Raga could tell that the clopping came from the path he had just passed, but he ignored it and did not turn around as the horse slowed and stopped right behind him.

"Raga! Why are you here?" Inya Telu's eldest son, Logo, shouted above the wind. "Let's go home. Come on!" Raga and Logo had gone in different life directions many years ago. Logo was known as the thief of livestock and family land. He had harmed the extended family for his personal gain.

Raga rose and turned irritably. "What happened, Logo? Why do I need to go home? What are you up to? Are you here to steal land, horses, and buffaloes from our family? What do you want? Do you want to tell me that Galuh, the woman you planned on making your third wife, will be taken by our father as his seventh?"

Logo affected a worried look. "Can you stop Bapa?"

"You already know that's our father's character, Logo, so don't pretend to be worried. He is an elder, he is rich, and he is respected. So let the young woman be taken to the Big House to be his seventh wife. Should we be proud? Is this the time for you to blackmail Bapa?" Raga fought to stay angry with Logo instead of feel sorry for him.

"It cost just a few buffaloes!" Logo chuckled. "True, everyone already knows about Galuh." Logo grimaced at having to lose Galuh to his father. "Bapa is taking my Galuh!" Logo yelled to the sky. He clenched his fist and punched the air, cursing and shouting.

Then he looked at Raga and spoke again in a lowered tone. "Lara is angry! Lara was screaming in defiance of Bapa taking Galuh! Everything is messed up! Then Lara ran off somewhere! No one cares!"

Suddenly, Logo laughed. "Raga, your daughter is remarkable! Extraordinary! Did you teach her how to speak up for herself? I am very proud of her. Let Bapa feel ashamed!"

Raga looked at his half-brother's face. For the first time, Raga felt Logo was sincerely proud and speaking the truth, even though it was in Logo's best interest to flatter him. "Let her be." Logo continued. "She will eventually calm down and come home. In the end, she too will have to accept Galuh, just like the rest of us. Let's go back to the village now." Logo did not mention that Lara had been slapped for her impudence, in front of everyone.

"Who did Lara run off with?" Raga interrupted Logo's thoughts.

Logo looked extremely worried. "Come on. We'd better get home right away. You'll understand when we get to the Big House and you see what's going on." Logo turned his horse and with a jerk on the reins, broke into a gallop across the deserted field.

Raga followed reluctantly.

When Galuh arrived at the ancestral house as Waleka's future seventh wife, Lara was furious. She could not believe her grandfather would marry her best friend. Lara glared at Waleka. She wanted him to tell her that the rumors she had heard, and now saw, were not true.

"Galuh! Do you really want to be my grandfather's wife?" Lara stared as Galuh nodded.

"Kakek!" Lara gaped at her grandfather, who resolutely ignored her.

Galuh's parents and several members of Galuh's family stood before Waleka, Ndalo, and several other traditional elders. The crowd of curious people kept growing outside the ancestral home. Everyone wanted to know who Waleka's new wife was.

Lara suddenly lost control in front of everyone. She snatched the sarong to be worn by the seventh wife out of Koni's hand.

"You are my friend!" Lara screamed at Galuh, hot tears running down her face. She poked an angry finger into Galuh's face. "How dare you become my grandfather's seventh wife! You're evil! Get out!" No one could calm Lara as she continued to rant. "Everyone! Get out of here!"

Lara's unprecedented conduct shocked the gathering. She was the granddaughter of an elder, with a dream of graduating from college, fully supported by her parents. Her Uncle Uka was the first to raise his hand to her face. The slap left an angry red mark on Lara's cheek. Inya Telu slapped her next. How dare Lara defy her grandfather, a respected elder!

When Lara saw Koni and Duyo crying, she became frantic to defend her two grandmothers and charged at Galuh, attacking her until the surprised girl fell to the ground. Village men immediately surrounded the fighting girls, pulling Lara back and trying to restrain her.

"Lara!" Koni rushed to hug and protect her granddaughter. But Uka and Telu blocked her and dragged Koni away. No one sided with Lara.

The sixteen-year-old Lara ran away from the ceremony under watchful eyes. "She doesn't respect her elders! She didn't respect her elder's name, which is her grandfather's name!" Those were the voices that accompanied Lara as she jumped on a horse and fled the village.

"Just let her go! Don't chase her!" some of the elders exclaimed. They had just witnessed what would turn out to be a historic event for Waleka.

After the commotion died down, the wedding ceremony was set to resume, but Galuh's family refused to accept the shameful spectacle they had just witnessed. Galuh and her entourage all left the village, ignoring the pleas of Waleka and other elders not to go.

"We are withdrawing," muttered Galuh's family, as they left the village. "We ask for time. We will return, only if we are taken care of properly! We are very embarrassed. Where can we hide our faces?"

Logo watched Galuh leave, with a pounding, jealous heart. "How dare you take my woman, Bapa," Logo whispered. He, too, left the village, spurring his horse in the opposite direction from Lara's escape route.

Through it all, Wula stood transfixed, face flushed, blood pulsing in her tightly clenched fists. She stared at Waleka, but he was not paying any attention to her. When Wula glanced at Ndalo, she caught him already looking at her. She glared, unblinking, until Ndalo looked away.

Wolli touched Wula's hand. "Stay here. I will go after Lara and bring her back." Uka watched Wolli mount his horse and ride away from the village. Waleka and several elders left to meet at Ndalo's house and discuss how to get Galuh back.

Later, while everyone was eating, Uka saw Wolli return alone, looking worried. Everyone came out of the ancestral house to hear what Wolli had found out about Lara.

"Why did you chase after Lara?" Uka attacked Wolli. "She's Raga's daughter, not yours! Why did you bother?"

"No, Gha Uka!" Wolli replied. "Lara's gone!"

"With whom?" Uka persisted.

Wolli did not have an answer; he did not know. He didn't dare tell the truth: that he'd seen Lara galloping full speed along the beach before turning a corner and disappearing from sight.

CHAPTER 8

Raga was deep in thought as he rode his horse slowly behind Logo. He wanted to search for Lara, but he held back. Deep inside, he was proud that his daughter had dared to openly defy her grandfather. Up ahead, Logo had slowed his horse to think about how he could extract some benefit from his own father.

From afar, at the same time, the half-brothers both caught sight of smoke billowing high, enfolding a writhing, flaring fire. "Ratenggaro!" Raga shouted, whipping his horse, as Logo spurred his into the race for time.

The gusting wind fanned the blazing fire as it grabbed the roof's edge of Waleka's ancestral house. Throughout the village, neighbors ran helter-skelter, trying to help one another but not knowing where to start. Screams of fear and anger mingled with the blowing smoke. Relentlessly, the wind swirled and danced, embracing piece after piece of the ancestral home. The roar of the wind became one with the roar of the fire and the crackling sound of the tall, thatched roof burning. The bamboo cracked before being consumed by the fire. There was nothing that could be done other than allow the fire to continue devouring the Big House.

Cries filled the air. "Water! Water!" Containers were gathered from each home. Most contained only a small amount of water leftover from what had already been used for household needs.

Some of the men threw water on Waleka's burning roof, but there was not enough water to quell the flames as they crept up towards the peak. The village had no water source nearby. Several men mounted horses and rode to the spring they used, even though it was too far from the village to do any good. Everyone knew that at this very urgent time, it was impossible to secure the water they needed in time to save Waleka's home.

"Who started the fire?"

"What have we done wrong?"

"Oh, Waleka, whose fault is this?"

"Bo kolo mata – mbe leko roka tilu! Please help!" Koni shouted, and several men ran into the stilt house to carry out Bapa Tua and Mama Tua.

Chaos ensued as every villager worked desperately to save whatever essential items they could from Waleka's home. All looms, threads, unfinished weaves, clamping tools, traditional sarongs, clothes, and other crucial belongings were moved away from the fire. People ran everywhere, saving whatever items they could find. No one paid attention to Lamura, stabled beneath Waleka's house in the kambu luna.

Fear and anger quickly turned to accusations and remorse.

"There were children playing with fire!"

"The wind was blowing! Why did you play with fire?"

"Hey! The wind whipped up suddenly!

"Do you blame the wind?"

"How could this happen?"

Conjecture and assumptions led to confused interpretations of how the fire started. One story held that the fire started at the base of Waleka's roof, reinforcing the widespread allegation that someone had lighted a flare, which the wind had carried to the roof.

The coming of the fire was as fierce as the jab of a Pasola javelin flying from the galloping to-paholong on horseback. The thatched roof made a perfect partner for a fire dancing to the rhythm of a war dance.

Amid the angry screams, pleas for help, and cries of despair, Mada Wolli jumped up the stairs and entered his father's burning house.

"Wolli, no! Wolli!" Koni shouted.

"Gha Wolli! Gha Wolli!" Tila Wula screamed. Others also yelled Wolli's name.

"Wolli —" Koni sank to the ground.

The following minutes felt like hours. Finally, Wolli appeared through the smoky doorway carrying a set of looms, still clamping woven threads, and his and Wula's school bags. He threw everything out on the ground and rushed back inside for another few long, terrifying moments. He reemerged, hugging a small trunk to his chest, and jumped off the home's porch to safety.

Wolli ignored the grumblings of scorn by some of the men, jealous of his bravery. Duyo and Wula held him tight. Koni reached out to hold his feet.

Suddenly, Wolli yelled. Lamura! The kambu luna beneath the house was on fire! Inside, Lamura, snorting and whinnying, reared up and pawed the air, fighting to escape the fire and smoke engulfing the stable. Wolli raced to the kambu luna's door. It was locked. *It has never been locked before. What is happening?*

The floor of Waleka's home — the roof of Lamura's stable — collapsed in a fireball of smoke and sparks.

"Lamura!" Wolli howled, as several men grabbed and restrained him. The burgeoning flames, intense heat, and the imploding roof would have killed Wolli if he had recklessly obeyed his heart.

The men dragged Wolli to safety, as everyone moved farther away from the fire. Amid the crackling and popping flames, Wolli could hear Lamura snorting and blowing as he struggled to breathe, endlessly, until all sound disappeared along with the *whoosh* of the fire as the entire house collapsed in on itself, burying Lamura's body.

The fire crept higher and higher. The fire would soon reach the top of the ancestral house. The blazing flames easily devoured every dry reed.

Wolli stood in the distance shaking. There was nothing more to be done, and he wept.

Slowly, the frenzied atmosphere calmed, leaving the sound of sobbing women. Among them were two of Wolli's mothers — Koni, his adopted mother, and Duyo. Both women tried to stop him as he walked slowly toward the smoldering fire.

"Mama! I'm fine," Wolli told them hoarsely. The other women reacted angrily to Wolli's risky efforts. He had put his life in danger. He could have died! But Wolli focused his quiet attention on Kakek, Nenek, Duyo, Koni, and Tila Wula, who kept worriedly hugging him. Everyone was ordered to stay away from the fire and stay near Kakek and Nenek.

"Inya," Wolli said softly, handing his mother the trunk he had saved from their home, "this is the chest you keep your sarong in."

"Lamura," Koni murmured. "Lamura."

"I will take care of him, Inya."

The charred remains of the fire clearly showed that the wind had prevented the fire from spreading beyond Waleka's house. It looked like the wind and fire had conspired to aim their destruction solely on the very last house in Ratenggaro — Waleka's.

Waleka stood trembling. He had watched the flames grow, flatten, and devour his ancestral home. He had proudly watched Wolli trying to save everything. He thought about another fire, almost ten years ago, in 1966. It had destroyed all the houses in Ratenggaro, and killed the first Lamura. He had been asleep with Nomo, his sixth wife, in a field house. Waleka remembered all the villagers — men, women, and children — running outside, then running for their lives as flames soared into the air.

Waleka bit his lip. In the most shameful moment of his life, people were bringing him the news that his granddaughter Lara had run away. They said she had jumped on her horse and galloped away along the coast.

Wolli approached Waleka, as if reading his thoughts. "That's right, Bapa. Lara is gone."

Waleka believed Wolli. This beloved son was comforting his first and second wives and his parents. Waleka froze as his wives wailed not far from where he stood. The fear-filled screams of children and grandchildren stabbed his heart.

The soaring flames had been seen by the surrounding villages. People came to witness what was happening — some on horseback, others on foot. Speculations about which ancestral house was on fire were settled as soon as they arrived at the gate of Ratenggaro. Almost everyone agreed that the ancestors were very angry because Elder Waleka had been publicly shamed by his granddaughter.

"Where's Raga?" "Where's Logo?" "Where are the men?" "Why are there only little children?" "Where are the elders?" "They don't care?" "Is your only hope Wolli from Lamboya?" Anxious questions came hurtling in from those wanting to see how Raga and Logo would react to the burning of their ancestral house.

The thunder of galloping horses between the cemeteries and toward the village gates grew louder. Logo was right behind Raga, who immediately jumped off his horse. He threw the reins to a villager and told him to tether his horse to the corner post of the gate. He immediately looked for Bapa Tua and Mama Tua and made sure his grandparents were safe. He caught the clear and direct accusations aimed at Lara, his child.

"Let her go! Don't bother looking for her!"

"Your impudent daughter doesn't know how to respect an elder who is also her grandfather!"

"This fire is the result of your daughter's bad behavior! The ancestors are in a rage!"

"There is no mercy for her and no mercy for us if we allow this!"

The angry voices continued, each one searing a wound in Raga's heart. He tried to calm himself. He tightened his fists and steeled his resolve.

"Lara wasn't wrong!" came a voice from the crowd. "You have to search until you find her! The ancestors are angry because we don't listen to our children and grandchildren!"

The enraged voices rose and again filled Raga's ears.

"Our ancestors are angry because you let her go and no one knows where she is!"

"Of course your daughter doesn't like it that her best friend is going to become her grandfather's wife and she has to call her "grandma" while bowing her head!"

Then a familiar, high-pitched voice pierced the crowd. "Raga, are you just standing there with your mouth open?" old Ndalo's voice was hoarse. "You'd better think about the ceremony we must hold right away to avoid more bad luck! You are useless, you sissy!"

Shaking, Raga fought to stand strong. He squeezed his eyes shut, imagining the fire reaching the top of the roof and perching there on the rafters that had become food for the fire. The peak of the roof was the peak of the fire that reached for the clouds and the sky.

Everyone was stunned as their eyes focused on the same point — the missing peak of the ancestral home. The wooden and bamboo walls collapsed, burying everything in the house in embers and dust.

Slowly, Raga sat. His shoulders shook from holding back the pain that threatened to explode. Logo sat down beside him. Hamoli, Koni, and Duyo surrounded Raga along with others, including a speechless Waleka. Wolli entered the circle and stepped slowly towards Raga to comfort him.

Angry, condescending voices continued pummeling Raga. Some people needed their anger to be heard. Others were satisfied just to speak their opinions, regardless if they reached Raga's ears or were blown away by the wind without anyone listening.

Spontaneously, several women started preparing food. A soup kitchen soon materialized, and all the villagers tried to take part.

The wind died down and the smaller, outlier fires along with it. Ratenggaro felt silent amid the crowd of people. They came one after another to ascertain what had happened and to confirm everything that was uncertain about the cause of the fire disaster. The embers slowly faded. The men who had ridden to the spring returned. They worked together to pour water from the bamboo containers and douse the remains of the fire and extinguish it completely.

Wolli and the villagers pulled Lamura's charred body from the debris. They poured water from the bamboo containers to drench his burned body. Wolli stroked the remains, his vision blurred. He had no more words. Lamura, the famous Pasola steed, was dead.

Wolli and Wula sat quietly next to each other. Not once did Wolli look up to see where Lamura's carcass was being taken to be skinned and butchered for food.

Some of the water containers were placed where the women had built the soup kitchen. Groups of men formed to talk about anything and everything that they heard, saw, believed, and hoped. The largest group formed around Waleka.

A myriad of words came attacking for various reasons. No one could guess what Waleka thought about the woman who by now should have been by his side as his seventh wife. Waleka firmly believed the fire would not have started, and Lamura would not have died, if Lara had not misbehaved. *But are you sure?* his inner voice asked.

Chapter 9

Waleka did not know exactly when the original ancestral house, with so much grandeur, had been built. He remembered his grandfather's story that the ancestral house was built when Waleka's great-grandfather was still in his mother's womb. It had been several generations since the ancestors built the house. Back then, homes were built with materials that were believed to become stronger through time. The house that burnt to the ground, along with all the other houses that burned ten years ago, was rebuilt by all the villagers together, hand in hand, with the pain they all shared.

At that time, everyone lived in their respective traditional ancestral house in the village. A house was not occupied by as many residents as it was now. Now, the occupants were scattered among houses because one wife did not get along with another wife. Or because one child competed with another child. Or one grandson wanted more than the other. So many wives and their offspring were now spread out to form new settlements with rows of field houses.

Waleka could not remember it well, and there were no written records that could be read. And even if there were anything to read, it would not help Waleka; he didn't know how to read.

The ancestors had passed down their history verbally. The spoken language was extraordinarily beautiful if it was used cleanly and authoritatively, if the stories were not based on wealth, the number of wives, children, and grandchildren, but rather on loyalty and ability to share attention in a balanced and honest manner. It was something, Waleka realized, that he was unable to do.

Waleka stood in front of the rubble and dust of his destroyed house. His chest tightened as he glared at the remains of the fire. Standing with the men were four of his wives: Telu, Potoh, Lime, and Nomo. One by one, Waleka's children and grandchildren — he could never properly remember who was who — joined him.

Uka stood next to Waleka. "Lara's behavior caused all of this." He gestured with his chin. Ndalo stood silently near Waleka, with a cold look in his eyes.

"Lara's behavior is inexcusable! Bapa Ndalo, don't you agree?" Uka was looking for support. His words echoed exactly those of the wives who accused and cursed Lara mercilessly. The women started clucking again, trying to explain in their own way how embarrassed they were to witness Lara's shameful behavior when she so strongly opposed Galuh's position as her future grandmother. Lara did not seem to know anything regarding the pride of her ancestors, they said, the pride of her grandfather, the pride of the chairman of the board of elders, the pride of the extended family, and the pride of the ancestral house. Their voices rose with suspicions about who was behind the girl's behavior.

"The important thing is you have received the belis," Ndalo whispered triumphantly in Waleka's ear. "How much more do you need? You are taking good care of Wula, right? I hope you will give Wula to me soon!" He was sure Waleka would need his help to make Galuh his Inya *Pitu*, his seventh wife.

"About Wula," Waleka also whispered. "You have to keep *your* promise."

"My man, Ama Dula, will be the best watcher," Ndalo murmured, a few moments before walking away with the rest of his entourage.

Waleka stared into space with an empty anger. He had paid a large dowry to make Galuh his seventh wife. Waleka was sure he didn't have to worry about Logo fighting him for Galuh because, as an elder, Waleka had more rights.

"Ten buffaloes." Waleka remembered Logo's voice as he argued with him.

"You are crazy!" Waleka had snapped.

"Bapa, you stole my woman. Galuh should be mine, not yours!"

Waleka's head reeled. He shook his head to chase away the image of Logo yelling about the ten buffaloes.

Everything was supposed to have gone according to plan. Waleka could not believe that Lara — his granddaughter! — had dared to oppose him and had openly, publicly, thrown out Galuh. *Oh, she doesn't care about the ancestral house burning down, not ten years ago or now. Back then, I had Nomo. Now all I want is Galuh. Galuh is more important to me than the ancestral house that burned down.* Defeated, Waleka hissed, "All because of Lara!"

Waleka shook his head remembering Lara's anger. "Go away!" she had shouted. "Get out! You are my friend! Why do you want to be my grandmother? Go!" Lara had pushed Galuh towards the open door, her fury a gale of flames.

Shocked, Galuh and her parents had gathered their whole entourage to return home, disappointed and humiliated.

Waleka was powerless to stop them. He could still see the woman he now missed crying in her mother's arms while glancing at him. Their eyes met briefly, but Waleka had to look away.

"Damn Lara! Let her go! No one is allowed to bring her back here!" he growled, his wrath escalating when he discovered that Wolli had tried to chase after her. In his fury, Waleka forgot all about everyone around him.

Now, Raga stood in front of him with his head bowed. Waleka was terse. "I thought Lara — your daughter — would be the one to help with settling my seventh wife into the Big House! Instead, she fought me and acted a fool! Why didn't you raise her better than that?"

"I taught her loyalty, honesty, and respect. Just that." Raga replied.

"Then let her disappear! Never bring her back to the village, never is she welcome in my house! Prepare everything to build a new ancestral house. We have been humiliated! How can a tom mtona like me not have a house!" After referring to himself as an important elder, Waleka licked his suddenly dry lips. He carried on, but with a feeling of uncertainty he did not want to admit. "We will see! The house burned down because the ancestors are angry at her shameless act!"

And thus, Waleka placed the blame on Lara for his having abandoned his ancestors.

Now, his plan to spend heavenly nights with his seventh wife had to be delayed. Worried, Waleka tallied up the number of cattle he had already given to Galuh's family for the original dowry. He shook his head, imagining how much more it would take to buy her back into his house. And not just that, but how much more would it take to keep this large village safe from any more calamities?

"How dare Lara raise her voice in front of so many people!" The high-pitched squawking of the women buzzed in his troubled ears.

The night after the big fire, Waleka sought solace from Nomo, his sixth wife. But the woman lying next to him was grumbling, disturbing his tired heart. "Bapa, there must have been someone coaching Lara to do what she did. I bet Inya Koni and Inya Duyo are behind it." She pouted. "They always make a mess of things around here. They are old, but they still don't know how to take care of a village elder's dignity and our home's reputation." She stroked Waleka's back.

Nomo thought she was more beautiful than any of Waleka's other five wives and more beautiful than Galuh, too. "Lara really doesn't know her manners," she said sternly, pretending to be angry at Lara while actually feeling very happy with how things turned out, because it meant she would remain Waleka's favorite wife. "Oh, Raga and Logo could also have been the instigators. Just think where they were when it all happened. Logo immediately left when he found out Lara had run away. Raga must have waited somewhere for Lara and taken her."

Nomo snuggled into Waleka's arms. Her dream to be Waleka's final wife was in the balance. "Don't be sad, Bapa," she said, disguising her angst. "We'll do whatever it takes to get Galuh to return. I will help you bring her back here."

Waleka turned her to face him. "Do you remember the story of the uma parona?" he asked quietly.

"We will build the Big House again," said Nomo. "You used to tell us that the Big House is a sign that we are a rich family — owners of meadows, horses, and buffaloes. Our uma parona was the biggest, tallest, most impressive of all the houses in the village. Tell Inya Koni and Inya Duyo to leave. They are of no use. Let me and Galuh take care of the Big House."

The words of his sixth wife burned Waleka with sorrow. His thoughts turned to the past, when he was only ten years old. His grandparents, parents, sisters, and many other villagers were at a restoration ceremony for their ancestral house that had burned down. He had sat among the traditional elders and the men, wearing his headband and other traditional attire, being honored as the eldest, even though he was born the youngest.

Now, he, alone, was expected to take care of the rebuilt traditional ancestral house, to protect the family, guard his self-respect, and honor the ancestors from generation to generation. "Our uma parona is gone," he whispered, feeling a mixture of sadness about the burned-down ancestral house and a longing for Galuh.

"We will rebuild the uma parona after Galuh is here." Nomo did not understand what was going on in her husband's mind. This sixth wife only understood that soon, Galuh would replace her body under Waleka's.

Ever since the traditional ancestral house had burned down, Waleka had not been able to sleep well. His pride had been tarnished in front of everyone, especially Galuh. It was not only the loss of the ancestral house that worried him, but also Lara's fury, which he could not erase from his mind. Galuh's family's taking offense embarrassed him, and he deeply regretted the entire incident.

Walking outside his burned home, Waleka held his head high, as if trying to touch the top of the tall roof that was no more. When he lowered his head, his eyes met Koni's, sitting atop a rock amid the ruins of their uma parona.

Waleka looked away. For him, Koni was the same as the best sarong that covered him day and night. Wherever he went, whichever wife he fell asleep with, Koni's face always appeared. After years of living together with no children, she had brought Wolli home. Still later, she had given birth to Wula. During his days filled with love and happiness in their ancestral house, in the garden, in the farm field, on the nyale beach, at the Pasola field, and everywhere else, this woman's face was always with him.

Because Koni had married him, the chairman of the board of elders, she had been forced to accept the local custom of the first wife having to give birth to a son, a direct descendant from the male elder. Waleka remembered clearly how Koni was made to accept Inya Duyo as a wife to bear the son she couldn't for her husband. Thus, Raga and his younger siblings had been born, and Raga, as the first son directly descended from Waleka, became heir-apparent. As expected of her, Koni had helped raise Duyo's children.

Still, Waleka felt unsatisfied. His male prowess and pride, backed by his wealth and power, were unstoppable. His machismo grew stronger after he started kidnapping his wives. Waleka never thought his hunger for women hurt Koni. When he took Inya Nomo, his sixth wife, Koni had been pregnant with Tila Wula.

Many people expected Waleka to stop acquiring new wives after Koni had given birth. Others suspected that Waleka would continue because he was a descendant of a long line of well-respected elders, well-known for their wealth of livestock and acreage.

The ruins of Waleka's uma parona became a testament to Koni's wounds over the years, each time she had to accept the introduction of her husband's new wives. After the fire, the house turned into dust — which, when doused with water, turned into mud. Now, the mud baked in the sun.

Waleka approached his first wife. He stood strong, but looking down at Koni's stabbing eyes, his heart beat wildly. She sat in solemn silence.

"We will soon rebuild our Big House, complete with a tall roof." Waleka's voice shook slightly. "The roof will be higher and stronger. Our home will be built with the best materials."

Koni remained silent, looking at him.

"We will also have a new uma parona party. A big and merry party." Koni just looked at him.

"Where's Tila Wula?" he asked. When Koni didn't answer, he continued, "You should also know that Wolli's family from Lamboya is coming with a large donation to help us build the house more quickly."

Koni sat silently, gazing evenly at him.

Waleka started to feel annoyed. "Inya Duyo's family is also giving donations to rebuild our house! Our children and grandchildren do everything they can to help so our new house will stand soon. Everything will be fine. So, now you don't have any reason to be sad and angry!"

Wanting to goad Koni into responding, he added, "Everyone will help except for Raga and Logo. They won't be there. Raga is unreliable and Logo always wants to fight. But all the other children and grandchildren will be ready to help build it. Oh, and Lara won't be there either, of course!"

Waleka's voice rose. "Let it be that Raga and Logo won't participate in building the traditional house! Let Lara go! I hope she never comes back. How dare she disgrace her own grandfather!"

Koni finally looked away. She would not even turn her head to give her husband her attention. Nor did she turn when she heard her husband stalk angrily away. After Waleka's steps had faded, Koni prayed for Lara and hoped Raga would find her safe and sound.

After the fire, Koni moved into in a temporary house that the villagers built outside the village fence, just a few feet from the burned ruins of her traditional ancestral house. The roof of the temporary house was flat, not tall and pointed like a real ancestral house. She lived there with Wolli, Wula, Bapa Tua, and Mama Tua. This way, the Big House could be re-built directly on the site where their ancestral house had stood for so many years.

"Kakek and Nenek are staying here." Koni's voice had been flat the night they moved in. It was a sad time. She knew how much the loss of their ancestral home had impacted her in-laws, and she could see how heartbroken Wolli was over Lamura's death. But she tried to stay calm and comforting to her small family.

"Hopefully, the new horse will arrive from Lamboya soon," Koni said hesitantly, as Wolli arranged the few belongings he had been able to save.

"Yes, Inya." Wolli turned to Wula. "Take care of your school bag," he said. "Take it everywhere while you're at school. You won't have Lara there with you, but you still have Ida. Try not to worry."

"But we don't have a house," Wula said.

"Bapa will build a new house later," Wolli replied.

Before sunrise the next morning, Wolli asked Wula to accompany him on a walk with Kakek and Nenek, both very old and feeble. Nenek, now blind, wanted to visit the edge of the cliff. Wolli and Wula held Kakek's and Nenek's hands as they guided them. Not far from the cliff, Kakek pulled Wolli's hand toward the place where Lamura had usually been tethered.

"Be careful and just sit near Lamura," Nenek told her old husband. Kakek raised his hand as if to pet Lamura's back. Tears sprang unbidden to Wolli's eyes. "Lamura is no longer here, Bapa Tua," he said quietly. "He died in the fire."

"Lamura is dead?" Kakek and Nenek cried.

"Please, sit here, Kakek." Wolli helped his grandfather to a flat rock where Lamura was usually tethered. Wula led Nenek. The siblings took a seat on either side of their grandparents next to the house that had burnt to the ground. They were very close to the ashes of Lenggu Lamura. Everyone felt the horse's presence, and it seemed he, too, was grieving the loss of his master's legacy.

The sun crept up. The reddish-yellow light drifted away from its bed. The horizon refracted the lighter colors of the sea, welcoming the sun. The waves broke and chased each other up the Waiha River, which looked like a mere stream at the foot of the cliff. The land breeze blew slowly, covering the village with a peaceful chill — just the opposite of the hot flames that had brought so much destruction.

CHAPTER *10*

Koni and Wolli both understood Lara's anger and Wula's sadness over the circumstances surrounding Waleka and his seventh wife. Koni was aware of Wolli's attempts to face reality more calmly. The memories of their shared past were very strong between mother and adopted son.

For a long time now, their family had been scattered in field houses outside the village. Specifically, for the Waleka family, there were three field houses. Each housed the second, third, and fourth wives. The fifth and sixth wives respectively, lived in houses farther up the side of the road towards the city. Each wife lived with her children. Meanwhile, Koni, the first wife, along with her in-laws and children Tila Wula and Mada Wolli, still lived in a temporary house in Ratenggaro, a house with a flat roof. But Wula and Wolli were leaving for Anakalang. Wula to resume high school, and Wolli to complete his last year of teacher education.

During the three months after the fire, Wolli travelled between Ratenggaro and Anakalang. In Ratenggaro, he always stayed in the temporary house with Koni, Kakek, and Nenek.

One afternoon, Koni and Wolli left the spring where two of their buffaloes were tethered. They planned on herding the livestock to a flatter area so it would be easier to move them to their pastures later.

Wolli rode the new horse from Lamboya, with Koni in the saddle behind him. Wolli held a small whip in his right hand, which he occasionally used to direct the buffaloes to the field. His left hand held the reins.

"It's not difficult, Inya," Wolli answered when Koni asked if he was comfortable riding a new, unfamiliar horse to the pastures. "It is safe. Just watch how this horse obeys."

"The important thing is that you are happy with it," Koni said. She still grieved the second Lamura's death. She was grateful that a week after the fire, the family from Lamboya had brought donations, including a black horse with a white spot in the middle of its forehead. Wolli had not reacted when he saw the horse, so Koni wasn't sure whether he was pleased or not.

Koni leaned in. "What name would fit this horse?" Her lips almost touched Wolli's neck.

"You name him, Inya," Wolli replied.

Koni thought back to the first time she met the man she married. Waleka had looked so handsome and proud on the first Lenggu Lamura's back.

"Lenggu Lamura!" Koni said. "It's a suitable name. Do you agree?"

"Yes, I agree. Lenggu Lamura the third, it is."

They were both silent as they made their way to the grazing grounds through a shortcut behind the hill. The grasses grew high, flanking the rarely used path. The sun was already leaning into the west. Its reddish-yellow light refracted over the vast field stretching below it. The breezy wind rode alongside mother and son on their journey.

"Wula and Ida are participating in a competition at their school for Education Day on the second of May," Wolli said to lighten the mood and cheer up his mother. "If they win, they participate again in the competition on Independence Day, next August. I'm sure, they will win!"

"Oh, I see!" Koni laughed proudly, but then could not think of anything else to say.

"Both of them are smart," Wolli tried again. "Lara is very intelligent too. She would have participated in the competition. Inya, Lara is so resourceful, she definitely won't get lost. You have to believe that."

Then both of them fell silent to the rhythm of the hooves clopping through the quiet. They were halfway there. The wind blew slowly, offsetting the sunlight piercing the open fields.

Wolli flinched when he realized what he saw. "Inya, get off quickly," he whispered tersely.

Without asking why, Koni slid off the horse.

Wolli quickly dismounted after his mother. He motioned her to sit down in the tall grass while he dropped the reins and Lamura began to graze. The two buffaloes joined Lamura. Wolli sat next to his mother and put an index finger to his lips.

"What? Did Lamura see something?" Koni whispered. "Did *you* see something?"

Wolli put his arm around his mother's shoulder and brought her close.

From their hiding place, they heard hooves quickly approaching. They could see Logo, Uka, and Ama Dula on horseback, leading five horses carrying heavy loads. Eight men followed on foot, each pulling a buffalo. The group stopped about one hundred yards from where the tall grass hid Wolli and Koni.

Lamura and the two buffaloes did not attract any attention. It was not unusual to see herd animals that belonged to other villagers grazing in the fertile hills.

The wind carried Logo's voice to Wolli and his mother. "Let's go straight to the harbor."

"All is well, Bapa!" one of the men replied. "Everything is moving along smoothly."

"Meet me on the ferry dock before the third signal of the ferry horn," Logo said. "All of you will receive your share there."

Wolli and Koni listened as the group moved on downhill toward the main road and out of sight. They quickly mounted Lamura again, leaving their two buffaloes grazing with the others. Wolli spurred Lamura to a fast gallop until they finally arrived at their family's farm.

Koni dismounted and stood stunned. The crude slaughter of livestock was apparent everywhere. Severed heads, tails, and legs littered the bloody ground. She now understood what she had seen from the tall grass. The butchered meat must have been what the horses were carrying. She immediately knew how many stolen horses had been used to carry loads of stolen meat, and how many cows, horses, and buffaloes had been stolen unbutchered. What Logo and his men had been doing that afternoon was not a one-time act. *So is it true what people from our village are saying? Logo and Uka have truly become evil thieves like this?*

"Inya," Wolli called softly, "Logo and Uka don't think twice about stealing. They don't just steal from their own family, but also from other people. You mustn't worry about it. Let it be, Inya." Wolli helped Koni walk away from the carnage.

"They are stealing from our own family and from other people," Koni repeated quietly. *Don't take anything you don't own.* She heard Bapa Tua's words from so many years ago. Koni took a deep breath to ease the tightness in her chest. In silence, she and Wolli thought about what Telu's eldest son and Potoh's eldest son had done.

All this time, Koni had thought Logo and Uka were only taking one or two head to sell or give to other parties. She thought they were only selling one plot of land here and there. But, no. Logo and Uka had been stealing everything.

"Let's go home, Inya." Wolli did not want his mother to linger on the farm. His mind flew to Lara. No one knew where she was. And Wula. The sister he loved was now at school in Anakalang. He, himself would have to leave soon to Kupang to complete his college education. It hurt him to think of his mother being alone.

"Inya, please be patient." Wolli tried to comfort his mother. "Lara will definitely come back. Wula is studying well. I'm also going to be a teacher, soon. Don't be sad. All of us will definitely come home."

Wolli swung up onto Lamura's back and reached down for Koni's hand. She put her foot into the stirrup, and Wolli pulled her up behind him. They rode back to Ratenggaro, together in the saddle, accompanied by the golden rays of the setting sun.

The traditional ceremony to prevent the village from experiencing more bad luck was carried out before the rebuilding of Waleka's ancestral house. The village at the top of the cliff was filled with the extended family of wives from generation to generation and elders from neighboring villages far and near. This included the envoy of Waleka's prospective seventh wife's family. Seeing Galuh's family representative made Waleka feel like he had the upper hand.

"Look at that! They still respect me!" Waleka said to Ndalo at the ceremony.

"It is a great honor to be a respected tom mtona parona," wheedled Ndalo. "If you were not a respectable elder, how could they offer you their young, beautiful daughter?" Ndalo's words flattered Waleka.

His arrogance and greed skyrocketed again when, one by one, family members came bearing a wealth of gifts: livestock, including horses, pigs, cows, and buffaloes; materials needed for rebuilding the traditional ancestral house, such as wood, planks, and poles; and subsidies of money, gold, and fabrics. All of this was collected easily. Waleka knew that some of the traditional sarongs would fetch a very high price.

Mada Wolli's extended family also came with a large entourage. They brought several cubic feet of wood, as well as two logs of kadimbil wood, a type of forest mahogany. The logs were large, long, and strong — perfect for the home's framing posts.

"This is the share Mada Wolli's family can give," one of the delegates from Lamboya said earnestly. Such an extravagant gift was understandable, because until this ceremony, Wolli's family had not found an occasion where they could adequately express their gratitude to Waleka, Koni, and the entire family for adopting Mada Wolli as an infant. They were grateful to Koni for taking such good care in raising the boy.

"We adopted Mada Wolli because Wuri Wona and Inya Biri were good friends of our family," Waleka said, as the delegate presented the gifts.

"Mada Wolli's birth mother, Inya Biri, was like a sister to Inya Koni," the Lamboya delegate said. "They were friends since childhood — in the village, at school, and at the convent."

"Because of Inya Biri's last words before she died, Wolli is not someone else's child. He's our son." Waleka said proudly.

Thanks to the gifts everyone brought to the traditional ceremony, an elaborate inauguration ceremony could be organized quickly, without a penny from Waleka's pocket.

Waleka and Raga worked quickly to design the new ancestral home. The new house would be brown and sturdy and reflect the high quality of the materials used. The roof was designed to match the height of the original. Building materials arrived quickly in the village with the support of the many people working under Ndalo's supervision. In no time at all, the long post was ready to be erected.

It was at that time that Waleka made a surprising decision. "We're staying in the temporary house," he said, ignoring the shocked looks of those around him. "Don't build the roof of the Big House yet!" Waleka presented himself as a good planner. "Let the wood for the framing studs age and cure in the sun. For now, let's finish building a house that will be just a little better than a temporary house, because we have no more funds to do anything else." The villagers complied because Ndalo, as a traditional elder, supported Waleka's decision.

Seeing the construction come to a halt, Koni approached Waleka one afternoon while he was sitting on the stairs of the flat-roofed temporary house.

"How many head of livestock do you need to sell to have enough money to build an appropriate tall roof for the new Big House?" Koni asked.

"We don't have any livestock to sell anymore," Waleka answered curtly.

"Where did all the donations from the extended family go?" Koni asked.

"You saw that everyone helped us."

"Yes, I know. We don't have to pay any bills." Koni was silent for a moment before pressing on. "The huge expenses, including those for the ceremony after the Big House is rebuilt, are covered by the donations we received. What else do you need money for?"

When Waleka didn't reply, Koni looked at him sharply. "It's fine to sell land and livestock, but marapu, the altar for the gods, must be there in the Big House. We can't have the proper altar in a house with a flat roof." Koni looked at her husband suspiciously. "What will you say when tribe members ask what happened, why you aren't building? How should we answer when all the extended family ask? The important thing is that this Big House, marapu's house, is completed quickly. The roof must be erected immediately. Where are all the donations?" Her words stabbed Waleka.

"The wood beams, the planks, all of the building materials are here!" Waleka snapped. "Everything except for the livestock. All livestock seems to be lost. They must have been stolen! Perhaps Logo and his brothers sold the animals. Why don't you ask them instead of me!"

Waleka gathered himself. "Where am I going to get the money from if they steal and sell everything and then disappear?" Waleka spat and looked away.

"I can't believe it's all gone!" Koni was angry. "And still, you don't dare to face Logo, your son? Is that why you kept quiet when Logo took everything that didn't belong to him?" Koni enunciated every syllable of her next words: "You have only one goal in your mind, Waleka: to bring Lara's friend — your granddaughter's friend — into the house. Do you know that she's the girl Logo wants?"

"Don't talk nonsense!" Waleka glared at Koni.

"You can never trick me with your lies!" Koni stared him down.

"Please be quiet! Be quiet!" Waleka rose. "I will try to have the uma parona built soon. The Big House is coming soon. The ceremony is coming soon. Don't lose any sleep over it!"

"You already know I haven't slept well since you started bringing other women into our family. I haven't slept well since our Big House became nothing but a charade for your marriage matters and desires."

Waleka turned away from his wife. He was face-to-face with the responsibility and consequences of his decision to take a seventh wife in the full meaning of the words. He had made sure of getting his way by allowing Logo to steal livestock and land. If he confronted Logo, Logo would not back down and respect him. Waleka did not want to be humiliated again. He would do anything to make up for the mistakes his granddaughter Lara had made. But when Logo and Uka stole almost all the livestock in the field and pawned the land, Waleka had panicked. He had planned to use the cattle and land as Galuh's second dowry.

"Build a house with the proper roof." Koni said calmly.

"Yes!" Waleka responded, agitated.

"The marapu altar must be in the house," Koni insisted.

"Yes!" Waleka's mind drifted, looking for the right way to save face — from being humiliated by his own children and grandchildren.

That day, the air was cooler than usual. The wisps of clouds moved fast to the west and quickly turned leaden. Koni felt a deep loss, caused by the person she loved. Waleka had taken something that did not belong to him.

Waleka tightened the sarong around his waist, smoothed his headband, and straightened. He walked to Ndalo's house and took a seat on the terrace.

Koni said nothing more as her husband left her sitting alone at the foot of the stairs of the temporary house with a flat roof.

A few minutes later Ndalo joined Waleka, and when Koni looked up, she caught the two men looking at her.

CHAPTER *11*

The revelation that buffaloes, cows, and horses were disappearing from the grazing pastures and the stables behind the village spread rapidly through the community. Almost all Ratenggaro villagers regretted the discovery that Logo, Uka, and their followers had cunningly conducted these thieveries as a normal daily activity.

"You have to ask your children." Ndalo stroked his beard as he and Waleka sat under the shade of the banyan tree between their houses. Ndalo and Ama Dula exchanged meaningful glances while Ama Dula fed the horses. Ndalo grinned. "Ask Raga and his wife Hamoli. Their daughter Lara is the cause of all this."

Ndalo stopped talking when he saw Hamoli enter Waleka's house. "You are suffering a lot," he resumed after Hamoli was inside the house. "The cattle are gone because Lara misbehaved. Maybe someone else stole them. Our fellow villagers are usually quite concerned about other people's misfortune!" Ndalo laughed triumphantly.

Ama Dula had told Ndalo everything that had happened, because Ama Dula was also in on Logo's stealing at the cattle ranch. He knew that Uka and the port guard watched the harbor closely to see what the ships loaded and off-loaded as they came and went. Everything had to go through the harbor. Ama Dula had also told Ndalo that he had seen Koni and Wolli in the field, and therefore, they probably also knew what had happened.

"The thieves are not my children!" Waleka declared. "The thieves must be people with a complete lack of empathy."

Four months had passed since the fire that destroyed Waleka's ancestral home. Wula was still away at school, and there had been no news about Lara, whose rebellious behavior was still fresh on everyone's minds and tongues.

Ndalo acted concerned. "How could anyone have the heart to make the Waleka family suffer again?"

"You must help me," Waleka pleaded. He did not have enough time to meet the demands of Galuh's family. He needed to offer many head of livestock as an offering of regret and to restore the family's good name.

Ndalo was well aware of Waleka's situation. This was his opportunity to show that he was more important than Waleka.

From the front yard of her house, Koni saw the two men, and they saw her. Koni ignored them. A short time later, one of Koni's stepsons brought a horse to his father. She saw the two old men mount their horses. Koni watched them, the village elders. They were always the main figures at village events. *What inheritance are they passing on to their descendants?*

That day, Waleka and Ndalo left the village. Waleka did not say a word to Koni about leaving, but that was not unusual. Waleka's unexplained journeys just needed to be accepted. There was no need for Koni to ask where, what for, and how long he was traveling. Koni only needed to wait until he returned with an old or new story.

Koni's heart hammered. There was something odd about her relationship with her husband. No matter how bad the situation was between them, no matter how silent one was towards the other, her husband always left from their own house, never from someone else's house, never from Ndalo's.

"Have you asked Bapa who gave him that sarong?" Hamoli suddenly appeared, startling her.

"Oh, which one?" Surprised, Koni thought back to what Waleka was wearing: the sarong with a bright, eye-catching color and a slithering snake pattern. "He's wearing the snake sarong that he wore at the past Pasola. Why?"

"Nothing, Inya," Hamoli said, not wanting to agitate her mother-in-law, as the two walked into the kitchen. "There are two other dark brown sarongs that Bapa can change into. I hope he will remember to change."

"Which dark brown sarongs?"

"The ones you weaved."

Koni, an unpretentious woman, smiled. She was unable to express exactly how proud she was of Hamoli's smart mind and heart. Hamoli, Lara's mother. The dark brown sarongs had white bone-colored threads arranged in a horse pattern at the bottom and a chicken pattern at the top, framed with a border pattern of tiny turtles. That pattern was a stark contrast to the snake sarong Waleka wore when he left the village.

"Here, put this food in the *remba*." Koni pointed to the special place to store food for Waleka to eat whenever he arrived home.

"Bapa won't be coming home tonight," Hamoli replied, and taking the container filled with food, she added, "But Wolli will definitely eat it tomorrow morning. Will Wolli come back from the city this afternoon, Inya?"

Koni nodded. "We'll save another plate for breakfast later." She watched Hamoli put the food in the remba.

"Bapa is away a lot," Hamoli mused. "Why do you keep on storing food for him? You store food in the morning, afternoon, and night."

"The food should always be there for whenever Bapa does come home," Koni answered calmly. "It would be bad if Bapa came home hungry and there was no food."

It was the custom. Whenever Waleka went away, food was always stored for him. Whether he came home or not, food was always ready for him. If the meal time had passed and Waleka had not come home, Koni always replaced the food with a fresh portion. It never entered Koni's mind to change the habit, even though Waleka had hurt her so many times.

"What if Bapa doesn't come home?" Hamoli noticed her mother-in-law smiling at her.

Koni changed the subject. "Have you heard from Lara?"

"Not yet, Inya. Inya Duyo always cries and now sleeps more because she is sick with sadness." Hamoli rubbed her eyes, trying hard to be steadfast so she would not add to the burdens carried by Koni, Duyo, Kakek, and Nenek.

"How are Kakek and Nenek?" Hamoli stepped into her old grandparents' room. Koni followed her. There, the two of them sat for a while, keeping Kakek and Nenek company while they ate. The aging Bapa Tua and Mama Tua ate quietly, living in their solitude and the pain caused by their own children and grandchildren.

Koni felt something was about to happen. Something far more hurtful than the mocking of neighbors and the pain of living in a temporary house with a flat roof. Even a roofed farmhouse carried more status than this flat-roofed house.

According to the rumors, Waleka and Ndalo were spending a week in the seventh wife's village. After that, Waleka would bring Galuh to Ratenggaro.

Koni's mind and heart had come to terms with the news that her husband was away to woo another wife. What made the world collapse on her was what Waleka said when he returned from his trip.

"You wanted the roof of the new Big House to be built immediately, right?" her husband had said. "Well, we have nothing more to sell to start the roof-building work. But we have received a belis of forty buffaloes, forty cows, and one hundred horses to build our Big House.

More dowry money will be added for as long as we need it." Waleka looked restless.

Koni gasped. "Who paid the belis and who is it for?"

Waleka bowed his head for a moment before speaking. "We received the belis from Ndalo. For Tila Wula." He raised his head and his voice. "Ndalo paid the dowry a long time ago, when Wula was seven or eight years old. He won't take Wula now. He will wait until Tila Wula finishes school. That's the deal."

Koni gaped in astonishment. Waleka shot her a sharp glance. "She will be Ndalo's seventh wife, or whatever number of wife, that's all!" Koni continued to stare, unable to find words. "What's the problem?" Waleka barked. "Is it too hard for you? Your job is to just agree, just keep quiet, and just follow what I've decided!" Waleka spat.

"Bapa!" Koni screamed in horror. "Have you gone mad?"

"Shut up!" Waleka warned. "Don't fight me! How dare you call me crazy!" Agitated, Waleka rolled his eyes and thought, *You're the only one who always opposes me.* "Ndalo will wait until Wula finishes school, whenever that is. So don't worry about anything. Any number of things could happen between now and then, so shut up! Just shut up and accept my decision!"

"You have just killed me." Koni couldn't breathe. "You sold your own child when she was only seven or eight years old! How could you?"

Koni raised her head and looked around for Tila Wula. Instead, she saw Wolli standing there. "Wolli! You're home from the city!" Koni hugged him, sobbing.

Wolli was startled. "Why are you sad, Inya?"

"She's not sad," Waleka answered abruptly. "She's happy that the roof of the Big House will be finished soon. Yes, Inya is so glad because we will soon build a tall roof so all of you don't have to stay much longer in a temporary house with a flat roof. We will have a party soon to celebrate the tall roof for our Big House. Kakek and Nenek will be so happy!"

"We already have a good house, Bapa!" Wolli said. "Even though it is only a temporary house without a tall roof like the other houses, there is still a roof. It's fine, Bapa. We don't get rained on, and Kakek and Nenek must sleep well because they are protected from the weather."

"Wolli!" Koni choked.

"Our house already has a roof, Inya," Wolli said. This was Wolli's way of reasoning whenever someone made fun of his family's house because it did not have the tall roof of a traditional ancestral house. "It is fine if we don't have the money for a soaring roof. It's really fine." Wolli wanted to cheer up his parents. He repeated, "The important thing is that our house has a roof, Inya! There's no need for a soaring roof. It doesn't matter!"

Waleka listened in silence with his head lowered. Wolli stood frozen in front of his parents. His mother kept crying, and his father kept warning her to shut up.

CHAPTER *12*

Koni went into Bapa Tua and Mama Tua's room. She cried silently in front of her two old parents-in-law. Kakek and Nenek had been like her parents ever since she left Lamboya and became Waleka's wife.

Bapa Tua's hand trembled when he touched her head. Mama Tua's did the same.

One could not talk, the other could not see, but both heard and felt what had happened. Both of them could only keep track of time based on the Nyale and Pasola. During these events, family members filled the ancestral house. Even though a year was a long time to wait for both of them, the time passed quickly when hopes and longing brought together all of their children and grandchildren. Now, time had slowed because Waleka kept bringing in one problem after another. The two old people cried silently with their daughter-in-law.

Raga entered the room. "Kakek ... Nenek ..." The room was less than ninety square feet, but it felt plenty spacious for those with a wide mind and heart. Bapa Tua and Mama Tua touched Raga's head in blessing. Moments later, Raga left the room. He stood for a moment in front of the fire pit, collecting his thoughts, before returning to his grandparents' room.

Raga knelt beside his grandfather's bed, in front of Nenek. Without a word, the two old grandparents stroked his head several times. "You take care and look for Lara until you find her," Nenek said.

Raga stood. When he walked out of the house through the front door, he found Waleka smoking on the terrace. "Bapa, come with me," Raga said.

"Where to?"

"To the fields!" Raga replied coldly, as he strode off toward the shade of the banyan tree where his horse was tethered. He untied his horse and mounted quickly. "Hurry up!" he called to his father.

"Go!" said Koni from the doorway. "You'd better see the situation in the fields for yourself." The tone of Koni's voice convinced Waleka to climb onto the saddle behind Raga.

Villagers watched Raga leave on horseback with Waleka sitting behind him in the saddle. Along the village alleys, people commented, "That's the way it should be. The greatest elder and his eldest son getting along and facing problems together!"

One of the village women asked Koni directly. "When building an ancestral house, the family must be in harmony with one another and sincere to each other. Isn't it like that, Inya Koni?"

Koni didn't answer. She turned slowly and walked back into the house. She lay down in a *koro* — one of the special bedrooms for women that Wula usually occupied — with her face toward the wall. The cold outdoor air sliced through Koni's mind and heart, like the sharp knife used to slice nyale for palowor. Koni wept bitterly.

Raga spurred his horse so fast that Waleka had to hold on tight to his son's waist. They rode through the grasslands that stretched as far as the eye could see. The bright blue sky was a stark contrast to Waleka's heart, which was cloudy and black with fear.

He knew why Raga was not talking. Raga's birth as the eldest son had been celebrated with a big party, and Waleka had been very proud to have a biological son as the successor of his lineage. Raga had been taught how to position himself and convey feelings, especially fury. Raga's silence indicated the depth of his rage. Waleka hugged Raga's waist. Raga, his eldest son — the father of Lara, his granddaughter.

They came to the farthest pasture, far away from any settlements. The shepherds rarely passed this pasture on their way taking the cattle to graze because these fields were farther than their now empty pastures. Raga stopped. He felt his father's old body trembling, but the old man was trying hard to maintain his dignity.

Raga dismounted. He looked up at Waleka. "Get off!"

"What do you want?" Waleka slid off the horse's back. He walked stiffly to the nearest lamtoro tree and sat down in its shade.

Raga dropped the end of the horse's rope into the grasses and sat down beside his father. A strong breeze bent the tall blades. For a while, greatest elder and eldest son sat silently, occupied with their thoughts.

Raga broke the silence. "Bapa, where did you take the buffaloes, horses, and cows that were supposed to be used to pay for rebuilding our Big House?"

Waleka did not answer.

"Bapa, where did you take our horses, buffaloes, and cows?"

Waleka still did not answer.

"Bapa! You knew that Logo and Uka were stealing from us. Who else did you pay to steal buffaloes, horses, and cows? Who did you pay to create a problem so that the Big House could not be built because all the people's gifts had been stolen? Where are you taking it? Why did you let Logo and Uka do whatever they want?" Raga ripped out a handful of grass and twisted the blades around his hand so he could pluck at them.

Waleka was shocked into silence to see Raga's unusual behavior.

"Why and for whom are you selling our acreage?"

Waleka remained silent.

"Bapa!" Raga yelled. "What made you so mean?"

Waleka's eyes widened. "What made you so rude?"

"I don't want my father to lose self-respect because of fraud and greed! That's why I brought you here to ask you questions and get the truth from you!"

Raga's questions infuriated Waleka. "Listen! I am a kabani pa ate, a wise man, a tom mtona parona; we are descendants of rato; we have the biggest house; we have a huge influence. I'm rato, and you are a future rato! I have Nyale rights, I have Pasola rights. I'm a to-paholong. So don't ask me all kinds of impertinent questions!"

Raga threw down the clump of grass in his hand. "Bapa brought horses, buffaloes, and cows to make up for the shame of that woman's family who have asked for many dowry payments. Bapa wants to marry up to seven women. Bapa snatched the woman Logo wanted." Raga glowered at Waleka, trying to hold back his anger. "Bapa! You are willing to sacrifice everything to satisfy your greed and lust!"

"Now you wait!" Waleka's voice matched his son's. "You remember! I am a traditional elder! I can do anything I want! You have no say in what I do!" Waleka looked away.

Raga continued delivering his merciless accusations. "Bapa, you sold our land and took the money to that woman's family as another dowry. You allowed Logo and Uka to steal because you were afraid Logo would be angry that you stole his woman and would create an even bigger problem than what we already have. You have turned a blind eye to them robbing us of everything we have because they know you are determined, no matter what, to marry Galuh — the young woman Logo wanted to take as a new wife and a friend of your granddaughter!"

"Eh, you're a pansy! You only have one wife. So you're talking nonsense!" Waleka wouldn't look at Raga.

"Bapa, please answer my question! Why are you so mean?"

"If you want a second, third, or whatever wife, I'll look for you." Waleka started to stand. Raga grabbed his father's arms tightly and twisted them behind his back, forcing Waleka to sit back down.

Waleka was shocked into silence.

"Do you know where Lara is?" Raga demanded.

"No. And there's no need to search for her. She embarrassed our family! She embarrassed the Big House. Because of her, the Big House burned down. You failed to teach her proper manners because you don't know anything yourself!" Waleka rubbed his arms.

Raga roared with anger. "You'd kill your grandchildren to get a seventh wife, Bapa! You are greedy!"

"Shut your mouth!" Waleka hissed. "Do you want me to curse you? I'll tell the sky to fall and bury you alive!" Waleka trembled with fury. "It'll be nyale season soon, and I'll tell the nyale to twist around your legs! I'll command the nyale horse to chase you down and trample you! You just wait for the Nyale and Pasola; I'll curse you! Let everyone know! Let the whole world know!"

"If you want to curse me, do it now!" Raga's chest was about to explode.

Waleka spat. "You are a useless eldest son." He looked away.

"You, my father, are also the firstborn and eldest son." Raga was shaking. "Why did you sell Tila Wula?"

"Because she is indeed a daughter, fit to be sold to Ndalo, a tom mtona parona, a famous traditional elder. He is wealthy and respected. You should be proud." Waleka raised his eyes but immediately lowered them again as Raga resumed his verbal attack.

"Bapa!" Raga's voice thundered across the field and echoed into the distance. "Why did you sell Tila Wula? You killed Lara! You sold Tila Wula. Where is your heart?"

Waleka watched Raga struggle to control his exploding anger. There was not a drop of regret in Waleka's heart for what had happened or what he had done. He had acted in his firm belief that elders were rulers. No one could stop him. Especially not his children or grandchildren.

Now, Waleka started to wonder. Except for Koni and Duyo, he had obtained his other four wives by simply kidnapping them. He had entered their village with his horse entourage and brought several heads of horses, buffaloes, and cows as a dowry. He stayed there until the woman was handed over to him with great respect. *Why is it so difficult to obtain this seventh wife?* His male stature was challenged every time he thought about Galuh's beauty. Waleka had promised himself to make the seventh wife preeminent on the bamboo bed of the ancestral house. He strongly believed that as an elder, he should have anything he wanted, at any cost. He no longer cared about anything or anyone else.

Raga continued to mourn over Lara's and Tila Wula's fate. Lara was his favorite child. She had big dreams for school and goals for the future. Tila Wula was the half-sister he and his mother, Inya Duyo, loved. The smart girl had been sold by her own father! The beautiful teenager was already in Ndalo's claws.

"Bapa, what makes you so heartless?" Raga asked without turning around. "You have corrupted the village for so long. The elders and the villagers have begged you to complete building the Big House. You are a tom mtona parona but live in a temporary house with a flat roof. How can you hold your head up?" Raga paused for a moment to catch his breath. When he continued, his voice was more calm. "Please, Bapa, build a house that is truly the home of a tom mtona parona! For the sake of respecting other elders, please, Bapa!" Raga knelt before Waleka.

Waleka straightened and attacked. "All you can do is whine! You don't understand anything. All you do is complain. You don't know what it means to chair the council of elders, to be a rato. You don't know how to respect a rato. You don't do anything!" Waleka spat again.

Raga shot to his feet. He grabbed his horse by the halter and swung up onto its back. Waleka quickly jumped up and swung onto the saddle behind Raga. With one whipstroke, the horse went flying into a full gallop. Raga barely had time to adjust the reins. His heart ached; his self-esteem was crushed.

As the horse pounded home, Raga thought about the past. He remembered Tila Wula running to meet him every time he visited the ancestral house. Wolli was always diligently watching over their little sister. He could hear Lara laugh, persuading him to agree to her enrollment at a vocational school for teacher education, with Wula. His pride came from the respect that the sons and daughters he loved so much regarded him with. Now, his heart was fraying. How could the old man — his father — riding behind him, hurt him so badly? Because Waleka was his father, Raga would never be able to hate the man. He could only try to hold him accountable for his actions.

Raga continued to spur his horse across the fields. The grasses seemed to part themselves to make way. After arriving at the top of one of the hills, Raga pulled hard on the reins. From this height, they could see Ratenggaro in the distance. The sun was starting to set. A flock of small birds swayed on the grasstops.

"Get off here," Raga said.

"What else do you want to talk about?" Waleka asked, jumping off the horse.

Raga yanked the reins toward his chest and spurred his horse. The stallion reared up, pawing the air with its front legs high. Its indignant neigh travelled far into the expansive meadow below, loud enough that it might have reached the house tops in the distance — including the flat top of the temporary house.

Raga bent close over the horse's neck. After a final neigh broke the silence of the field, he whipped the horse's flank once and it bolted.

Stunned, Waleka watched in disbelief as Raga, his eldest son, galloped away, leaving him alone in the middle of nowhere. He started to walk hastily toward Ratenggaro. His old body carried the burden of itself, as he staggered hurriedly along the path's grassy silence.

A hornbill flew low and alighted on the lowest branch of a lamtoro tree by the path. Waleka had only encountered the large black birds with their colorful beak when sling-shotting them with other hunters for target practice — picking them off one by one for no reason other than sport. Many birds in the forest were quickly becoming memories because their homes were turning into human homes, including the new settlements for his wives. Fear trickled uncomfortably into Waleka's mind.

He paused. The sun had sunk. An owl flew low and perched on another lamtoro branch. "An owl," Waleka whispered to himself, looking at the bird's big red eyes and small beak. The bird returned the look, unblinking, as if laughing at him. Waleka straightened his shoulders and, swearing, hurried away.

He reached the main road around midnight. The night was darker than usual. It was still about an hour's walk to his village, but at least he was closer. Tired, he sat for a moment by the road. His mouth was dry. He had no cigarettes and no water. There were neither stars nor moon. Darkness covered the earth. The wind swept through the weeds and rustled — *a sign of longing? Or sadness?* It was difficult for the old man to interpret nature's voice because his heart was clogged with revenge and hatred. It was impossible for him to accept that his eldest son had abandoned him. For the first time in his life, Waleka felt belittled by his son. This hurt so much more than what Lara had done.

Waleka heard the thunder of hooves approaching and rose expectantly. Ndalo and a group of his cronies reined in and stopped in front of Waleka.

"Hey! Where have you been, old man?" Ndalo jeered. "Who left you here?" Laughing louder, he joked, "You're supposed to take a woman to a house, not to a deserted field! Where is your horse?" Ndalo pulled Waleka up behind him on the saddle.

"Hah! They brought me here, and I told them to go home ahead of me," Waleka joked back. "Now, hurry up and quit asking all kinds of questions! You already know what happened!"

Ndalo responded with a crack of the whip, and the group of men galloped off toward Ratenggaro.

Waleka was grateful no one had witnessed how Raga had treated him. He arrived back in the village with Ndalo and a satisfied look on his face.

"Where's Raga?" Koni asked. "Did you come home alone?"

"Raga is in his house," Waleka answered and immediately went to sleep in a corner of his own house.

CHAPTER *13*

Despite their father's promise, Mada Wolli and Tila Wula continued to live with their mother in the flat-roofed temporary house.

Koni did not say anything more except to agree with what her two children had said about not being wet when it rained, not being hot when the sun reached the top of the sky, and not being exposed to cold dew at night. Even though the appearance of the house looked ridiculous — the flat roof looked like a bottle cap — it reflected the truth. The flat-roofed house looked like nothing else in the village.

"Waleka's house is not any better than his wives' field houses," Ndalo squealed every time he talked about Waleka's temporary house. Ndalo had only one goal: He wanted the woman in the flat-roofed house on the other side of the fence to hear him.

"It's not a problem that our house does not have a tall roof," Wolli said one day while cleaning the kambu luna beneath the home. "The important thing is that the kambu luna remains a safe stable for Lamura."

"True. We don't want Lamura to be too far away; he will guard our house," Koni said. "Your job is to clean the stable and take care of Lamura." She took a deep breath, knowing that Wolli was not referring

97

to their flat roof. For Wolli, the most important thing was that they had a roof over their heads and Lamura had a safe place to rest.

"Your other job is to take care of Wula, too," said Waleka, sitting not far from them. He did not expect Wolli to speak his true feelings about the flat roof, but he didn't want the discussion to lead into *why* they still had a flat roof. *Had Koni already told Wolli about Galuh?* Trying to distract Wolli from broaching the actual problem at hand, Waleka said, "Just focus on taking care of both Lamura and Wula."

"Of course, Bapa," Wolli answered confidently.

For a moment, the faces of Wula, Wolli, and Lara flashed through Waleka's mind. From the time they were children, the three of them had always been friends with Galuh, now the woman of his dreams. Waleka shook his head, thinking about how bravely Lara had defied him. Wula, a much calmer person, had shown her disapproval with her posture. Wolli, stunned and silent, kept many things to himself.

Waleka never thought he would have to face his children and grandchildren like this. He thought it would be easy to bring Galuh to his ancestral house. Waleka convinced himself that Galuh had to be in this house to be Inya Pitu — his seventh wife. He would show everyone that his self-respect came first.

Waleka was standing with Wolli in front of the kambu luna, ready to take Lamura out, when Logo arrived looking unhappy. Waleka immediately left the stable to meet the eldest son from his third wife.

Logo glanced briefly at Wolli before looking away. Wolli looked very different compared to his other brothers and sisters. The young man was patient, willing to learn, and obedient to his parents. Tall and handsome, he had also gone to high school. Logo did not like it. It felt like his father cared more about Wolli and Tila Wula than his other children.

"What is going on?" Waleka asked while while walking up to the terrace with Logo.

"What, am I not welcome to come here?" Logo answered indignantly.

"You know that's not what I mean. You usually only show up when there is a problem. So, what's wrong now?"

Logo answered his father's question with silence. After a while, he said, "Big problem."

"The important thing is that your 'big problem' has nothing to do with you asking for Galuh." Waleka glared. "She is my woman! You have already received the buffaloes I promised, and all the villagers know Galuh is mine!"

"Big problem!" Logo repeated forcefully.

Waleka was not worried that Logo or any of the other children had found out about his problems with Raga. The old man knew Logo's character. Logo always had his way of conveying his thoughts and feelings whenever there was a problem. Waleka sensed that this time the problem Logo was referring to was not small and simple.

"When will the roof of our Big House be built?" Logo asked.

"Just wait." Waleka replied.

"When?" Logo persisted. "Everyone knows a traditional Big House must have a tall roof. Our house doesn't have a tall roof. We are the only ones without a traditional Big House. It is very embarrassing!" Logo spoke while looking at Ndalo's house and the houses around it. "Nyale is coming soon, and what if it's Pasola time and our house still looks like this?" He snorted. "Everyone will come here for Pasola and ask, 'Why has the roof not been finished yet?' Why hasn't it? How many more years will it take? How many more Nyales and Pasolas do you want to wait?"

Waleka looked away. "How much money do you have to build a roof?" he asked. "How much money do you have for the party? Can you build it yourself?"

"Sit down with the family," Logo urged. "Talk and share so we can all bear the burden together. This is embarrassing! Everyone has a traditional house with a high roof. We are the only ones that look different. Can it be built soon?"

"We don't have enough money," Waleka answered. "The livestock have all been stolen. Perhaps you know who stole them?"

Logo was silent for a moment, then said, "Ndalo was drunk."

Waleka took a deep breath and exhaled loudly. Was his and Ndalo's tightly held secret coming loose? At the time they made the secret pact, both of them had made sure no one knew anything about it. It had been their secret for eight years. *How could it unravel now, at the exact time I am preparing to pay for my seventh woman? Do my other children know the secret? Does Raga?* Then a rebellious thought filled his mind, *Am I not an elder?*

"So what?" Waleka said cautiously.

"Don't pretend, Bapa! I already know!"

"You already know what?" Waleka glanced at Wolli cleaning the kambu luna.

Logo moved closer to Waleka and hissed, "I already know about my Bapa and Ndalo having a group of thieves at the farm, stealing family property that is supposed to pay for the roof! How many plots of land have you sold for your personal gain?"

Relief washed over Waleka. *So this isn't about my secret deal with Ndalo. Logo doesn't know about the belis I received for Wula.*

Noticing his father's restlessness, Logo pushed on. "You want to marry again? You want to take a seventh wife? You're taking Galuh, the woman I want. You already know Lara doesn't like it. Now she's gone. You still don't care?"

So this is about Galuh. Waleka found himself on familiar ground. When it came to explaining why he needed a new wife, he was very practiced and prepared in answering questions and explaining himself. After all, he had done this routine for five wives before.

"It's enough, Bapa! How much livestock? How much land? And how many more children and grandchildren are you willing to sacrifice? While you're spending all this money, there are so many children and grandchildren who are not being taken care of properly."

"How dare you disrespect your parents!" Waleka answered. "If I marry again, it's because I can afford the belis. I am a rato!"

"And what about me, Bapa? What about *my* wife and children? You do nothing about Uka stealing and selling cattle. He wants to leave Ratenggaro and abandon his two wives here. Why don't you say anything? Are you too busy looking for another wife?"

Waleka did not answer. Logo, too, fell silent. They both knew Wolli could hear what they were arguing about, but neither of them cared.

Logo pictured his father taking Galuh to be his seventh wife. He thought about Wula, too. Of all his siblings, Wula was the fairest. Her beauty had been apparent since childhood. Logo assumed that this was the reason Ndalo dared to pay the belis for her to his father. Logo knew something had happened between Ndalo and his father, that the two men bartered and negotiated agreements they could use to pressure and benefit from each other when attempting to obtain a woman.

Logo looked at Wolli and jealously flared. "So how long is Wolli going to stay here, anyway?"

"Why are you asking that?" Waleka's voice rose. He saw Koni raise her head, and knew his first wife had heard Logo's petulant question.

"You don't care about Wula, Lara, my children, or your grandchildren," Logo said, wondering what he could extort from Waleka in this situation.

Waleka tried to distance himself from Logo's attack. "You can't do anything. You can only steal and cause trouble for your parents."

"So, Bapa," Logo whispered meanly. "How much did Ndalo pay you for Tila Wula?"

Waleka gasped and shouted, "Get out! Get out of here before I curse you!"

"Go ahead!" Logo snapped, then chuckled. "Curse me!" Logo steeled himself as he mustered up all his courage to confront his greedy father. "You received a lot of cattle from Wolli's family. Where are they? Do you want me to tell your dirty secret to Wolli, so that Inya Koni, Bapa Tua, and Mama Tua's favorite child knows what you've done? You sold Wula to be Ndalo's wife. How much did you receive for your daughter?"

Waleka flinched. "Shut up!" he roared.

"Please stop, Bapa!" Logo shouted. "Don't bring another woman into our house. Just stop! Finish building the Big House instead. The dowry you received from Ndalo is more than enough to pay for that. Raga knows about what you did, too! So your tricks won't fool us!"

Spent, Logo descended the terrace stairs. "I'm leaving Ratenggaro, too. Give me five head of livestock. I'll leave tomorrow, and you can do whatever you want!"

"Logo!" Wolli found the courage to speak. "Kakek and Nenek are inside. Please don't let them hear you."

Waleka's eyes followed Logo as he walked away without saying goodbye. His thoughts turned to Galuh. He still had time to build the pillars and a magnificent roof for the Big House! His bravado blazed like a bonfire in the middle of the grazing grounds. But … his farm was empty now. Logo and Uka, his own sons, had stolen the livestock. Thank goodness he had already sent some of the cattle to Galuh's family as an apology for Lara's behavior. Waleka felt sure the girl would soon be delivered to him. Briefly, he regretted Lara's disappearance. Like Wula, Lara could have been sold for a large dowry, replenishing his grazing grounds with much livestock.

Waleka walked to the edge of the cliff, not to look at the sea, but to turn around and survey the village. It was the best spot to see his temporary home clearly. Even without a tall roof, the sturdy-looking house would benefit with the presence of the soon-to-arrive seventh woman.

Waleka thought back to Ndalo's advice after Raga had deserted him on the side of the road. "Just kidnap Galuh and take her with you," Ndalo had said at that time, grinning contemptuously. "It's much better than her being snatched away by Logo or some other guy!"

Now Waleka stood on the edge of the cliff and looked at his temporary house, smiling. He swore he would build the roof just as soon as the seventh woman had arrived. In that new ancestral house with a tall roof, he would be young again — and Koni would just be the old, annoying first wife.

Waleka gasped — shocked at his thoughts. Koni was already far from his mind and heart. Adrenalin tightened his chest. Waleka gazed at the parched, bare ground where his traditional ancestral house once stood. "Galuh …" his voice trembled.

CHAPTER *14*

Waleka left his temporary house and calmly walked to the village gate. His horse was already tethered at Duyo's fieldhouse. Waleka liked Inya Duyo. She always kept her mouth shut and never opposed his decisions or caused trouble with the first wife.

Duyo stood at the back fence of the house, which separated her garden from the vast fields. She turned when Waleka came and immediately walked toward him.

Duyo looked closely at her husband's appearance. He wore a new sarong and destar and appeared to be in a cheerful mood. His white teeth meant he had used young betel nut shells to clean them — and no wad of tobacco bulged beneath his lower lip. His hands and feet were freshly bathed; his body was rubbed with fragrant oil.

"Where are you going?" Duyo asked, although she already suspected the answer. Like Koni, she had learned to manage her feelings internally. This was just like the old days, when her husband would leave and, in no time, a third, fourth, fifth, and sixth wife returned with him. *Has the time come for the arrival of the seventh wife?*

Duyo took a deep breath. She hoped that Galuh had disappeared, in shame, forever. Duyo's main concern, however, was not about a new woman coming to their home. Her real worry was Raga's plan to

105

search for Lara. Even though Raga had become a reliable, respectable, young man, Waleka did not seem to care if his eldest son left before the roof of the new ancestral house had been erected. Soon, there would be another harvest time. The family would all gather for the Bau Nyale and Pasola. The house would be quiet without Raga. She decided to speak, even though she knew that whatever she was about to say would be useless.

"Raga is leaving." Duyo told her husband.

"He's not!"

"He sold some of his livestock and land." Duyo continued. "Raga has never stolen anything, and he will never steal anything. Still, Logo swears that Raga is stealing to get money so he can just travel around — not to find Lara."

"He's not leaving," Waleka repeated. "He has a wife and children here."

"Don't allow Raga to go!" Duyo pleaded. "Please tell Logo not to spread any more gossip about Raga."

"Raga will not go," Waleka insisted. "Many people leave their village to live in the city and work there. Many people leave to attend school far away in Flores, Timor, Java, and wherever else. But Raga won't leave. He's an important man here. We have plenty of cattle to build a new ancestral house. You keep Raga here so he can start leading the construction of the new roof."

Duyo, watching her husband's face, suddenly gasped, "Bapa! Why do you have a coiled snake on your head!" Throughout her life with Waleka, Duyo had never seen a henggul with a snake pattern wrapped around her husband's head. *Inya Koni once told me about a henggul with a snake pattern! So, it's true!* Duyo's fear deepened.

Waleka jumped into the saddle and whipped the horse's flanks hard. He ignored the children and grandchildren watching him. On the path behind his house, he whipped the horse again. In the next second, he was flying on the rhythm of the galloping horse as it raced into the embrace of the grasses that spread far and wide.

"The traditional house, again!" Waleka shouted, spurring his horse mercilessly. "The traditional house, again and again and again! Raga! Logo! Uka!" His whip smacked the horse. "Galuh!" he shouted even louder, as if only she could solve his problems. The image of Galuh's face consumed him with desire.

The wind whipped against Duyo's face. For a moment, she bowed her head. After her husband disappeared around the corner of the path, she silently watched her grandchildren. One by one, everyone returned to their activities. The women returned to their weaving looms or went to the fields. The children went to fetch water or play in the garden.

"Nenek, why did you scream, earlier?" one of Duyo's grandchildren asked. "Where is the snake?"

"Where did Kakek go?" asked another grandchild.

"He had to take care of some business." Duyo replied curtly. Fear consumed her. Her husband was wearing the wrong henggul. *Where did he go?*

Duyo gathered her grandchildren and took them on a walk into the village to visit Koni, Kakek, and Nenek's house with the flat roof. *Does Inya Koni know that Waleka left with a snake on his head?*

Moments after Duyo arrived at the temporary house, all were surprised by the arrival of Hamoli, Raga's wife, and their youngest child. The house became crowded in an instant, as villagers came quickly to find out what was happening in the flat-roofed house.

Everyone knew that Raga had gone to look for his daughter Lara, but the stories that explained *how* Raga had left the village were less clear.

"Did he sell one cow shed's worth of livestock and two plots of land near the beach?" one of Ndalo's family members asked. "If he didn't sell them, how did he pay for his expenses? Where does he think Lara is?"

"Don't talk nonsense," another man grumbled loudly, showing his regret at Raga's leaving. "It's no secret that Logo, Uka, Ama Dula, and their followers stole from our farm!"

"Someone said that Raga is staying with Father Bili in Weetebula, and that Father Bili said Raga might take a boat to Java, Sumatra, Bali, and maybe even Malaysia!"

"Men are like that." Ndalo joined the group and laughed. He was very happy that Raga had left. "Raga has to be a worldly man!" he sneered. "Travel to Java and Bali! If necessary, go to the Netherlands, go to America! Don't forget to visit England and Japan!"

"Yes, yes!" Ama Dula and the men in his group laughed.

"Raga is not going to move abroad." Hamoli spoke softly and politely, showing proper respect to the elders. "He went to look for Lara."

"Going is going," Ndalo chuckled. "The destination doesn't matter. If you're going, it doesn't matter why and where. It's called emigrating!" Koni looked away when Ndalo's piercing eyes found hers. She shivered.

Koni, Duyo, and Hamoli went inside the temporary house to Bapa Tua and Mama Tua's room.

"Hey, Wolli! Ndalo shouted.

Wolli calmly greeted him with a curt nod before stepping quickly away to join the others in Bapa Tua and Mama Tua's room.

Every Independence Day, Duyo wove special sarongs for Lara and Wula to wear for the occasion. Raga always presented the sarongs to the two girls. But on Independence Day, in August 1974, Raga only presented one sarong, for Wula. Lara had been gone five months. Although Father Bili had assured him that Lara was fine, Raga wanted to see Lara for himself, wherever she was.

It had been overcast on the day Raga left to look for Lara. Koni was the only one who felt guilty about Raga's leaving. She felt responsible for his leaving the village. When Raga said goodbye to her, he repeatedly begged for Koni's understanding and help in explaining to Duyo why he had to go.

"I won't be gone long, Inya," he said softly. "I can't rest easy until I see Lara and know for sure where she is and how she is doing."

"Are you sure you'll be able to find her?" Koni asked hopefully.

"Yes, Inya!" Raga smiled. "Now, don't worry. Please take care of Mama Inya Duyo, Hamoli, and the grandchildren." Raga bowed and apologized to Kakek and Nenek for leaving without Waleka's permission.

Koni held him one last time before he left. She handed him the small shawl she had just finished weaving. The shawl could be used as a henggul.

"Put this on," Koni said, and Raga accepted — thanking her repeatedly.

"You can stop by Bapa Bili's house or go directly to the convent in Weetebula. I am sure Bapa Bili knows where Lara is." Koni spoke what her heart told her. She felt Lara had been saved by someone — someone who knew her family's plight. Things were becoming increasingly difficult with Waleka always thirsting for a new wife. "Bapa Bili can help."

Koni sent Raga off with a mixture of sadness and confidence that he would return with Lara. Koni now shared the information with Duyo, Hamoli, and her other children.

CHAPTER *15*

Raga was no stranger to Father Bili's house. When he was a student, he lived with Bapa Bili while helping to farm and raise livestock at the monastery. But family relationships had worsened over time. Now, Waleka was angry at Father Bili for helping the son and the granddaughter who had defied him. Waleka shied away from any contact because of his shame and anger at Raga for leaving the village without his permission. Bitterly, he avoided Father Bili by no longer selling cattle to him — especially if the monastery would somehow benefit from the sale.

Waleka was worried that people who knew Koni would side with her. He was even more concerned when he found out that Raga was staying at Father Bili's house for a few days while looking for Lara.

As he spurred his horse, Waleka tried to surrender his mind to the wind. He could not allow every memory to influence his mind and heart. Now, the important thing was to walk forward without looking back. He left Duyo's house riding his horse, wearing a red destar with a snake pattern. Ndalo's voice sounded again, stirring his heart. "What makes a man braver is his conquering of women." Waleka thought about his visit to Galuh's village with Ndalo soon after the fire, and receiving the destar he wore from the woman he now longed for.

111

Waleka did not care what kind of destar he wore. The only thing that mattered was to make the seventh woman completely his. Just as when he had found the third, fourth, fifth, and sixth, he did not want to talk much about it with the previous wives. As it turned out, Koni and Duyo had been the only obstacles. *They are ill-behaved and disrespectful wives*, he thought indignantly.

Ndalo's words had a profound effect on Waleka's attitude, making it tough and resolute. "Just look at me," Ndalo had boasted. "Who dares to oppose me? No one! A woman is lucky to be an elder's wife. All she has to do is be proud of her status and honor her husband! That's all!"

"You're right! Waleka had agreed.

"I'll soon take a seventh wife just like you! Ndalo added slyly.

"Now, wait, Ndalo, you promised to wait for Wula to finish school in three to five years."

"There are other girls besides your children!" Ndalo had chuckled.

Waleka had laughed. "You know what will happen if don't keep your word? You will face me on the Pasola field! Remember, wehave a deal: If I win, Wula is free from any obligation to be your wife."

"Yes, but you won't defeat me," Ndalo had replied.

Now, the thought of Tila Wula awakened an anxiety in Waleka's heart. He pulled hard on the reins and turned his horse back to his temporary house. There he found his first two wives and daughter-in-law crying over Raga.

"Raga is gone!" the words fell on Waleka like a chorus as he entered the house.

"Everyone already knows it. Let him go. He's useless!" Waleka accentuated each word. His feelings were complicated. He felt hatred for those getting in the way of his having Galuh, regret at having put himself and Wula in the position that they were now in, and shame at the way Raga had treated him. He would never, he vowed, forget how Raga had abandoned him at the top of a hill in desolate grassland.

Waleka could not hide his anger as he faced Koni, Duyo, and Hamoli. He sat rigidly while pounding betel nuts in the small mortar he carried everywhere.

"Did you ask Raga to leave?" Waleka looked at Koni while putting the mashed betel nut into his mouth. "Or did Raga leave because you were crying like a fool?" He chewed until the betel nut juices filled his mouth, then spat red saliva through the lattice of the house floor.

"Bapa, please … please find Raga and Lara," Hamoli pleaded, wiping her tears. "Tell them to come home. Raga might have gone to the monastery where he used to study, where Inya Koni also studied. Or maybe, right now, Raga is still at the harbor, waiting for the ship to leave. Please tell the other children to go after Raga and bring him back. Please ask people to find Lara. Please, Bapa, bring them home."

"Bah! Let them go! No one is allowed to look for either one of them. Good riddance!" Waleka continued to chew and spit. He still couldn't understand why Lara had dared to defy him. Surely it was better to bring his own granddaughter's best friend into the house as a new wife than to bring in a stranger? Lara could have been persuaded to accompany his new wife. All she had to do was call her by a different name: Nenek or Inya Pitu. There was nothing for anyone to complain about. His children and grandchildren should be proud to have a father who was an elder, but no, that didn't happen. Waleka could still see Galuh gasping and turning deathly pale as Lara raged uncontrollably at her.

And Raga! Waleka was stunned by how defiant Raga had been. Thank goodness, no one but Ndalo knew what had happened between him and his eldest son.

Waleka rose and walked out of the house. When he reached the bottom step of the stairs, he heard Mama Tua crying, "Leka … Leka." Mama Tua's illness had made her even more frail.

Waleka paused for a moment, realizing that his old mother was still able to hear and feel what was happening. He took a deep breath.

Anger and pent-up desire for Galuh stopped Waleka from returning to see his parents.

Instead, Waleka chose to go meet the seventh woman. Even though he knew that the bad-omen birds, *pungok wengi* and *julang*, always appeared at night, he braced himself to saddle up and spur his horse onward. The owl had no power to stop him, nor did the hornbill that cawed while traveling through the sky.

Hamoli stayed for a few days with Koni, Duyo, and her grandparents in the temporary house before returning home to resume her own life.

Raga's departure in search of his daughter became the daily topic of village gossip. Just like every other parent in Sumba, Raga wanted to see for himself that his child was doing well while living away from home. In time, all children who left the village to study returned for one reason or another.

In years to come, Lara would come home at Nyale and Pasola time, even though the meaning of the two ceremonial rituals was beginning to slip away from Waleka's, Ndalo's, and their women's minds.

Some women accepted whatever kept them down while others used their inner strength to hold their heads high. Hopefully, Lara would arrive back home as a woman with the same attitude, mind, and heart that made her so precious. Whatever she set her eyes on, she would always do so in the spirit of the love, self-respect, loyalty, and honesty, which the Nyale and Pasola were meant to convey.

Chapter *16*

After Kakek and Nenek had finished eating, Wolli left the house with Lamura, taking his horse to bathe in the river at the foot of the cliffs. Koni was still cooking on the stone stove when he said goodbye.

After giving Lamura a good washing, Wolli let the horse graze on the river bank. He sat there alone, feeling empty and troubled by all the family problems that kept coming. He knew that his mother felt the same sadness. It seemed that the happy times of their togetherness as a family in Ratenggaro were gone. "Ah, no." Wolli murmured. "There are many beautiful memories that can heal a wounded heart."

Those memories took Wolli back to when he was a ninth grader in middle school, and two little girls — second graders of the elementary school — rode with him on horseback across the fields to school. The sun would still be behind the small hills next to their uma parona and the tip of the small cape at Ratenggaro Beach. Soft golden rays gradually climbed over the cliffs and sliced into the dark sky above. The rooster had already crowed under the trees and was pecking at the corn scattered there. An oil lamp illuminated the Big House from within. Its weak light penetrated the lattice of the wall, but struggled to reach the farthest corners of the house. Mada Wolli was in the saddle on Lenggu

Lamura's back, waiting to take the two little girls to school: Wula, his sister, and Lara, his niece.

"Take care of them," Koni had said as she lifted Lara into the seat behind Wolli. Koni strapped two small jerry cans on each side of the saddle. "Don't forget to get water after school," she said.

"Yes, Inya," Wolli replied.

"There are two bags of food," Koni said, as she lifted Wula to sit in front of Wolli. Koni hung two bamboo water containers near Wolli's feet and said, "Help the girls get water."

"Yes, Inya," Wolli replied.

Every morning, at dawn, and every evening, at dusk, the three of them had passed through the village gate. The crashing waves accompanied the hoofbeats along the path between the large gravestones that rose above the field's surface. Most graves had tightly closed doors; but some graves had open doors, ready to receive the dead. The wind whistled gently between the stones. Swirling lightly, it sang notes of sorrow that told of every farewell that found a stopping place at the cemetery.

"Gha," Tila Wula said in a small voice, "I'm scared." Her voice trailed off and dissolved into Lara's laughter behind Wolli.

"What are you afraid of?" Wolli asked. "I am here!" He held the reins in one hand and wrapped the other around Tila Wula. The little girl pressed her head back against Wolli's chest and closed her eyes.

"I'm afraid of passing this road," Tila Wula said. "There are open tombs."

Wolli and Lara laughed, but they could not dispel Wula's fear. The little girl turned her face away and hid against Wolli's chest.

"The open tombs are there so that when someone dies, there's no need to make a new grave because the grave is already prepared," Wolli said. "Those two open graves belong to our family."

"I don't want to go by the new graves," Wula replied. "I'm afraid." Wula pushed her face harder against Wolli's chest and burst into tears.

Letting the little girl cry against his chest, he tapped Lamura's neck with the reins, and the horse began to trot.

"You can open your eyes! We've passed it!" Wolli let go of the reins and allowed Lamura to enter the path beyond the graveyard freely. He placed his hands on either side of Wula's head and gently turned her face forward. "Look! We have passed the graveyard. Don't be afraid anymore." At times like these, Wolli felt so important to the little ones. "The Almighty, The Wide-Eared and Big-Eyed One, is watching over us," he comforted Wula. "Don't be afraid."

"I am still afraid," Wula repeated and grasped Wolli's arms with her two small hands.

"Hey, hey, hey! Don't be afraid, or Lamura won't want to take us to school," Wolli said lightly. They passed the Maliti Bondo Ate field, where the Pasola was held. It was a special place for Wolli, Wula, Lara, and all the other children, because it was on this field they would meet their kin and friends from near and far every year.

"Do you want to go to school and be a smart student?" Wolli asked.

The two little girls answered in chorus, "Yes, yes!"

"One times one," Wolli began, and both girls replied, "One!"

"Two times one," Wolli continued, and thus the multiplication tables of one to ten became a rhyme on the way to school.

"Hold on tight, we're going faster! One, two, three!" Wolli lightly tapped the reins on Lamura's neck and the horse sprinted onto the road through the middle of the field, leaving Ratenggaro behind. On their way, they saw children from the neighboring villages on horseback with their fathers or older siblings. Some were headed to school, but most of them followed their parents to work in the fields.

"Gha Koda! Ida!" Wula and Lara called out, waving at their classmate Ida, sitting behind Koda, Wolli's classmate. They were also riding to school.

"Galuh!" Lara called out when she saw Galuh, another classmate, walking toward her.

"Are you coming with us?" Wula asked.

Wolli rode over to Koda, and the two friends positioned their horses side by side. As usual, Wolli lifted Wula with both hands, and she immediately settled into the saddle in front of Koda. Galuh took her place in front of Wolli.

Every school day, they met like this at the crossroads at the Maliti Bondo Ate field.

In this open part of the field, hoofbeats sounded faster and freer. In the part of the field where the grasses grew tall, the horses moved slower. From afar, only four heads were visible: Wolli's, Koda's, and their horses'. The four heads moved in concert with the beat of the horses' hooves, the gusts of wind, and the dance of the tall, wild grasses.

Wolli opened the snack bag and took out the roasted corn — one for each of them. Koda also opened his snack bag and shared it with the others. Next, the water bottle was opened and passed from mouth to mouth. Koda and Wolli were last.

"You will get to rest in front of the school," Wolli told Lamura.

Koda told his horse the same thing.

Lara, Wula, Ida, and Galuh would always laugh. They thought it funny that the two kind-hearted older boys talked to their horses, but it made them happy.

The sun continued rising slowly, revealing the morning in all its glory. The air was clear. The sky stretched like a bright, blue canvas. Before entering the larger road, Wolli and Koda dismounted and helped the four little girls down so they could walk together into the elementary school. The two middle school students would ride on to their school.

"Gha," Tila Wula's voice was the softest. "We go home together!"

"What?" Wolli teased.

"We go home together!" Tila Wula's voice was soft even when she shouted. She couldn't shriek no matter how hard she tried.

"What?" Wolli asked, still pretending he couldn't hear what Tila Wula was saying.

The four girls now shouted in unison: "We go home together!"

"Oh!" Wolli replied, laughing. "Yes!"

"I don't understand why they're always yelling about going home together," Koda would chuckle. "We always go home together!"

Wolli turned for a moment and saw Wula, still standing in front of the school, waving at him.

That had been when Wula was still in elementary school. She had since graduated from junior high and was now enrolled at the vocational school in Anakalang — where he had once studied — to become a teacher. Wolli smiled and drifted back into memories.

After school, Ida and Koda would let Galuh off at the side of the crossroads, where they had picked her up on their way to school, and then went straight home.

Wolli, Wula, and Lara headed for Waimalu, the spring. Sometimes, there would be a line of people waiting to get water. Wolli tethered Lamura to a tree on the flat ground above the arch that held the natural spring. Wolli walked ahead with two large bamboo water containers on his back. Wula and Lara each held two smaller ones. The spring was right beside the trail, making it easy for everyone to collect water.

Wula and Lara would join their friends to bathe in the spring's small lake, Lake Waimalu. They would leave their clothes piled on the rocks while they played. Women and small children also bathed, and this enlivened the mid-afternoon atmosphere at the spring. While he waited for the girls, Wolli collected firewood not far from the spring.

As soon as he heard a voice call, "*Paghogha*! Big brother!" Wolli knew that they were ready to go home together.

Go home together... The memory of those voices always made Wolli smile. He felt both valued and proud to be so meaningful to these very young girls. He shifted his seating on the riverbank and returned to the past.

"Gha, I'm not going with Lamura," Lara had told him. She ran in front of the horse to be with the children and women who were collecting water, before walking home with them.

"I'd like to ride the horse with you, Gha!" Wula raised her arms, ready to be lifted. Seated in front of Wolli, she leaned against his chest.

"We still have some roasted sweet potatoes. Want some?" Wolli took another roasted sweet potato from the bag on Lamura's side.

"Yes, please!" Wula replied. "Thank you, Gha."

Her small hand was in Wolli's grip as she joined him to hold the reins. Wolli smoothed Wula's wet hair, pulling it behind her shoulders to lay down on her back. He tucked her wet bangs behind her ears.

In doing so, Wolli was repeating the same motions that he remembered as a child, when he went to the spring with his parents. After he finished swimming in Lake Waimalu, Koni would smooth his wet, messy hair. He remembered sitting on Lamura's back, in front of his mother, and leaning against Koni's chest. Her two loving hands would move his hair back from his temples and tuck it behind his ears. Then Koni would touch the top of his head with her pointed nose.

Bapa always walked in front, holding the reins.

"Don't let your hair fall on your forehead!" Koni warned.

"Why? Wat will happen?" he always asked, looking up to see his mother's face.

"It will cover your eyes!" Koni would laugh and take the rubber band from around her wrist. She smoothed the hair off his forehead again, and banded it. "This way," she said. "Tie it like this. Now you look very handsome." She would hug him tightly and continue, "A horseman must be dashing!"

"Like who?"

"Like your father, Bapa Waleka!" Koni would exclaim laughing. "Dashing during Nyale with very beautiful kawoking. Dashing in the saddle. Dashing holding the reins. Dashing on the Pasola field as a loyal and honest to-paholong. Dashing everywhere!"

Koni would continue, "Inya will weave a henggul you can wear around your head. Not a single hair should spring lose! Oh, you'll be very handsome. Handsome in the head, handsome in the chest. Handsome in mind, and handsome in the heart."

"Manly indeed!" he'd interrupt before his mama could finish.

"Well, that's it! You're a smart boy!"

Still sitting on the riverbank, Wolli again felt the stirrings of sad nostalgia. The situation at home now was so much different from the past. He returned to the happier memories of when he was a middle-schooler.

"Come on, jump! We've arrived!" Wolli would say when they approached the village gate. Wolli dismounted. "Do you dare jump?" He laughed when Tila Wula held out both hands for him to help lift her down. "Come on! Jump!" Wolli said again.

But Tila Wula shook her head. "I'm scared!"

Wolli quickly turned his back to Wula, and the little girl immediately wrapped her arms around Wolli's neck and climbed onto his back. When Wolli leaned backward, she slipped off to the ground.

Lara and the other children ran to get their water containers from Wolli. Some of the mothers and children expressed their gratitude as they walked back into the village.

"Go straight home," Wolli instructed Wula and Lara. He remounted Lamura and rode to the estuary at the foot of the village. He always bathed his horse in the same place he and his father had bathed him. He had just reached the center of the lower cemetery when he heard Lara calling after him.

"Gha Wolli! Gha Wolli!" Wolli did not want to turn around and go back. It would soon be dusk, and he had never bathed a horse in the dark. But Lara's voice grew louder and was joined by Wula's cries.

"What's wrong with Wula?" Wolli muttered, turning Lamura around. He quickly spurred his horse back towards the little girls.

"Wula is scared," Lara said when he arrived.

Wolli jumped down. "Scared of what, *ade*, little sister?" he asked.

Wula ran into his arms and pointed toward an empty grave.

"Aw, it's all right," Wolli soothed. "Ambu Marapu, the Great Grandfather, is watching over us. Here, let me take you to the gate." Wolli crouched down and Wula climbed onto his back. "Hold on tight!" he said as he stood up. Wolli held Wula's two small water containers in one hand and wrapped the other arm around her legs.

"Where are the school bags?" Wolli asked.

"Here." Lara pointed at their bags.

"What are you afraid of?" Wolli asked again when Wula pressed her face against his back and would look neither left nor right. At the village gate, Wolli leaned backward and carefully loosened the two small hands around his neck. As Wula ran toward home, he quickly turned back toward the estuary.

At the side of the cemetery, Wolli stopped for a moment. He tried to sense what Wula was so afraid of. He looked around, recognizing some of the tombs, as well as their family's two empty graves up on higher ground. These graves were for his grandparents, when they died. In the layer below, his paternal ancestors — whom he knew from stories and names — lay to rest. Almost every week, Wolli came to the cemetery with his friends and younger siblings to clean around the graves. There was nothing to be afraid of here. He, himself, had not been afraid to play here.

Wolli spurred Lamura through a shortcut to the estuary. The sun would set very soon. He would have to bathe Lamura quickly.

When Wolli was a child, Waleka always took him along when they bathed their horses in the estuary or on the beach. Wolli clearly remembered sitting proud in the saddle on Lamura's back, in front of Waleka, while he and his father held the reins together.

The speed of Lamura's gait depended on Wolli tightening or flexing the reins. Wolli would bend forward until his head lay against Lamura's neck, and his father would bend over on top of him. The two of them would circle the open, wide, flat fields.

"Hold Lamura! Love him! Put him in your heart! Put him in your head!" Waleka's words rose above the pounding hooves and whistling wind. "It is not you who makes Lamura gallop! It is Lamura taking *you* galloping. When you're riding him, it's no longer you or Lamura. You are inside Lamura, and Lamura is inside you — the two of you are one!"

"What does that mean, Bapa, to be one with Lamura?"

"When you grow up, you will know what it means." Waleka spurred Lenggu Lamura through the open fields. "Be a true winner!" Waleka pulled back hard on the reins. The horse whinnied loudly and reared several times. Then, with lowered ears, Lamura snorted and began grazing.

"Let Lamura rest!" Waleka jumped off Lamura's back."Come on," he said to Wolli. "Jump!" Confident that his father would catch him with just one hand, Wolli threw himself out of the saddle.

That was back then when the tension in the house was not so high as it was now. Now, his father didn't have time to spend with him anymore. Wolli knew that these childhood memories had shaped him to feeling responsible for looking after Wula, especially, and the other little ones, including Lara. That instinct came naturally to him. Wolli hoped that his father felt the same. Despite everything going on, Wolli still hoped for the best.

Now, some eight years later, Wolli rode toward the estuary to bathe Lamura on the same path through the cemetery, located right in front of Ratenggaro. Wula was away, studying hard to become a teacher. No one had heard from Lara, and the fulfillment of the hope that Raga would return with news seemed a long way off.

"Did you just arrive, Wolli?" Several men, including Ama Dula, were already there, bathing their horses. "You are very diligent about bathing your horse. You're just like your father!"

"Did Raga leave?" asked another. "Logo and Uka also left. I hope you won't leave too!"

"School first," Wolli replied.

"What do you want to be?" the first man asked.

"A horse breeder and school teacher," Wolli replied.

The men laughed. "Why do you spend so much time bathing horses?" Ama Dula sneered. "Aren't you tired of it? Do you really want to be a teacher and a horse breeder?"

Wolli usually answered this kind of question with a little laugh and no words. He would spend the rest of the time soaking and bathing his horse until Lamura was clean and shiny.

"Let it be," Ama Dula continued meanly. "No need to go to school. Just become a horse breeder. Your older brother has left the village. Who will take care of the horses? I think Raga wants to find a new wife somewhere."

Ama Dula chuckled. "Your brothers Uka and Logo are useless. They sold all the cattle and land so they could move away. Is that what good men do? No! Only the person who doesn't steal livestock and doesn't pawn land that isn't his is a good man!"

Throwing a shrewd look at Wolli, he said, "Tell Lara to marry me. I'll give you a dowry of horses to replenish the stable Uka and Logo emptied." He paused, then continued mockingly. "Your father's behavior most likely caused everything! He already has six wives and still wants a seventh. What a greedy man!"

"Raga did not sell our livestock," Wolli replied calmly. "Raga did not steal. Raga went to look for Lara."

"Oh, what do you know? You're always away at school and only come home for short periods of time. You don't understand!"

"I do understand, Ama Dula." Wolli replied and lifted his head to look at Ndalo's goon.

"No, you don't. You are not from here. You don't have any legitimate right to live in the Big House." Ama Dula hooted. "A big house, that is, with a flat roof."

Wolli tensed. "Ama Dula, don't say that."

"A flat-roofed temporary house isn't a traditional ancestral house," Ama Dula jeered. "Hell, if it weren't for Ndalo, your father couldn't build any kind of a house."

The people bathing horses and themselves lifted their faces to gaze at the flat top of the uma parona in Ratenggaro, where the roofs of ancestral houses were built tall and soaring.

"So tell me, where is your ancestral house?" Ama Dula needled. "Ask your father when he plans to build the high roof of your house so we can see it from here." He narrowed his eyes. "Do you understand why all of this is important? If you don't, then just leave Ratenggaro. Go back to your village in Lamboya."

"Hey, watch your mouth!" one man warned. "Waleka will be angry if he finds out you were talking like that. Wolli is considered their biological son."

"Don't accept that, Wolli," Ama Dula said slyly. "Just go home to your own village. Would you want to be Waleka's biological son? I definitely wouldn't, if I were you. That old man can only cause trouble."

Ama Dula paused for a moment before attacking again. "Greedy old man. Imagine selling a child who is only eight years old without anyone knowing." Ama Dula chuckled and spat, enjoying the confusion creeping across Wolli's face. "Now it's all revealed. It's just a matter of two or three years before Wula becomes Ndalo's wife. Waleka has already received several herds of livestock and plots of land from Ndalo as her dowry." Ama Dula moved to leave the bathing spot. "Tell Lara to run away with me. I have a lot of livestock for a dowry, and tell your old father not to be greedy."

Wolli was stunned. He understood what Ama Dula had said about Raga, Logo, and Uka leaving the village. He also understood the comment about the horses and how he should choose and determine his future. But he did not understand what Ama Dula said about his father accepting a dowry for Wula. *So Logo's and my father's argument about the dowry for Wula was true.*

Wolli saw Ama Dula and his two men disappear around the corner of their respective homes. He dried Lamura and himself.

"Horses must bathe every day, just like you do." Waleka's voice from long ago rang in his ears. He remembered sitting on the horse's back and his father, holding the reins, walking in front. On the way home from the pasture, the garden, or the spring, he and his father would always see a horse that was tied up to graze.

"Look at that," Waleka would say. "Horse flies swarming all over. Look at those flies between the hind legs." Concerned, his father watched the horse fidgeting and swishing its tail to chase away the flies that kept biting again and again. "That's a horse that rarely bathes."

"Poor thing," Wolli said.

"Do you feel sorry for it?" his father asked, and Wolli nodded. "Don't ever let your horse be swarmed by flies. The horse will be embarrassed, and you'll be embarrassed too."

"Come on, let's take a bath!" his father urged. "Horses take baths, what about you? Let's take a bath!" Father and son splashed each other playfully. The estuary felt fuller at high tide. The breaking waves created a continuous echo.

Wolli's memories of his father had made vivid imprints. Sadly, he realized that day by day, he and his father were growing farther apart. He tried to recall when the distance was first created, but all he could remember was that since Inya Nomo's arrival, his father had kept himself apart.

"Bapa," Wolli murmured, "did you really receive the dowry? For which sister? Wula?" Wolli gasped, fully realizing he was no longer as close to his father as he used to be. Each time his father acquired a new wife, Wolli had further separated himself from Waleka. After Lara stormed away from the village, after the Big House burned down, and after Raga had left, his father had moved even farther away. Wolli took a deep breath. The tension among his father, his mother, Inya Duyo, and the other wives had intensified. Wolli began to understand better why his grandparents kept moaning the names of Waleka, Raga, Wula, and Lara.

"Go home, Wolli!" One by one, the men still bathing in the estuary returned to the village.

Wolli held Lamura's reins and stood for a moment before leaving the waterhole. In the silence of the beach and the darkening estuary, the rushing water churned all the way to his heart. The spring gurgled so loud, its sound reached everyone nearby. Tears were even louder than spring water. Only sensitive people could appreciate the rhythm of both.

Wolli hoped that later, at home, there would be no more tears from Kakek and Nenek, nor from Inya Koni, his mother. Wolli wished with all his heart that what Ama Dula had said was not true. That it was not Wula who Ama Dula was referring to, not Wula who Ndalo had paid a dowry for when she was just eight years old. Wolli's heart ached thinking of Lara, Wula, Ida, and Galuh and the way they rode horseback to school during their childhood, when everything was simple.

CHAPTER *17*

At the entrance gate of Ratenggaro, Lamura seemed reluctant to move through. Wolli jumped down. The sun had already set. A bright moon and twinkling distant stars lit the cold and silent coastal sky. The sound of the waves washed in so close it reached the gate.

Suddenly, Lamura brayed loudly, just once, and planted his feet. This was not normal. Wolli could not get Lamura to move, even when he slapped Lamura's hip hard. "Come on!" Wolli commanded. Lamura answered with a snort. "What's wrong?" Wolli looked cautiously all around the graveyard. They were right next to an open grave.

"What's wrong?" Wolli asked again. "Are you afraid?" *When Wula was a little girl, she was afraid to pass here too.* Wolli tried to reassure himself, "She's not afraid anymore," he muttered. "Now Tila Wula is a young woman studying to become a teacher."

Lamura snorted again.

"What did you see, Lamura?" Wolli asked, then saw the flickering lights inside the open tomb. "Oh, those specks of light are probably fireflies," he answered himself, heart pounding. "Just fireflies," he whispered slowly. His heart began to race again. It was only for a second that Wolli felt something was off. The momentary feeling disappeared when Lamura stepped forward on his own. A group of men and women, talking among themselves, was just entering the village, returning from a day of fieldwork.

"Good evening," Wolli said, as he joined the other villagers, walking next to his horse.

"Are you home on a break?" Someone asked. Wolli answered the question friendly and politely.

Ratenggaro was quiet during the day, but it came to life after dusk. Men sat on the porch. Women prepared food by the fire. Children played in front of the house.

Wolli tethered Lamura to the banyan tree outside his house. He quickly picked up the bamboo water container he had left at the village entrance a while ago and took it home. He was surprised to find Koni sitting sadly by the fire.

"Is Bapa not home yet?" Wolli asked quietly.

"Eat first," Koni replied, wiping her eyes.

"Ambu?" Wolli asked.

"Your grandparents just finished eating," Koni's voice quivered.

"What's wrong, Inya?"

"Poor Ambu!"

His mother cried a lot now. She usually sat near the fire that warmed the house from its central location. She chose the side of the fire where she could look out of the back door, which was always open.

"After you finish eating, take some grass to Lamura," Koni said softly.

"Yes, Inya. Is there food in the remba for Bapa?"

"Yes," replied his mother. "Don't be too long out there." Wolli loved to play the flute, especially while sitting next to Lamura after cleaning the stables and feeding his favorite horse.

Wolli helped Koni light the lamp and place it in the center of the room. "There is only a little oil left," Wolli said. "Why don't you just go to bed while waiting for Bapa to come home." He took the food meant to be his father's lunch from the remba. He was touched by how his mother always saved food for his father. No matter how long his father was away without news, no matter when or at what time he came home, food always awaited him. "I'll just eat this, Inya," said Wolli.

"You always do that," his mother replied. True, Wolli always wanted to eat the food his father had not eaten. After he finished, Wolli took the food prepared for dinner and put it in the remba for his father. He went to see his grandparents before going downstairs.

"It's already late!" Koni said. "Come back soon. You must have some rest. Tomorrow, you have to go to the harbor and return again to Kupang to wrap up your schooling. Come home to Ratenggaro after you've received your diploma and taken care of all the university matters."

"Yes, Inya," Wolli replied. He made several trips to the back of the house until the pile of straw filled the entire back corner of the kambu luna.

Lamura waited patiently under the banyan tree. He was not like the other horses, who stood placidly in their stable stall under the stilt house. Lamura preferred to be free. Other horses accepted the floor of the stilt house as their roof; Lamura insisted on the sky as his — except during the rainy season, when he took shelter in the kambu luna. Wolli grabbed a bale of hay and dropped it near Lamura. He then took a seat on the hay bale and began to play his flute. The instrument produced clear, bright, high tones, as he blew with measured force. The notes became staccato and punchy when he blew in quick, short spurts. The overall rhythm of his song mirrored the galloping of horse hooves, running free, leaving everything behind. The music floated through the silence of the night.

As he played, Wolli smiled inwardly whenever the light inside the house occasionally disappeared. He knew that meant his grandparents and mother were taking turns peeking out at him. Although their eyes could not penetrate the night's darkness, their hopes and peaceful hearts united them with an awareness of each other as they enjoyed the sounds that came and went through the night. The light slipping between the bamboo slats in the back of the house brightened when he stopped playing.

Wolli placed his flute next to him on the hay bale. He looked up at Lamura. "Are you tired?" Lamura gave a low snort. Clouds covered the moon; the night was inky black. The young man who loved Lamura fell asleep next to the snoring horse.

"Paghogha! Gha!" In Wolli's dream, Wula had fallen into the corner of the cemetery.

"Gha Wolli! Gha Wolli!" Wula screamed.

"Wula!" His shout bounced around the cemetery. "Wula, where are you?"

"Here, Gha Wolli!" Wula sobbed.

"Wulaaaa!" he called loudly.

"Gha Wolli!"

In his dream, Wolli couldn't find Wula. Then he saw Bapa Tua and Mama Tua in the cemetery, cleaning graves.

"Wula must be scared to be alone," Kakek said as he helped Nenek tidy the gravesite. "Take her away and look after her. Don't leave her. I am entrusting her into your care, Wolli."

Wolli gasped as the grave door closed. "Wula! Wula!"

His own voice woke him up. Wolli rubbed his eyes, momentarily disoriented. He realized he had fallen asleep on the hay bale next to Lamura, but he still felt frightened by his dream.

The night was silent. A dog howled far away, the only voice bearing news.

In the shadows, Wolli caught the movement of a man rounding the back of the temporary house and tying his horse to a tree not far from Lamura. The man quickly stepped over to the back side of the kambu luna, just a few meters from where Wolli sat motionless.

The man was not alone. Wolli recognized the tall shadow as his father's. The shadow following him on tiptoe was someone he had brought with him. The two shadows disappeared behind the house.

It's Galuh! Wolli choked. Quietly, he followed from behind. His mother and grandparents were alone in the house. Crouched at the foot of the back stairs, he heard the floor creaking before it stopped at the far end of the room parallel to the back door — only about six feet away from his grandparents' room.

Wolli stood still, trying to catch any other suspicious sounds in the back of the house. He walked to the edge of the cliff and looked around. He saw no one and heard nothing except the relentless waves breaking.

Quickly, Wolli returned to his house and climbed the back stairs. He halted abruptly in front of the door at the height of his parents' argument. He heard crying — it was his mother, Wolli knew. During the past few months, this had happened often.

The glow from the stove inside the house grew fainter. The oil lamp had died. Wolli sat quietly on the steps of the house. He had to remain silent if he did not want to invite trouble.

"Don't bring another woman here!" His mother's voice.

His father: "Just shut up and obey. Don't complain! All my other wives have left the Big House because of you, all except Inya Duyo, who is in cahoots with you! Inya Telu left because of you. Inya Potoh, Inya Lime, and Inya Nomo — all left because of you. You were hostile to all of them! Do you have any idea how many horses and buffaloes I've had to sell to build fieldhouses for them?"

"Don't bring another woman here!" Koni persisted.

"Watch what you say! Remember, you have to be good to her! Tonight she sleeps with us here, to feel the traditional house even though it hasn't been built yet. To feel the house even though the roof is flat. Do you know how many buffaloes and how many horses I gave her family in addition to the plots of land?"

"Poor Wula! Poor Lara!" Koni pleaded again. "That woman is a friend of your daughter and granddaughter!"

"Huh! After more than twenty years of marriage, you could only give me one daughter. Now, where are my other women? Where are my other children? You don't even realize your ancestors saw what you did, you fool!"

"Take her to a fieldhouse — anywhere, but not here!"

"Shut your mouth!"

Wolli heard a slap followed by a sob. He shook with anger but could do nothing except keep silent.

"Leka! Leka!" Nenek's hoarse voice cried. "What have you done ... Leka ... Why Leka? ... Why have you become like this? Leka, you're lost!"

Steps approached the corner room. "Inya, be quiet. Mama Tua, be quiet. You can't see what's going on, Mama Tua. You don't understand." Waleka's voice had turned whiny, trying to convince his mother that, as a descendant of traditional elders, he knew what he was doing and how to maintain dignity.

"Leka ... you brought another woman here," Nenek cried. "You must find Lara ... you must listen to Raga!"

"I am an elder, Inya!" Waleka blustered. "I will protect my elder's honor and do as I please."

"No, Leka ... no, you are wrong. You are not an elder." Nenek choked on the tears trying to break loose from her old body and burst into a coughing spell.

"Drink this, Ambu," Koni coaxed, guiding a glass to the old woman's lips. "Drink." Then Koni hissed, "You heard what Nenek said. You are not an elder!"

Wolli shook his head. Although Nenek was blind and couldn't hear well, and Kakek could no longer speak, they always seemed to know exactly what was taking place. Years later, Wolli would realize that his grandparents had the sensitivity to know what was going on — something Waleka was unable to cultivate, knowing only how to use his authority, carelessly and heartlessly, to give more importance to his own best interests.

Midnight had passed and Ratenggaro's silence felt thicker than usual. The waves lapping at the foot of the cliffs gave testament to the constancy of nature's voice that spoke the same language for everyone. But nature's messages were not always interpreted the same when the heart was wounded.

The towering rooftops in the village rose black and shadowy against the dark sky. Beneath the one flat roof that should have been soaring like the others, the hearts of elders and women were in turmoil.

Koni could no longer accept her husband's habit of adding wives. Twice, three times, and now for the seventh time. And what did it say for Galuh, this measuring the value of a woman's life in herds of livestock and acres of land? Or perhaps Galuh didn't care. Perhaps she was just happy to be the current favorite in Waleka's arms.

"You dared to accept Ndalo's dowry for Wula when she was only eight years old!" Koni's harsh words startled Wolli.

"Shut up, you old woman!" Waleka snapped.

Nenek shrieked, horrified that the fate of her family was being determined by lies. Her repeated attempts to explain the need for honesty and integrity failed to overcome Waleka's desire to acquire more women. Galuh, his seventh wife, who would sleep with Waleka that night in a corner of their temporary house, would later give birth to yet another child.

Wolli remained seated on the stairs under the back door of the stilt house. A breeze blew in from the sea. The great ocean in the distance undulated in copper-black swells. If it were not for the song of the waves, no one would have known that Waleka's house sat on a flat cliff. The ebb and flow of lapping tides blended with the river emptying slowly at the foot of the cliff. This night, the steep cliff walls echoed the voices rising from above, as if they shared Wolli's heartache.

Wolli was young enough and strong enough to easily overpower his father and drive Galuh away. But he held back. His father would not be defied when it came to women.

Through the moon, the stars, the breaking waves, and the river at the foot of the cliff, Wolli realized that discourse was always present, always with different interpretations. He was forced to understand everything happening in the temporary stilt house that had been rebuilt without the tall, traditional roof as it should have.

"Stay there!" Waleka's voice broke into Wolli's thoughts.

"I want to go get Wolli!" Koni said. "He's probably asleep next to Lamura."

"Don't go looking for him."

"Do you want to find Wolli or do you want to spread rumors in the village?" Waleka said irritably and threatened, "Try it if you dare!"

Wolli pressed his hands tightly against his ears, but no matter how hard he pressed, the arguing voices still reached him. As the commotion inside reached a breaking point, Wolli jumped up and hid behind the stairs.

"Is she angry?" he heard Galuh ask.

"No! She's a fool!" Waleka replied. "Don't you be stupid like her!"

Then, a giggle from the corner of the house, surely from Galuh.

The bamboo floor creaked, and suddenly Koni jumped down from the back door and fell by the stairs, very near to where he hid.

Waleka was right behind her. He dragged her away from the house shouting, "Go ahead and find Wolli! You can't come home tonight!" Then Waleka bounded up the stairs and went back into the house. Koni tried to follow her husband, but she fell again as she tried to climb the back stairs.

Lamura whinnied. Wolli stepped out of hiding and hugged Koni tightly, calming his mother. Suddenly, they heard steps nearby. Lamura whinnied again. *Lamura never whinnies in the middle of the night.*

"Lamura ... are you okay?" Wolli murmured anxiously. Lamura snuffled softly for a long time in the silence.

"Nenek ... Kakek," Koni wept. "Wolli, please go comfort your grandparents."

"Yes, Inya." Wolli's voice shook with anger. He wanted to scream, but shouting would wake those in the village who were still fast asleep. Worse than that, it would cause more pain and embarrassment for Inya, Kakek, and Nenek.

They heard Nenek crying for her son. "Leka! Leka!" Her wailing penetrated the walls of the house and was absorbed by the silence and darkness of the night.

"Please go up to the house, Wolli," Koni urged again, crying. "Poor Nenek and Kakek." But when Wolli moved toward the house, she suddenly held him back. "No, wait, don't," Koni whispered. "It will only cause more trouble." The two held each other in the darkness, behind the stairs, by the back door of their temporary house with a flat roof.

Koni and Wolli passed the night with Lamura, sleeping against the hay bale, while Lamura stood guard over them. He didn't move at all, giving his two masters a chance to rest.

But Wolli could not sleep. He felt uneasy and wanted to look after his mother and horse. Listening to Koni's soft sobs as she fell asleep, Wolli bore the sadness of the woman who had been his mother since he was only one day old.

Wolli had a big family in Lamboya who he did not know well. Because he had never experienced having biological parents, he didn't know if there was a difference between having biological parents versus having adoptive parents. All he knew was that Waleka and Koni had raised him as their own, and from early childhood, he felt how much they loved him. Even after Tila Wula was born, when he was seven, Bapa Leka and Inya Koni only grew more loving toward him.

The family grew bigger over time with new wives and new births. All that time, Wolli enjoyed a blissful childhood, where both parents and extended family worked together to overcome problems. From time to time, he sensed a sadness in his mother, especially as children and grandchildren from Waleka's other wives left the village to live elsewhere.

But Wolli knew that his mother was not sorrowed by the children's courage to leave, but rather because their comings and goings were always followed by quarrels and tensions over livestock lost or sold, or land sold or mortgaged.

Of his father's seven wives, only Inya Duyo, Raga's mother, had a good relationship with Koni. So did Raga's wife, Hamoli, and her children, especially Lara, who was the same age as Tila Wula. Problems arisng from dissatisfaction with material possessions were not uncommon, but tensions had never been as bad as they were now.

Wolli slowly began to understand that although the turmoil in the house revolved around his father's desire to take multiple wives, his mother had known all along that having more than one wife was customary among the elders.

Regardless, his mother was angry. Lara was angry. His grandmother cried bitterly that his father no longer qualified as an elder. His father took a dowry from Ndalo for Tila Wula. *My father sold his own daughter.* Wolli ached with sadness.

"Oh, Inya," Wolli whispered. He sat up. The sky was still black. Koni's hand had slipped from his shoulder. Very slowly, Wolli moved his mother's hand.

The back stairs creaked, and Wolli's senses sharpened. He saw Waleka and Galuh tiptoeing toward his father's tethered horse.

Wolli moved quickly to the tree where the horse was tied.

"Wolli!" the old man jerked back, startled.

"Yes, Bapa," Wolli replied calmly.

"Why are you here?" Waleka's voice was barely audible, but he quickly regained his composure. "So you must have heard!" he said sternly. "But remember! Keep the secret. No one should know." He quickly mounted and pulled Galuh up to join him in the saddle. They did not pass through the main gate. Instead, they left through the *binya wawa*, the lower gate rarely used by villagers. Wolli watched as they left; there was only starlight in the distance.

Feeling empty, he returned to Lamura.

Koni woke up. "Where did you go?"

"Looking around the night, Inya," Wolli replied.

"Don't let anyone know, Wolli," his mother said softly.

Wolli quietly bowed his head.

When morning broke, Wolli and Koni returned to the house and entered Bapa Tua and Mama Tua's room. Nenek was still fast asleep, her breath catching occasionally from stifled tears. Kakek lay wordlessly against his pillows. Wolli gasped when he touched Kakek's foot. It was very cold, much colder than it should be.

CHAPTER *18*

Kakek's death gathered the entire family. Family members from Kakek's side, and kin from Nenek's home village, came together in Ratenggaro. Kakek's body was placed in Waleka's temporary house.

Now, all the family members who had come from afar joined the villagers in voicing their opinions about whether the flat roof was the cause of Kakek's death.

"You didn't build the traditional ancestral house with the right roof, so disasters will come again and again," one of the elders said.

"When will you rebuild the traditional roof of the ancestral house?" asked another elder who had come from the most distant village.

"You should be ashamed!" another elder admonished. "Your parents, the oldest of our elders, sleep in a house with a flat roof! We are so ashamed and very embarrassed. Where is your pride? You must build the new roof immediately!"

"You have enough money to pay the dowry for a young wife, but not to build the roof over your house?" exclaimed another. "How is it possible for this house to be stark naked? Is this how you want it?"

To all accusations, Waleka answered convincingly. "I guarantee that before you return for next year's Nyale and Pasola, the roof of the ancestral house will be erected."

"You dare to talk about Nyale and Pasola?" shouted an elder. "Before you can talk about Nyale and Pasola, you must have the courage to be loyal and honest. Remember that!"

Waleka was struck silent by the elder's words.

"Don't forget the promise you made to Kakek, at his wake, to build a new roof," the elder continued. "Remember! Don't anger the people of this village because you fooled them. We elders are ashamed, and the whole village is ashamed! If it's that hard to build a proper roof, then just dismantle this house and move into a regular village house!"

Many questions were raised and became the main topic of conversation among the extended family. The issues with properly rebuilding the ancestral house was used to bring up other embarrassments.

"How could you, at the end of his life, make Kakek sleep in a naked house?"

Such were the types of accusations thrown around freely that made Waleka bow his head.

"Do you have a new wife?" Waleka answered this question with a confident nod. "Where is your son's wife? Where is Raga? Where is Lara? How much did you ask for Tila Wula's dowry?" The questions pummeled him relentlessly.

"How many children do you have? How many grandchildren?" asked an elder. "Where are they? Please, point them out to us, one by one."

For the first time, Waleka realized that he did not know the number of children and grandchildren he had. Except for the children born to his first and second wives, he could not name the rest with certainty. He also couldn't say where some of his children had gone, or where his grandchildren were scattered.

Waleka faltered. What *were* the names of his children and grandchildren? His tongue felt thick. He paused for a moment, then recovered. "All" was the safer word to use, not names and numbers. *All* the children, *all* the grandchildren, and *all* the great-grandchildren.

Stories about Waleka's extended family grew more confusing and complicated by the events that kept happening. The most discussed news was that Kakek, who had always served as the family's backbone and unifier, was not just dead, but that he had been mute for a long time.

The naked house Waleka lived in became another part of the various predictions of his family's future. Villagers questioned each other quietly, "How long will Waleka be able to uphold his dignity as a village elder?"

And so, the village on the cliffs became crowded with families no less numerous than the families who would come for Nyale and Pasola. They slept scattered in each of the village houses. Some stayed in the homes of Waleka's children and grandchildren, in houses around the village. Others stayed in the fieldhouses with Inya Duyo, Inya Telu, Inya Potoh, Inya Lime, and Inya Nomo.

CHAPTER *19*

Bapa Tua went to *praing marapu*, his heavenly home, without delay. The family decided to bury him immediately, because the roof of the uma parona had not yet been built. It would not be appropriate for Bapa Tua's body to be kept in a house without a proper roof. Moreover, because the flat roof was considered a *naked* roof, it was inappropriate for Kakek, a tom mtona parona, a village elder.

"Let Bapa rest in peace in praing marapu instead of an inappropriate house," the extended family decided.

Waleka said nothing.

Bapa Tua's funeral took place when the appointed time arrived. Families who had not arrived by that time were no longer expected to come.

Drummers and wailing women accompanied Kakek on his final departure from the temporary house. Some women wailed to express the deep loss they felt from losing Kakek. Hired mourners cried to express grief, and it was their duty to cry throughout the procession to the graveside.

Wolli had picked up Wula from the school in Anakalang with the news of Kakek's death.

Tila Wula's wept through the entire the funeral ceremony. Wolli watched as Wula pulled free from her mother's embrace and ran to the door of the grave, calling out for Kakek. "Why did Kakek die?" she cried.

Waleka grabbed her hand, pulling her away from the pallbearers and back to her mother. "Take care of her!" Waleka told Koni curtly. "No crying! The ancestors are watching all of us. We must be happy. We must party. The dead go home to the dead. They have reached praing marapu, the home of our ancestors."

Koni glared at her husband with the most withering gaze she had ever shown Waleka throughout their marriage. Her eyes seemed to swallow the man alive.

"Keep Wula from crying," Waleka said. "You know better than I do what must be explained for the common good!" Waleka was so unnerved that a small amount of his betel juice spurted onto Koni's face. He looked away from the hateful eyes that pierced his soul.

In the next instant, Waleka turned to Galuh, who sat among the females near the pallbearers. Nodding, Waleka sent her a thin smile, a token of a deep sense of sorrow as well as an acknowledgment of anticipated joy that ran deeper than the sorrow.

Only Galuh understood the meaning of that faint smile. She was very proud to be a part of the old man, who was not only respected for the land and livestock he owned, but also for the commanding role he played in the Nyale and Pasola, rituals that influenced the entire life cycle on the lands of the ancestors who had already given so much.

In the midst of the grief engulfing her husband's family, Galuh remembered her parents' words and smiled slightly. "Take everything you can," her parents had said. "Cows, buffaloes, horses, land, money, everything! His wealth will never run out." She remembered her relatives grumbling. "They have shamed us! We must make sure that they restore our dignity in a way that can be apparent to all!"

Thus, Galuh, the seventh wife, felt satisfied that she had received everything she wanted. So when she lifted her face and saw the old man who had held her all night, gripping Wula by the arm and talking to his old wife, she did not care. She looked away and pretended she didn't know Wula, who still wept mournfully.

Waleka spoke to Galuh. "Don't say anything," he told her. "It's much better that way." He took care to keep the tobacco wad, clamped between his upper lip and lower jaw, in place. "You know you have to stay here until the ceremony is over."

Then, turning to Wolli, he said quietly, "Wolli, don't forget what I said."

"Yes, Bapa." Wolli's voice was barely audible. Standing next to his mother, he had heard and felt all the words spoken to his mother and himself. Even though she said nothing, Wolli knew what his mother was thinking and feeling. He watched Koni look down and wipe her eyes.

Waleka became exasperated. "Wolli, take care of Wula! She must not cry anymore! This is a joyous occasion, not a sad one. Understand?"

Wolli nodded. "Let me talk to Wula." Wula was still huddled in her mother's arms. Calmly, Wolli approached Wula. When he shifted his gaze to Kakek's grave, he saw Ndalo chewing tobacco and staring at him. Wolli held Ndalo's gaze until Ndalo looked away.

"Wula, please stop crying," Wolli whispered in comforting tones. "You know Kakek went to praing marapu. There's no reason to cry anymore. Tomorrow morning you have to go back to school."

Wula nodded.

Wolli wiped Wula's tear-stained face, affectionately. "There, there, don't cry anymore. Look over there; the door to the grave is closing. Kakek went to praing marapu."

"Kakek went far away and won't come back," Tila Wula said.

"No, where he went is close by," replied Wolli. "It's right here. All of our ancestors are here now. We can't see them, but they can see us. They're here; they're very close by."

Tila Wula sniffled. "You're right, Gha Wolli. Kakek now lives with his parents."

Wolli nodded. The ceremony continued solemnly. *"Men are like horses. Men are manly …"* Wolli listened, thinking, *Have they ever understood a young girl's love for her grandfather and the pain and loneliness she feels when she loses him?* Wolli hugged Wula's shoulder tightly, as if he were embracing his own fear, longing, and loneliness. "My dear sister," he whispered, looking around for Waleka.

A breeze blew in from the sea. The cemetery was silent, even though almost everyone in Ratenggaro and the surrounding villages were there in mourning, crowding the cemetery grounds.

"You must have the courage to let Kakek go," Wolli continued quietly, still holding Wula. "Kakek is going to our ancestors' home. They're all looking after us." The feeling of love and knowing he was being taken care of by his father and mother had made Wolli grow into a strong, young man and a protector of his younger siblings. He was convinced that his ancestors were with him wherever he went. He believed that his parents would be with him under all circumstances.

After Kakek's funeral, some mourners stayed in the cemetery, sitting on gravestones or cleaning graves. But most of the mothers and children left the graveyard and returned to the ancestral house to prepare the animal sacrifices and food for the festivities that would take place to honor the death of a 90-year-old elder.

A cold wind kicked up as the sun began its lean into the west. The cemetery was quiet except for Duyo's wailing outside the grave that had closed only moments before. Koni and Nenek sat beside her. Hamoli, Wolli, Wula, Koda, and Ida surrounded the three older women.

Duyo did not cry for Kakek. She cried for the return of Raga, her eldest son, and Lara, her granddaughter, who had left the village and were still missing. She wept with anxiety and longing for them.

Koni put her arm around Nenek's shoulder. "Let's go home." The sad group of women and children walked slowly through the cemetery toward the village's lower gate.

"Mama, please don't cry anymore," Wula said. "You will run out of tears and you won't be able to sleep."

The group shuffled home, Wolli moved to help support Nenek. Wula stepped between Koda and Ida. "Thank you for coming," she said to Ndalo's two grandchildren. Not once did Wula look in Galuh's direction while returning to the village. Because Wolli understood Wula's deep-seated anger at Galuh, he vowed that Wula would never find out what had happened on the night Kakek died.

Wolli and Koda's friendship, the love for their younger siblings, their journeys to school, along with the ups and downs they endured together, became the underpinnings of a future generation.

The period of deep mourning following Kakek's death continued, especially by his youngest sister, who had left home long ago to follow her husband and settle in his village.

After the funeral, Kakek's out-of-town relatives circled into a meeting with Kakek's Ratenggaro relatives. They questioned the Ratenggaro family about Kakek's death. They had assumed Kakek was in good health. What had happened? What had his son Waleka done for the family?

At first, the heated conversation was fueled by shame that Kakek had died in a temporary house with a flat roof. The discussions quickly slackened, as no one really wanted to talk about the traditional ancestral house. For reasons they kept hidden within themselves, the issue of the traditional ancestral house was of no consequence, in their minds, because it did not provide anything of worth directly for anyone. Therefore, Kakek's brothers and sisters mentioned it only briefly before re-igniting the meeting with more important topics.

Some of his siblings claimed they had been excluded from the family, that their parents had never given them anything. Demands were made regarding who had rights to what land was still left after such a large amount had already been sold.

"Raga is gone," one of Waleka's sisters said passionately. "Logo, Uka, and the other boys have already taken their share and sold it to live a life of luxury somewhere else. Now it is our turn. Even though we are women, we still have rights."

Koni remained silent during the discord among Waleka's extended family. Among all the things that were in dispute, their most worrisome concerns were about Inya Pitu, the seventh wife. How much land, livestock, and money had Waleka spent on her, while the roof for the ancestral house had gone unbuilt?

"I remember, *clearly* remember, Kakek saying to divide the land equally between every family member," said one relative. "No one but real family has any rights to it!" He glanced at Wolli.

The family council finally ended with an unexpressed accusation. There had to be a scapegoat — someone to blame — so they turned accusatory eyes to Koni as the cause of Kakek's death.

Koni gripped Mada Wolli's hand and squeezed it hard.

CHAPTER *20*

Koni sat on a hill. From there, she used to watch hundreds of horses and buffaloes grazing on the vast fields — fields that never really belonged to her. The livestock never really belonged to her either. These vast fields and all the animals belonged to her husband's family, for generations. All that wealth was attached to Waleka's great name, and with that important name, he could lure and conquer women as he wished. Cows, buffaloes, horses, women, and vast fields were the mark of manhood. Even now, Waleka's greatness was measured by his wealth.

From the heights of the hill, Koni's gaze swept to the foot of the horizon and the vast, dusky blue ocean. She heard hoofbeats approaching but did not turn her head or acknowledge their presence as the horse halted next to her and Waleka dismounted. He tethered the horse to a nearby lamtoro tree and sat down next to Koni. "One hundred horses, one hundred buffaloes, and one hundred cows," he said without preamble. "That's the price."

"That's the selling price for Tila Wula, your flesh-and-blood daughter?" Koni's voice shook.

"Yes! Is it not enough?" Waleka stiffened, ignoring the voice of alarm from his greedy heart.

151

"And you used the money from the sale of your daughter to buy a seventh wife." Koni's voice was flat.

Waleka tried a different tack. "Her price was much cheaper than yours!" he exclaimed. "I paid *twice* as much for your dowry! Why aren't you ever satisfied? What makes you so difficult? Inya Pitu is already ours, period. She can help you weave, fetch water, carry wood, take care of the horses, and help with your children and grandchildren. She can also teach Wula everything."

"Teach Wula everything?" Koni snapped. "No need!"

"You're still not satisfied!" Waleka shouted. "No one lives in the ancestral house but you. Only you rule in the Big House! And you are not satisfied?"

"Are you not satisfied sleeping in rotation from one fieldhouse to the next?" Koni spat back. "You don't even know how many children and grandchildren you have. Tell me, how many? Tell me now!" Koni looked away in disgust.

Waleka's slap was swift and hard. "How dare you say that!"

Koni gasped and faced her husband. "You own fields!" she screamed. "You own cows, buffaloes, and horses. You employ all the shepherds. You own the ancestral house ... the uma parona that will be rebuilt!" Koni paused to catch her breath. "You have all these things to pay for women! One woman is not enough. Two are not enough! Three are not enough! You have become a briber and a thief to get the fourth, fifth, sixth, and seventh!" Koni straightened herself before launching her final accusations. "There will be an eighth. There will be a ninth. Never mind the number of children, grandchildren, and great-grandchildren that these wives produce. I ask you again: Tell me how many children you have and their names. Where are they now, what have they become?"

Shocked, Waleka stared bug-eyed at Koni. If it were not for his eyelids, his eyes might have popped out of their sockets. "Do you know who I am?" Waleka's voice rose dangerously. "Shut up and obey me! I am an elder!"

Quietly, Koni said, "You don't care about Tila Wula."

Waleka shrugged. "Eh, she is your daughter."

"What? Is Wula not your daughter as well?"

Waleka rose, walked quickly to his horse and untied it. Without speaking, he mounted and loosened the reins. He clucked his tongue, and the horse bolted, carrying Waleka away and leaving Koni alone on the hill.

The wind caressing the waving grasses witnessed Koni's tears. Slowly but surely, nature reminded Koni of the resilience all life must possess. Koni's intelligence told her there was no need to shed tears for a man who would always bring other women into their home. Nor was there any reason to pity a woman who took pride in taking a man and adding more problems to an already complicated household. Everything happened as it was supposed to happen. She must accept it because it had to be accepted. She would not give up, because her defeat meant a victory for another woman.

Koni realized that as the first wife, she had to survive. Even though her heart was scarred, she needed to endure, because despite Waleka's livestock, bringing home a nyale nest, winning at the Pasola, and appearing at every ceremony as an honorable man, her husband was nothing but a naked man who had never really owned anything.

Koni stood and listened to the hoofbeats descending the hillside rapidly. From the top of her hill, she watched her husband turn his horse to the left, and she knew he was heading for the house where Inya Pitu lived.

Alone among the grasses waving in the breeze, Koni heard a gentle rumble. *Thunder?* Sun brightened the sky; wind pushed clusters of clouds. A kettle of eagles circled low, then perched on the branches of a solitary lamtoro tree standing in the vast open field. Their high-pitched whistling pierced Koni's resolve, and she burst into resentful tears again.

Koni pounded the ground repeatedly with both hands. Her parents' advice to remain resolute in establishing herself as the old wife, the *first* wife, didn't erase the painful mental wounds inflicted by her husband, with each new woman he brought into the family. The trauma felt fresh every time she had to brace herself to allow the man she loved to sleep with other women, even if he did so under different roofs.

Koni gathered all her strength to rise again. The sun was leaning to the west, signaling the right time for her to pause and chant a plea to the Big-eyed and Wide-eared One for the success of Tila Wula, Wolli, and Lara.

Afterward, Koni was eager to return to Ratenggaro and share the sad experiences of the day with Duyo. She stopped just outside the gate and wiped her face with the tip of her sarong. She forced a smile on her lips, straightened her spine, and took a firm, confident step into the village.

Chapter 21

Straighten up and keep smiling. With those words leading the way, Koni returned to her home, filled with the new courage she had gathered within herself. She quickly climbed the back-door stairs. The only thing she heard was Nenek's coughing. "I'm coming, Inya," Koni called out. She found her mother-in-law lying on her back, eyes closed. "Nenek," Koni called gently.

Nenek opened her eyes briefly then closed them again. "You're home," she said slowly. "Where's Leka?"

Koni did not answer. Such questions could never be answered accurately.

Nenek was only seventy-four years old — not so old for a farmer and weaver. But lying sick in her bed like that, she looked Kakek's age. "Where's Waleka?" Nenek's voice was barely audible.

A clatter of steps on the back-door stairs interrupted Koni's answer. She turned and saw Duyo and Hamoli.

"Is that Leka?" Nenek's voice was filled with hope.

"Mama Tua, it's Hamoli. I'm here with Inya Duyo."

Koni moved to make room for Hamoli and Duyo to enter the room and sit by Nenek's side.

The four women sat in silence for a long time. Nenek rarely spoke anymore. Her words began to dry up after Waleka started bringing in new women. And after their uma parona burned down and was rebuilt without a tall roof — like the houses of other elders — she had become almost as mute as her husband, Kakek, had been. After she found out that Kakek died on the same night that Waleka had brought home a seventh wife, she rarely left her bed. Despite their silence, Koni and Duyo knew how much Nenek suffered because of her eldest son's behavior. Through the years, Wula, Wolli, and Lara had been her constant joys. The fact that Waleka rarely came to the ancestral house did not bother Koni and Nenek much at all.

From before sunrise until midnight, a Ratenggaro woman had so many things to take care of. Her schedule was set to fulfill her family's daily needs according to the passing of time: preparing food for breakfast, lunch, and dinner; weaving the best clothes as gifts to loved ones and to sell; gathering firewood and lighting the cooking fire; fetching water from the spring; watching after the children; and so on. These daily rituals shaped each woman's personality into a steady pattern that promised good results for the group as a whole. For generations untold, women carried out these expected chores.

A horse whinnied at the side of the house. "Is that Leka?" Nenek asked.

Hamoli left the room to see who was there. "Bapa," Hamoli greeted Waleka at the front door. "Nenek asked for you."

Waleka did not believe Hamoli. His mother had become practically mute. He walked through the front door and into his parents' room.

"Leka ..." Nenek's voice was barely audible. Her efforts to speak louder and clearer were obvious. "Leka ..."

Waleka took a seat next to Koni and bowed his head.

Koni and Duyo were paying close attention to what Nenek was trying to say.

"I ... only ... gave permission ... for one. Only Inya Duyo ..." Nenek gasped and visibly gathered her energy before she could continue.

"But … you … broke your promise." Nenek's voice rasped hoarsely. "Pa … so … la …" She could barely speak between her sobs.

Nyale and Pasola had not been the same since the arrival of Waleka's third wife. The rituals were no longer treated as a space and time for the family to gather and solve problems together. Instead, the events only added problems, because the people who were supposed to solve problems moved away. The arrival of the fourth, fifth, sixth, and seventh wives had only complicated the rift.

Nenek had quieted. "Uma parona … take care of it," she said calmly. Suddenly, with a surge of new strength, she struggled to sit up. Nenek's blind eyes looked at Waleka and asked in an accusatory tone, "What were you doing with that woman?" She fell back and sighed before stammering on, "That night … when your father died early in the morning." Her breath quickened, her blind eyes still fastened on Waleka, she added, "You … what did you do, Leka?"

Waleka rose, and without a word or a look at any of the four women, he strode out of the house. The front stairs creaked under his quick descent, and the clatter of hooves signaled he was gone.

"Waleka has been gone since he sold Wula to Ndalo." Koni's voice was barely audible. The thought of a father marrying off a daughter who was both educated and obedient to her parents' wishes, made Koni's adrenalin pound.

"Waleka is really gone," echoed Nenek, speaking her last words before joining Kakek in the ancestor's home in praing marapu. A home with a tall roof.

Waleka stepped closer to Nenek's grave. The door had just been closed. He sat and leaned back against the door, spent with sorrow. Nenek was the last backbone of Waleka's immediate family.

Occasionally, Waleka lifted his downcast eyes to gaze up at the sky, calling out to the ancestors to accept Nenek in her eternal place.

The circle of Nenek's extended family around the grave continued to expand until it filled the narrow courtyard between the other graves.

The village of Ratenggaro was eerily quiet as it dealt with the loss that would be imprinted on Wolli's memory for the rest of his life. Wolli had interrupted his studies in Kupang, and Wula had taken a leave from her school in Anakalang, to return home as soon as they heard the news that their grandmother had passed away.

Now, standing at Nenek's gravesite, Wolli searched each woman's face. Some of them he knew well; others he knew only casually. He found very few expressions of sincere sorrow for the woman who had loved Inya Koni and Inya Duyo as if they were her own daughters.

Wolli sat down next to Waleka, who turned and leaned against him. Wolli stiffened with discomfort at Waleka's behavior. It went against village custom. Waleka should not be sorrowful during the traditional burial ceremony, when the spirit was entering the praing marapu. Waleka was supposed to remain strong to prepare the way for Nenek's spirit to enter heaven. His father's behavior was abnormal for an elder.

Wolli could not find any meaning in his father's sorrow. When Waleka tried to stand up, the other men, including Ndalo, supported him. Wolli noticed that Ndalo, throughout the funeral, kept glancing at him.

Waleka tried to compose himself, but then he saw Tila Wula weeping. "That's enough!" he said sharply to Wula. "Stop crying! Ndalo is looking this way, and he won't like to see you cry. Don't embarrass me!"

Wolli stared at the closed grave. *How much pain had Bapa Leka inflicted on Kakek, Nenek, and Inya?* Tears welled up as he remembered the night his mother had fallen and hit her head on the wooden beam at the foot of the stairs. He felt his mother's pain deeply and knew how hurt Wula would be if she knew and understood what had happened that night.

Wolli wasn't the only one who felt uneasy. Many people were unsettled by seeing such overt weakness in a man who lusted for young wives, disregarded tradition, and had ignored what he needed to do for his parents' journey to praing marapu.

Waleka straightened when he saw Inya Pitu enter the cemetery with her family. Waleka greeted them with a sad face and red-rimmed eyes.

"Yes, Nenek went ahead of us." Waleka lied to his seventh wife's family. "We watched over her day and night. I never allowed her to be left alone. But in the end, she still left." Inya Pitu and her family expressed their condolences simply by shaking hands with the family members.

Koni and Duyo kept their heads bowed in deep sorrow. They also bowed with shame for the humiliation witnessed by their children, family, and everyone else at the funeral ceremony.

The family bickerings and disagreements that erupted after Kakek's death resurfaced after Nenek's, causing more violent arguments between close and distant family members. One distant family member, related by marriage only, felt it was important to have his say in the decision-making.

Wolli was dispirited — not because of the squabbles over livestock and land, not because their ancestral house still had a flat roof, but because Waleka had clearly lost his authority. His voice and say-so was nullified by the incessant demands of his young wives, who each exerted influence and wanted bigger shares.

Chapter *22*

Koni took a seat at Duyo's bedside. Duyo looked weak, becoming thinner by the day. Tears pooled beneath her sharp cheekbones, into the pockets of her sunken cheeks. Her watery eyes stared lifelessly from deep sockets.

"You must recover," urged Koni. "We must do Nyale; we must cook for the many children and grandchildren who will definitely come." Koni poured a little oil from the betel container sitting on a table next to the bed and rubbed the oil on Duyo's hand.

"How many Pasolas has Lara missed?" Duyo wept. "Another Pasola is coming soon, and I don't even know where she is. And where is Raga? There is no word from either of them. And," her voice grew even softer, "what is happening to the roof of uma parona?"

Three months had passed since Waleka had left the village with Ndalo and the other elders. They had always traveled together from one village to another. Since the beginning of her marriage, Koni had never known where they went exactly. She only knew that Waleka would return. How long he would be gone or how soon he would be back was not something a wife needed to know. Therefore, she had never been told. That was the reason Koni never answered questions about Waleka's travels from anyone who asked, including her children and grandchildren.

The sun had started its westward lean when Wolli returned from Kupang. He tethered Lamura to the banyan tree in the corner of the yard. Koni looked outside and, while watching Wolli and Lamura, became lost in thought.

Fortunately, we have Wolli and Lamura in this flat-roofed house, she reflected.

Wolli is figuratively the roof of the house. With pride, she remembered Wolli's modesty when he spoke his opinion about the house's flat roof. Koni would never forget how she was enlightened by the voice of a man who came from Lamboya, from Biri's womb, who was placed into her arms when he was barely a day old.

And Wolli was right! Koni realized. *The children and grandchildren make this house a Big House and function as its tall roof. They are the ones who "dress" the Big House. They are also the soaring roof. When family members, guests, and villagers return home for the Pasola, they will see that the house is not naked. Instead, they will see that it is surrounded by and filled with children and grandchildren who are smart, polite, well-mannered, and know how to conduct themselves as offspring of an elder in the family.*

"Waleka hasn't come home yet?" Duyo asked, breaking into Koni's reverie. "Raga hasn't come home yet, Lara ..." Duyo closed her eyes.

Suddenly, they heard approaching hoofbeats. Startled, Hamoli rushed out of the house and stood among the children and grandchildren. Everyone was watching to see if the horse and rider would head straight, toward their house, or would turn and take the path to another house.

The horse went straight. The rider sat tall on a shiny saddle. A large hat perched on his head, with the strap tied under his chin. He wore a thick shirt, thick trousers, and a heavy jacket. A small shawl, that could also be used as a henggul, wrapped his neck.

It was the shawl that made Hamoli scream. "Gha Raga! Bapa Raga!"

Raga stopped the horse right in front of them and dismounted in a single bound, as Hamoli and the children rushed to meet him.

Koni gasped when Duyo rose from her bed and took a shaky step. Koni grabbed her, and the two staggered toward the door. As soon as she saw Raga, Duyo stretched out her arms and sobbed, "Raga! Where's … Lara?" She shook from head to toe and would have fallen if Raga had not caught her in a tight embrace.

"Inya, Lara is fine." Raga looked lovingly at his mother's face. "She's at the nuns' convent in Denpasar. She is working there while going to school. The priests in Weetebula are helping her."

"Who is helping her?" Inya Duyo asked in an almost inaudible voice.

"Father Bili," Raga said brightly, trying to encourage his mother. "Father Bili, who used to help children who wanted to go to school, helped her. Lara is very smart, Inya. She'll come back after she graduates as a teacher."

"Oh Apu, oh Big-eyed One," Duyo sobbed. She looked at Raga with feverish eyes. Her gaze moved briefly to Koni, to her children, and to her grandchildren. Then Inya Duyo closed her eyes forever.

Waleka cried at Duyo's cold feet. Inya Pitu stood quietly nearby, surrounded by her family. Despite the loose-fitting sarong Galuh wore, Koni could tell how far along she was in her pregnancy.

Raga became withdrawn and silent whenever Waleka was around. He never knew that Waleka had taken Inya Pitu to the temporary house on the night Kakek died. Koni had kept quiet about it, and Wolli, too, kept that sad story to himself.

One of the saddest things for Raga was that Inya Duyo had died on the day he returned to his home village. Pain now filled his heart. He had so many things he wanted to tell his mother about Lara, but that opportunity had passed. He felt even more bitter when Waleka dared to bring a pregnant Inya Pitu with her three toddlers to the temporary house.

Logo and Uka suddenly appeared, looking overwhelmed with grief over the death of Inya Duyo. After Duyo's funeral, the two half-brothers worked together to receive a number of livestock deliveries from Duyo's family and other extended family members.

"Thank you," Logo said, as he received the gifts. Uka took the horses, cows, and buffaloes to the side of the village where they could graze. Then, when the numbers had grown quite large, he moved all of the livestock to the family's grazing pastures. "It's safer there," Logo told Waleka and Raga.

Wolli had also come home for Duyo's funeral, and stayed close by Wula and Koni. Wula was devastated and kept crying.

Prior to the seventh day of Duyo's passing, Raga and Wolli went to the farm. They found an empty field without a single animal.

"Every day, three head of cattle were taken from the field," the herdsman there told them.

"Who took them and where did they go?" Raga asked.

"To Ratenggaro, for Inya Duyo's burial ceremony," the herdsman replied.

"Who took them to Ratenggaro?" Raga urged.

"Waleka's sons Logo and Uka took turns," said the herdsman. "Yesterday, they both moved the last buffalo."

Anger flushed red across Raga's stunned face. He had suspected all along that Logo and Uka were planning to profit from the funeral. Their outpouring of grief had been merely a foil. They had pretended to secure the gifts of livestock in the grazing pastures, and now it turned out that every single animal had disappeared without a trace.

"They both took what they didn't own!" Wolli exclaimed.

Raga bowed his head. "Inya always said, 'Don't take what doesn't belong to you, unless the owner gives it to you because you deserve it. If you don't deserve it, you can't take it even if the owner gives it to you!' That's what your mother and my mother said!"

"I remember, Gha," Wolli replied.

"When you grow up …" Raga stopped himself.

"… you will understand." Wolli finished Raga's sentence with a chuckle. "Gha, you are just like Bapa Waleka when he gives advice!"

"When you get married, don't be like Bapa Leka!" Raga's words made Wolli burst out laughing. It was funny to see his brother looking so serious.

"Why are you laughing?" Raga asked, but he laughed too. They both laughed at the sadness and troubles that neither could stop.

"I've grown up, Gha! I've graduated from college."

"Yes! You've already grown up and you're smart!" Raga tapped Wolli on the shoulder. Thinking again about Logo's and Uka's deceit, his heart re-filled with anger. Raga paused and took a deep breath.

On the way back to Ratenggaro, the two of them stopped at Duyo's house, which was now Raga and Hamoli's home. Raga took two of his own buffaloes and joined Wolli, who continued to ride Lamura to the temporary house. The ceremony of Inya Duyo's seventh-day passing would soon begin.

CHAPTER *23*

Wolli rode Lamura with Wula behind him in the saddle to the stop where the bus passed Ratenggaro on its way to Anakalang. Wula had to return to school after attending Inya Duyo's funeral.

When Kakek died, Wolli started to understand what a family gathering meant. His mind churned, trying to find the proper words to record the events of the night before Kakek died. He wanted to be able to retell the story in its entirety at a later date. But he never managed to find the right words — not because he was afraid to voice them, but because he knew he would not be heard. Overtly or secretly, the good and bad deeds of the human race were sensed by creatures perceptive to signs — just like Lamura's whinny, which told about sad human activity. Both, the first and second Lamura, as well as the present Lamura III, possessed an innate sensitivity to be proud of.

Wolli waited until the bus arrived and Wula was safely on board. "Be careful!" he called.

"Yes, you must be careful too, Gha." Wula waved as the bus rumbled off.

Wolli was returning home when a group of men led by Ama Dula blocked his way. "Are you dating Ndalo's future wife?" Ama Dula

167

chuckled. "It must be great fun to ride with a woman you have a crush on."

"What do you want?" Wolli asked politely.

"Shut your mouth!" Ama Dula shouted. "You're just an adopted child. Wula isn't your real sister. I know you have a corrupted brain. You're waiting for Wula to finish school to take her to Lamboya! You devil!"

Ama Dula whipped Lamura's flank. The horse startled, almost throwing Wolli out of the saddle. "Be careful!" Ama Dula threatened. "If you don't want Wula to get hurt, be careful! If you continue seeing Wula, you'll see what I mean. Wula will be the one who will be finished." Ama Dula whipped his horse, and the group galloped away.

After Wolli arrived in Ratenggaro, he tethered Lamura by the side of the house. He pulled a handful of salt from his pocket and let the horse lick it directly from his palm. After that, he filled a container with water for Lamura and bade his horse goodnight.

Upon awakening the next day, Wolli immediately descended the steps from the house and untied Lamura, still tethered in the shade of the banyan tree. His thoughts returned to the fire that, a few years ago, had destroyed the uma parona and killed the family's favorite horse, the second Lenggu Lamura. While it was easy for his family in Ratenggaro to get a new horse from the family in Lamboya, it was hard for Wolli to forget what happened to the second Lenggu Lamura.

"It must have been so hot and hurt terribly," Wolli said to Lamura III. He tried to hold back his grief, but tears fell regardless. The still, early morning allowed him to hear the sea thunder and the breaking waves lap hungrily. Wolli also heard the river emptying at the foot of the cliff.

"Lamura," Wolli said to his horse, "can you tell me why Ama Dula is always threatening me? I feel sorry for Wula." Wolli turned. A short distance away, the edge of the Indian Ocean marked the island's boundary. The silvery horizon clearly marked the cloudless blue sky. The sea wind swept across his face.

Ama Dula watched Wolli from the terrace of Ndalo's house. He saw a tall youth, well-built, and tanned. His hair was neatly cut. Everyone thought he looked like Soekarno, the first president of Indonesia, who had passed away a few years ago. Ndalo, Ama Dula, and his men envied Wolli's good looks.

Wolli had quietly tried to find out who was behind the death of the second Lamura. He was almost sure that Ndalo and Ama Dula had something to do with the disastrous fire that had killed his horse. The stable door was never locked. Lamura could have saved himself by running out. But that night, someone had locked the door of the kambu luna.

"Does anyone really care about Lamura's death?" Wolli whispered to himself. He still ached about the loss of the second Lamura, imagining the pain of being burned alive. He realized that only two people truly understood the loss he felt: his mother and Wula. Wolli smiled as he recalled the years with Wula riding Lamura to school.

Wolli shook his head hard. "Wula," he said softly, "they had the heart to hurt Lamura. I will not allow them to hurt you!"

Wolli looked up at the blue, cloudless sky. An eagle circled high above Ratenggaro near the Maliti Bondo Ate field, then soared away, calling shrilly.

Wolli stroked Lamura's back. "Inya was right to stick with the name," he said. "Lamura. Lenggu Lamura the Third!" He pushed away his intimate feelings for Wula. He had always thought of Wula as his sister. He still wanted to keep thinking of her in that way. Koni had always divided her affection evenly between him and Wula, as siblings. Therefore, Wolli was always conscious of maintaining his position as an older brother. He suspected that if Wula knew his innermost feelings, his beloved sister might respond in kind. But Ndalo had already paid Waleka her belis, and Wula would be taken away from their uma parona. Besides, people would notice the unusual relationship developing between the siblings, and he and Wula would be the subject of endless gossip.

Koni approached Wolli standing by the pile of hay. "Are you feeding Lamura?"

"Yes, Inya." Wolli tidied up some of the scattered straw.

Koni stroked the white mark on Lamura's forehead. "Don't take Lamura to the kambu luna. Let him stay here."

Wolli laughed. "Yes, Inya, we'll let Lamura stay here. It is spacious under this tree. He will be free in the open air and can break his tether to run away fast if anyone disturbs him."

Both of them turned toward the house when they heard Waleka arrive. The old man walked up to the terrace and entered the house. A few moments later, he came back out with a piece of woven cloth in his hand.

Koni narrowed her eyes. "Bapa!" she shouted. "Where are you taking that cloth? It is a new piece for Wula!"

Ignoring Koni, Waleka strode quickly to the gate, jumped on his horse, and left.

"Where is Bapa going, Inya?" Wolli asked, without needing an answer.

"Don't take anything you don't own," Koni said.

They both knew that many of Nenek's old weavings of various patterns had disappeared. Now Koni's new weavings were disappearing, too. If Waleka could make land vanish, he could certainly do the same to items that were easy to carry off.

"The important thing is that Bapa did not take Lamura," said Koni, keeping her voice strong.

Wolli snorted. "Lamura wouldn't budge if anyone besides you or me tried to take him away."

"Lamura only obeys you!" Koni's voice finally crumpled. With tears running down her cheeks, she said, "If you take anything that doesn't belong to you, for whatever reason, the item you took will return to the real owner in whatever way and form! Everything that is not yours will move away and disappear. Everything that is yours will return and stay with you."

Wolli would remember Koni's words as long as he lived.

*C*HAPTER *24*

Koni typically spent her days in the vegetable fields, at the spring, at the grazing pastures, and at Raga's house. This morning, she walked home from the vegetable fields with her hands empty, because Lamura was carrying the heavy harvest of corn, squash, beans, and greens in saddle bags slung over his back. A bundle of dry wood from the pasture and a bamboo container filled with water from the spring rounded out the burden on Lamura's back.

Six years had passed of enduring the ups and downs and comings and goings of waiting for Tila Wula's and Wolli's school graduations. During that time, Lamura was Koni's best friend. The horse not only carried the burdens of goods on his back, but he also eased the burdens of Koni's mind and heart.

Walking home with Lamura that morning, Koni thought about how proud she was of her two children. Wuli and Wolli rarely saw each other while both were continuing their studies. But they always came home to Ratenggaro on school holidays to visit the family. When Wula was home, she liked to sit next to Lamura and read or draw.

Likewise, when her two children were off to their respective schools, Koni relied on Lamura's constant companionship. Koni smiled, remembering how she and Wolli decided to name this horse

Lamura, after the two previous Lamuras had died in the fires that had destroyed their traditional ancestral houses.

Wolli now lived in Lamboya with his biological relatives, but he had wanted Lamura to stay with Koni. "Let him stay here with you, Inya," Wolli said before leaving for Lamboya. "I will come back, and he will still know me as his master."

Wula was now an attractive young woman, and the thought of her leaving soon made Koni miserable. Yes, Wula would still live in Ratenggaro, but she would be surrounded by a much different environment. And despite the number of times Koni had been pressured by her own surroundings, it was not enough for her to succumb to the circumstances.

Walking through the village gate, Koni saw from afar a group of Waleka's wives gathered in the shade of the banyan tree. Koni slowed to calm herself and, squaring her shoulders, forced herself to approach them.

"Inya Koni!" Potoh greeted her loudly. "Do you realize that Waleka has fallen into poverty? Wula will be better off staying with Ndalo's first wife, Inya Tua. You might as well accept it and prepare her to be Ndalo's wife." Potoh sneered, "What is Wula's higher education doing for her?" Ignoring Koni's cold stare, she clucked, "After all that fancy education, she still falls into the claws of an old, rich man! Now, why would a smart girl like her do something like that unless it was to acquire some of that old man's wealth?" Potoh laughed out loud. "Wealth is good, isn't it? Let Wula go! She can be very proud to be Ndalo's ninth wife!"

Inya Potoh had always made sure that she, her children, and the other wives participated in preparing food for family and guests who came to watch the Pasola or attend other traditional events that brought them into the temporary house. She was completely unafraid of Waleka's eldest wife and her anger.

"It's been a long time ago since Waleka received the dowry for Wula!" she continued, still laughing. "Let's see, I believe Wula was only eight years old when Waleka sold her for one hundred and fifty horses? Oh, and all the buffaloes and land he received after that."

"Yes!" Telu bravely chimed in. "It was Inya Koni who told Waleka to accept the belis from Ndalo!" Banda Iha, Waleka's ninth wife, nodded in agreement.

"Fortunately, Ndalo's first wife will surely love Wula, because Inya Tua knows how to respect her husband, a rato, an elder."

Koni had long ago become accustomed to the vicious chatter of Waleka's other wives. Silence was her way of surrendering to the fate that hurt her so deeply. While the other wives threw taunts, Koni calmly unloaded her belongings from Lamura's saddle bags.

Banda Iha delivered another stab. "Even if there are a thousand Pasolas and a thousand wins, Wolli won't be able to marry Tila Wula. And, after all, why would she want to be with him?" Banda Iha paused meaningfully before delivering the coup de grace. "Moreover," her voice rose to make sure Koni heard, "Ndalo's ninth wife-to-be is already in his house. Tila Wula and Ndalo must have already slept together. So, it's done!"

No one spoke for a moment.

"Wolli will still ride in the Pasola!" Telu joined in. "Let it be! It has to be. He's a man from Lamboya, the neighboring village, right? So it has to be." Looking at Koni sharply, Telu sneered, "But even if Wolli wins, he'll still be a loser if his goal is to get Tila Wula. Such a pity for him! Does he even know that Tila Wula has already slept with Ndalo?"

Banda Iha laughed out loud. "It's impossible to live in the same house and not sleep together!" Banda Iha's shrill voice was joined by laughter from the other wives.

Potoh raised her voice above the others. "Ndalo's grandson, disagrees! Even with his high school education, Koda still doesn't understand that Tila Wula can't be with Wolli. Koda should realize that Ndalo, his grandfather, is not on Wolli's side!"

Potoh glanced at Koni before continuing. "Wolli is shameless. Waleka and Koni adopted him when he was one day old. They treated him as if he were their biological son — and Tila Wula's biological brother. How could he fall in love with his own sister?"

Koni's eyes swept over the faces of Waleka's young wives, who continued to babble loudly, ignoring the feelings of their husband's first wife and mother of Wolli and Wula. Koni had endured many things in silence. When facing the young wives who were always vying for attention, it was much better to be silent than to talk. Likewise, now, Koni only listened. She quietly tethered Lamura, then picked up her bags and climbed the stairs to her house.

"Bapa ..." Potoh woke Waleka on the morning of the Pasola. "Did you know that Wolli is participating in the Pasola? He wants to fight Ndalo. Does he want to take Tila Wula? Please don't allow him to embarrass us! Take care of Tila Wula. You must warn him that she has to become Ndalo's wife no matter what."

"She is already at Ndalo's house," Waleka snapped. "Inya Tua must have taken Wula under her wing. Inya Tua is a great wife. Ndalo is a wonderful man. Tila Wula is amazing. They'll make a great couple with no compare."

"How many more head of cattle did Ndalo add?" Potoh asked slyly. "Enough so you could pay the dowry for your seventh, eighth, and ninth wife? You must be careful. Wolli will fight Ndalo at the Pasola, and Inya Koni supports him. She has permitted Wolli to ride Lamura at the Pasola, so we must be careful; if Wolli wins, he will take Wula."

Waleka did not answer Potoh. He knew Wolli was riding in the Pasola. He rose quickly and put on the old sarong Nenek had woven for him along with the destar on his head and the sash that covered his body. He always wore these garments when he went to enjoy a Pasola. He walked to the field under the banyan tree where his horse was tethered. For the past few days, he had heard the rumors that Wolli would represent Lamboya at the Pasola. Wolli would lead his entourage for this match against Ndalo and his entourage from Ratenggaro.

From under the banyan tree, Waleka could clearly see Wula leaving Ndalo's house to meet Wolli, who had apparently just arrived from Lamboya.

Wolli immediately embraced Tila Wula but quickly released her. The two then pressed their palms together in greeting. A light breeze carried the conversation between the two young people who loved each other to Waleka.

"Is it true that you are representing Lamboya at the Pasola?"

Wolli nodded. "Yes, it's true, I'm joining the group from Lamboya."

"Of course you're riding Lamura. But which Lamura? You must choose! The Lamura you rode from Lamboya or the Lamura who lives here in Ratenggaro?"

"I choose the Lamura of Ratenggaro," Wolli replied.

Wula smiled. "You will definitely win with the Lamura of Ratenggaro!"

Watching them, Waleka took a deep breath. He tried to push away the memories of receiving the belis from Ndalo when Wula was only in the second grade of elementary school. Ndalo had assured him that he would wait for ten years, twelve years, or even fifteen years — however long necessary "until Wula finishes her school." Waleka clearly remembered those words when he made the deal to satisfy Ndalo and himself, each for their own reasons.

Waleka smiled for just a moment but immediately pressed his lips tightly together when he saw Ndalo, staring at him from afar.

Koni, who had walked onto the house terrace when she heard Wolli coming, stood transfixed. Only after seeing how much her children had grown up did she realize they were now adults!

An education! That was the only thing that really made Koni proud. Although her worries never completely disappeared, she always made sure that both Wolli and Wula were going to school — a dream she had never been able to attain for herself.

Solitude gave Koni time to reflect on the uselessness of trusting in people who never gave her hope. Since childhood, Koni had witnessed how a family with one husband and multiple wives functioned. She never asked whether the wives were happy. Actually, there was no one *to* ask. And later, when the time came when she could ask herself that question about happiness, she could not answer it, other than to say that she was content to see Wula and Wolli grow up and go to school.

When someone asked her if she was happy to deliver Wula into the folds of Ndalo's blanket, Koni did not know what to answer. She was like the moon in the field that only existed to provide light.

Chapter 25

Tila Wula was received with a great ceremony at Ndalo's uma parona. On either side of the stairs leading up to the ancestral stilt house, Ndalo's eight other wives, dressed in full traditional clothing, stood at attention. Two accompanied Inya Tua on the right side of the stairs, while three others stood on the left side. The two youngest wives stood in front of the entrance where Ndalo, accompanied by other elders, was waiting.

Adults, young and old, gathered with the children, in front of the house, on the footpath, and even underneath the stilt house. They were filled with a curiosity that could not be contained. Tila Wula's escorts stood waiting in the small street that was also part of Ndalo's property.

Tila Wula stood next to Koni, trying to keep a calm demeanor. Her eyes, searching the crowd, were met with sullen looks sparked by jealousy. Briefly, her eyes locked with Koda's and Waleka's, two men she cared for deeply. Wula grasped her mother's hand tightly, and the hand of the woman she loved was clammy.

Long ago, Koda had promised Wolli that he would come to Ratenggaro when the time came for Wula to be taken to Ndalo's house. Ignoring his grandfather's glares, Koda appeared calm. He was Ndalo's eldest grandson, and his presence was natural and welcomed with joy by his entire extended family. His attendance showed that the relationship between son, father, and grandfather had improved over time.

Waleka kept his eyes lowered, unable to look Koni's only daughter in the eye.

Koda gazed at Tila Wula, sending her his inner strength and support for maintaining her dignity, as Wolli had advised.

"If only I could stop Kakek Ndalo's power," Koda had told Wolli, as the two sat on the beach discussing the news that Wula would be handed over to Ndalo.

"That power has gone too deep," Wolli had replied. "Its roots have twisted around the rocks at the bottom of the sea."

"It is also the reason my father, Zoga, never comes home anymore," Koda said. "But I am okay. And so is my inya. She has become used to living and working alone."

"I feel sorry for her," Wolli said.

"I can't hate my grandfather, just like you can't hate your father," Koda said.

"Please take care of Wula." Wolli cast his eyes far out to sea.

Now, in front of Ndalo's house, Koda's heart pounded as Tila Wula released her mother's grip and stepped forward, while Inya Tua, Ndalo's first wife, also stepped forward and took Wula's hand. Koda took a deep breath as he watched Inya Tua wrap her best sarong around Tila Wula as a sign of acceptance and approval from the first wife to the newest wife-to-be.

The two women climbed the stairs of Wula's future husband's house. Koni entered the house as Inya Tua dressed Wula in her best clothes. The main garment, the *lamba leko*, sarong, was wrapped around Tila Wula's upper body and tied with a belt. She looked beautiful, with gold earrings in her ears and an array of bracelets on both arms. A *hamoli*, a gold pendant, adorned her chest, and a *henggul katipia*, a gold crown, was placed on her head.

"You finally came," Inya Tua whispered, grasping Wula's hand. Wula squeezed Tua's warm hand. Ndalo's other wives took turns mumbling "Welcome" while extending their hand with a nod. Not one of them smiled.

Wula murmured, "Thank you."

"Thank you for what?" one of the wives muttered, glaring hatefully.

Koni could not stop weeping. The two families now sat cross-legged facing each other in Ndalo's stilt house. She gripped Tila Wula's hand so tight, it was as if she would never let her go. Dazed, Tila Wula couldn't follow the ceremonial words her family spoke as they delivered her to Ndalo, as a woman whose dowry had been paid for. According to the agreement, she was supposed to have been Ndalo's seventh wife. In fact, she now would be his ninth. Wula could not clearly understand what the officiant from Ndalo's family had said about the belis that had been paid off and increased over the years, but he expressed his respect to Waleka for fulfilling his promise. He then expressed his respect to Tila Wula for being willing to enter Ndalo's house as a young woman who understood and was devoted to her parents.

But those were not the only voices Tila Wula heard. In the eyes of the wives, she saw both acceptance and hatred. Two of them whispered together before pursing their lips and spitting a spray of betel through the floor lattice of the house.

Inya Tua was the only wife who remained calm and sincere, even though everyone knew how difficult it had to be for the old women to accept the bitter reality that her husband was taking yet another wife.

Ndalo's wives weren't the only ones who disapproved of his desire to take another wife. The children, both girls and boys, also looked grim. It seemed that no one approved of Ndalo's decision to marry again.

"Are you all right, Wula?" Koni whispered.

"Yes, Inya," Wula replied as her mother squeezed her hand tighter. Wula knew she was unwelcome in Ndalo's uma parona, but she learned an important thing: In a family, something that made one member happy could make another member miserable. The same things were not always accepted in the same ways. Wula knew Inya Tua was unhappy, but she tried to be understanding. Yet no matter what, no matter how strong the controversy was between likes and dislikes, happiness and suffering, no one could rid Ndalo's deepest desire to arrogantly continue acquiring more wives. Nor was there anyone who could dissuade Wula from upholding the promises that Waleka had made a long time ago on account of a dowry that he had already accepted.

"As for the wedding," the officiant from Waleka's side was saying, "this means that Tila Wula and Ndalo's official marriage will take place after the Pasola ceremony." Ndalo's side agreed. There was no need to wait too long, because the wedding would be followed by the construction of the new roof for Waleka's house.

"Yes," Waleka spoke up. "According to the fourteen-year agreement between Ndalo and me, my daughter, Tila Wula, will enter into all the proper ceremonies leading up to a traditional marriage. Our agreement was that Tila Wula would be the seventh wife, but under current circumstances my daughter will be the ninth wife. Regarding the issue of being the seventh or ninth wife, I will make an agreement with Ndalo on how ..." Waleka broke off for a moment. His eyes pounced on Ndalo, and he continued firmly, "The words 'after the Pasola' must be seriously considered. Before the Pasola, Tila Wula will not be Ndalo's wife. She will stay in Ndalo's Big House, but she will be accompanied by Inya Tua at all times!" Waleka shifted his gaze to Inya Tua to make sure she heard. He continued in a hoarse voice, "I trust that Inya Tua will take good care of my daughter until the time comes for Tila Wula to become a wife in in the true sense of the word."

After Wakela's words, the officiant continued with other routine matters. What was said was met with approval from Waleka's side, and hmms and whispers from Ndalo's side.

Koni leaned on Tila Wula's shoulder. "Wula ..." Unable to express her feelings about delivering her only child into the arms of a man who was older than Waleka, Wula's father, she could only whisper, "I am sorry."

"There's nothing wrong, Inya!" Wula insisted. "Everything is fine!"

"Bapa ..." Koni faltered.

"There's nothing wrong with Bapa either," Wula replied. She turned her head for a moment to look at her father, but her gaze met Koda's instead. He smiled and nodded.

With the permission of Waleka and the other elders, Koni excused herself. She made her way to the door, led by Inya Tua and several other women.

Tila Wula rose to escort her mother out, but Ndalo stopped her.

"Stay here with Ndalo," Koda said. He immediately joined the group to help Koni leave the meeting.

The procession of people accompanying Koni's departure from Ndalo's house moved slowly. Some of the people gathered outside followed, others just watched from afar. Many minds and many mouths voiced various interpretations about the same thing: The bride-to-be was educated and beautiful; the couple's age difference was more than forty years; the belis had been paid almost fourteen years ago when this ninth wife was not even eight years old.

"Inya Koni, you knew this would happen." Inya Tua cast a stern look at Koni. "Why are you carrying on about it now? Why do you feel sick? You must accept the situation gracefully."

"Inya Koni is sick because she doesn't agree," one of Ndalo's wives said.

"So why did Tila Wula agree to be Ndalo's wife?" another woman added. "Tila Wula is the one who could refuse the marriage if she wanted to!"

"Tila Wula is better suited to marry Wolli," blurted out another wife, "not an old man who already has eight wives and dozens of children and grandchildren! She would also be better suited for you, Koda!" The other wives nodded.

The group arrived in front of Waleka's house.

Koni and Tua were both first wives, both old, and both traditionally educated. The two women used time to mend their hearts with patience and fortitude from the unspoken pain they endured, as their husbands collected wives. Now the two old women swallowed the bitterest pill that could either heal or break them as first wives.

"Let me take Inya Koni upstairs," Koda said calmly.

"So Tila Wula is sleeping at Ndalo's house?" Hamoli asked.

"Tila Wula knows what she has to do." Koda's voice was even. "She knows how to honor her father's decision of fourteen years ago. A promise is a statement that must be fulfilled."

After Koda, Inya Tua, Hamoli, and everyone else left, Koni leaned against the corner of the house where old people rested. Her days were now filled with sad stories about her children and grandchildren. She felt exhausted, far more exhausted than she had ever felt before — even more than after the long journey she had traveled after Waleka abandoned her in the desolated field.

Chapter 26

The next morning, Ida arrived early to meet Wula at Ndalo's house. Together, they went to the cliff to sit and talk. "After the Pasola, I will have to call you Nenek, even though you are my friend," Ida said carefully. "You mustn't enter my grandfather's room, even if he tries to force you. Just don't! Hold out until you are officially married." Ida looked down. "I'm sorry ... Gha Wolli would have protected you if he were around!"

"Don't worry, I'll be fine." Wula smiled. "I'm fine!" she reassured her doubtful friend.

It was true that morning, noon, and night, Ndalo was always at home. But Inya Tua, the first wife and matron of the household, kept a close eye on her wherever she went. Ndalo was furious at his wife for not delivering his bride-to-be into the folds of his blanket.

"You are useless, Inya Tua!" he berated her for all to hear.

"Don't listen to him, Inya!" Tila Wula remembered covering Inya Tua's ears.

"Tila Wula, only you have the power to keep him away," Inya Tua had told her slowly. "Don't give up! I'll help!" The woman was too tired to go through receiving yet another wife into the household. "You must win — and you can, if you follow your parents' advice."

Inya Tua's voice had broken into the silence in Wula's soul — an eerie stillness filled with nocturnal sounds, where owls screech, dogs bay, horses whinny, and the waves lap sadly in the moonless night.

The two of them then heard a woman's light footsteps crossing the bamboo floor and vanish quickly into the silence of the night. It meant that a woman had joined Ndalo in his bed of bamboo stalks.

"You will still become a teacher," Ida's voice brought Wula back to the present.

"Yes, certainly," Wula assured her. "At the right time." Certainty! That's what Wula wanted and planned for. She completely understood her parents' message. She was grateful to Ida and Koda for having such high hopes for certainty. She resolutely rejected Ndalo's persistent advances. She would do whatever it took to prevent what typically happened to a woman after being delivered to the man who had paid for her dowry.

Now, sitting on the cliff with Ida, Tila Wula listened to the familiar sighs of the sea breeze blowing ashore. She shivered and felt grateful that she would never be in the same place as the javelin throwers on the Pasola field. The man who took pride in being a to-paholong and leader at the Nyale, truly believed that he could seize all he wanted, whatever he wanted, at any time.

"Never!" Wula vowed. She was wise enough to know that reality could not be rejected unilaterally. That's why she had to walk each path that had been set for her. Never had anyone asked her if *she* had agreed to being sold for the dowry her father had received. She shuddered. Here she was, already in the house of the man who was to be her husband! The thought that, in due course, she would join Ndalo in his bed of bamboo stalks made her shake violently.

The next morning, Wula left Ndalo's house and headed for the field under the banyan tree. When she and Wolli had lived with Koni, he went to see Lamura there, every morning. Wula walked up the path, keenly aware of eyes staring at her from behind the walls and lattices of houses that were deliberately designed for peeping. She kept her stride as steady as the steps of a student passing the lecture hall terrace, completely focused on passing the course.

Lamura whinnied at her arrival. Tila Wula offered him the salt on her palm. Lamura's ears perked up at the sight of the salt, and he licked Wula's hand clean. Although she had never figured out which way a horse's eyes were actually looking, Wula always felt Lamura was looking at her. "Gha Mada Wolli," she whispered, "where are you?"

"Come on, let's go!" Hamoli surprised Wula by suddenly appearing beside her.

"Did you sleep in Waleka's Big House with Koni?" Wula asked.

"Yes!" Hamoli replied. "Let's go to the spring."

"Are Bapa and Inya home?" Wula asked. She smiled, remembering Wolli lecturing her: *Honor your parents. Whoever they are! No matter what they do. Whether it is good or bad for us, only we can put them in a place of honor. No one else.*

"Why? What's wrong?"

"Are Bapa and Inya home?" Wula repeated.

"They are still sleeping!"

It was a cold morning, and the wind was blowing toward the sea. Wula, Hamoli, and a few other women left the village and headed for the spring. Ndalo always forbade her to fetch water, but Wula always politely replied that because she was young, she should be the one to fetch water, not Inya Tua.

"Raga went to Weetebula." Hamoli said. "You know that, right? Lara will come home for the Pasola. How many Pasolas has it been since she left?"

"Let's see, this will be the fifth Pasola," Wula replied. "Lara left before the 1974 Pasola, and now it's 1979!"

"I'm nervous about her coming back," Hamoli confided. "What if Lara gets angry and leaves again?"

"I wouldn't worry about it, Inya," Wula soothed. "That all happened five Pasolas ago! So much has changed since then. I'm sure Lara has changed too."

The two of them walked side by side among the other water fetchers, each carrying three bamboo containers across their shoulders. Everyone they saw along the way paid closer attention to them than usual. Looks of admiration, regret, envy, disappointment, anger, and the whole gamut of complicated feelings were aimed at Wula. As usual, Wula remained silent or smiled.

"Does Mada Wolli know about you and Ndalo?" one of the women asked her.

"Yes," Wula replied calmly.

"Is he angry?"

"Not at all."

The woman was confused by Wula's calm demeanor. "Mada Wolli is educated and so are you. Will he be at the wedding ceremony?"

"Yes!" Wula smiled.

That day, as Wula walked with Hamoli to the spring, there were not too many probing questions. For the most part, the women only asked how she was doing and how her parents were.

At the spring, Wula slid easily into her childhood memories with Wolli, Lara, and Lamura. Time had passed so fast, and those childhood days would never return. The self was the only one with the power to manage distance — how to bring what was distant closer or push what was near farther away — in the heart that remained or changed the way it felt.

CHAPTER 27

A gentle sea breeze cooled the heat of the midday sun, making the tall grasses in the vast expanse of field dance. Wula carried bamboo containers, filled with water, on her back and in each hand. She paused to set the containers down and wipe the sweat off her face. Taking a deep breath, she resumed the steady rhythm of her steps as she made her journey home. This was her third trip to the spring since ten o'clock that morning. She should have started at six, so that by ten o'clock, she would have been done. The water containers she had already brought from the spring to the house had not yet filled the main holding vessel for water. She had to go back again with the other women to fetch more clean water. Most of the others had started early that morning. Wula's late start was the cause of her uncomfortable journey after the sun had become hotter.

"Why are you the one who always gets the water?" Inya Tua asked her.

"Because we need water, Inya." Wula smiled.

Inya Tua believed that Tila Wula's smile was sincere. Wula had never once complained in front of her. "That's enough water." Inya Tua glanced at Wula before returning to the weaving she had started earlier that morning when the other women left the village for the spring.

189

"What are you making, Inya?" Wula asked.

"Just finishing the last part of this cloth," Inya Tua explained. "I've only got a few inches left to do. It is for my husband's family. They are definitely coming to the Pasola."

"It's beautiful, Inya," Wula said.

"The time will come when I'll weave the best cloth for you," Inya Tua said sincerely. "The color, the motif, the thread — everything will be the best!"

"Thank you, Inya!"

"Are you still planning to get more water?" Inya Tua lifted her face and looked at Wula.

It was important for the home's water vessel to be full. In a few days, families and guests would begin arriving at the village to celebrate the Pasola. *And prepare for the wedding ceremony,* Wula thought.

Drawing enough water from the spring was a common occurrence she faced every year. Although January and February were the rainy season, it did not rain very often, so the villagers lacked clean rainwater for kitchen use — especially when many families and guests came to take part in the Bau Nyale and Pasola ceremonies.

"That's enough, get some rest," Inya Tua said, as she continued to weave with a steady rhythm. *Shush-click, shush-click, shush-click.*

Wula said, "I better go back one more time." Walking back to the spring, Tila Wula thought of Inya Tua's concern for her, and felt a sense of regret that the old woman, who was even older than Koni, seemingly could not express her true feelings. It was difficult to explain, just as it was difficult to measure the distance between smiles and tears for some things that seemed equal on the surface, but were not equal in meaning for each person. From the look in Inya Tua's eyes that never really looked at her directly, Wula knew that Inya Tua was struggling to decide between expressing her true feelings or not. Wula dealt with it calmly and took her time to make a judgment.

Don't be in a hurry, take your time, and let the wind and the sun help carry your blessings. Wula heard her grandmother's voice, giving advice to her as a child. It was the secret that belonged to the women who fetched water. *Water is a blessing, carried home to sustain all life inside the home. One should never tire of carrying water.* Koni didn't; Wolli didn't; and neither did Wula. Maybe, one day, water would be piped to the village, and women would not have to travel so far to bring the blessing home.

That time will come. Tila Wula heard her grandmother's voice again. A voice she had not heard since Nenek died, six years ago, shortly after Galuh became Inya Pitu.

One of the largest bamboo containers was perched on Tila Wula's back. She carried a basket of water in each of her small hands. Sunlight greeted her more boldly as Wula left the spring and stepped onto the path toward home.

The wind carried the sound of distant hoofbeats to Wula's ears as she walked back from the spring. Many paths wound among the villages. In the fields, where the wild grass grew tall, Wula could not see anything; she could only hear sounds. Where the grass grew shorter, she could see just the heads of a rider and horse poking out above the vegetation, moving slow or fast in accordance to the cadence of the horse's hooves. Whether far or near, sounds always thrilled her. They signaled that she was not alone in returning home across the vast fields that often sang a silent song. Sounds came and went, loud and soft, depending on the direction and purpose of the journey.

Today, the horsemen sounded like they were heading for Ratenggaro or one of its surrounding villages.

"If only Gha Wolli was coming home," Wula said to herself. As she walked toward Ndalo's house, she thought about how different her journey was now, compared to the journey she traveled on this same road when she rode on Lamura's back, leaning against Wolli's chest, flanked by his strong arms.

Remember! Her father's voice rang clear in her mind. *It's meant to be. It's been arranged by the ancestors. Whether you are first, second, or whatever number wife, it is your destiny. Accept it so the ancestral honor can function as a light for our home. Understand?* She could hardly distinguish her father's voice from that of her half-brothers. Wula remembered how she dared to raise her head very slowly, as if she knew where Mada Wolli sat among the other men. Their eyes met for only an instant, but she understood the sign of fortitude Wolli was sending her, a reminder that respect demanded a loyalty and fulfillment from her as the daughter of an important elder.

Suddenly, Wula was very tired. She stopped walking and allowed the tears to come.

"You know, Wula, we're both just children of parents we must honor," Wolli had told her. "I must leave Ratenggaro for the best of all of us." And so Wolli had left, riding Lamura, not turning to look back even once, despite how loudly Koni called after him.

Now, Wula tried to free herself from fear. Her faith in Mada Wolli gave her strength. He had set a brotherly example of how to keep secrets, yet honor the promise of a future that had to be faced. Bitter and sweet were now part of their life. There was no other way. Mada Wolli had indeed proven to be a brother-like mentor, gallant in the way he left impressions and conveyed messages.

Again, Wula wiped the sweat from her forehead and neck. She straightened her shoulders and back and adjusted the water containers she carried. She was alone under the wide blue sky. The sun had grown brighter.

Once again, the wind carried the sound of hoofbeats from afar. As the rhythmic beats pounded closer and closer, she heard neighing and barely had time to realize that the horse and rider were heading toward her when, suddenly, they were behind her. She tensed, trying to remain calm.

Oh, please, don't let it be Ndalo, she thought fervently. *I'll refuse him with all my might. I will beat him with this bamboo container! If he dares to try again, I will fight him! I will fight!*

"Oh, the Almighty the Big-eyed and Wide-eared One, please ..." Wula murmured, then stopped when the horse stopped. She bent to place the water baskets she carried on the ground and slowly lowered the bamboo container from her back. She mustered her courage and turned around.

Stunned with relief, Wula saw that the tall man riding the well-groomed horse was not Ndalo; it was Koda, sitting high in the saddle. He wore an eye-catching henggul. The hanggi around his waist was made of the finest threads, woven by a craftswoman who had spun the yarn and made the coloring dye with her own hands. A bundle of javelins, blunted for the Pasola, hung from each side of the saddle. Behind him sat Ida, his younger sister, who could not hide her sadness.

"Gha Koda! Ida! Where are you coming from? What's going on?"

"I have a message for you from Wolli," Koda said slowly, "and it is this: Don't give up. Do what you need to do."

"Yes, Paghogha!" Wula still could not believe it was Koda. He had come to the village as if guided by the wind that always kept her grounded in her surroundings.

"You can run away from Ambu Ndalo," Ida said confidently.

"Don't say that again," Koda said, silencing Ida. "We promised we wouldn't say anything more about our grandfather."

Koda motioned for Wula to move the water containers she carried onto the horse.

He then held out his hand, and Wula took it without hesitation, placing her foot on top of Koda's in the stirrup and swinging up between him and Ida.

Koda and the two young women left, taking the path that did not lead directly to the village. Instead, they crossed the field. The tall grass waved in the wind, and the corn fields stretched between the open fields. The flat landscape made it possible to take in the entire area. For a while, the three rode away from the towering roofs between the tree tops and the waving coconut trees around the village where Koda would take Wula and her filled water containers.

Wula felt a sudden alarm. Here she was, sitting behind Koda and in front of Ida — Ndalo's grandchildren. Her longing for Wolli had brought her to this place, so close behind Koda's back, riding a horse that could tear off through the silence of the field. Wula's forehead bounced against Koda's back, and each time, her heart pounded.

"Have you seen Ndalo yet?" Wula broke the silence.

"Yes, we saw Ambu Ndalo." Koda laughed lightly. "Soon, Ida and I will have to call you 'nenek' — the beautiful Nenek Wula!" The three of them laughed out loud.

"So you have already seen your grandfather?" Wula brought herself back to reality.

"We saw each other at the Big House." said Ida. "Inya Tua told us you were fetching water from the spring. That's how we knew where to catch up with you. Our grandmother said you had made several trips to fetch water. She also said to take care of you because, 'as grandchildren, you should be with Nenek Wula.'"

"We just wanted to convey Wolli's messages to you," Koda said calmly. "He had five of them: One, take care of Bapa Waleka's name; two, take care of Inya Koni's name; three, take care of the Big House's name; four, take care of your own name. Those were Wolli's five messages to you."

"Those are only four messages," said Wula. "What's the fifth one, Gha Koda?"

"Number five, take care of your grandchildren, Koda and Ida!" The three of them shrieked with laughter.

"Wolli wants you to sit at the left end of the Pasola stand," Koda said quietly, "so he can see you!"

Wula smiled proudly at the messages Wolli's best friend delivered. Her smile turned into a grin when she thought about Koda also being Ndalo's grandson — Ndalo, the old man she would soon be living with as husband and wife.

For three consecutive years, Koda, who always came home at every Nyale and Pasola season, had been the undefeated winner on the Pasola field. Each year, Koda always delivered a message for Wula to sit at the left end of the stand. Wula was never certain whether the message came from Wolli or Koda himself.

They were just rounding the last bend on the road into the village when the horse suddenly shied and whinnied loudly.

"Oh!" Wula cried out as she grabbed Koda's waist to keep from falling. Ida hugged Wula's waist tightly. Koda pulled out a javelin. "Don't be afraid. I'm looking after you!"

In front of them, across the road, lay a manmade barrier of stacked logs stuffed with sharp, thorny thistles. Someone had deliberately blocked the passage of horses.

Ama Dula reined in from the side. "Wula is your grandmother!" he barked. "Don't ever try to bother her!" He pulled Wula onto his saddle, and his horse sped off toward the village like a demon in flight.

"Gha Koda! Ida!" Wula screamed. "Gha Koda! Ida! Ida!" Wula kept screaming until her voice dissolved into the silence of the path.

Koda jumped off his horse, helped Ida down, and collected the water containers that had fallen and spilled on the road. Other villagers, passing on horseback, dismounted and helped remove the roadblock.

"Turn around and leave quickly before your grandfather finds out and gets angry," said one of the horsemen. "How could you dare bring Tila Wula! You've been warned several times, but you're stubborn!"

The galloping of approaching horses came closer. "Go away now!" urged the man. "They must be coming to confront you! They won't care even if you both are Ndalo's grandchildren. Go quickly!"

"Nenek knows I went to pick up Wula," Koda replied clearly.

The man shook his head. "Not everyone will understand that! Now, go! Go! It's much better to meet them at the Pasola field than to meet them here."

Koda jumped onto his horse, grabbed Ida's hand, and pulled her up behind him. Spurring his horse to a fast sprint, they quickly disappeared among the grasses. When their pursuers arrived at the spot, Koda and Ida were already far away. Only their heads were visible, racing quickly among the reeds that waved in the wind.

Dusk turned to night, and the air turned cold. A pale moon hung in the corner of a gloomy sky. Wula angrily forced her way to dismount in front of Ratenggaro's gate. "Don't you ever disrespect me." Wula eyed Ama Dula.

"I am only carrying out Ndalo's orders," he replied indifferently.

"And don't you ever touch Gha Wolli, Gha Koda, or Ida," Wula snapped. "You'd better be careful!"

Ama Dula was surprised. When he saw Inya Tua glaring at him from the porch of the house, Ama Dula immediately turned his horse around and quickly left the village.

CHAPTER *28*

In a flat place not far from the elementary and junior high schools where he and his younger siblings used to study, Mada Wolli stopped and dismounted from Lamura's back. He let Lamura graze while he sat down to rest for a moment. He wanted to return home to be with Waleka and Koni, his father and mother, but it was so hard to do. He only went to Ratenggaro on the days of Bau Nyale and Pasola. And even then, he went only for a short time, to see Koni and Waleka.

The wind picked up, and Wolli closed his eyes. He lingered in his memories of all those years, long ago, when together with Koda he picked up Wula, Galuh, Lara, and Ida after school.

Seeing and *feeling* were two words imprinted in Wolli's mind and heart. Two words that, in their own time, place, and circumstance, could spread like a deadly disease. The outcome was very much determined by how one dealt with these two emotions.

Mada Wolli rose when he heard a horse approach. The man on horseback was still in the shadows, but Wolli knew immediately who it was. "Kak Raga!" Wolli ran to greet Inya Duyo's son and helped him tether his horse to a lamtoro tree near Lamura. "Where are you going?"

"Let's go home," Raga replied. "We're almost there, and Inya is waiting. Every time you and I see each other at Lamboya, you always say, 'I'll be home later.' Now there is no 'later.' There's only now. Let's go."

"Where are you coming from?" Wolli asked.

"I said Inya is waiting at the Big House," Raga said with such firmness, it seemed pushy. "Bapa is waiting there too. They're not well. We must go back to Ratenggaro." Raga moved to untie his horse. "Surely you must want to go home yourself. Let's go!"

The two of them trotted slowly toward their village, side by side. Along the way, Raga talked and Wolli listened, answering when asked a question.

"We all know Lamboya is your native village," Raga said. "Everyone also knows Bapa Leka and Inya Koni adopted you when you were only one day old. Yet your home is not in Lamboya, but here — in Ratenggaro."

Raga restlessly wiped his dry forehead. He turned to look at Wolli before saying, "Only Ratenggaro and the folks in the house there have taken care of you since you were born. It was Inya Duyo who breastfed you, because at that time, she had a three-day-old newborn. You were accepted into the family." Raga rubbed his chest hard several times. "You were taken care of by Inya Koni and Inya Duyo. Now Inya Koni is alone in the temporary Big House with Bapa Waleka. So, you must go home."

Raga fell silent, and for a while, the only sounds belonged to the horses' slow trot. "You've been away for a long time, and you only came home for a day or two for Nyale and Pasola. You didn't come home to specifically see Bapa and Inya. Why? It's been a few weeks now that you've been back in Lamboya. How could you not go to Ratenggaro? Ratenggaro is your home!"

Raga kept talking and Wolli remained quiet. He missed his parents, siblings, family, and Ratenggaro. But he had chosen not to go home, as his staying away seemed best for his parents and younger siblings — especially for Wula, the younger sister he loved.

"Do you understand?" Raga asked. "Surely, you understand."

"Yes, Wolli replied. "Ndalo —"

"Ndalo?" Raga interrupted and took a deep breath. "Oh, he won't dare to disturb your presence in our village again."

"But his people," Wolli said frankly, "have always been like shadows — and they still are."

Raga spoke calmly. "Tila Wula is your younger sibling, your sister. Ida is also your younger sibling, your sister. Koda is your best friend. There is nothing wrong with a big brother protecting his younger siblings. There is nothing wrong with two friends always meeting each other. Go home and take care of them. You've graduated from college. You're a teacher now. Don't leave again. Go home."

"Yes, I will," Wolli replied.

"Come on!" Raga loosened the reins and slapped his horse's flanks. The horse surged to a gallop, and Wolli followed suit. The two of them continued their journey, escorted by a faint moonlight that grew and brightened the open fields before them, acting as a guiding beacon, aided by the faithful reflection from the sea of grass.

Nature always seemed to work in tandem to give as much as possible to each of God's creatures. Raga and Wolli stopped at the highest part of the field. It was the same place where Wolli, Koda, and their younger siblings had taken a short break on their way home from school; the same place where both Wolli and Lamura were hurt for the first time. Raga dismounted and Wolli did the same.

The two of them sat side by side, gazing at the silvery black sea in the distance. A few flickering lights swayed on the surface — boats, fishermen looking for fish.

The people of Ratenggaro were not fishermen. Almost all were farmers or raised livestock. A few worked in nearby towns, or migrated to work on land belonging to others. With the exception of gathering nyale on the coast every season, not a single villager made a living fishing. Generally, fishermen came from coastal villages, fishing their way to the waters of Ratenggaro.

"The years are flying by," Raga said wistfully. "Wula, Lara, and Ida graduated from teacheing school last year. Ida now teaches at the elementary school where you all went. Lara will return to Ratenggaro soon. She now teaches on another island."

"Is it true that Wula has moved into Ndalo's house?" Wolli asked, though he already knew the answer.

"Yes, Wula is already in Ndalo's house." Raga took a deep breath and let it out slowly. "Wula ... poor girl."

"Wula must fulfill Bapa Waleka's promise," Wolli said.

"Yes, yes, because he's a traditional elder, a kabani," Raga said dismissively. "His promise is the promise of an elder, and Wula doesn't want Bapa Waleka to be accused of being a dishonest kabani. Bapa Waleka received the belis almost fourteen years ago, back when you were in junior high school and the girls were only in elementary school. It's been a long time."

Raga sighed before continuing. "Ndalo called in their agreement, and Bapa Leka has to deliver the goods to preserve his dignity as an elder along with the good name of his wife, children, and extended family — and also his ancestral house, of course."

"Yes."

"Inya Koni is making herself very sick about Wula being taken to Ndalo. I'm worried about her. Do you remember how Inya Duyo cried until she couldn't catch her breath because she wondered why I hadn't brought Lara home? Inya was so worried, and she wanted Lara to come home. She got sicker and sicker and, in the end, she died." Raga fell silent.

Wolli was also silent. The song of the cicadas sounded frail, as if only one or two could muster a song, too weak to carry into all corners of the vast field. The night wind blew listlessly. On this hilltop, it was hard to tell a sea wind from a land breeze. Just as it was hard for Wolli to distinguish between the mother who gave birth to him and the mother who raised him, because both were present in his mind without needing explanation.

Raga broke the silence. "That's why you must return to the house in Ratenggaro." Sensing Wolli's concerns, Raga continued, "Your family in Lamboya will understand and give permission — hasn't their permission been there since Inya Koni took you as a newborn to raise you in Ratenggaro? And don't worry about Ndalo and whoever he sends."

"Poor Wula is forced to follow a path that Bapa Leka carved for her," Wolli said, as the pain of agreeing to a path and choice that he did not agree with churned in his chest.

"That's why you should stay in Ratenggaro," Raga's voice broke. "For the time being, don't go far. Don't return to Lamboya. Your family in Lamboya is already aware of what is happening. You must take care of Inya and Bapa in the temporary Big House."

"Don't cry," Wolli said, draping a comforting arm around Raga's shoulder.

"I'm not crying!" Raga quickly wiped his face.

Wolli kept his arm around Raga's shoulder. Indeed, the eldest brother in this large family cried very easily. "Let me tell you what Inya Duyo once told Inya Koni," Wolli said. "She said, 'Raga's tears are very close to the surface, so they spill easily.'"

"Really?"

"Yes. Then Wula said to Inya Koni, 'Mama, please don't cry anymore. You will run out of tears and you won't be able to sleep.'" Wolli chuckled, reminiscing about happier times.

Raga rose. "Let's go home."

Wolli also rose, but did not move. Clouds crowded the moon.

"Come on," Raga urged.

"Where is Lara?" Wolli had wanted to ask this question for a long time, but he had waited until he could ask Lara's father directly.

"You'll find out in due time, but know that your niece is doing very well."

"Is Lara coming home for the Pasola this year?"

"Yes. She'll stay in Ratenggaro for Wula's wedding ceremony, then she will leave again."

Raga jumped onto his horse and Wolli mounted Lamura. The two rode quickly down the hill. They were soon accompanied by the distant sound of galloping horses. Raga and Wolli knew that this group of horses would neither join them nor pass them. Instead, they purposefully followed from a distance.

CHAPTER 29

Wolli's return to the temporary Big House in Ratenggaro spawned arguments that were intended to be kept secret. But gossip crept from house to house, out the village gate, onto the highway, and far beyond. Wherever the story of Ndalo and Wula landed and spread, people embellished it to their own liking. Everyone in the village wanted to get the news first, because they wanted to be the first to start spreading it.

"Wula has already been taken to Ndalo's house," Koni said, as soon as Wolli and Raga arrived at the ancestral house. "Wula is not here; she has left." Wolli knew his inya's chest was tight as she relayed the news to him.

"Wula hasn't left, Inya," Wolli reassured his mother. "Wula is here, near you. Every day, she can come here to visit her Bapa and Inya. And whenever you have time, Inya can go to see Wula. Wula has not left."

The news of Wula moving into Ndalo's house had spread faster than wind traveling in the open fields. "I already knew about it, Inya," Wolli continued. "Don't be sad. It's normal. It'll be fine. It's the path that Bapa has carved for Wula."

Waleka stood uncertainly next to Koni. "Wolli ..."

"Yes, Bapa."

"Wolli ..." Waleka's voice faltered again. "You've grown taller. You're as handsome as your father, Wuri Wona. Wula must be happy to have you home."

Wolli had mixed feelings about being back in Ratenggaro. During his college years, he had been beaten by Ama Dula for the second time. His uncle had taken him away to Lamboya for treatment. After he healed, he had returned to college and only went home once a year during the Nyale and Pasola season. It was only during this time that Wolli began to understand that his returning to Ratenggaro was not good for his family or for himself.

Everyone involved in the Pasola — participants and spectators alike — knew that Ndalo was a cheater. His cheating was carried out by Ama Dula and his retinue. They were the ones responsible for the violence that befell the innocent, even though they never admitted it.

Wolli understood what his Lamboya family had told him. There was no point in prolonging the problem. There was nothing to gain by trying to deal with Ndalo, because Ndalo would always win. He was a wealthy, influential elder, not only in his home village, but also in the eight villages where his wives came from. Ndalo would defend his position to get a ninth wife from his own village at all costs — a ninth wife that his other wives were expected to support. The small community would bow deeply and back Ndalo in whatever he wanted. They would defend the man who stood mighty and triumphant on the Pasola stand, even though that same man did not honor the historical, prestigious meaning attached to his great name, *Ndalo*, that his ancestors had given him as an elder.

There was one bright light in the ancestral house. Raga had brought a kerosene lamp from his house so that Wolli had enough light to read at night.

Early the next morning, a large group of Waleka's extended family headed toward the temporary Big House after hearing the news that Wolli had returned home.

Hamoli went straight to Ndalo's house to deliver the news that Wolli was home and pick up Tila Wula.

Without stopping to ask questions, Tila Wula hurried out of the house. She saw Ndalo's thunderous look, but continued on decisively. "Wolli came home, Bapa!" she called back to Ndalo.

The old man spat.

Outside the house, Wula took off running. Ndalo ordered Inya Tua to follow her. He changed into a clean garment, smoothed the clump of tobacco under his lower lip, and descended the stairs of his stilt house to follow Wula.

From afar, he could clearly see Ida and Wula embracing Wolli. All three of them — and the others around them — were crying and laughing. Tears of emotion and joy mingled.

"Please don't leave again, Gha Wolli!" Wula exclaimed, trying to sound strong. "You must stay here. Bapa and Inya are by themselves."

"Wula can come here every day," Ndalo said loudly as he approached, trying his best to hide his hatred and jealousy for Mada Wolli. "You don't have to worry, Wula." He smiled to keep the tobacco wad from falling out from under his upper lip and to buy a few seconds to secure it with the tip of his tongue.

"May I really come here every day?" Wula asked.

"Sure! Who said you can't?" Ndalo was the picture of understanding and generosity. "Wolli has finished college. He now needs to think about his future. It's good if he's going to work. Wula will take care of Wolli's parents here. There's a lot of family who can help, and I can also take care of them. After all, aren't the parents of my bride my parents, too?" Ndalo laughed.

"Of course, Bapa." Raga bowed his head and held the respectful stance as long as possible to smooth Ndalo's ruffled feathers.

Wolli shook hands with the visitors, one by one, and thanked them. Ndalo was no exception. "Thank you, sir," Wolli held the old man's hand with a confusing mixture of reverence and contempt.

"You're very handsome, son," Ndalo forced a cheerful tone. "You're home at last. Wula must be very happy that you're home!"

"Don't leave again," Wula repeated. "You have to take care of Bapa and Inya."

"Yes, yes, he will definitely take care of our parents," Ndalo continued with a chuckle. He noticed people paying attention to him, and he basked in his importance.

"For sure, Bapa Ndalo?" Wula asked again.

Ndalo's affirmative response was greeted with a round of applause from all the other family members. "Yes, Inya Tua will also be here," he continued expansively. "She can be here every day to help and be together."

Ndalo chuckled, covering his annoyance with his best smile. He spit out his chewing wad and said, "So, Nyale and Pasola are coming soon." Turning to Wolli, he asked, "You're still the to-paholong from Lamboya?"

Betel nut was passed around. Ndalo was given a container especially prepared for him. He took two betel nuts and chewed them. A few moments later, he picked up a whole areca nut and, with his knife, cut pieces for himself, Waleka, Raga, and some of the other elders, as a way to show brotherhood.

"Pasola is just around the corner," Ndalo repeated, stealing a glance at Wula, who was chatting with Wolli, Koni, Hamoli, Ida, and other relatives.

"Surely the Pasola participants and audience will be better than those in previous years," Raga said.

The men entered into a deeper conversation. Ndalo arrogantly barged into the discussion. "Wolli's homecoming should be celebrated at the Pasola!" he crowed. "I will face the young man in a friendly match, and we'll make the Pasola field a place of peace for all parties. All past misunderstandings will be resolved!"

"Oh, that's wonderful, Bapa Ndalo!" Raga clasped his hands together on his chest and bowed towards Ndalo.

Flattered, Ndalo preened. "Wolli and his Lamboya family may appear on the field. Wolli is Wula's elder brother." Ndalo emphasized the words *elder brother*. "We are all family. I will show you myself what role Pasola plays in maintaining our strong family relationships. That way — thus, yes, thus ..." Ndalo faltered.

"What are you trying to say, Bapa?" asked the elder sitting closest to Ndalo.

"The Pasola will be successful," Ndalo continued, relieved at finding his words again. "My wedding ceremony with Wula must also be grand. Me as king, and Wula as queen. Yes, the king and queen will get married soon and be supported by all family members."

Suddenly, everyone was chiming in.

"Inya Tua will remain the queen," Koni said.

"Yes, Inya Tua will remain the queen!" Wula said in a bold, clear voice. "I will be the ninth wife — not the seventh, let alone the first. Although I am the only child of Inya Koni, Bapa Waleka's first wife, I still will not dethrone Bapa Ndalo's first wife."

Wula's words were met with a buzzing among the gathering, which, after a few moments, solidified into a variety of responses.

Raga spoke first. "Yes! Therefore, respect Inya Tua. She is the first wife. Tila Wula, my younger sister, will be the ninth. The ninth."

"Not the first," Wula added.

"Yes, yes, yes," Ndalo laughed and nodded in a show of indulgent patience. He was not in the habit of correcting himself. As an elder, he ruled more in thought than in deed. He looked down just long enough to smooth the tobacco wad with the tip of his tongue.

Ama Dula felt the need to speak. He said loudly, "For Bapa Ndalo, all his wives are first. When the ninth is the first, it means the most recent. He is a kabani, our father."

"Yes, yes, that's why it's called the first," Ndalo resumed, thankful for Ama Dula's rescue. He stole a glance at Wula. "That's right, that's right — everyone is first. The ninth is also the first."

Ndalo tried to make light of the situation so that everyone present at Waleka's house that afternoon would be affected by his words and those of his followers. Wolli and Raga — unlike Waleka — accepted Ndalo's words as a way of underscoring the influence of a wealthy elder who was influential throughout the world in his power.

"Yes, yes, yes," Ndalo repeated. He wanted to say that Tila Wula was the most special among all his other wives. Although his eldest son, Zoga, was almost three times the age of his ninth future wife, Ndalo would still regard Wula as the most important. "Wula will come with me wherever I go. She will be present, morning, noon, and night. She will be there whenever and wherever I want her. No matter what I want, she will always be there!"

"I am not the first wife!" Tila Wula repeated emphatically. "Mama Inya Tua is the first wife, not me. No one can take her place. She is Mama Inya Tua. She's my mama. She's our mama. You can't upset Mama Inya Tua like that. That's enough! Don't ever say that again!"

Tila Wula's outburst brought silence, broken only when the food was served.

Wolli's unexpected return to the ancestral house was celebrated in a big way. All the villagers who occupied the traditional houses were there, along with rato and other elders. The first day of Wolli's presence in Ratenggaro provided a welcoming atmosphere — like welcoming a Pasola — when family came together in each other's traditional ancestral houses, and matters could be discussed openly and honestly.

But basically, the villagers all wanted to know who Mada Wolli was now. Had he indeed finished college? Was he returning to Ratenggaro to live in Waleka's house? Most of all, was Wolli really going to allow Wula to become Ndalo's ninth wife? And, would Tila Wula stick to her decision?

Waleka, Koni, Raga and the rest of the extended family accepted Wolli's return with trepidation.

Shortly after Inya Tua went home with Tila Wula, the gathering at Waleka's house dispersed. Some of Ndalo's wives, children, and grandchildren went to Ndalo's ancestral house, while others walked or rode directly out of the village gate and onto the road through the cemetery to continue their journey home.

Wolli walked by Ndalo's side until the old man arrived in front of his own house, occasionally stopping along the way to listen to people's questions and answer them, as if he had no worries at all.

That, alone, convinced everyone that Ndalo's marriage to Tila Wula would take place as planned.

Chapter 30

Koni re-arranged several small wooden boxes stacked in the corner of her room. The last time she had moved the boxes, Kakek and Nenek were still alive. She took out one of them and opened the small chest. Her hands trembled as she removed the piece of cloth, as if the cloth were a thin, fragile glass cup with a very expensive gold rim.

"Inya ..." Wolli approached her.

There were no words Koni could utter when Wolli stood in front of her. All she had were hugs and tears. Wolli had not been home for a long time. Koni had traveled to Lamboya several times to see him, but they were never there at the same time. Now, however, Wolli was home.

Koni looked at him and stroked his face, the high cheekbones. He stood tall, with his straight shoulders and broad chest. *Dashing, like his father.* Wolli had inherited all of Wuri Wona good looks, except for his eyes — those were Biri's, his mother.

Wolli rubbed his mother's shoulder. "Inya, it's late. Everyone has gone home. Go to sleep, please."

Koni looked down, stroking the cloth she had just taken out of the box next to Nenek's bed. "How are you doing?"

211

"I'm fine, Inya!" Wolli replied. "You can see for yourself that I'm healthy."

"Did you escort Ndalo to his house?"

"Yes, Inya. I did not escort him inside his house, but I did stay until Ndalo had entered."

"What about Wula?"

"Wula also went into Ndalo's house. She has to stay there. She will never be able to come live in this home again. We must be sure to maintain a good relationship with Ndalo. Everything has to go smoothly, Inya. That way, Wula and all of us can be comfortable, too."

Wolli patted his mother's shoulder. "This is the fate our ancestors passed down to us. Now, let's go to bed." While tucking Koni into her bed, Wolli whispered, "Please go to sleep, Inya. Bapa is already asleep. Please Inya, go to sleep."

The night was moving on. Alone, Wolli closed his eyes and leaned against a wall in the *katendeng*, a special place just for men in the Sumbanese traditional ancestral houses. The image of Wula came to him, and bitter memories filled his mind.

Ama Dula's old threat still rang clearly in his ears. "Go home to Lamboya if you don't want any harm to come to Wula. As long as you're in Lamboya, we'll keep her safe until she finishes school. But if you stay in Ratenggaro and hang around Wula, we will destroy her. Choose!"

The threat was followed by personal assaults. "After all, you were not born in Ratenggaro. Aren't you ashamed to live in other people's *uma parona*? Go back to your own village! We don't want to see you hanging around here anymore. We're watching you! If you mess with Tila Wula, you will die!"

Wolli's heart raced, thinking about Wula sleeping under the same roof as Ndalo. "Ndalo and Wula will be married soon,"

Wolli whispered. "Why does Wula have to go through this?" Then he relived the incident that had made it clear that he had to give up Wula for the sake of Bapa and Inya, and for Wula's own sake.

On the day the incident happened, he was returning to Ratenggaro after picking up Wula from Anakalang, where she had graduated from the vocational school for teachers. She had some time off before entering the university in Kupang. The sun was almost up when they left Anakalang on Lamura.

"You'll be busier after you go to university," Wolli said.

"Yes, I want to be a teacher like you, Gha Wolli!" Wula leaned forward against Wolli's back. "Inya and Bapa will be very happy. I can't wait!"

Suddenly, the pounding of hooves thundered toward them from every direction. Frightened, Wula hugged Wolli tightly around the waist. "Gha, who are they? Run!"

"Don't worry," Wolli said in a trembling voice. And then dark horses surrounded them and everything happened fast.

Wula was dragged off the horse and gagged. Wolli, too, was dragged off the horse, gagged, blindfolded, and hands bound behind him. Darkness surrounded him. Wolli screamed for Wula. He begged the captors not to hurt her.

Of all the men surrounding them, only Ama Dula had spoken. He firmly reminded Wolli that Ndalo had paid a belis for Wula and, according to custom, she was to become his wife. Before leaving, Ama Dula emphasized that it would be best for Wolli to leave Waleka's house, leave Ratenggaro. If he wanted Tila Wula to be safe, he should go back home to Lamboya, where he belonged.

Wolli was beaten and then, they were gone. For over an hour he lay crumpled on the ground, shaking in pain and fear over Wula's fate. Then, he heard the pounding of hooves again. *Was Wula being returned?*

Wula's lip was split, her face swollen. Her wrists and ankles were chaffed and bruised from the tight rope restraints. Sobbing, Wula begged Wolli to take her home to Ratenggaro.

Wolli would never forget Wula's pain and her helplessness to retaliate. He quickly untied the ropes around Lamura's mouth and legs. With a loud snort and an indignant shake of the head, the horse immediately scrambled to its feet. Swishing his tail and stamping his hooves, Lamura was telling them to hurry up.

"Please, we must keep this a secret between us," Wolli had said in a trembling voice. "We mustn't let Inya and Bapa know what happened." Wula sobbed harder, and Wolli hugged her tightly. They would both be silent. Neither he nor Wula would ever discuss the incident again.

Inya Koni had been terribly worried when they arrived home later that afternoon. But whatever questions Bapa Leka, Inya Koni, Raga, and other relatives posed, the answer was the same: He and Wula had fallen off Lamura's back when the horse got spooked and reared up.

Thus, the assault became an anxiety without resolution — the same type of anxiety that Inya Koni had displayed when he and Wula had come home injured, she showed tonight talking about Wula's stay at Ndalo's house.

"Inya, please don't cry," Wolli approached his parents' room, which had been Kakek and Nenek's room. He saw Koni sitting next to Waleka who had fallen asleep. She clutched a cloth to her chest.

"Wolli ..." Koni cried, stroking the cloth she had worn at her wedding to Waleka. The same cloth Raga's wife had worn. The same cloth she wanted to hand down to Tila Wula, the only daughter, a descendant of Waleka, an esteemed elder, and his first wife who was also the daughter of an elder from Lamboya.

Deep inside, Koni wanted Tila Wula and Mada Wolli to stay in Ratenggaro. Both of them could take care of the house. Both, with their family as the heirs, would maintain the dignity of the ancestral house.

When Wolli and Wula had come home wounded a few years ago, Koni felt that the most appropriate follow-through was that Waleka investigate why the two had arrived home hurt and bleeding. Unfortunately, Waleka remained silent and preoccupied.

Koni was grateful to the ancestors because Wolli had been raised as her own biological son. She begged the ancestors for forgiveness because Wolli had missed various ceremonies that ensured he indeed was Tila Wula's adopted sibling. However, she and her husband could not provide full protection. Although neither Wula nor Wolli ever told her the truth of what happened, her mother's heart sensed why Wolli had left Ratenggaro and returned to Lamboya, and why Waleka allowed it to happen.

Koni held the sarong to her chest and cried. Wolli and Wula — they were two biological children born from her heart.

"What's wrong, Inya?" Wolli asked softly. "Let me air the cloth. Are you crying for joy? Wolli is home, Mama. This is Wolli." Smiling, Wolli pointed at his own chest.

"You don't understand," Koni said, still crying. "If only Bapa Waleka had not accepted the dowry from Ndalo a long, long time ago ... oh, poor Tila Wula."

"But it did happen, Inya, and you mustn't cry. You've cried enough over this. Pay it no mind, Inya; everything will be fine. It's to be Tila Wula's fate."

"But she will be the ninth wife." Koni burst into tears again.

"Yes, Inya, we've known that for a long time. Actually, she was going to be the seventh wife. But because of the waiting for almost fourteen years, there were a seventh and an eighth wife who preceded her."

"Don't you feel sorry for Tila Wula?" Koni sobbed. Regret and a deep sadness filled her chest.

"Inya, we all do. We're all very sorry." Mada Wolli's voice was barely audible. "But Wula must do what Bapa Leka determined. Wula is now protecting Bapa's honor so that Bapa will not be humiliated for breaking promises."

Wolli's throat closed. After a moment of silence, he continued calmly. "Let it be, Inya, let Wula live with what Bapa Leka has determined. We all need to deal with this, for the sake of Bapa's good name and the good name of all our family."

"Wolli, you don't understand." Koni wept quietly to keep the sound from filling the ears of those desperately trying to get news from inside her house — information they could use as delicious fodder in the chattering gossip of jealous men and women.

"This is a beautiful cloth," Wolli said. "Let me fold it and put it back in the chest. If Inya wants Tila Wula to wear this sarong at the wedding, we can tell Ndalo." Wolli hugged Koni's shoulder. "He will agree. Believe me, I'm sure. Let me put it back in the chest."

Wolli reached for the cloth on Koni's lap, but Koni held on tightly. She rested her head on her knees to hide her crying.

Wolli took a deep breath. He was genuinely shocked when he saw Waleka sitting up with his head on his knees. The old man's shoulders shook violently as he tried to hold back the tears that exploded. "Don't cry, Bapa," Wolli patted Waleka's shoulder. "Pasola is coming up. The extended family will come to gather here. We must be well prepared for everything. The ceremony for Wula must be the best. Isn't this the sarong that Wula will wear at her wedding?"

Waleka and Koni didn't look up. The wind blowing inland from the sea rattled the walls of the house. It gusted in from underneath, spun around, then rushed away. The flat roof of the house shook. It did not rise to the height that was the norm for a house of an elder. A form and norm that could be interpreted in different ways. Giving an alternative way of looking at the situation, was what Wolli was now trying to execute in his mind and heart.

Wolli sat between Waleka and Koni, his adopted parents, who were holding back their tears. A sense of sadness pervaded his heart. When one grew older, when the energy was no longer strong, the burden of life should shift onto the shoulders of children and grandchildren. His two old parents had been carrying an increasingly heavy burden alone for more than ten years.

Although Waleka was older now, he still had to support his young children born to his seventh and eighth wives. There was nothing he could do when his children left Ratenggaro and scattered all over the world. He didn't know where they were and whether they lived in prosperity. He did not even know how many children and grandchildren had left the village. He felt as if he were leaving his position as an elder.

"Don't leave again," Koni whispered to Wolli. "Don't leave Bapa alone again. There are many things to take care of. Besides Tila Wula, there is also Lamura. Your inya will not allow you to take Lamura with you. If you leave, Lamura stays here."

"Yes, Inya." Wolli smiled. He was amused that Koni used Lamura to threaten him. Trying to comfort her, he said, "I'll take care of everything." In his heart, he said, *I will not leave again. I will stay here. For Wula, I will stay here.*

CHAPTER *31*

The news that Ndalo and Tila Wula's wedding would take place after the Pasola was what all villagers were most eagerly awaiting proof of. The extended family, scattered in their own homes outside the main village, prepared everything to make sure the ceremony would go well for everyone. As usual, many family members who had moved away would come home for Nyale and Pasola. This time, however, that number was higher than usual.

Many people believed that Ndalo's and Waleka's children and grandchildren would determine the success or failure of Ndalo's ninth marriage. The gossip became more evocative when word spread that Lara was also coming home.

According to rumors, Father Bili had come to her rescue when she ran away from Ratenggaro six years ago, introducing Lara to the head of a local convent with a mission to improve education on the island of Sumba. This information did not come from Raga, Lara's father, but from someone who knew a little about what had happened.

The midwife who was helping Galuh deliver her sixth child in the smoke hut said, "Lara has really become an important person." Galuh's mother, who came to accompany her daughter during her stay in the smoke hut and help care for the newborn, remained silent.

Galuh, who had become an Inya Pitu six years ago, responded, "Oh, really?"

"But what good did it do for her?" the midwife added. "She's still not married!"

Galuh weighed her own thoughts and feelings. Lara had been her best friend from elementary school through junior high. Both of them had wanted to become teachers. But fate drove them into an unresolved enmity that began with a shocking confrontation. *If Lara returns, would Waleka reunite me with Lara?* Galuh wondered. If her memories of the events that took place six years ago were any measure, it seemed impossible.

"Lara is really coming home!" It was this last piece of news that led to the suspicion that Lara would be as upset as when Waleka, her grandfather, married her friend for his seventh wife.

"She must be coming to apologize to you," The midwife comforted Galuh. "She will apologize to her grandfather, Bapa Leka. She will definitely come to apologize."

Galuh grinned. There was now an eighth and ninth wife that Lara didn't know about. And what would Lara think about Tila Wula becoming Ndalo's ninth wife? Wula and Ndalo would be the most celebrated couple during this Pasola season.

In the six years since Galuh had become Waleka's seventh wife, much had happened. When Galuh entered Waleka's ancestral house six years ago to become Inya Pitu, she had lived up to her parents' expectations and pride of becoming the wife of a rato and giving birth to the elder's children.

The appearance of wives eight and nine, Inya Panpotoh and Inya Banda Iha, when she was giving birth to her second and fifth sons, did not bother her.

Ratenggaro's smoke hut, built in the middle of the field, had now witnessed five times Galuh and her newborn being roasted by the smoke of the fire. The windowless stilt house was about 130 square feet, with a bamboo floor, thatched roof, and door. The fire and smoke were tended at all times so the mother and her baby would be healthy afterward.

"Just so the rato remains proud of you," Galuh's mother said. "You have five sons, and the sixth is on his way. You must be proud," Galuh's mother wiped away tears caused as much by the smoke as the pain in her heart.

"Yes, this is already the sixth." Galuh looked down holding back a spasm of pain.

"You did a great job birthing boys!" her mother said. "You're a rato's wife giving birth to a rato's son. You have everything and will be given everything."

The cry of a newborn interrupted her. Galuh's mother immediately went downstairs to add dry wood to keep the fire burning and the smoke minimal.

Galuh brought the naked baby, her sixth son, to her breast. She was exhausted. Her pride of six years ago seemed to dissipate with the smoke around her. She was still holding on, only because her maternal instinct prompted her to breastfeed. To her, breastfeeding was as meaningful as nurturing and raising a child to the best of her ability. Galuh took a long breath, watching the baby cling to her breast, as the other five children noisily climbed up the ladder and spilled boisterously into the hut.

They gathered around Galuh, munching on sweet potatoes their grandmother had given them. A few moments later, the children ran off, jumping from the top of the hut's porch to the ground without taking the stairs.

"Hey, now! Don't go too far!" Galuh's mother called out to her grandchildren. She climbed back up the ladder and entered the hut carrying a container of water to clean the infant being warmed by the embers. But Galuh refused. She went straight to sleep with the baby in her arms.

A few days later, Galuh asked her mother, "Is Lara really coming home, Mama?" She closed her eyes and took a deep breath. Six years ago, when facing Lara's rejection of her, she felt so sure and strong. Back then, she was so proud of her position as the wife of a rato. She expected to be regarded as righteous and important. She was so sure that her title of Inya Pitu would elevate her status above Lara, who was only a granddaughter.

Galuh sighed. Even though it happened six years ago, Galuh could still feel Lara jerking her hand roughly.

"So you want to be Kakek's wife?" Lara had shouted.

Galuh had tried to joke. "Hey, we'll really be a family. You will call me Nenek!" She never imagined that Lara would become so angry and scream so loud that no one's forceful attempts could stop her. Galuh was shocked by Lara's fury, as she watched her run away, crying. People told her that Lara had jumped onto a horse and spurred the horse into a frenzied gallop.

And, except for the return of the horse, there had been no news of Lara for months afterward.

Galuh's thoughts shifted to her extraordinary wedding. After she married Waleka, her family's living conditions had improved. They owned more horses, acreage, and a house. Even more remarkably, her family was welcomed into the circle of respected elders.

But that was then! Now, Galuh felt empty, an emptiness she had felt since the birth of her first child. As a newlywed, Galuh did not care about the sharp, mocking stares from the other six wives, whom she considered old and no longer beautiful. She only respected Inya Koni and Inya Duyo. But then came the eighth wife, followed by the ninth. With each additional wife, Galuh's life felt more meaningless. Waleka spent more time at the two new wives' houses. He seemed to have forgotten her.

Recalling all that had brought her to this moment, Galuh wept. Her tears fell on the head of her baby, sleeping comfortably in her arms.

"What's wrong?" her mother asked, massaging Galuh's arms and legs. "Are you afraid Lara will disturb you? No matter what happens, she can't kick you out. You are her grandfather's wife! There's nothing to fear." Galuh's mother was not used to giving advice. She could only share what she knew about the customs of life in her village.

"Bapa Leka never comes to see his children," Galuh whispered.

"That's the way it is," her mother said. "It's better this way. You just had a baby and are not yet clean, not yet strong. What would he come for? It would not have been any different if you had married his son, Logo. And what does Logo own? And who would guarantee that you'd be his only wife?"

"Waleka doesn't even know his children," Galuh said. "He doesn't know which is his child and which is his grandchild ..." Galuh closed her eyes and drifted back in time.

When she was heavily pregnant with her fifth child, Galuh had come to the temporary ancestral house. That day, there had been a ceremony for the late Inya Duyo and the ancestors. Koni, Raga, and his wife and children acknowledged her coldly. Galuh forced herself to join in and behave casually. She helped with the kitchen work and did her best to attract Waleka's attention by bringing her children up to the house. But when Waleka and the first wife's family continued to ignore her, she found a seat at the foot of the stilt house and watched her children play.

Telu, Waleka's third wife, had taken a seat next to her. "So, what did Waleka say?" she asked. "Did he ask you how the children are?" Telu laughed when Galuh shook her head. "You're the same age as Lara, Inya Duyo's granddaughter! You must accept the way things are."

That day, Galuh and her children had gone home and didn't return to the ancestral house until after she'd given birth. Waleka visited every night while the baby was still breastfeeding, then never came again — even when she found out she was pregnant with the next child.

Six years, six children. Galuh sighed.

"Maybe your husband has a lot of problems to deal with," her mother continued, trying to comfort her. "Maybe that's why he hasn't visited you."

"This is the sixth time, Mama!" Galuh cried. "I feel bad for my children. It's as if they don't have a father!"

Galuh's mother said nothing more. The experienced mother understood what her daughter was feeling, but what was happening was normal — something that did not need to be discussed. Why complain and cry?

"Lara is coming, Inya," Galuh suddenly spoke up again. "I'm so scared. I'm afraid she'll find a way to kick me out."

"What can she do?" The older woman repeated, picking up the betel nut holder. She quickly rolled a wad and chewed it.

"Well, she went to high school." Galuh placed the baby by her side, and wiped her tears with the tip of her sarong.

"People who go to high school are useless if they come home just to get rid of you.

What are you really afraid of?" The wind blew smoke into the hut. "Don't talk anymore." Galuh's mother spat betel juice and coughed.

During the next few days, Galuh listened as her five children ran in and out of the smoke hut, telling her various stories they'd heard in the village. The most interesting were about the ancestral house. Stories about Wolli, Wula, Waleka, Koni, Hamoli, Raga, and Lara. Galuh was most drawn to the stories her children told about Wolli, Wula, and Lara. These three names always became the topic of conversation whenever the family gathered at Waleka's house. Galuh eagerly listened to her children.

Galuh looked at the face of her baby, fast asleep after feeding until he was full. Waleka had not visited his new son, who was now one week old. She heard her children running up the stairs and into the hut.

"Bapa Wolli is coming!" her eldest son shouted. "Bapa Wolli is home!"

"Don't call him *bapa*! Galuh scolded, irritated.

"But he is!" another son argued.

"He has the same position as you in the family." Galuh tossed the worn pillow near her. "Just like you, he is Bapa Leka's son. So call him *paghogha*, not *bapa*! Or just call him Wolli."

"But Bapa Raga says —"

"Raga also has the same position as you in the family," Galuh interrupted. "You and Raga are both Bapa Leka's children. Don't call him *bapa*, either. Call him *paghogha* or just call him Raga." Irritable, Galuh continued, "Wolli, however, is not the same as all of you. Wolli is another person altogether. He has no blood relation to this family at all. He's Inya Koni's adopted child."

But Galuh knew that her anger was trying to erase the whispers of her heart. Gha Wolli had always been very kind and affectionate — a paghogha who had been part of her childhood, the big brother who had always been there through her elementary and middle school years with Lara, Ida, Wula, and Koda.

Galuh's eldest son panted with excitement. "Everyone is waiting for Inya Lara! Who is she? Why is she so important?" Too impatient to wait for his mother's answer, he pressed, "Is she smart? Why are people waiting for Inya Lara to come? They say you are afraid of Inya Lara. Are you afraid of Inya Lara, Mama?"

"You shut up!" Galuh snapped. "You don't understand what you're hearing!"

"But people say that —"

"You have to be quiet now," Galuh's mother interrupted. "Just be patient, just wait."

She took the children out of the hut and sat with them at the bottom of the stairs. "Tell me who is at the Big House?"

Overhearing her mother's question, Galuh rose and took a seat by the door opening at the top of the stairs so she could pay close attention to her children's stories.

"Many!" the eldest said.

"Did they ask about your mother?"

"No!" they answered together, with the simple honesty of children.

"Did anyone ask about your new little brother?"

"No!"

Eyes sparkling, the eldest reported, "We ate meat. We ate a lot of it!" He hopped around excitedly before he could control himself and continue. "We saw Bapa Raga, Bapa Wolli, Kakek Ndalo, Inya Koni, Inya Tila Wula. Lots of people! Everyone was happy that Bapa Wolli was back at the Big House. They are having a Pasola party. After that, everyone will have a party for the wedding."

"Whose wedding?" Galuh's mother asked.

"Inya Tila Wula and Kakek Ndalo. There will be lots of parties!"

"Oooh, that sounds nice!" Galuh's mother brought food out for her grandchildren. "Eat some more," she encouraged, glancing at her daughter sitting in the door opening. Galuh had not received any food parcels from the Big House since her second son was born — not even when they had celebrations.

Galuh's mother climbed the stairs to sit next to her daughter. "Do not be afraid of Lara," she said firmly. "Would Lara dare to cause a scene at Ndalo and Tila Wula's wedding? No! Besides, Tila Wula is already living at Ndalo's house. She must have already slept with Ndalo; after all, what can she do?"

"Yes," Galuh replied, still nervous at the thought of another confrontation like the one six years ago. Lara's angry shouting and chasing her away, the commotion triggered by Lara's furious outburst, the image of her riding out of the village while crying her eyes out — it was too much.

Galuh pictured the same scenario happening at Tila Wula's wedding and gathered herself. Galuh raised her head. Her fear and resentment turned into hope that Lara would behave the same way she had six years ago. She wished fervently that Lara would return to Ratenggaro with the same grudge and fury that she had displayed at her wedding to Waleka. She longed for Lara to shout angrily at Inya Panpotoh and Inya Banda Iha, Waleka's eighth and ninth wives.

He had brought them into the ancestral house before building a field house for each so he could freely visit them. She wanted Lara to slap Bapa Leka's face in his old age and separate Tila Wula from Ndalo. Then, Lara's intelligence would figure out a way for Wolli and Wula to escape smoothly. This would bring great shame to Waleka's house and cause the ancestral house in Ratenggaro to be stripped of all dignity. Galuh raised her head. Her fear and resentment turned into a hope that Lara would behave in the same way she had six years ago. Galuh hoped that Lara would also shout angrily at Inya Panpotoh and Inya Banda Iha, Waleka's eighth and ninth wives, who he had brought into the ancestral house before building a house for each so he could freely visit them.

Galuh's children sounded joyful as they returned to the smoke hut. Rain began to pelt the roof. Thunder exploded, followed by lightning flashing over the vast field. The baby started to cry, and Galuh brought his head close to her heart.

CHAPTER *32*

Wolli and Raga were preparing to travel to Lamboya to deliver the official news of Tila Wula and Ndalo's wedding following the Pasola. The family in Lamboya already knew, but Wolli, according to tradition, needed to make the formal announcement. Hamoli had prepared provisions of grilled chicken, corn, and boiled sweet potatoes, which were packed in bags that hung from each horse. Wolli's bag also carried four bottles of water.

"Please, tell Lara not to fly off the handle again," Hamoli pleaded while Raga and Wolli were getting ready. "She does not have the right to be angry. I'm afraid she'll lose control again. After six, almost seven years, I don't want a repeat of what happened. Please, Bapa, tell Lara."

"Mmm," Raga replied, distracted.

"Don't worry, Gha," Wolli said, as he continued packing.

"You must tell Lara that it is useless to lose her temper," Hamoli continued. "Ndalo and Tila Wula already live in the same house. Bapa Leka doesn't care what Lara thinks."

When Raga and Wolli remained silent as if ignoring her, Hamoli's voice rose. "Lara cannot leave again! Lara must not be cursed!" Hamoli grabbed Raga's arm and urged, "Everything I say is because people talk. Please! Don't you have anything to say?"

Raga took one look at his wife's face and chuckled. "Yes," he replied, "Lara will be fine." Raga gazed at his wife's face with a sense of gratitude for the beautiful woman he had kept as his first and only wife. "Just like you, Inya! Lara will be just fine!"

Wolli and Raga mounted their horses, and the two left the house, taking a shortcut to speed the trip. They rode up the hills and out onto the mile-long big road, then re-entered the path. Along the way, and at every stop where the horses grazed, the two of them said little, wrapped in their own thoughts.

Raga knew that Hamoli was anxiously waiting for her daughter's return. He also knew that his wife opposed her father-in-law's marriage, just as vehemently as Lara. But Hamoli had remained quiet — not for lack of courage, but because she knew her place as a wife.

Yes, Lara had lost control of herself, some six years ago. Raga shook his head. He was proud of his daughter. She encompassed his heart and mind. *Would Lara act the same way to Ndalo, who would soon marry her girlfriend Tila Wula?* The question weighed on Raga's mind. He muttered, "If that happens, it happens."

"What's wrong?" Wolli asked.

"It's nothing," Raga replied.

"Come on, I heard what you said. What's wrong?"

"It's nothing," Raga repeated. He clicked his tongue and urged his horse into a gallop down the path in the middle of the field.

Wolli followed close behind. He hoped that when they passed the smoke hut where Inya Pitu had just given birth, Raga would stop and they could all visit for a while. Doing so would open up just a little bit of heart space and reduce the grudge that had been wedged in long ago. But when the smoke hut came into view, Raga spurred his horse even faster, as if he couldn't pass the house fast enough.

Onward they sped, bodies flattened against their horses, the synchronization between hoofbeats and heartbeats only they could understand. Tila Wula filled the minds of the two men.

Both Wolli and Raga understood that Wula had grown up into a Ratenggaro Sumba woman in the true sense of the word. Sumbanese women were always faithful to their parents' promises. A Sumbanese woman knows that her parents' self-worth could not be exchanged for anything. Sumba women might appear weak for doing what they were told without resisting, but in this weakness lay the Sumbanese woman's strength.

CHAPTER *33*

Wolli hugged Lamura's neck tightly. The heat of his horse's body warmed his. Lamura's mane brushed his chin every time he leaned forward. The clatter of Lamura's hooves echoed his own desire to run faster. If he could, he would fly far beyond the fields and horizons that lined the ocean. Wolli knew he could not stop Wula from entering Ndalo's arms. He knew he had to gain control of himself to accept the situation.

Wolli thought back to the first words he had spoken to Wula after they had reunited at the temporary Big House after not seeing each other for a long time. "Are you okay?" he had asked. Wula had grown taller. She still had long hair that, as far as he knew, she had never cut.

Tila Wula had hugged him tightly and cried with joy, an embrace that Ndalo caught with a look of jealous hatred. He tried to mask his feelings with the best smile a rato could give with a mouth clamped shut by a betel nut wad.

"Gha Wolli has been gone for a long time," Tila Wula had said. "Where did you go? Why did you leave Inya and Bapa for so long?"

"Are you okay?" Wolli had repeated.

"I'm already living in Ndalo's house," Tila Wula had said. They released each other's embrace and turned their heads to look at Ndalo, who, trying his best to appear gallant, stood staring at them.

Wolli had known then that the old man was trying to win over Tila Wula so that all his wedding plans would go smoothly. After the wedding, he would mercilessly take possession of her.

His thoughts were interrupted as he and Raga stopped in a valley not far from a spring. They used to stop here for a water break on their trips to Lamboya, years ago. Wolli took out a water bottle for Raga and one for himself from his saddle bag, then they took a seat near the drinking horses.

They were getting closer to Lamboya and planned to head straight back to Ratenggaro early the next morning.

Raga was troubled, but he couldn't speak the words churning inside him. *Wolli, take Wula away. Take her away, as far as possible, from our village. Don't let Wula fall into Ndalo's claws. I want to give Wula to you! You are the best person to guard her.*

Raga longed to shout these words to reach Wolli's thoughts and feelings, but his lips only released a sigh. It was too difficult, like trying to catch a seagull flying high over the edge of the horizon before sunset.

"Can we postpone Wula's wedding?" Raga suddenly spoke.

Wolli turned to stare at Raga. Then he shifted his gaze to the two horses by the spring.

Raga rose and paced anxiously. "The traditional ancestral house isn't finished yet," he said. "We can use that as the main reason to postpone the wedding." He was confident that Lara would not make trouble when told that Tila Wula had been delivered to Ndalo's house. Secretly, though, Raga wished Lara would be as angry as she had been six years ago. "We can politely suggest that the wedding be postponed until the roof of the Big House is finished," Raga continued. "I'm sure that would make Wula very happy."

"There's no way Wula would do something that would embarrass and sadden Inya and Bapa," Wolli said.

"What about the traditional ancestral house?" Raga asked. What he really wanted to ask was, "What about your own heart, Wolli? Do you love Wula more than a brother loves his sister? If you love her, take her and go. Go to Lamboya! The fence there is strong enough to protect you."

"You, Paghogha, must believe that, in due time, all of us can build roofs on our houses," Wolli said calmly.

"What about Tila Wula?" Raga insisted. "It's hard to watch her being forced to live under the constraints of custom, being forced to live in Ndalo's house, become his wife, and forever remain his ninth wife!"

"Wula can take care of herself," Wolli said gently. "Wula cannot be restrained. She has gone to school to become a teacher, and she will always remain a teacher." Wolli looked into the distance.

The two continued their journey onto the downhill path that descended toward Lamboya. The towering roofs of the traditional homes were already visible. Those, too, represented generations of spirit and imagination. The owners' minds had been clean and clear — unclouded by dust. Even the dust kicked up by the horses on the Pasola field would not reach them.

"If there's something you want to talk about, just say it!" Raga said, as he let Wolli pull up even with him.

"I have nothing to say." Wolli held Lamura's reins as the two horses trotted side by side.

"Nothing?" Raga looked at Wolli. "Is there another woman you like?"

Wolli met Raga's look. "No."

"You're old enough to get married."

"After Wula gets married ..." Wolli paused before he continued, "only then can I think about it." Wolli turned his head, dug in his heels, and spurred Lamura toward Lamboya. Raga followed at the same pace.

The two arrived at Lamboya late that afternoon.

The Lamboya Council of Elders and Koni's extended family welcomed Raga and Wolli. Everyone already knew that Wula would be Ndalo's ninth wife, and that the dowry had already been paid and had, over time, increased.

Still, disappointment filled the elders' hearts. "Wula is grown up now," said one. "She is educated; she is a teacher! She can't become the ninth wife. She must be the first and only wife. What happened? We hope Lara will come and speak up so Wula can go back to her own house."

Another elder rose. "How could Wula agree to be taken to Ndalo's house? How could Wula want to marry such an old man? Wula has gone to university, but she just blindly obeyed her father's wishes. How can that be? That's not right!"

"Tila Wula is right." Wolli replied.

"What?" the astonished elders asked simultaneously.

"Tila Wula is right." Wolli repeated.

The Lamboya elders were dumbfounded. "What do you mean?"

"If indeed she must marry Ndalo, the old man will only receive her body." Wolli's voice trembled as he spoke. "He will never possess any part of her heart and mind."

"What are you talking about?" Raga asked impatiently.

"He's talking about Wula!" clarified an elder. "Is that who you were talking about just now?" The elder's question attracted everyone's attention.

"Yes, Wula is right." Wolli repeated and slowly lifted his face. "As far as I know, Wula will fulfill Bapa Leka's promise to Ndalo. She will obey and honor her parents, she will obey and honor the ancestors." He spoke in a flow that seemed to be orchestrated to immerse the listener in the thoughts and words he was conveying. Wolli fell silent. What he was saying now was what he had said many times before to his mother and to other family members who regretted the reality.

Annoyed, Raga listened to Wolli's explanation, which, in his opinion, did not solve the problem they faced.

"What about yourself, Wolli?" the council chairman asked loudly and sternly.

Startled, Wolli's heart raced as Wula's face flashed through his mind.

"Don't you regret Wula being put in this position? Are you going to allow Wula to become Ndalo's ninth wife? Are you, really? Don't you love Wula?" The accusing urgency in the elder's voice made Wolli lower his eyes. His true thoughts and love for Wula were buried deep. He was not prepared to speak frankly.

"Can't you explain to Wula that you don't see her just as your adopted sister? That you love her? Don't you want to marry Wula? Answer, Wolli!" The elder's voice silenced the meeting completely. Everyone waited for Wolli's answer.

Raga breathed very slowly. What he had wanted to say had just been said.

"Answer, Wolli!" The elder repeated, his voice cutting through the silence. "Take Wula out of Ndalo's house. Marry her! Wula definitely wants to. If you answer *yes* and dare to take responsibility, we will do whatever it takes for you and Wula."

Wolli bowed his head deeply. His eyes filled, and he quickly wiped the tears before they fell. When he slowly raised his head, everyone held their breath.

"Wula has made the right decision." Wolli's voice shook with the deep affection he had for the woman who was the center of attention of the entire family. Wolli tried to master the turmoil of his thoughts and feelings for his beloved adopted sister. "She deeply respects Bapa Leka and Inya Koni. I know Wula won't back out. For Wula, the honor of Bapa, Inya, and family comes before anything else. She is prepared to do it."

Wolli looked down as the silence was broken by disappointed groans and disgruntled voices.

"Are you sure?" one of the elders asked in disbelief.

"I believe Wula can handle it," said Wolli. "Wula has gone to university, but it's not because of her education that she can rebel.

Quite the contrary. It is her education that made her realize how to live a life of filial piety."

"By becoming Ndalo's ninth wife?" an elder exclaimed incredulously. "Is that what Wula is showing?"

"Wolli!" another elder snapped. "What we want is for you to bring Wula here, to Lamboya, to be your wife!"

"Give Wula a chance to get through this," Wolli replied. He raised both hands and rubbed his forehead, swallowing the words that filled his throat: *I love you, Wula. I love you so much. I would love to take you to Lamboya to live here forever.* Aloud, he quietly said, "We must also believe in the path that Wula has to follow. If it is not her path, there will be signs that show this. If there are no signs that are clear to all of us, I am sure Wula will get a sign. Wula will walk the right path, the path that is destined for Wula, not for us. The ancestors of praing marapu will look after Wula while she lives in Ndalo's house."

Wolli's voice was calm, but he was uneasy about denying his true feelings.

"And you are absolutely sure?" The Lamboya elder scrutinized Wolli.

"Yes. I'm absolutely sure," Wolli's voice was barely audible.

Many heads bowed in the silence that suddenly blanketed the family gathering in Lamboya that day. Everyone was confused and disappointed at the words Wolli had spoken.

Wolli understood that perhaps his explanation had been too modern for the traditional elders to understand. He felt sure that the elders, including Raga, were still not satisfied with his answer.

"Wula will get through everything just fine," Wolli reassured everyone, including himself.

CHAPTER *34*

The report from his lackeys angered Ndalo. The old man chewed his wad of betel nut rapidly. His blood surged with anger. Sweat trickled slowly, wetting his body. He ordered two of his men to guard the entrance of his property. No one was allowed to enter the house. His wives, children, grandchildren, and other relatives were all in the courtyard helping the workers prepare tents and everything else necessary to celebrate the upcoming Nyale, Pasola, and wedding.

"Is that so?" His question was accompanied with a spit.

"Yes," one of the lackeys lied, "we met Wolli and Raga on the road, on their way to Lamboya. We believe Wolli is going there to ask the elders for his ancestors' blessing to prevent Tila Wula from marrying you. Even though we made it clear that the equipment we rented from Weetebula was to receive all the families who will come to celebrate the Nyale, Pasola, and wedding party."

"So what did Wolli say?" Ndalo asked.

"He said —" the lackey turned to the other and asked, "What did he say?"

"What did Wolli say!" Ndalo yelled.

"He said, 'A party? What party? A wedding party? Why would Tila Wula want to marry that old man? Do you think Wula wants to marry an uneducated man whose mouth is always full of betel nut spit? Hey, Wula is going to be my wife. We have known each other all our lives. We've loved each other since birth, and we're both educated.'" The man delivered this deception without a pause, and now he was short of breath.

"I'm sure the two of them went to Lamboya to garner support from their families," Ama Dula continued excitedly. "Wolli must want to mobilize all his family members to help him pay the belis compensation. It must be like that. I'm sure. He thinks it's *that* easy!"

Ndalo's eyes bulged. "What did that sissy Raga say? He only has one wife. He's jealous and wants to fight me, a man who has many wives. Huh! He thinks it's easy to pick a fight when he likes. Who does he think he is?"

Ama Dula continued his tale. "When we asked Raga if they were going to Lamboya, he glared at us and said it was none of our business. We also heard that his daughter, Lara, is coming home. We'd better check with Waleka so she doesn't make another mess. We'll threaten him before Lara arrives, because once Lara is here, it could be bad! She could ruin the party. She'll conspire with Raga and Wolli to kidnap Tila Wula."

Like Ndalo, Ama Dulu chewed a wad of betel nut to hide his anxiety.

"You think so?" Ndalo chewed hard on his wad, then spat. "That's it! Waleka better not mess around. If he can't manage his family, he'll see!" Ndalo spat out the entire betel nut wad he had been chewing, then picked up some tobacco and stuffed it roughly in his mouth.

"That's right!" Ama Dula and the other lackeys encouraged him.

"Where is Tila Wula?" Ndalo rose and looked around anxiously.

"At Raga's house. That means Wula must have met Wolli again, and they must have made plans. They must have already met Lara. That means we're all finished!" Ama Dula smacked his forehead.

He and Ndalo immediately left for Waleka's house. As they neared, they saw a crowd of old people and children standing in the open field under the banyan tree. A young, beautiful woman stood in their center.

It was too late for Ndalo to retreat. There was no other way to get to Waleka's house but through the side of the road near the banyan tree. He stood rooted, trying to decide what to do, when the woman saw him and smiled.

"Kakek." Lara walked slowly towards Ndalo. Her voice was calm and her steps were sure.

Ndalo looked anxiously at Lara. She had become a very different woman.

The crowd opened up on its own, and all eyes fastened in amazed expectation on Ndalo and Lara. The rumors and conjectures about Lara's return, and what she would do when she arrived, had spread far and wide. The shame of Lara's disobedience six years ago had festered in all who felt dishonored by Lara's conduct.

"Kakek," Lara said once more. "Nice to see you again. Remember me? I am Lara!" she continued to smile.

"Lara ... Lara ..." Ndalo finally stammered. "Raga's daughter? Who has been missing for how many years? Am I mistaken?"

Ama Dula stood wide-eyed. This woman was not the Lara of six years ago. That Lara was a tomboy, good at racing her father's horse. That Lara's skin was dark, and her unkempt hair fluttered in the wind. That Lara was much different from this Lara. Tall, clean, neat, and calm, dressed in a sarong with an *alambaleko*, Sumba motif, and a white kebaya as a top, she looked beautiful. Her hair was tied and draped over her right shoulder. What mesmerized everyone most were her lips. They were red, but not from chewing betel nut. They were red because she wore lipstick, and lipstick was expensive.

"Yes, I am Lara," she repeated, extending her hand politely, like a granddaughter who respected her grandfather.

"Lara ... Raga's daughter?" Ndalo repeated.

"Yes."

"You are home."

"Yes."

"Have you met all your family?"

"Yes."

"Have you met ..." Ndalo's voice trailed off.

"Met who?" Lara asked. But before Ndalo could answer, quick hoofbeats entered the path through the cemetery. Everyone turned to watch, stunned, as a horse with two riders came to a halt right in front of Ndalo. Both men quickly dismounted and one caught the rope to tether the horse to the side of the gate.

"Bapa," the first rider said, looking at Ndalo intently. "I've come home!"

"Who are you?" Ndalo stared at the man before him. He was tall and thin and had a slightly curved back. His long hair was unkempt, his lips were stained from nicotine, and his ear was tattooed. He wore flip-flops and looked like he would fall forward if he didn't make a concerted effort to stand straight.

"Bapa, it's Zoga!"

Ndalo jerked and stepped back. "Zoga?"

"Yes, Zoga, Bapa!"

"What have you come for?"

"To go home!"

"To go home where?"

"To go home to the Big House — our ancestral house!"

"Oh ... to the Big House?"

"What? Am I not allowed to come come home?"

"Why are you coming home?"

"I'm coming home to my ancestors' house, but I'm also coming home to see my children, Koda and Ida."

"Koda is at home with his inya!" Ndalo snapped.

"Which inya?" Zoga asked. "Is there another new inya in the Big House?" Zoga brushed past his father and strode toward their ancestral house.

Ndalo stood still, in shock. His face flushed. The comfortable atmosphere had disappeared. Lara turned and, looking straight ahead, she headed for Waleka's house with measured steps.

Seeing Zoga, Ndalo had been taken aback. He assumed Zoga had died in some distant, unfamiliar place. Never once did he think that his son was still alive.

Deeply shocked, Ndalo whirled around. He remembered Zoga clearly, the only son of his first wife, Inya Tua; the son who did not want to assume any responsibility, who had left when his son Koda was born. He had come back after his daughter Ida was born only to leave again. Zoga had abandoned his wife and children. He sold some land that wasn't his and left with some livestock. He only came home with problems, then vanished, leaving more problems. Koda and Ida had been raised by their mother's family, in a house not far from Ratenggaro.

Zoga came and went as he pleased. At last year's Pasola, he kidnapped a woman to be his wife. She was the sister of Ndalo's fifth wife. He took her away, leaving behind the burden of shame that Ndalo had to make up for with cattle and a piece of farmland.

After that, Ndalo had told his son, "You can go and never come back!" Zoga had stomped his feet and promised never to step foot in the ancestral house again.

Ida had been in first grade. At that time, Ndalo had been really angry, not only at Zoga, but also at all the people who had anything to do with Zoga, including Zoga's son Koda, Wolli's close friend, and Zoga's daughter Ida, who was best friends with Lara and Wula.

Since then, Ndalo's anger had cooled, and Koda and Ida often came to his ancestral house. He had received Koda and Ida with pride. His grandchildren were students who would support him as a grandfather who would marry an educated girl. "The important thing is that Koda and Ida are here to replace Zoga," he had said on several occasions.

Now Zoga had decided to come home, after his children had become educated people, and he, Ndalo, was about to marry an educated girl. "Let Zoga disappear forever," Ndalo grumbled to Ama Dula as they made their way back to his house.

"There must be a conspiracy," Ama Dula whispered.

"You think so?"

"Yes! It must be! Wula is at Raga's house. Lara is at the Big House. Koda visited often, and now, suddenly, Zoga comes home. There must be a connection!"

"How so?" Ndalo asked, his heart burning.

"There's a connection! Wolli will take Wula away with Lara's support. Wula could also be taken away by Zoga with Lara's support. It's dangerous. Zoga might even want Wula for Koda."

"You really think so?"

"What's even more dangerous is if Wolli runs away with Wula. Be careful," Ama Dula whispered. "Be very careful."

Later, all eyes were on Lara, and her presence brought the bustle in Ndalo's courtyard to a halt. Lara's parents had already told her about the rumors spreading throughout the village that she would go on a rampage. She smiled and looked around her.

Ndalo's wives watched Lara anxiously, wondering what she was going to do. They were hoping to see Lara lose control, just as she had done all those years ago. Because if Lara did lose control, it would mean watching Lara do what Ndalo's wives really wanted to do, but could not and would not. Their hopes were suddenly shattered by Zoga's arrival.

Ndalo returned to the courtyard of his house with Ama Dula and some of his men.

"You must remain vigilant," Ama Dula said. "You saw, yourself, that Tila Wula is spending more time with Wolli at Waleka's or Raga's house. What is she doing there? What is she planning?"

"People who have lived in the city for a long time usually have a lot of street sense," another lackey warned. "Be careful! Wolli will run away with Tila Wula. They won't use horses, they'll use a car. It is faster, and there's no way a horse can catch up with a car. They will go on a plane with Lara."

"Don't worry about Zoga," Ama Dula said to Ndalo. "Just look at him slumped down and sleeping on the porch of the Big House. What we need to think about is the whereabouts of Wolli and Wula. Why are they staying in Raga's house so long? What are they doing there?"

Ama Dula and Ndalo's lackeys knew with certainty that making Ndalo nervous was one way of showing that they were earning their pay. For men like Ama Dula, chaos was work. He added words to fuel Ndalo's anger, "We're sure Waleka knows about it."

"Oh, really?" Ndalo's frown deepened.

"I will kill myself if you fail to marry Tila Wula, Bapa Ndalo," Ama Dula wheedled. "Her beauty matches your extraordinarily handsomeness. It's true that you are old, but you're like an old coconut: the older it gets, the more oil it yields!"

Flattered, Ndalo preened. "Really?"

"Yes! You must make sure that Waleka does not embarrass you. Where will you hide your face if that happens? Wolli wants to take the easy way out to get Tila Wula — you have waited fourteen years!" Ama Dula knew the importance of flattering Ndalo, but at the same time, his own insecurities made him uncertain. He now faced university students, teachers, and college graduates!

CHAPTER 35

The large ancestral house that belonged to Ndalo's family was located near the coastal cliffs, next to Waleka's house. The house was taller than the other houses in Ratenggaro. The roof, straight and slender from the top to the bottom, was almost 50 feet high. At the bottom, it formed an arch with a slope that made the 50-foot roof appear to be soaring into the sky.

The walls and floors of the stilt houses in Ratenggaro were built with the finest bamboo. Everyone knew that Ndalo's house, with its soaring roof, indicated that the owner was rich, that he owned a lot of livestock and land, had many wives, and commanded a great influence in important decisions that affected the village and its relations with the surrounding villages. The owner was also known for having so many children and grandchildren, he was unable to recognize all the offspring born to his eight wives — and soon there would be more children born to a ninth wife.

Ever since being ushered into Ndalo's Big House, Wula had always slept vigilantly next to Inya Tua, who assured her that the other wives slept in their respective homes, the field houses, that Ndalo had built for them.

"He wouldn't dare sleep with you," Inya Tua said. "You've heard the agreement yourself; he can only sleep with you after the Pasola, after the official marriage!"

Wula simply nodded.

"Besides, he's free to stay in whichever field house he chooses," Inya Tua said, as if to make herself realize once again that Ndalo would have nine wives just like Waleka. With the existence of eight wives, he did not need to rush to sleep with the ninth. "Do you understand?" she whispered.

Wula was grateful for that. Ndalo owned a lot of land and many houses for his wives around the village, where he was free to come and go as he pleased. However, approaching the Pasola, all the wives and many family members took turns sleeping in the ancestral house, where Wula and Inya Tua slept every night.

The morning that Zoga returned to Ratenggaro, Inya Tua had invited Wula to weave with her on the terrace. As soon as they walked out Ndalo's door, they saw the crowd under the banyan tree.

"It's Zoga, my son!" Inya Tua whispered. "Zoga has been missing for a long time. He's Koda and Ida's father. But he left his wife and children some time ago."

"Poor Koda and Ida," Wula whispered sincerely.

"Zoga might hate you," Inya Tua said. "He might not approve of his father marrying a ninth wife. The same goes for the other children. None of them want their father to marry again."

Wula felt the sharp tip of a javelin in Inya Tua's every word. Despite the old woman's kind demeanor, the girl could sense that her kindness was not heart-felt. Wula understood Inya Tua's words as a message that she should be prepared to deal with the attitude of the children and grandchildren who were returning for the Pasola that year.

Yet Wula knew that it was neither Zoga nor Ndalo's other children she needed to fear. The ones who posed a threat were Ndalo himself and his wives, especially the seventh and eighth wives who, since she first arrived, had always faced her with a sour look.

Tila Wula sat beside Inya Tua on the terrace, both weaving. The eighth wife silently spun yarn. On the other side of the terrace, three women winnowed rice. Meanwhile, near the stove and in front of the kitchen door, several other women prepared food.

Wula and Inya Tua were weaving and watching the busy work when Koda's arrival caught everyone's attention. "Gha Koda!" Wula was stunned.

"Did Bapa Zoga come?" Koda's voice trembled. "Is my father here?"

"Yes! Your father has come home," Inya Tua replied. "From where, no one knows!"

"Who is that?" Zoga rose and staggered toward the door. "Who is that?" he repeated, before collapsing limply on the floor.

"It's your son," Inya Tua said, as Zoga rolled onto his back, muttering incoherently.

"Are you Koda?" Zoga's voice was hoarse and disjointed. "Where is my daughter Ida? Koda ... my son? Are you a college student?"

"Bapa ..." Shocked, Koda remembered the warnings from his mother's relatives: "It's true that your father came home. He's at the Big House in Ratenggaro. Don't go see him! Don't go there!" His mother had remained silent, quietly dabbing at her tears.

"Bapa!" Koda called again.

"Take him away from here," Inya Tua's voice sounded cold and sharp. "Immediately! That's Kakek's order!"

"Bapa ..." Koda climbed up the ladder and into the house toward his father.

"She's yours!" Zoga said, out of control, as he tried to raise his hand and point at Wula. "That's Wula, Bapa Leka's daughter. She's not Ndalo's. You are the one who has to have Tila Wula! Take her away ..." The crowd at the foot of the porch continued to grow.

"Let's go, Bapa." Koda picked up his father and carried him downstairs. "Sorry," he said to Tila Wula.

Tila Wula was shocked. She immediately looked down when Koda addressed her. It saddened her seeing how Koda carried his father.

The crowd opened up on its own.

Koda lifted his father onto his horse, jumped on behind Zoga, and galloped out of Ratenggaro.

Wula heard the hoofbeats as father and son left through the gate. The sound made her shaky. Wula knew Koda's kindness. Koda would take care of everything his father needed before bringing him back to the Big House.

Inya Tua turned to Ndalo, who had acted haughty and indifferent toward Zoga. It saddened her to realize that her biological son had come home and did not recognize her anymore. Inya Tua watched Koda carry Zoga away "I hope he comes back here soon," she whispered.

"No!" Ndalo barked. "No, he cannot come back home! Not now, not after I am married, not anytime!"

"He's your own son!" Inya Tua cried.

"He definitely can't come home until after I have married Wula." Ndalo said firmly.

"He's coming home to this Big House soon!" Inya Tua countered with equal resolve. We can't let him be sick!"

"Who told him to leave?"

"He's coming back soon!"

"He sold my land, he stole my cattle, he ran out on his wife, abandoned his children, and left no news!" Ndalo shouted. "And now, all of a sudden, he wants to come home! No! He is just using sickness as an excuse! He's probably come to rob me again. It's enough!"

Inya Tua was not surprised to see her husband's tantrum.

Ndalo raised his chin high and continued to blabber, while Inya Tua looked down and wiped away her tears with the edge of her sarong. "What good is your property without the family?" she asked

"After I marry, the ninth wife must get a share too!"

"May there be no marriage!" Inya Tua snapped.

"Shut up!" Ndalo's voice was dangerously sharp.

"If Zoga can't come home, I'll be the one to leave." Inya Tua rose, challenging her husband with a sharp gaze.

"Go away!" The low tone of Ndalo's voice did not match his words. Tila Wula witnessed the quarrel between Ndalo and Inya Tua in silence. It was clear to her that Ndalo was worried that his marriage to her would fail if Zoga returned. Tila Wula was secretly happy that Zoga had come home — not to break up the marriage, but to return to his wife and the children he had abandoned at birth. Koda and Ida's father should return and receive *pandaluhari*, the water of prayer, from the *lete*, altar of the Marapu, in this Big House.

CHAPTER 36

Ndalo dressed to go to Waleka's house. He was on fire with jealousy. Ama Dula had told him that Koda and Zoga were scheming to separate him from Wula. Ndalo was furious. He strutted out of his house with some of his retinue following him. They had made sure that Lara and Koni were still at the Waimalu spring.

Ndalo walked to Waleka's house with confidence. He would kill the man if he dared to prevent the marriage. He had already lost a lot of dowry money for Wula, as well as dowry money for Waleka's seventh, eighth, and even ninth wife. He had only asked for one guarantee: Tila Wula would be his wife.

Ndalo arrived at Waleka's front door at the same time Waleka happened to be going outside. For a short moment, that felt like eternity, the two men stared at each other intently.

"Everything is ready," Ndalo said calmly after catching his breath. We'll have the best wedding ever."

"Yes," Waleka replied, equally calm.

"I heard you're scheming to sabotage it," accused Ndalo. "I heard that you, as a family, want to take back my Tila Wula. Is it true that Wolli will run away with Tila Wula, before she becomes my wife?"

253

Ndalo paused to catch his breath again. "Leka, remember! Don't forget the dowry and how much more has been paid! You must keep your promise!"

Waleka looked sharply at Ndalo. "You are the one who has broken your promise! Have you forgotten? If you break your promise, everything is canceled!"

"Fourteen years is a long time," Ndalo complained.

"You promised to wait," Waleka's voice rose. "You said that Wula would be your seventh and last wife forever. Have you forgotten?"

"You also broke your promise!" Ndalo argued loudly. Equally agitated, both reiterated the terms of the agreement they made fourteen years ago. There was no time to resolve it, so the two old men agreed to meet on the Pasola field. Whoever lost would surrender to the winner's decision.

As Ndalo and his retinue left Waleka's house, Koni arrived from the spring with her children and grandchildren. Everyone carried water containers of appropriate sizes according to age and strength. They all watched Ndalo and Waleka silently.

Ndalo turned his head and found Koni's cold eyes. Ndalo looked back at Waleka with a look of hatred.

"What's wrong?" Koni asked her husband after Ndalo left looking grim. Some of the women who had also just returned from the spring with their water containers, whispered to each other while glancing at Ndalo's retreating figure.

"Everything is fine," Waleka replied. "He invited me to take part in the opening of the Pasola. Ndalo wants to make sure that the opponents show togetherness in the Pasola match. It is only for the warm-up. An example for other Pasola participants. I have already accepted. So you just need to support it."

"Ensuring togetherness in the Pasola competition?" Koni looked at her husband. "What kind of togetherness? You're old, and you're also not feeling well! You need to rest."

Koni climbed the ladder to the back door and headed toward the stone stove. Waleka moved to the side of the small bamboo cot by the stove. He was silent as his wife knelt down to light the fire and heat the water.

Out of nowhere, love filled his heart — a feeling he had lost when he started adding wives. Only now did he realize that it was Koni who witnessed and withstood all the coercion of his wills: his will to bring one woman after another into this house; his will to sell Wula for the fulfillment of his own lust. This was his chance to give his first wife the best. Just once in their old age, he had an opportunity to redeem himself by returning Wula to her mother.

"What's wrong?" Koni asked as Waleka approached her.

"If you don't want me to face Ndalo on the Pasola field, I won't go," Waleka said.

Koni glanced at her husband. She understood there was something else that he really wanted to say, but could not.

"Go, if that's what you want. If you're sure that you'll only face Ndalo in a warm-up, go ahead. You must set the example of an elder on the Pasola field."

"Are you sure, Inya?" Waleka sat down beside his wife.

"As long as I have lived in our village, there has never been a single Pasola match with opponents of the same kabisu, tribe. What kind of warm-up is this?" Koni asked with an effort to convince herself. She added quietly, "We'll wait for the Nyale results tomorrow morning."

After forty-six years, the nyale arrived in a nest, and Mada Wolli found it. It was completely unexpected. Koni remembered vividly how Waleka had found the nyale nest when she came to Ratenggaro for the first time. She had come with Inya Peke, Waleka's eldest sister. Koni still remembered clearly how Banu, Peke's little boy, had asked all sorts of questions about nyale and expressed his desire to be like his uncle Waleka — to be a to-paholong and find a nyale nest. Waleka had found the nyale nest once. Now it was Wolli who found it. It was a sign, and Koni's heart fluttered with hope. *Is this a sign that Tila Wula's*

marriage will go well, too? Koni asked herself. *Actually, there should be no nyale nests. Oh, the Wide-eared and Big-Eyed One.*

She untangled the nyale nest that was brought home from the beach. Fat, plump worms in all colors: red, yellow, black, white, blue — all nyale colors were accounted for. The worms looked bright and shiny. Plenty, fat, and bright nyale were a sign of prosperity, happiness, and success. "This is an extraordinary nyale harvest," Koni exclaimed. "There hasn't been one like this for decades. Wolli found a nyale nest!"

"Yes!" Waleka joined in. *What sign is it?* he asked himself. He had not cared for a long time about signs — neither Nyale nor Pasola signs. What the Nyale predicted was mimicked by the Pasola. They both would address the goodness of the future. He suddenly shivered. *I once found a nyale nest.*

"Honest and faithful ... that's Nyale ... that's Pasola." It was as if Bapa Tua, his father, stood before him. Waleka couldn't pull his gaze away from the container that held the nyale nest that his wife, children, and grandchildren were talking about. He approached Koni. "Do I have your permission to fight Ndalo in the pasola?" Waleka asked with his heart pounding.

His wife nodded with a fleeting smile. Waleka had never asked for her permission before. *What did this mean? Would this be his last Pasola before Tila Wula becomes Ndalo's wife in every sense of the word?* Koni took a deep breath and exhaled slowly.

The voices of her children and grandchildren became louder as everyone watched the nyale worms. The harvest of a nyale nest increased the number of side dishes that would be eaten later that day, after the Pasola. There were many requests from her grandchildren. Everyone wanted Nenek Koni's cooking, including Lara, who had ordered bodho, the special nyale jerky, to take with her to the city when her vacation was over.

"Gha Wolli is great!" Lara said. "He found the nyale nest!" They were all proud because everyone who joined the nyale harvest knew that there was only *one* nest. And Wolli was the one who had found it!

"Please make bodho for Bapa Bili too, Nenek," Lara said. "I haven't visited Bapa Bili yet."

"Of course!" Koni smiled. "I want to see that sweet old man, too. To thank him for all his kindness."

"Yes," Lara replied with a proud smile.

"Where's Tila Wula?" Koni asked her grandchildren as they busily watched the worms in the container. Everyone was grateful for the plentiful harvest, which evoked the highest hopes and deepest faith.

"Wula went straight to Kakek Ndalo's house," Lara answered, "with Nenek Inya Tua." Grandmothers, aunts, cousins, and younger siblings continued the food preparation in front of the back door. Lara remained seated, dividing the nyale into several containers to be distributed to the relatives' homes, including her own.

"Where's Wolli?" Koni asked.

"Still on the beach with Koda," Lara replied. "Don't worry, Nenek. I won't embarrass you or make any of the family ashamed of my behavior. Not anymore. Please, believe in me."

"You're so beautiful," Koni said, stroking Lara's arm. "Nenek Duyo would be so proud. She missed you until the last moments of her life." Koni took Lara into her arms. "Tila Wula!" she cried. "I hope she can be like you — strong, steadfast, and successful!"

"Yes!" Lara assured her. "Wula will definitely be all those things!"

Koni held Lara tightly to suppress her true heart's desire. Deep inside, Koni wished Lara would behave the same way she had before. She wanted Lara to be angry and shout like she did when Waleka wanted to marry his seventh wife. Koni wanted Lara to be furious and thwart Wula's wedding. Koni had such mixed emotions. She was really disappointed to see the positive changes in Lara but, at the same time, she could not help but admire the maturity in her granddaughter.

"Kakek will also ride in the Pasola," Koni said.

Lara gaped. "Against whom?"

"Kakek Ndalo!"

Lara's eyes grew wide. "What? Members of the same tribe can't fight each other!"

"He said it's just a warm-up. Just giving an example of how to behave at the real Pasola. This might be the last Pasola for your grandfather. The last memory!"

"Why his last?" Lara asked.

Koni did not answer her.

"What's wrong?"

Koni answered with a question. "Do you agree with Wula moving into Kakek Ndalo's house?"

Now it was Lara's turn not to answer.

Lara asked her parents for permission to seclude herself in her room and not be disturbed all day. She was very angry and poured all of her anger onto a piece of paper. Her anger bordered on hate, if it were not for trying to see Waleka, her grandfather, in just one way: to obey.

She had been raised to obey the parents who had brought her into this world. Anger, let alone hatred, was pointless. When she realized that Wula had been sold fourteen years ago, Lara had no words. She rested her head in her hands. She knew what it meant to run very far away, what it meant to be hurt on the run and not have the strength to put everything back in place.

In her solitude, Lara reluctantly realized that she had been away for too long. Short trips away or long trips away, all yielded the same outcome: She was powerless to stop her grandfather. The promise had been made. That promise influenced every subsequent decision. Regarding what Wula still had to go through, Lara was convinced that Wula did not go to Ndalo's house empty-handed. Wula brought her strength of character. If she hadn't, Wula would never have found the courage to enter Ndalo's Big House.

Lara had been away from her village for five years. She returned to find her grandfather's ancestral house standing under a flat roof. All family members should have taken responsibility for rebuilding the roof. It was not just about rebuilding the high peak of the house, but about the *Marapu Rato,* the Marapu altar, that should have been placed there. Yet no one ever mentioned this. Lara wondered what had happened to Waleka and the rest of the extended family.

Lara marveled at Koni, who never seemed to tire physically or mentally. She vowed to be as steadfast as her grandmother, as sincere as Tila Wula, and as tough as Mada Wolli. Lara also knew how to be compliant to her parents, Raga and Hamoli, who had been devoted to each other all these years, no matter how tough the challenges were that came their way. With those convictions, Lara left her room and returned to her grandmother's side.

"Why were you staying in your room?" Koni asked.

"You promised to make sambal nyale!" Lara laughed and hugged her grandmother tightly.

"Do you agree with Wula moving into Ndalo's house?" Koni wanted a definite answer from Lara.

Lara looked down for a moment. When she looked at her grandmother's face again, she changed the subject. "Oh, Wolli has come too. He wants to ride Lamura at the Pasola." To comfort Koni, she added, "Trust me! Believe me! Everything will be fine!"

Then she rushed out of the house to find Wolli, grooming Lamura. Standing next to Lamura, they both looked at the flat roof then turned to face the house where Wula now lived.

CHAPTER 37

Near the edge of the cliff, Waleka sat contemplating. Ratenggaro was eerily quiet, as almost all the villagers were at the beach for Bau Nyale. Some women were in their homes, cooking and preparing food for family and guests. Waleka wished he could bring back the old days. Things were no longer the same.

For many years, Waleka had played an important role in the annual search for sea worms. He and Ndalo had always accompanied the rato in performing the sea worm summoning ceremony, held right before the villagers flocked to the beach at low tide and plunged into the sea to search for sea worms. Groping under the rocks and mud of the seabed, everyone tried to catch as many nyale as possible.

From the edge of the cliff, Waleka looked across the village. He could see the women bustling around their fire at the back door of every ancestral house.

Waleka did not look up; he did not want to catch the shadows of the tall roofs that buried the flat roof of his own uma parona. The shadows cast a smothering sense of pain on his shoulders.

His eyes travelled to his uma parona — to the pile of long round logs, sturdy beams, and bamboo stakes stacked against the side of his house. He startled, realizing how long those building materials had been piled there without the roof work ever being started. The wood had weathered from years of exposure to rain and sun. The wind had sprinkled them with the dust of time and deteriorated the material. The wooden poles, peeling and black, were now anchoring clotheslines. The stacks of building materials were now seats for old people and places for children to play hopscotch. Passersby chewing betel nut spat wherever they wanted, so parts were sprinkled with dried betel spit.

Occasionally, in the past, he had seen Koni wash off the red stains. But Koni had long stopped paying attention to the materials to rebuild their house. Waleka did not have time to take care of his roof. His time was spent traveling from village to village. As an elder, he was always invited to family events in the villages of his wives' relatives. He had become the head of the household in each of his nine wives' homes. Time had passed very quickly, and he was shocked when he realized he could no longer solve the problems that befell his children and grandchildren.

"Why has the roof of our ancestral house not been repaired yet?" one of Waleka's grandchildren had asked, without Waleka knowing for sure if the child was indeed a grandchild and, if so, which of his children was the child's parent. "It's been a long time," the child continued, and Waleka did not know which wife was the child's mother.

Waleka remembered how Raga, his eldest son, had left him without looking back. He remembered how Raga returned several years later. To this day, Raga had never initiated a conversation with him. Raga only spoke when he was asked a question. And, as a parent, Waleka was very careful in choosing his questions. He always worried about what Raga's answers might be to certain topics.

"Waleka! He's just a child! Raga is just a son! Why are you worried?" Ndalo's words sprang into Waleka's mind. "Children and grandchildren can replace us when we've been buried — when we're living with our ancestors, in the praing marapu, in the afterlife. Before that, we are in charge!"

"Really?" Waleka had asked.

"You have to be firm, Leka," Ndalo had continued, with full calculations of the benefits and costs to himself. "If you are not firm, your children and grandchildren will trample you. I'm telling you this because it's been proven! Remember! You are a parent, you are an elder held in high esteem by the whole community. How can you give in?"

"Giving in does not mean losing," Waleka had replied.

"Nonsense!" Ndalo scoffed. "Who told you that? Hey, father-in-law! Don't think about anything else. Don't pay attention to children and grandchildren who like to oppose your decisions." Ndalo paused for a moment and looked at Waleka with gleaming eyes. "Do you want to rebuild your uma parona? It's easy! After the wedding, I will rebuild your uma parona with a towering roof as a reminder of the occasion!"

Waleka had shuddered at the reminder of the upcoming wedding. He regretted that his actions had been based on his own selfish benefit.

"Hey, Father-in-law!" Ndalo's jeering voice had jolted Waleka. "Only a few more sunsets after today, and you'll be my father-in-law!" Ndalo had chuckled triumphantly. Patting Waleka's shoulder, he had said, "It's just a matter of hours before all our dreams are realized. Thank you, Rato, for being true to your promise. Keeping a promise equals self-worth. Right?"

Ndalo had left him, tightening his sarong and folding it around his waist. Then he had adjusted his headdress and spat.

The memory caused Waleka to rise. For a moment, he looked at the sea. The breeze blowing inland felt stronger. He summoned all his strength to walk back into his house. He was going to stop Ndalo. He was going to pour his heart and mind out to Mada Wolli, whom he believed could solve this problem.

At the Pasola that day, Mada Wolli, Waleka's favorite son, would replace him. Mada Wolli had to be expert in both riding and javelin throwing. Waleka had to make sure that Wolli had enough courage to fight Ndalo. He would take care of that himself. Ndalo would never be his son-in-law. He wanted Mada Wolli to make that happen so that he would not lose face in front of anyone. "You have to defeat me at the Pasola!" Waleka remembered shouting at Ndalo. "If you win, Wula will become your ninth wife! But if you lose, I take Wula back!" His chest had burned as he said that.

"You will never defeat me!" Ndalo had grinned and spat. "Just watch!"

Now, Waleka's knees shook. He sat back down and dropped his head into his hands. Ruffling his whitened hair, he finally cried. He realized his regret might have come too late.

Although his hearing had started to diminish with age, Waleka could still catch the voices coming from the beach — those returning on foot and on horseback. The children's voices always arrived first, followed by those of women and men.

Waleka changed into the outfit he was going to wear when riding in the Pasola. Feeling boisterous, he stacked three destars on top of one another. The first headdress was red, topped by a black one, crowned with a blood-red one. His black sarong had a horse motif, and the sash that crossed his chest covered his black T-shirt.

Waleka felt the same as he did some forty years ago when he brought Koni into his ancestral house. He had felt invincible after defeating a sprinting opponent with the javelin he had thrown from the back of Lamura at a full gallop.

*C*HAPTER *38*

The morning of the Pasola, Koni sat alone in a corner of her room. Trying to organize her thoughts, she held her head tightly. Zoga, Ndalo's son, had suddenly returned to the village. She vividly remembered how, decades ago, the news that Ndalo had kidnapped a young woman and brought her into his ancestral home had spread like wildfire. Zoga had been courting that sixteen-year-old girl, with the intention of making her another wife of his. When he found out what his father had done, Zoga vented his anger by selling cattle and land. He rummaged through heirlooms, then fled from Ratenggaro, leaving behind his pregnant wife. The event was especially clear in Koni's mind because it had happened at the same time Waleka brought home a new wife in the same way. This had made his son, Raga, so angry that the boy chose to go away to school in Weetebula.

The rumors about Zoga's son Koda, and his role in Tila Wula's life, never bothered Koni. Instead, she had been puzzled by Zoga's shouting, at the gate of their ancestral house, about Wula belonging to Koda. The rumor had quickly spread throughout the village and farther afield.

Then, Koda's biological mother had come to visit her. The woman had wanted to tell Koni that she would accept Wula into her home if Wula married Koda. "The only good that Zoga can do for his son Koda is to arrange a marriage between Koda and Wula," she had said.

Now, alone in her room, Koni felt alarmed. *Was there really a conspiracy to kidnap Tila Wula? Would Wula be saved from Ndalo in this way?*

She opened the chest in the corner of her bedroom and took out all the cloths. Unfolding them one by one, she stroked each one gently, then folded and returned them. From another small chest, she took out a sarong and cradled the cloth against her heart. "I wish you well, Wula." Koni placed the sarong on her knees and buried her face into it.

"Inya, why did you agree to Waleka riding in the Pasola against Ndalo?" Logo and Uka suddenly appeared in front of her.

Koni lifted her face and looked at her two stepsons.

"Will you take responsibility for anything that happens, Inya?" Logo's tone was challenging and arrogant. "You should have stopped him, instead of agreeing with him Inya; everyone is surprised and angry!"

"Did you ask Waleka to ride in the Pasola against Ndalo, Inya?" Uka probed. "Or perhaps Raga and Wolli are planning to kill Bapa Leka!"

"Yes! They want the rights to our ancestral house!" Logo shouted. "They want the rights to all our property! Let them try! If they think they can, they have another think coming!"

Uka's eyes bulged in his reddened face. "Everyone is saying that Wula is secretly in love with Koda. Now, wouldn't that bring shame to the entire family!"

The hateful haranguing continued, even after Hamoli arrived with news of Lara. "Lara went to visit Inya Pitu in her fieldhouse," Hamoli said breathlessly. "She brought gifts for Galuh's baby; she brought notebooks and school bags for her older kids."

"What?" Koni asked in surprise. "Lara is visiting Galuh? She's sending Galuh's children to school?"

"Lara will send all of Inya Pitu's children to school!" Hamoli smiled proudly. "Lara is paying for their education! She has contacted Bapa Bili in Weetebula to ask his help for a scholarship."

"Father Bili? A scholarship?" Koni could not believe Lara's change from hate to love.

"Yes, Inya! Father Bili is an advisor to a foundation that helps advance education." Still smiling, Hamoli placed her hand on her chest as an expression of gratitude for what her daughter was doing.

Koni was still trying to process the change in Lara's and Galuh's relationship. It was such a contrast to the events of six years ago!

"Oh, Lara has come back?" Logo chuckled meanly.

"It's a conspiracy," Uka grunted.

"Tell Tila Wula not to make trouble!" Logo warned. "Also tell Wolli! Don't let him fight on the Pasola field to take Tila Wula away from Ndalo and bring shame to us all!"

Koni said nothing.

When distant voices from the Pasola field drifted into the house, Logo and Uka left. The two women — Lara's mother and grandmother — watched them go in silence. Koni rested her head on the small chest. Quiet tears trickled from her closed eyes. The sounds carried by the wind from the Pasola field shrouded her with sorrow.

"Inya, don't worry about Uka and Logo," Hamoli said to comfort her. Before leaving to join the other women preparing food at the cooking fire, she added, "And remember, Wolli found a nyale nest!"

Koni sat back and thought about the nyale nest Wolli had found that morning. Something of great importance was going to happen to the lives of her children, her husband, and her extended family. Decades ago, the nyale nest had been in Waleka's hands. Today, the nyale nest was in Wolli's. *Something is going to happen.* Nature always gave signs in accordance to the reality humans faced. The nyale nest was a clear sign that the best Pasola ever would take place that day.

Wula fingered the balcony rail as she walked down the stairs behind Inya Tua. At the foot of the stilt house, she turned to look at the houses closest to the coastal cliff. Although there were several towering roofs lined up there, she could see where her parents' house was located, because its roof had never been rebuilt to look like that of a traditional ancestral house.

It should have been rebuilt fourteen years ago, she thought. *It's a pity the belis was used to pay for another wife and not to rebuild the house!* "Inya …" she said aloud.

"What's wrong?" Inya Tua turned to look at her.

"Nothing."

"Don't worry. You will be a good wife. I will take care of you, guide you, accompany you!" Inya Tua's voice was flat, making it hard for Wula to gauge the mood of the older woman.

"Yes, Inya," Tila Wula replied with a calmness that differed from the demeanor of the other wives.

Inya Tua sensed it. *This girl seems calm, decisive, and certain.*

Tila Wula's heart fluttered as she thought about her current circumstance. Becoming a wife was an unspoken wish of every woman. But becoming the ninth wife was something totally different.

Tila Wula felt as if she were floating, as if her feet never touched the ground. She had known for many years that her father had betrothed her to Ndalo, but never did she think she would actually have to carry out the pre-arranged marriage. She steeled herself to walk with confidence. Ahead of her, Inya Tua walked, head held high.

The grasslands stretched on either side of the road, giving the wind freedom to play. Wula looked at the tall grasses swaying. *Who says the wind can't be seen?* Startled, Wula heard the words Wolli and Koda had spoken long ago. *The wind can be easily seen when it plays with the grass, the treetops, leaves, and even the sky-high palm fronds behind our village.* But now, she was definitely not playing with the wind nor the grasses nor anything else around Ratenggaro.

As she followed Inya Tua into the Maliti Bondo Ate Pasola field, Wula straightened and walked in with measured steps, feeling everyone's eyes fastened on her.

The stands were still filling with spectators. Wula followed Inya Tua to their seats on the western stands, in the top row, on the left. From there, they could clearly see the entire Pasola field. The sidelines were densely packed with spectators from both competing villages.

From the moment she entered the field, Wula felt all eyes staring at her with a mixture of wonder, admiration, and disappointment, reflecting each person's individual beliefs. Some were astonished that the young 22-year-old college graduate was willing to be the ninth wife. Some admired her willingness to fulfill her father's dowry-paid promise made more than a dozen years ago. Some were disappointed and resentful because the marriage was continuing the old custom of polygamy.

In Ratenggaro, nothing was a secret. People preferred to speak frankly, whether it was about gossip they had heard or something they had experienced first-hand.

"Hey, Tila Wula!" One of the nearby women immediately took a stab at Wula. "Are you already staying in Ndalo's house? Ugh! So you're going to marry that old man? Aren't you the same age as his grandchildren?"

"Yes, Wula," said another. "You're beautiful — a teacher too! Why would you want to do this?"

"How rich is he?" asked a third. "Don't you find it disgusting to be his ninth wife?"

Tila Wula remained quiet.

"Inya Tua, did you give your permission?" asked another woman.

"Disgusting! It's because of the dowry, isn't it, Inya Tua? So you just gave the old man to Tila Wula." The first woman continued blabbering, not caring who heard her. "He did not have enough with eight wives? Now he wants a ninth? The ninth is the prettiest and youngest. Oh, but wait! I'm younger —"

Inya Tua interrupted calmly. "It's better to be the ninth wife than to be you."

"Oooo, Inya Tua is blind with jealousy!" one of the women crowed. She spat on the grass at the side of the stand.

On both ends of the field, a number of horses from the two competing villages stood ready. Some riders had warmed up by riding their horses around the field. Meanwhile, the spectators were still arriving.

Tila Wula's heart lurched when she saw Koda and Wolli in the center of the field. "Are they both riding in the Pasola this time?" she whispered to herself.

Perhaps it was only Koni who understood what was going on when Waleka had suddenly asked for her blessing to face Ndalo during the warm-up. She knew there was a secret agreement between the two men that involved Wula. Koni was placing a lot of faith in the nyale nest Wolli had found.

Koni couldn't do anything else but tell Raga what Logo and Uka had said before they left. Raga had not replied, but his face hardened as he left for the Pasola field.

Although Raga had never ridden in a Pasola, he knew it was the best place to test one's riding skills and ability to unhorse opponents by throwing javelins from atop a galloping horse. Pasola was considered a ceremonial activity to express friendship, kinship, harmony, togetherness, and a prediction of the future. That was why everyone looked forward to it. Pasola also brought together those who were separated, reconciled differences, and promoted forgiveness with hope for a better future.

Raga's heart pounded when he arrived at the Pasola field with Lara and her siblings. He saw police cars and a number of police motorcycles. Some policemen sat under the stands' awning; others were scattered at several points around the field; still others roamed the crowd, wearing civilian clothes. Raga recognized some of them.

Surprised by the police presence, Lara asked, "Why are there policemen, Bapa? Is it not safe? What's wrong?" Lara and her group quickly made their way to the empty stand at the upper section. All eyes watched Lara with various thoughts and judgments.

The atmosphere was already tense when Zoga entered the field. His thin, lanky body bent over the horse he rode. Tila Wula could see the old man. Zoga held the reins with one hand, while holding a fan in his other, fanning himself continuously. The air was hot, despite a strong, dry wind. Koda quietly ushered Zoga off the field.

Wula watched him. *Poor Koda*, she said to herself. Wula startled when she saw Ama Dula and a number of his men loitering around the stand where she sat with Inya Tua. Wula re-centered herself and focused on Koda leading Zoga's horse, while Zoga sat limply in his saddle.

The sun crept higher until it hung like an umbrella over the Maliti Bondo Ate Pasola field and covered it with its heat.

Cheering crowds encouraged the riders warming up. Spectators now filled the stands and the edges of the field. Ndalo's fifth wife was among those who crammed into the stand.

Tila Wula rose as soon as she saw her father enter the field. Mada Wolli walked beside Lamura, the horse Waleka rode. Behind him, Koda walked alongside Wangga, the horse Ndalo rode.

"What happened?" Wula asked. "Who is going to compete?"

"Ndalo will fight Waleka," Inya Tua replied. "It is only for a warm-up. It's not a real fight because both of them are from the same team representing our kabisu."

"So then why do they look like they're going to compete in a match?" Wula asked worriedly.

"It's fine," Inya Tua explained. "It's just a warm-up to set an example of how to fight properly in a Pasola."

"Bapa didn't say that," Tila Wula replied. "He didn't plan on being here today. He isn't feeling well. What's going on?" Agitated, Tila Wula stood, ready to leave the stand to see her father and brother.

"Sit down!" Inya Tua commanded. "Everything will be all right!"

"I'm afraid Bapa will get hurt," Wula said, sitting.

"There are only one or two rounds in the opening of the Pasola. His participation is a sign that he supports your marriage after this Pasola."

"But ..." Wula's throat closed.

"It's okay." Inya Tua patted Wula's shoulder. Tila Wula felt a strange sense of love in the gesture. *Is Inya Tua sincere?*

"Bapa!" Tila Wula shouted when Waleka passed by the front of her stand.

Waleka did not turn his head, but Mada Wolli did. He waved while holding Lamura's reins tightly. Koda did not turn his head, but Ndalo did, waving and grinning big.

Wula immediately dropped back into her seat and shuddered. The old man was not giving her a friendly smile, he was leering at her!

"Bapa Ndalo! You must win!" Ndalo's eighth wife called out. The fifth wife joined her. "Bapa! You must win!"

Ndalo turned to wave and smile at the eighth wife. Only the two of them understood the meaning of his smile.

"Gha Mada Wolli!" a woman shouted among the voices responding to what was happening in today's Pasola. Mada Wolli, however, did not respond to her call. He kept his eyes on Tila Wula and continued to wave until Lamura and Waleka passed the stand and entered the field.

Mada Wolli and Waleka headed to the right side of the field; Ndalo and Koda headed to the left.

Tila Wula's heart pounded at the thought of what was going to happen.

The tense atmosphere on the Pasola field heightened without anyone knowing about the agreement between Ndalo and Waleka in this Pasola warm-up. A friendly encounter before the actual Pasola competition was unusual. The two old, strong-willed men forced their way to perform.

Ndalo's spirit was burning to bring Waleka down on the Pasola field. He promised himself he would defeat Waleka in a friendly round and set an example of a proper Pasola. His manhood was challenged to the core. He did not want to lose.

Waleka trembled in the face of accusations from the Pasola crowd that he was the cause of all the village's problems. But he dared to face Ndalo on the Pasola field for the sake of his daughter's dignity.

Waleka and Ndalo were both consumed by anger. This would be the last Pasola for both, regardless of the outcome. They would risk their lives out of a dual sense of regret and a need to unload a heavy burden. Both were as anxious as a twisting caterpillar on a smoldering piece of wood. Under the guise of performing a friendly match to set a good example, the two would actually fight with everything they had, on a sun-scorched field, to either save or possess Tila Wula.

The sun crept higher and the air grew even hotter. Cheers erupted as the two men faced one another. The whinnying sounds of women's kayiliking colored the annual event that could bring rain or fire.

"Ririri ... ririri ... riri ... riri ... ririri ... riririri ...." The neighing women from all corners of the field stirred everyone's hearts.

CHAPTER 39

Thus, the 1980 Pasola would open, with a friendly performance by Waleka and Ndalo. Both would demonstrate the proper equestrian skills. Both would show how to hold the reins, how to control the horse, how to move while sitting high in the saddle, and how to throw the javelin while in full gallop.

Waleka stood out among the other horsemen. He wore a colorful headdress. A sarong with horse patterns wrapped his waist. A brownish-red sash crossed his chest and back. He held the reins in his left hand, while using his right to pull out javelins fastened to both sides of Lamura, his favorite horse.

On the left side of the field, the opening of the Pasola was being prepared by the elders. Cheers erupted when Ndalo entered the field spurring Wangga into a gallop. Waleka, riding Lamura, did the same.

"Bapaaa!" Tila Wula shouted every time her father passed in front of her stand.

But Waleka never once turned his head to her.

It was Ndalo, the old man who would become her husband soon, who turned around and raised his hand.

Inya Tua watched Tila Wula and repeated, "They are not in a fight. They are just setting an example for children and grandchildren.

Neither will be unhorsed by a javelin." But her voice trembled and her heart raced.

"Yes, I know, Inya," Tila Wula replied.

"Both are in their sixties. They have been friends since childhood and lived in the same village for generations."

"Yes, I know, Inya," Tila Wula repeated.

Inya Tua looked tense as she surveyed the Pasola field with a pounding heart. She mumbled, "I hope Waleka defeats Ndalo."

"Why, Inya?" Wula asked.

"I hope Ndalo loses!" Inya Tua rephrased her words.

"I thought you said this was just a warm-up?" Tila Wula asked.

"Who do *you* hope wins?" Inya Tua replied. "Your father? Or Ndalo?"

Tila Wula, not understanding what Inya Tua meant, shook her head. From the movement of her hand, Tila Wula knew that Inya Tua had quickly wiped away tears.

"Look over there!" Inya Tua said. "The two of them look dashing on the field!"

"Is it really just a warm-up?" Tila Wula asked. "Is it really just a demonsration?"

Inya Tua answered by taking a deep breath.

Tila Wula raised her face. She tried to send her thoughts to the rider of Lamura, the black horse with the white mark on its forehead. *Bapa ... Don't be sad. I can get through this difficulty. Compete! Show your respectability by setting the right example of riding in a Pasola. Didn't you say that Pasola is a way to display our honesty, loyalty, pride, and respect to our ancestors?* Tila Wula straightened herself. She wanted to shout, *Bapa, I'm here to witness your skill in riding in the Pasola with pride.* Instead, she swallowed, and the words became only a whisper in her heart.

Waleka raised his face. Even though they were far away, he could clearly see Tila Wula in the western part of the field, standing next to Inya Tua. *Tila Wula,* he vowed, *Bapa will take you home.*

Waleka spurred Lamura. With a single tug on his reins, Lamura darted onto the field as Ndalo approached with equal speed. Waleka dodged and turned Lamura before, seconds later, heading straight toward Ndalo, who flinched as the javelin flew so fast it almost grazed his temple.

In the next second, Ndalo, chasing Waleka, pulled a javelin from its holster and threw it with all his might. The javelin narrowly missed Waleka's waist. The tense audience broke into cheers as Lamura proudly reared. This infuriated Ndalo and Wangga.

"Ririri ... ririri ... ririri ... riri ... riri ... riririiiiiiiii!" The sound of women kayiliking contributed to the excitement of the crowd.

A second round could not be stopped. The council of elders agreed to one more round of the warm-up match. All the young men felt pride. They wanted to be like Waleka and Ndalo, with their perfect posture and handling skills, as they controlled the reins and threw javelins while leaning forward to maximize speed. Both men were exemplary to-paholongs.

"Drop him, Waleka, drop him!" Inya Tua called out clearly. "Drop him now! Waleka come on, come on Walekaaa!" Inya Tua's shouting resembled a horse's whinny. The old woman grew short-winded, encouraging Waleka.

"Inya." Tila Wula reached for the older woman's hand, but Inya Tua gently pushed her away.

"Ndalo must lose to make my wishes come true." Inya Tua gasped at hearing her own words spoken aloud. "Oh, no! This is not the actual competition. They are just setting an example. After this round, the real Pasola will begin." She returned her gaze to the field.

Bapa Waleka, please don't fall. Be careful, Bapa! Tila Wula had caught a glimpse of excitement in Inya Tua's eyes when she said, "Ndalo must lose to make my wishes come true." Inya Tua's voice sounded hoarse amid the cheers. "This is just a warm-up," she repeated.

"He's old, but he's still so handsome," someone in the audience said.

"Waleka and Ndalo have always been good riders at a Pasola," another added, as the two horsemen attacked and threw javelins at one another with all their might.

Tila Wula stared transfixed when Waleka spurred Lamura toward Ndalo, who appeared undaunted in facing Waleka. Lamura and Wangga chased each other and carried their respective masters to thunderous applause and endless cheers.

Ndalo raised his javelin high and threw it just as Lamura came face-to-face with Wangga. The tip of the javelin struck Waleka in the chest, and he toppled off his horse.

"Bapa!" Tila Wula let out a long cry. "Get up, Bapa! Get up! This is just a warm-up."

"Get up! Get up!" Inya Tua shouted. "You know Ndalo cannot win! He mustn't!"

Tila Wula sat while Inya Tua kept shouting amidst the whinnying women in the arena. Wula covered her face with her hands, hoping that her father would not suffer an injury that could be paralyzing, even deadly. When Wula stood again, Waleka was getting up slowly with the help of Mada Wolli and Koda. Meanwhile, Ndalo's followers were cheering.

"Enough!" Mada Wolli said. "This is not supposed to be a match. This is supposed to be just a warm-up. Why did Ndalo throw his javelin as if he were fighting in a real competition?" Mada Wolli supported Waleka, who was bent forward in severe pain. As Waleka collapsed at the edge of the field, Wolli muttered, "And why were you trying so hard to fight back? Enough!"

The presiding elder and council of traditional elders immediately convened in a corner of the field. Mada Wolli accepted the assignment to continue the match. He was going to have to fight Koda who would replace Ndalo, his grandfather. The event was paused while Mada Wolli and some family members started to accompany Waleka home safely.

The warm-up match was considered complete, and the actual Pasola was about to begin. Ndalo led the Ratenggaro team against Lamboya, led by Mada Wolli, on the Maliti Bondo Ate field.

Tila Wula wanted to run to her father, but Inya Tua held her back. "Your place is here," the older woman said, "Not there. Just hope that Ndalo will lose in the next round against Wolli."

Tila Wula wished that the actual Pasola competition had ended. "I'll be back, Inya!" Without waiting for Inya Tua's reply, Tila Wula quickly climbed down the stand, ran across the field, and stopped the entourage that was taking her father home.

"Bapa!" Wula burst into the crowd. She placed her head on her father's left shoulder while trying to hold back her tears. "Are you all right?" she asked, although it was clear her father was hurt in the upper right part of his chest.

Waleka bent over and his right shoulder leaned forward. "It's all right," Waleka's voice was almost inaudible. "That was just a warm-up."

"Bapa ..." Wula's voice trembled.

"Go! Inya Tua is waiting for you there." Waleka looked down and signaled with his hand to be taken home to Ratenggaro. *I'm sorry your father was unable to take you home*, Waleka thought. Meanwhile, the crowd around them was growing, and still Wula did not move.

Wolli touched her shoulder and persuaded her to return to Inya Tua. "Everything can be resolved," he said almost in a whisper. "Many people here will be full of suspicions; you know that. It is best to leave now. Trust me!"

The two of them only exchanged a quick glance, but Wula had found confidence in those familiar eyes.

Koda joined them. Standing at Wula's other side, he assured her gently, "Listen to Wolli. Everything can be resolved. Trust me!"

Raga, Lara, and Ida stood behind Wula. Lara, followed by Ida, had been the fastest to run towards Waleka after he was unhorsed from Lamura. Lara was silent. Her look of sadness and disappointment was difficult to describe.

Raga was also silent. The quiet man's hands shook as he lifted his father onto the palanquin.

So her father had been unhorsed by a hard stab of the javelin. Wula sensed there was something behind the meeting between her father and her future husband. For a moment, she doubted the warm-up match story. She tried to understand and convinced herself to step up to defend her father's honor — no matter what.

Wolli, Raga, and other family members took Waleka home.

"Let's help take Kakek home," Lara said to Wula.

"I'm staying here," Wula replied quietly.

Wolli took a deep breath as he turned around to watch Tila Wula return to the stand with her head held high.

CHAPTER *40*

Seated firmly in his saddle, Ndalo circled the Pasola field. He had insisted on continuing to compete in order to convince the Pasola riders and spectators that ups and downs in a match were normal. This was how Ndalo cunningly turned other people's losses to his advantage.

When the Pasola started again, he wanted to go head-to-head with Mada Wolli. He did not want to be replaced by Koda. He was confident that he was still strong enough to unhorse Mada Wolli, the young man who had found a nyale nest that morning. "Who does he think he is?" Ndalo muttered and spit.

Ndalo did not care about anyone. He was very proud of himself. He knew where Tila Wula and Inya Tua were sitting on the western stand, and even though he also knew that his future wife walked with her head held high, he did not care. Victory was already in his hands.

He whipped Wangga's flanks, and the horse carried him around the field before stopping right in front of the western stand. Wangga reared high. His whinny split Inya Tua's disappointment over Waleka's defeat, and pierced Tila Wula's deep sadness over watching her injured father being carried off the field.

The cheers of the crowd rose when Ndalo remained on Wangga, unwilling to dismount, and insisted on riding against Mada Wolli and the riders from Lamboya. Ndalo did not want to relinquish his golden opportunity to his grandson Koda.

Let it be! Inya Tua hoped fervently. *May the old man get down on his knees and overcome his growing lust.*

Ndalo was thinking, *Koda might allow Wolli to win, That can't happen. My grandchildren cannot be the main obstacle to my marrying Tila Wula!*

Mada Wolli and the other horsemen were returning from taking Waleka home. Raga and Lara had also returned to the field. The Pasola continued. Mada Wolli and Koda were the stars — at least that was what the audience expected. But what the audience witnessed next was the rivalry between Ndalo and Mada Wolli.

This second round of Pasola was filled with screams and whinnying. Inya Tua sat down and cried. She was very afraid of the Pasola's outcome. *May the old man who knows no borders, lose! Lose!*

On the leftside stand, Ndalo's eighth wife jumped up and whinnied loudly, cheering on Ndalo.

Saddened, Tila Wula had returned to her seat. She heard a woman's shrill voice on Ndalo's side, among the other voices. Wula fixed her eyes on Mada Wolli, as if forcing him to return her gaze and hear her message. "Be careful," she whispered, as he led Lamura onto the right side of the field where the group from Lamboya had gathered.

Although they had only exchanged a glance, both Wolli and Wula knew with certainty that each was present for the other, and Tila Wula knew that Wolli had received her message. She watched some of the other women rushing to the stand to get the best spot.

When she saw Ndalo enter the field from the left gate, Tila Wula stared straight ahead. He sat high in the saddle, assuring Tila Wula of his presence.

"You're my wife," Ndalo muttered to himself. "I'll make sure of it today. Where can you run off to? You will bow at my feet!" Ndalo spurred his horse and galloped at top speed around the field, followed closely by the other horsemen, testing their opponents' steadfastness before returning to the left side of the field.

"Where's Gha Koda?" Tila Wula asked. Looking around the field, she watched the riders warming up in the center of the field. "Isn't Gha Koda the one who will compete against Gha Wolli?"

"Mada Wolli against Ndalo," Inya Tua said. Her voice was filled with noticeable disappointment. "This all happened because Waleka lost! Did he intentionally lose so he can get rid of you?" Tila Wula flinched at Inya Tua's sharp voice.

"What, exactly, do you mean?" Tila Wula asked. "What must happen? What decides whether I go back to my home or whether I stay with you and Bapa Ndalo?" Her voice was drowned out by the boisterous noise on the stands and around the field. Wula soon realized that something was very wrong in this Pasola match.

Ndalo rode Wangga, as the horse galloped and reared in the neutral area of the field, between the two competing teams. Mada Wolli, riding Lamura, also entered. Wolli raised his javelin high, swinging it in arcs back and forth before returning to the right side of the field.

The elders had just finished carrying out the customary rituals to approve the second round between Ndalo and Mada Wolli — the actual Pasola.

"The ancestors guard and protect."

"There is no grudge. No animosity."

"This is a friendly match for the sake of family and the future."

"For fertility. For the sake of love. For the land of Sumba."

"Ratenggaro and Lamboya. Let's begin!"

The Pasola began with cheers. Koda had dismounted and now stood in a far corner of the field. Anger at his grandfather flushed his face. Ndalo had not wanted to change places. He still wanted to fight Mada Wolli after unhorsing Waleka in an unorthodox way. Koda turned to look at the stand. All he saw were heads of people watching the Pasola. Koda knew where his grandmother sat with Wula, his grandfather's future wife. The night before, his grandmother had told him the secret behind the match between his grandfather and Tila Wula's father. If Waleka won, it would mean the dowry had been paid back and the marriage between Tila Wula and his grandfather would be canceled. Koda was in favor of this as a way of freeing his grandmother from repeated pain. His anger at his grandfather was as strong as his affection for his grandmother.

Ndalo, however, sensed Koda's true intentions.

The old man ignored Koda completely. He immediately jumped onto Wangga's back and sped around the field with a satisfied smile until he reached the stand where Inya Tua and Wula were seated.

Koda stood silently at the very back of the layer of spectators who watched, filled with suspense and partiality, unable to imagine what would happen after Waleka had been unhorsed. Mada Wolli was much younger than Ndalo. His chance to unhorse Ndalo was not only obvious, but could easily be deadly. Koda chose to stay away in the hope that no one would get hurt. Koda left the Pasola field, trembling. He did not want to witness any sad events that might occur. *Hopefully, Mada Wolli won't throw his javelin so hard that it kills Kakek. Even though someone has to be the winner, his win does not need to have deadly consequences.*

Koda led his horse leisurely down to the beach. "Ah, Tila Wula shouldn't be Kakek's wife," he muttered as he cast his gaze far out to sea. The horizon was firmly outlined against the blue sky. A pair of ospreys flashed across, both flying low and screeching loudly before gobbling the food they caught at the sea surface.

The two groups from Ratenggaro and Lamboya moved as close as possible to their respective opponent. Javelins flew. The chaotic atmosphere on the field, where throwing and dodging quickly crescendoed into a frenzy, accompanied the whinnying and cheering. During the heat and tension of the moment, protecting the horse from the opponent's javelin was also a skill. The cheers erupted when the rider sped up, the javelin moved through the air, and the target moved as well.

"Ririri ... ririri ... riri ... riri ... riririiiiiii!" The kayiliking of the women echoed. Wangga returned to the right field and Lamura to the left. The crowd screamed encouragement. The tension of the Pasola was part of the entertainment. Almost all the spectators expected Mada Wolli to defeat Ndalo, not only to restore his father's pride, but also for Tila Wula's sake.

"Fight! Fight! Fight!" Ndalo's supporters shouted. "Beat him! Beat him! Beat him!"

"A match for the sake of fertility, gratitude, and the future!" shouted the crowd who supported no one.

Every time he passed the main stand, Mada Wolli valiantly turned his head for a moment to catch the shadows of two women sitting there. He knew that Tila Wula sat with Inya Tua on the highest left side of the stand. Voices from the high stand resounded. The shouts got louder when Mada Wolli's javelin hit Ndalo's arm holding the reins, throwing Ndalo from his horse.

"Get up! Get up! Get up!" the shouts came from Ndalo's eighth wife, who had come down from the stand and now stood on the sidelines. It was hard to tell who this young woman was supporting with her screams. One was her husband, the other was a handsome man who deserved the love of a young woman like her. Jealousy filled the eighth wife's heart.

Tila Wula remained transfixed, looking at the entire field. In stark contrast to the anxiety that held her, the air was clear with a gentle wind. In the sky, clusters of white clouds spread thin, then disappeared. Just as it had at the Nyale, earlier that morning, the sky held no sign of sorrow.

Tila Wula thrummed with fear. She could not figure out the connection between the signs given by the Nyale and the ongoing Pasola. *I will become Ndalo's wife.* That was the only thought that really stuck.

Tila Wula and Inya Tua looked toward the center of the Pasola field. Tila Wula nodded, and Inya Tua, forty years her senior, nodded and smiled. Even though she did not know what Inya Tua really meant, Tila Wula knew the older woman was on her side.

The Pasola continued.

Tila Wula startled when she noticed a woman, who she knew had eyes for Mada Wolli, giving her an attitude from the bottom of the stand at the edge of the Pasola field. The woman whinnied to encourage her man. Wula met the challenge and returned the woman's stare with a steadfast gaze.

The woman's whinny filled the air, breaking above the cheers and thundering hooves rumbling around the Pasola field. The whinnies that sounded like a song accompanied Wangga and Lamura among those of other horses.

Wangga galloped side-by-side with Lamura. Suddenly, Wangga turned to block Lamura, then immediately reversed.

Lamura raised his head high at the same time that Wolli pulled the reins, and the flying javelin pierced Lamura's neck. Wolli fell, and Lamura bolted across the field alone. Neighing loudly in pain, the horse with the white blaze galloped, riderless, around the field.

Wolli hit the ground hard. Several of the riders tried to grab Lamura's reins, but the horse was too fast. Lamura reared as blood flowed from the base of his neck. It was clear to the audience and players alike that Lamura had been wounded by a sharp javelin tip.

"Lamura is hurt!"

"Mada Wolli lost!"

"You must be ready to surrender tonight."

Tila Wula trembled at the sound of those voices. She saw Lamura spin around in a desperate search for his master. When he came to the place where Wolli lay unconscious, the stallion bowed his head. The people crowding around Wolli parted and made room for the horse with the white blaze. Lamura snorted and touched his master with a gentle nudge.

Tila Wula could see the blood pulsing from Lamura's neck. "Paghogha Mada Wolli, Gha Wolli!" Wula shouted. She wanted to jump off the stand and run through the crowd to get close to Wolli. She wanted to scream Mada Wolli's name over and over again and hug the unconscious man with all her strength. She started towards the stairs, but a cold, firm grip clamped her arm and pulled her back.

"Be quiet!" Inya Tua hissed. "Stay put and calm down!" Without taking her eyes off the scene in the field below them, she growled, "Control yourself! Don't give them the satisfaction." Inya Tua tone changed. In a regret-filled voice that was almost inaudible, she said, "Why is this happening? Wolli should have won!"

"Ririri ... ririri ... riri ... riri ... riririiiiiii ...." The women's kayiliking blared again.

The cheering enlivened the event and celebrated the victory. A fall was something the crowd looked forward to; retaliation indicated another victory.

Wula forced herself to remain seated next to Inya Tua at the highest part of the stand. Some women comforted her with concern.

CHAPTER 41

Lara and Ida ran along with the spectators from the stand and in the field towards the center of everyone's attention — the unconscious Wolli.

"Lamura!" Lara shouted. She saw Raga trying to resuscitate Wolli and shouted even louder, "Bapa!"

"Let go of Lamura," Raga shouted, as several men attempted to calm the horse. "Leave him alone!" When the men dropped the reins, Lamura calmed. He stepped closer to his unconscious master and, blood still oozing from his neck, the horse stood by Wolli's side.

Lara took Lamura's reins and stroked the horse's forehead to ease her mounting anxiety. "Bapa, we should take Gha Wolli to Weetebula," she urged, alarmed that Wolli was still unconscious. "He needs to be hospitalized. Let's go!"

A galloping horse rapidly approached, and Koda jumped off his horse. After quietly exchanging a few words with Raga, Koda took off his shirt and wrapped it around Lamura's bleeding neck, then prepared to lead the horse home.

"There's something wrong with the tip of Kakek Ndalo's javelin," Lara said, distraught. "Look at Lamura! Look! His wound is from a sharp javelin point, not a blunt one. How is that possible? The javelins are supposed to be blunted! Who is behind this?" She searched the faces of the surrounding spectators.

"Now, now, Lara, don't blame others," said Ama Dula, as if speaking to a child. "This is Pasola." He turned away.

"Gha Wolli!" Lara dropped down next to his body. When Wolli's eyes fluttered open for just a moment, Lara's big smile and tears showed her relief.

"We will transport the injured immediately to the health center in Weetebula," the police officer said. He appeared to be the head of the Pasola security force. "Which family members want to accompany him? My officers will escort them."

"Thank you, sir," Lara and her father replied simultaneously. "We will go."

The commander turned to face Lara. "You won't be going; you're coming to the police station with me."

Confused, Lara looked up at the commander's face. "What? Me?"

Raga and a few others were already boarding the transport vehicle that held Wolli. Raga's face paled and his jaw tightened when he saw Lara being herded into a police car. "Lara!" he called to her. "Just do what they tell you. I'm going with Wolli now so we can get help quickly!"

"What did I do wrong?" Lara asked the commander as they walked to the car.

"You're under arrest on suspicion of masterminding this fiasco," the commander said.

"What? You think I'm responsible for this chaos?" Lara asked incredulously.

"You'll be given the opportunity to tell your side of the story when we get to the station," the commander said, and he ushered Lara into the car.

Tila Wula remained seated next to Inya Tua on the stand. She couldn't hear what the policemen and Raga were saying. All she saw was Wolli being placed in the transport vehicle, the police arresting Lara, and Koda guiding Lamura off the Pasola field.

The transport vehicle and police car with Lara passed the front of the stand and left the field a moment later.

News of Lara's arrest spread like a virus carried by the wind, landing, multiplying, and infecting everyone. The women and children cooking in the village ran to the Pasola field to find out what was happening.

"Ririri ... ririri ... ririri ... riri ... riri ... riririiiiiii ...." The kayiliking that rejoiced in Ndalo's victory was louder than usual. In such a state of chaos, Ndalo and his entourage were still cheered on the field. Even though the police had directed the teams to disperse immediately, Ndalo still took one more opportunity to circle the field while raising his Pasola javelin high.

Tila Wula lifted her head. Sorting through the crowd of people, she saw Ndalo on Wangga, making his way towards her. When he arrived under the stand where Wula and Inya Tua sat transfixed, the old man raised his javelin high again before he flung it up into the sky. The weapon soared through the air and fell to rest at the foot of the opposite stand, as if challenging anyone who dared to oppose him.

With his eye on Tila Wula, Ndalo made his horse prance. He looked up to the sky, bursting with pride. He reached to the heavens with his accomplishment in bringing a beautiful, young, and well-educated woman to his bed of a lifetime.

"What woman wouldn't want to kneel at the feet of the man who rules on the Pasola field?" Ndalo murmured with great satisfaction. "What woman would not be dazzled by the stalls filled cattle, the titles to vast acreage, and the great influence of a wealthy elder?"

The women's kayiliking fueled his desire. Ndalo cast his gaze at his eldest wife and his future ninth wife. The sky was bright. The sun shone directly onto the Maliti Bondo Ate field. The wind was whipping hard.

Ndalo waved with both hands at Wula and Inya Tua. The spectators also waved and cheered him on. With the support of so many people, Ndalo's hubris soared. Nothing could stop him now.

Fuelled by the crowd's adoration, Ndalo let go of the reins and stood up on Wangga's saddle. He clenched his fists and pumped his arms as high as he could, as if trying to punch a hole in the sky. As the crowd roared, Ndalo jumped straight up, as high and as hard as he could, using Wangga's saddle as a springboard.

When he landed astride the saddle, however, blinding pain shot up his groin. Ndalo gasped. He tried to grab the reins and straighten himself, but immediately collapsed forward onto Wangga's neck. Biting his lips to keep from screaming out, he tried to ignore the excruciating pain radiating from his testicles.

Ama Dula, ever close to Ndalo's side, immediately jumped onto Wangga behind Ndalo. He spurred the horse toward the village, Ndalo cursing steadily. "What happened to you?" Ama Dula shouted in Ndalo's ear.

"It's nothing!" Ndalo yelled through clenched teeth. "Just hurry up! Take me home!" Ama Dula clicked his tongue, and Wangga ran like he was flying over the earth.

Everyone wanted to know what had happened. The excitement and confusing circumstances became topics of conversation and conjecture — especially when they saw a pale, grimacing Ndalo leaning against Ama Dula's chest atop Wangga.

But no matter how many speculations split the skies of Ratenggaro, nothing could alleviate Ndalo's intense pain nor his even more intense desire to appear painless. When Ama Dula and Ndalo arrived at his home, Ndalo tried his best to walk normally as he climbed onto his terrace and entered the house. As soon as he was out of sight, however, he immediately started walking like a monkey on two feet, trying to reach for the ground, but not quite touching it.

After the Pasola crowds had cleared, Wula walked down from the stand with Inya Tua. They did not re-enter the field. The Pasola spectators were long back in their respective homes with their own speculations. When the two women arrived at the village, they walked toward Ndalo's house. Wula held on to Inya Tua, who walked with lips tightly pressed together. They ignored the stares of the curious.

CHAPTER *42*

Maybe the sign had changed. Or, maybe, the sign had remained the same, but the meaning had changed, because meaning was determined by purpose and interest.

Waleka was taken home, having failed and regretting what he had done to himself. He had been so sure that he could beat Ndalo on the Pasola field. Instead, he had been defeated and carried home on a stretcher.

Waleka didn't move as he was carried home. Koni greeted him with tears. She cried again when, next, the news reached her that Wolli had been unhorsed and carried off the Pasola field, unconscious. Meanwhile, Koda had walked the injured Lamura home, blood still dripping from a neck wound. If only Lamura could speak, Koda thought. The gallant horse would have told him how sharp the edge of the javelin was that had pierced him. Lamura blew and snorted in pain as Koda led him back to his stall under the temporary ancestral house.

Wailing could be heard from inside Waleka's ancestral house. Koni and all the family members immediately gathered for a conference. A number of Waleka's sons were also present at the meeting.

After spending a long time away, their failures or successes were apparent in their appearance.

Uka sat in a corner, looking thin. His dry, stained lips always held a cigarette. His neck sported a tattoo of a naked woman. With two wives in the village, he had been gone the longest. His third wife, thin and with a tattoo of a naked man on her neck, now accompanied him.

There was Logo, who talked a lot. As he gesticulated, the flashy rings on his fingers attracted more attention than the words he spoke. "There are only two options," Logo opened the conversation. "Yes or no. I think it should be yes. Because we suffered a tremendous loss, Ndalo should redeem the shame he brought upon us. He unhorsed Bapa Leka and victimized Wolli. Fortunately, Wolli was not wounded by the sharp tip of Ndalo's javelin, but Lamura almost bled to death because of it. And, most embarrassing, Lara was arrested. Ndalo must pay for the shame he brought upon us with a pen of cattle!" Logo's voice rose. "We are men! Where is our pride? All of us men should get a share to help remove our shame. Demand that Ndalo pay up immediately! He can marry as soon as the cattle have been delivered!"

Logo had also been away from the village for a long time. After Inya Duyo's death, he had stolen some of the family livestock and land, then left. He married another woman and settled in her village, abandoning his wife and children in Ratenggaro.

Everyone remembered Logo's departure all those years ago. They had not forgotten that he had stolen from his own family, that some cattle and plots of land had disappeared and somehow found their way into the hands of Ndalo and his lackeys.

"Why did you take what doesn't belong to you?" Koni had asked him at the time.

Logo had shouted that what he had taken belonged to Waleka, and that whatever belonged to Waleka was also his. "Whatever!" he had yelled in fury before leaving. "It's whatever I want!" He was followed by some of the brothers who agreed with him. The situation made clear that for too long, Waleka's family had been divided by different realities, challenges, and interests.

Now, Logo was taking the same stand. "Well, what do you think?" he urged the assembled group. "Do you agree with me or not? As a man, I'm truly embarrassed! How can anyone here not be ashamed? Ndalo has to pay us, and then we'll let him marry today. He can't take Tila Wula, our sister, as he likes. Ask him to pay now."

"Why are you still yelling?" Koni spoke slowly, but her soft voice silenced Logo, Uka, and the other squabbling siblings immediately. "Why do you dare take what doesn't belong to you? This family is broken because it's been left to languish by Waleka and some of his children and grandchildren for a very long time."

"What do you mean, Inya Koni?" Logo straightened his shoulders. "Is Tila Wula not my little sister? Is that not so?"

"What are you talking about?" Koni remained calm. "Tila Wula has always been your little sister and will be forever. But you've disowned her by partaking in the belis that Ndalo paid fourteen years ago. You ran off with a new wife. Your father, too, acted recklessly by marrying Inya Pitu. You two have sold Tila Wula many times."

"Inya, don't say that!" Logo held fast.

"So don't take what doesn't belong to you." Koni looked at Logo, unflinching. Finally, Logo bowed his head before rising and stalking toward the door. Raga's sudden appearance in the doorway, however, caused Logo to sit down again.

Uka spoke up, repeating Logo's words that Ndalo had to pay with a pen of cattle, an equivalent of about forty head, to make up for the family's shame.

Raga crossed the room to make sure Koni was doing well. He asked how Waleka was doing. Koni just shook her head tearfully and continued listening to the words from Logo and Uka which, she was sure, Raga would address.

Hamoli put her arm around Koni's shoulder and gently rubbed it to help calm her.

"So what do you say?" Logo asked, as if challenging Raga and Koni. He looked at Raga. "Before you came, Inya Koni and I had already talked about it!"

"Wolli is recovering," Raga said. "The injury on his left shoulder has been treated at the hospital. He is currently in Lamboya. He just needs a few days to heal." Raga paused for a moment before continuing slowly, "We are fortunate that Lamura raised his head and became a shield for Wolli. I don't know what would have happened otherwise."

"What about Lara?" asked Inya Pitu, who sat at the very back.

Raga took a deep breath. "Lara is still at the police station and after that, she will go to Weetebula to see Bapa Bili."

Uka, Logo, and several others began talking at once. "So what do we want to do with Lara at the police station? The police arrested her because she did something wrong! That girl is always causing trouble — always embarrassing the family."

Raga's jaw tightened.

"I knew it all along!" Logo spoke again. "We have been shamed, and we're in trouble because we angered our ancestors. Just look! It's been six years since our ancestral house has been completely naked with no roof. This is beyond embarrassing! Don't be surprised if another disaster befalls us! We are all cursed."

Saliva flew from Logo's mouth as he yelled. Conveniently, he overlooked that his disappearance from home had left a wound that never healed. He ignored the fact that he was Waleka's son, a notorious thief of livestock who had parceled out the ancestral land for his own benefit.

"Logo, why are you shouting?" Koni repeated. "How many times have you taken what was not yours?"

"What do you mean, Mama Inya Koni?" Logo challenged.

"You already know the answer," Koni replied. "You have undressed this house for a long time — you did so each time you took what didn't belong to you!"

"Inya!" Logo glared at Koni with mounting fury.

"Listen to what Raga has to say," Koni said. "Bapa Leka can't speak now, so let's hear what Raga, as the eldest son in our family, has to say."

Raga calmly began to share his news. "Lara is fine. The police believed her statement about the Pasola. They accepted her view as an educated person. She went to the police station to give a statement, not to be arrested!" Pride filled Raga's heart. He wanted to tell them that Ama Dula and Ndalo's attempt to frame Lara as the culprit was not believable. Everyone, including the police, knew the Pasola field was a man's territory, not a woman's.

Raga also explained that the accusation of Lara being the mastermind of the chaos on the Pasola field, was completely unfounded. The allegation that she had arranged to replace Ndalo's blunted javelin with a sharp one had been considered absurd. What Lara had done six years ago to thwart her grandfather's marriage with Inya Pitu was also regarded as unrelated.

"Who doesn't know Lara?" Logo grumbled. "This isn't the first time she caused problems. It's been proven." He pursed his lips before lighting a cigarette. Exhaling the smoke randomly, he forced the women to be quiet.

"I can assure you that Lara has handled this very well!" Raga still struggled to remain controlled. "In a couple of days, Wolli will also make a statement to the police regarding what really happened at the Pasola. I have told the police that the problem on the Pasola field is a matter for the kabisu and its elders, and we can all solve it together."

"Where is Lara now?" Koni asked anxiously.

"She is in Weetebula at Father Bili's house," Raga replied truthfully. "She is taking care of the scholarships for Ratenggaro children who want to go to school."

"Huh!" Logo grumbled. "So while everyone is dealing with the difficulties here, she's busy taking care of others. How inconsiderate!" He looked away.

Raga pointed out that the most important thing now was the postponement of Ndalo and Wula's wedding because Waleka and Wolli were sick, and Lamura needed to be cared for.

"Thank goodness!" Logo erupted. He stuffed a wad of betel into his mouth and began chewing. "Lara takes care of herself, Wolli gets better, and Bapa Leka is cured. So now the most important issue left is to redeem our shame as men of our ancestral house. Where are we supposed to hide our faces?" Logo paced the floor. "We need to prevent the ancestors from getting angry with us. This flat-roofed house has been around for a long time. Nenek is angry with all of us. So Ndalo and Wula will get married as soon as we get paid. That's the decision."

Uka nodded along with the other men and women who followed those who most easily gave away the world's treasures and spoke the words they most wanted to hear.

"Postpone!" Waleka suddenly spoke. Hamoli and Koni helped him sit up. Everyone looked at him, their eyes filled with various emotions.

Raga was relieved that his father's decision echoed his own wish. Even though he felt his father's pain, he could not say anything. It was not about postponing the wedding or executing it now, but about the hostility within the family that made all of this happen.

Now, the decision had been made.

Waleka's voice was going to be heard. The family decided to postpone the wedding until things were better — until Waleka was healed, Wolli was healthy again, Lara had returned to Ratenggaro, and Lamura's wound had completely closed. They decided that Raga, together with the elders in the extended family, should talk to Ndalo and his family.

Within a short time, word spread that the wedding had been postponed because Ndalo respected the troubles his bride-to-be's family was currently facing.

The wind blowing in from the sea shook every part of the flat roof. Relieved, Koni took a deep breath. She walked down the stairs to Lamura, who was tethered in the shade of the banyan tree at the edge of the cliff.

Hamoli followed close behind. The two of them brought Lamura a handful of salt. But that was not their real purpose of going there.

The door of Ndalo's ancestral house faced the beach, and it was easy to see the place where Lamura was tethered. Koni and Hamoli wanted Wula to see them.

"The worms at the Nyale were fat and colorful," Koni said, "a sign that the Pasola would go well and the events after the Pasola also would run smoothly. A promise of a bountiful harvest and sustenance in the years to come."

"Yes, Inya." Hamoli felt pain in her heart.

The two women sat quietly in front of Lamura. Neither could answer the question of why the abundance of the nyale catch had not been followed by a lively and meaningful Pasola. Neither could answer the question of why Lamura suffered and Wolli had been taken away in an unconscious state. It seemed that nature's plans were not always understandable to humans.

Chapter *43*

"She's as beautiful as the moon," Ndalo said. "Her name, *Wula*, the moon, suits her perfectly!" Without turning to Ama Dula, who stood next to him, hidden behind the lattice wall, he asked, "Why do you think they named her *Tila* Wula?"

"Like you said, she is as beautiful as the moon!" Ama Dula replied, impressed by Tila Wula's resilience and beauty. "Just like her name, Wula, she is the moon!"

"The moon …" Ndalo whispered. They stood behind the lattice wall of Ndalo's house, where it was easy to see Wula sitting with Lamura under the banyan tree.

"The moon is far away," Ama Dula commented.

"How beautiful she is!" Ndalo said, trying to reach Tila Wula with his eyes.

Stroking Lamura's neck, Tila Wula examined the horse's wound.

Ndalo swallowed as he followed Wula's every move. The girl had really brought him to his knees, and it was very difficult to get up again.

"She was worth waiting for, even fourteen years!" Ama Dula said.

"Fourteen years, three months, and seventeen days," Ndalo replied, covering his mouth for fear that his cough would startle the girl. "Oh, Wula, Wula …" He watched as Tila Wula stood. Her long hair was tied in a ponytail, almost reaching her knees. It made her look taller and slimmer, like a horse's tethering pole standing upright beside the house. Unlike the skin of other girls in the village, Wula's was milky white. Her beauty was a trademark from Lamboya, her mother's homeland. Almost all young women her age had already become wives and borne children. But Tila Wula was different.

"She's a school girl!" Ama Dula exclaimed. "A female teacher! Look at her holding a pen and writing — I mean, drawing."

"Actually, she didn't need to go to school," said Ndalo. "What for? What is being a teacher going to bring her? How much money will that make? What kind of fame? By marrying me, she will become the most popular woman in this area. Ndalo's wife! Ndalo's wife!" His voice trembled with a sense of power. He removed the wad of tobacco from his mouth as he continued trying to reach Tila Wula with his eyes. He gasped when Wula turned her head. Even though he knew she could not see him, Ndalo felt electrified.

"Connected by feelings," Ama Dula said.

"Do you think?" Ndalo grimaced. Three days after the Pasola, his groin still hurt.

"Sure!" Ama Dula chuckled. "She is your future wife; she can't run away anywhere. If it's not a connection of souls, what else could it be?"

Tila Wula lowered the school bag from her left shoulder and took out a sketchbook. She had promised Koda that she would draw Lamura for Wolli. Wula wanted to give the drawing to Wolli, so he could see how Lamura was doing. Koda would pick up the drawing before visiting Wolli in Lamboya.

Wula sat back down and began to draw Lamura's face up to the neck, which still oozed blood occasionally. The area around the wad of healing potion looked swollen and infected.

At the sound of hoofbeats, Wula rose to greet Koda. "Here's the drawing I promised!" Wula handed the drawing of Lamura to Koda. "Please give it to Gha Wolli — and tell him that Lamura is still not healed."

"It's a nice drawing," Koda said truthfully.

"Tell Gha Wolli that he must come home right away for Lamura!" Wula's voice trailed off.

"Don't worry, Wolli will return to Ratenggaro soon." Although Koda was saddened about Wula's fate, he was excited about what Lara was doing to obtain scholarships for the children in Ratenggaro. He was proud of the way Lara found the good in the midst of tenseness and sorrow.

Koda took a deep breath. He knew Lamura's injury from Ndalo's spear was not healing — and that was why Wolli had not yet returned to Ratenggaro. Wolli had heard about an old man in a remote area of Lamboya who made potions to treat serious laceration wounds — like those caused by unblunted javelins.

"Where exactly is Gha Wolli?" Wula asked quietly.

Koda smiled. "After he sees this drawing of Lamura, he will definitely come home soon."

Dusk had fallen when Ndalo woke up. Ama Dula was still sitting beside him.

Ndalo felt dizzy. The pain in his groin was becoming more frequent and was lasting longer. He took a long breath and exhaled loudly. Nausea roiled again, and he vomited through the bamboo grating of the floor. Grimacing, Ndalo peeked out to see Wula again. But Tila Wula and Koda were no longer there. Lamura stood alone.

Ama Dula explained to Ndalo that Wula had gone with Ida, each riding a horse and both wearing pants like men. And that they dared to ride alone in the saddle! Slyly, Ama Dula concluded, "They definitely left the village to go … who knows where."

"You said that Ida went too?" Ndalo asked.

"Yes," Ama Dula replied. "Wula wanted to ask for your permission, but you were sleeping. Maybe they went to catch up with Koda."

"Koda? My grandchildren don't know how to respect their elders," Ndalo snapped. "Why are you letting him near Wula, my wife? Leave immediately! Go after Wula and Ida. Do whatever it takes!"

Ama Dula departed hastily without another word.

Inya Tua approached Ndalo with a bowl filled with hot water infused with herbs. She dipped a small towel into the hot water, wrung it out quickly, and pressed it against Ndalo's groin.

Ndalo bit back a scream; Inya Tua smiled slightly.

"It's good you told Ama Dula to persuade Wula to postpone!" she said with satisfaction. "It's good you gave him permission to go to Lamboya and meet with Mada Wolli. How could you promise to get married in seven days? There are only four days left," Inya Tua emphasized the words *only four days*. She went up to the katendeng.

"Has Wula gone, Inya?" Ndalo asked, closing his eyes. The heat made his testicles throb.

Tila Wula and Ida rode quickly toward Mada Wolli's house in Lamboya. The tall grasses parted, opening a path down the middle of the field that vibrated under the horses' thudding hooves. Ratenggaro quickly fell far behind the two riders.

In Wula's eyes, Wolli was a real Ratenggaro man. It was true — he had come to Ratenggaro by way of Lamboya, but home to Mada Wolli was not Lamboya; home to Wolli was Ratenggaro.

Tila Wula spurred her horse on through the flat, expansive land. Ida was right behind her. The wind blew hard, pushing along the past that crashed endlessly like the pounding waves at Ratenggaro beach. Wula wanted Wolli to attend the upcoming confrontation between Waleka's and Ndalo's families. She wanted to confirm Wolli's stance towards her marriage to Ndalo. She wanted to make sure Wolli knew what decision she would make.

Suddenly, thundering hoofbeats surrounded the two girls, and a man jumped behind Ida in her saddle.

"Ida!" Wula screamed. But the wind carried her shouts across the field while the sound of the kidnappers' horses grew farther and farther away. Wula chased Ida's kidnappers, her courage overpowering the fear of being a lone woman under siege by men in the middle of a desolate field.

The kidnappers split up. Ida's horse suddenly vanished, and Wula lost the direction of Ida's disappearance. She dismounted. "Bo Kolo Mata – Mbe Leko Roka Tilu, the Big-eyed and Wide-eared One, please help!" Trembling with anger, Tila Wula cried and screamed Ida's name.

The sound of approaching hoofbeats quickly silenced her. Not just one horse, but many. She heard arguments, threats, and rustling sounds that circled, grew near, then moved away.

"We're going home," Wula said, mounting her horse and spurring it to a full gallop. She never looked back until she reached the top of the hill and could see Ratenggaro in the distance, directly alongside the beach, where the waves never stopped slapping and pounding.

As the road descended, she loosened her grip on the reins until they reached the flat path and the fieldhouses scattered around it. Briefly, Wula looked up to the hills. Although it was far away, she could see two horses and their riders standing there. Wula kept calm and assessed the situation. The recent troubles that had arisen kept her anger in check. Although her heart was burning, Wula knew she should continue on toward home.

Inside Ratenggaro, Wula dismounted. She tethered her horse near Lamura and hurried to Ndalo's house. She found Ndalo sitting up in his room, leaning against the wall. Inya Tua had just served him food.

"Please save Ida immediately," Wula said upon walking into the room.

Ndalo looked up briefly. He was furious.

Wula didn't flinch. "I know Ama Dula did this. So, now order him to bring Ida back immediately."

Inya Tua was stunned into silence by Wula's impudence. She left Wula to deal with Ndalo, who looked confused and had no words.

"Wula sent these pictures," Koda said as he took out the drawing Tila Wula had entrusted to him. He had just arrived to visit Wolli in Lamboya.

"Yes, she loves to paint horses — especially Lamura," Wolli replied, looking at the picture. His heart was torn by a longing he did not want to talk about. "When she was a little girl, she drew many pictures of horses. But everything went up in flames when she graduated from junior high school and the Big House burned. She didn't want to draw anymore for a long time. She started drawing again when she was about to graduate from community college." Wolli took a deep breath.

"This is her most recent drawing," Koda said. "Lamura is not healing."

Wolli looked at the drawing in silence.

CHAPTER 44

A strong sea breeze carried the sound of sobbing from Waleka's house. Lying on her bed in Ndalo's home, Wula knew that the tears the wind carried were from the mother who had given birth to her. "Don't cry, Inya," she whispered. "Out of love and respect for my Inya and Bapa, I will not back down." The wind also carried Lamura's low groans. "Until Gha Wolli returns, I will take care of you, Lenggu Lamura."

"Dolphin." She again heard Wolli's voice, explaining the name he had given his horse. "Lenggu Lamura means dolphin. Dolphins are created to help people and bring joy." It was Wolli's voice of so many years ago … when, together with his younger siblings, he bathed Lamura at Ratenggaro beach.

Wula smiled and folded both hands on her pillow.

"I want to be a dolphin," Lara had stated.

"Me too," Ida had joined in. "I like being a helper!"

"I also like to help Ida, Galuh, Lara, Gha Koda, and Gha Wolli," Wula had added. Now, she rose to sit up and lean against the side of the bed. She sighed and thought anxiously, *I can't help Ida now, nor the entire village of Ratenggaro and its surrounding villages.*

Wula was disappointed, watching Ndalo pretend to worry about Ida. She sensed there was something the old man was hiding about

Ida in order to smooth his own path. This convinced Wula to stick to her decision to get married. There was no need for a further delay.

"I want to be a dolphin," Ida's voice echoed from the past again. "Be a helper."

Now the pounding of the waves on the beach reached Wula. The silence amplified the sound. Wula laid back down, but before she could fall asleep, the roosters started crowing and the morning quickly lightened. Wula rose and walked to the terrace. The silvery rays of the new day's sun shot over the horizon, turning golden as they reached the high roof tops. Wula savored the sight while burying her pain deep in her heart.

Ever since the disastrous Pasola, Inya Tua no longer accompanied Wula. Instead, Inya Tua always stayed with Ndalo, in the master bedroom, right in front of the stone stove. In the room flanked by two large, sturdy, horse-carved pillars, Inya Tua took care of her husband.

Ndalo lay on the corner of the bed. His inflamed testicles had swollen even bigger, and he was extremely agitated. Every time he stood or took a step, he had to hold in the pain. Inya Tua had bandaged Ndalo's entire genital area with a cooling potion. Ndalo would feel comfortable for a while, only to complain more loudly a moment later. The nausea had returned and left him weak.

While helping her husband sit up, Inya Tua quipped bitterly, "This is great! You won on the Pasola field and gained a woman! Then, forgetting yourself in your moment of grand glory, you stood up on your saddle, jumped up, and landed on your balls. How do they feel now?"

"Inya ..." Ndalo whispered in Inya Tua's ear, "what do I do if Tila Wula wants to get married even though Ida is missing? What is going to happen? Let's find Ida, my missing granddaughter, first. Ida, my granddaughter who will become a teacher. As soon as Ida returns, we'll get married!"

"You care about Ida? About Koda?" Inya Tua asked sharply. She was very wise to the old man's tricks.

"Poor Ida," Ndalo whined again. "If Wula cares about Ida, I'm sure she will agree to postpone the wedding until Ida is back home."

"Stop pretending!" Inya Tua snapped. "It was you who told Ama Dula to kidnap Ida. You know that Ama Dula will return Ida home after your balls recover."

Annoyed, Ndalo moaned, "So what should I do? Don't make careless accusations. It's about Ida who was kidnapped. Find a shaman? Oh, what if the whole world finds out!"

"The whole world already knows!" Inya Tua scoffed. The old woman sat quietly by her husband's side, spinning yarn she would later use to weave. "The whole world also knows that you are hiding Ida, our granddaughter. You'd better be careful. If anything happens to Ida, the whole world will know everything — including what you did to the tip of the javelin you used to win the Pasola. In return, you fell and busted your balls on your saddle. I say, let the whole world know!"

Inya Tua continued spinning her yarn.

Waleka's family welcomed Raga and the council of elders he brought along. They sat down in a semicircle. In the other half of the circle sat Ndalo, accompanied by Ama Dula and elders of Ndalo's family.

Raga opened the discussion. "We sincerely apologize," he began. "We're not here to cancel the wedding. We only ask for your consideration to postpone it until Wolli recovers. Bapa Leka is also still unwell, as is Lamura. And Ida, Ndalo's granddaughter, is also still missing. Meanwhile, Lara is away, arranging scholarships for Ratenggaro's children."

"Postpone?" Ndalo straightened, grimaced, and immediately apologized for not being able to move from his seat because his leg hurt. He bowed his head silently, effecting an unwilling attitude. When he looked up, he arranged his face to display extreme disappointment. "It can't be!" he said theatrically.

"No, it can't be!" Ama Dula echoed. "You can't postpone it! We have already waited too long!"

"Stay out of it!" Ndalo scolded him, then moaned, "We can't postpone it! The wedding must be executed immediately!" Ndalo rubbed the corners of his mouth with the tips of his fingers and repositioned the betel nut wad in his mouth. "The dowry has been paid in full. Was the amount not enough? If that's the case, we can talk."

He tried to straighten himself again. Everything was fitting in nicely with his desire to have the wedding postponed to give him time to heal and make Tila Wula the young wife he would never allow to leave his side — not even for one night. He decided it was in his best interest to change the subject. "Ida, my granddaughter, is missing." Ndalo looked down sadly. "We must find her!"

Inya Tua shot a look at her husband. It pained her to know he would never change. Her husband would always want more wives, no matter how she took care of him — from night to morning, from morning to night, she had applied the cooling potion.

After a few moments of silence to steel himself and plead with the Big-eyed and Wide-eared One to save his parents, sister, and child, Raga said, "We're not asking for anything other than a short postponement. On behalf of the family, I beg you with all my heart. Bapa Ndalo, please help us. When you help Inya Koni and Bapa Leka, Wolli and Lamura, it's the same as helping your family. It means helping Tila Wula and Ida too."

After another moment of silence, Raga added quietly, "Also, how are you feeling, Bapa Ndalo? I believe that you, too, were injured at the Pasola. Have you recovered?"

Ndalo lifted his head and shifted the tobacco wad in his mouth. Ignoring Raga's question about his health, he said, "Yes, for Tila Wula's sake, I agree to postpone our wedding." He stared at the tall roof passage of the house. His eyes roamed slowly and caught the beautiful face of Tila Wula, who was watching him with a sharp gaze.

"What about Ida?" one of the elders asked. "That's your granddaughter. Is her absence not also a reason to delay?"

"Oh, that's right, that's right!" Ndalo grimaced. "Yes, yes, of course it is!" Ndalo shifted to a reluctant tone, conveying how extremely hard it was for him to make the decision to postpone his wedding with Wula. "Let's postpone the wedding to also look for my granddaughter. Please, please, let's postpone it if we must. It seems that we all have matters to take care of."

Wula looked deep into Ndalo's eyes and suddenly spoke, "There will be no postponing! Whatever the reasons may be, I don't want to postpone it. The wedding will still happen — immediately!"

"Wula!" Raga gasped.

Logo and Uka almost jumped out of their skin with excitement. Their wishes would soon be fulfilled. Both of them now stared hungrily at Wula.

Wula looked sadly at Raga and said, "Gha Wolli will be fine." She kept her tears in check by drinking a glass of water. After she caught her breath, Wula continued, "Ida will also be fine! I'm sure Bapa Ndalo can find Ida soon."

"Yes, yes, yes!" Ndalo puffed up, flattered.

"Wula!" Raga choked. "What's wrong with you?" Raga had expected Wula to accept Ndalo's agreement to postpone the wedding, but instead, here she was insisting that the wedding take place immediately!

"We should all be heartened that Bapa Ndalo is willing to postpone the wedding because he's concerned about everything that's going on," Wula continued firmly. "But Bapa, Ida, Gha Wolli, Lamura, all are going to be fine. Bapa Ndalo has waited too long already — ever since my father received the belis fourteen years ago. So now we shouldn't demand anything, including that our wedding be postponed."

Ndalo was pleased to hear Wula say "our wedding," but at the same time, he was distraught by the fact that under the circumstances, he couldn't have sex with Wula, no matter how much he longed to bring the young woman into his private room to become the real "we."

"Wula," Ndalo called in a pleading voice. "You are very kind. But you must also consider Bapa Waleka, who always worries about you. Your brother Wolli will need time to heal, and Lamura has also not yet recovered." Ndalo kept looking down as he spoke. The pain in his groin made him restless, and his restlessness only increased the pain.

"And what about finding your granddaughter Ida? Did you forget about her?" Tila Wula was furious that Ndalo had not mentioned Ida.

And so the tension rose, not only between Ndalo and Tila Wula, but also between Tila Wula and her family.

Wula knew that something had changed in the old man, who was typically loud, powerful, and wife-hungry. His choice to postpone the wedding and the glint in his eye when he looked at her had made that clear. Wula also knew that her older brothers Logo and Uka, only recently returned from living away, showed insincere concern.

"No, no, don't delay," Logo and Uka said triumphantly. "Wula is right!"

"If the wedding is delayed, then send me back to my parents' ancestral house!" Wula said. Her words were clear and deadly to Ndalo. "I am ready to fulfill what Bapa Ndalo wants and has been pursuing for almost fifteen years. Isn't this the time for you to get everything you want?"

"Wula!" Raga tried to calm her down.

"Don't postpone, Paghogha!" Wula replied confidently.

"Postponing is better," Raga insisted. "You'll marry when the roof is finished!"

"Yes, yes, yes, that's right," Ndalo said. "I agree. I'll help build the roof so the house won't be naked on our wedding day."

"Which roof do you want to help build, Bapa Ndalo?" Wula asked coldly. "Our ancestral house has had a flat roof since the 1974 Pasola, after I graduated from junior high school. It's been six years. But there was always a roof. I was the roof. Gha Raga, Gha Wolli, Inya Koni, Lara were the roof. All our family are the roof. Our house has never been without a roof!"

Raga shuddered. He tried to convince himself that Wula was really talking about the roof, just like Wolli once had all those years ago. "Wula!" he pleaded.

"Yes, Paghogha," Wula replied slowly. "But still, I insist that the wedding take place."

Ndalo trembled at Wula's words. He could not believe how firmly Wula stood by her choice. His fear of educated children like Wula was real. His anxiety about a student who took stationery from her bag and scribbled on her book in front of Lamura was real. All his life, Ndalo had traveled in response to the drive of his desires, which were easily fulfilled because of his power and position. Now he was brought to his knees by a harsh reality that he was completely powerless to overcome. It was the best kept secret in his relationships with his wives, and he intended to present it in a special way to Tila Wula.

He shook slightly as he pleaded with Raga and the rest of the family to go home and consider two possible options: hold the wedding now or postpone it. He said he and his family, including Wula, would discuss the matter privately before reconvening.

"Please go home," he repeated, holding his waist. *Go home, and go home quickly*! is what he really wanted to say, because the nausea in his gut was twisting along with the pain in his groin. The swelling of his testicles had only become worse as time moved on.

"No postponing!" Wula emphasized her preference once again. She looked at the members of Ndalo's extended family one by one. Her gaze stopped on Ndalo. With a sharp gleam in her eyes, she said, "If you dare to postpone our wedding, I will return to my family's ancestral house, and I will never come back here again! If the marriage is postponed, I must be returned to my parents according to the customary procedures!"

She didn't blink.

CHAPTER *45*

A sudden gale-force wind slammed into the village with a noise that equaled the thunder of hooves on the Pasola field. It rattled the ancestral house with the tallest roof to its core. But the shaking of the house was no more powerful than the shaking in Ndalo's chest, as he silently lamented his current circumstances.

Tila Wula did not want to simply end their relationship, she wanted to be officially released to her parents in the manner prescribed by local custom that assured she would never have to step foot in Ndalo's ancestral house again.

"Inya, what should I do?" Ndalo asked, grimacing in pain.

"Tila Wula must go home," Inya Tua replied matter-of-factly. "Do you know how well Lara is doing? Everyone in the village knows that Lara is taking care of scholarships for Ratenggaro children who want to go to school. All the villagers know that Lara will take care of educating Inya Pitu's children." Inya Tua smiled bitterly as she continued her attack. "Do you think Lara cares about your problem? Lara and Wula are the same! Do you dare to tangle with educated folks? Do you dare to oppose a teacher?"

"Where is Ida now?" Ndalo asked softly, averting his eyes.

"Ida is wherever you are hiding her." Inya Tua snorted. "You are shameless! Do you think I don't know that you know where Ida is?"

Defeated, Ndalo looked down. All of his acts of deception on the Pasola field had failed. The police had not believed Ama Dula's nonsense. Instead, they had believed Lara and Wolli's explanation of what had happened. His anger at Ama Dula and his disappointment with reality agitated Ndalo.

"Allow her to go home Inya?" Ndalo's voice was barely audible. "We could just send her straight home. There's no need for a traditional ceremony."

"Wula wouldn't want to return home without the traditional ceremony!" Inya Tua's voice shook. "Our granddaughter Ida is Wula's friend. Our grandson Koda is Wolli's friend. Both of them have been Tila Wula's big brothers for a long time. Don't you care about your grandchildren and children?"

"Allow Wula to go home, Inya?" Ndalo asked again.

"Not *allow* her," Inya Tua replied, "but return her home by custom. Just fulfill her request. Let her go home and never come here again." Inya Tua smiled with satisfaction. She happily picked up a lump of cotton and calmly started spinning it with her thumb and forefinger.

"Is that so?" Ndalo asked. He let out a long groan and retched again. His testicles were throbbing. Tila Wula's refusal to go home without the ritual ceremony made Ndalo gloomy.

Just as Ndalo, the elders, and the rest of the family had welcomed Wula into Ndalo's house on his front porch, he was now expected to hand her back to her parents on their front porch. Ndalo felt like he was being tossed around between the winds blowing inland and those going out to sea. Spun in a vortex, he was dragged to the center of the earth. He was embarrassed to realize he had to walk bow-legged. His enlarged testicles hung like ripe papayas between his legs. There was no way to conceal the dangling fruit with a sarong. Everyone would be able to guess easily what he was suffering from.

At Wula's family's ancestral house, Waleka was stunned in disbelief at Wula's choice.

Koni, bent over a small crate, pulled out an old cloth that had traveled through many generations and witnessed many weddings.

She would weave a new cloth for Wula. She also wanted to weave a new cloth especially for Wolli. Hopefully, he could wear it at next year's Pasola.

For a while, Waleka watched his first wife in silence. Then he walked down from the house to Lamura. The wound on the horse's neck had still not fully healed. Waleka stroked Lamura's back and looked at the flat roof of his ancestral house. He remembered Wolli and Wula's words with pride: *We all are the roof of our house.*

"Lamura! Don't be sad." Waleka whispered, stroking the horse's forehead. When Lamura did not raise his head, Waleka coaxed. "You know that Wolli found a nyale nest. This year, the nyale were colorful. The nyale harvest was unusually good." Waleka shook his head. "What happened, Lamura? Why did the Pasola bring disaster to you? Do you want to participate in the Pasola again next year?" Hoping to see Wula, Waleka stole a glance at Ndalo's front door.

Wula did come down from Ndalo's house, but she ran to Koda and Ida, who had just entered the village gate. They hugged each other tightly.

"I'm fine! I'm fine!" Ida said. "It's good that Gha Wolli and Gha Koda had the courage to act. Without them, I don't know what would have happened to me! Please don't be angry at my grandfather," she whispered. "In time, Kakek will realize his follies."

"Where is Gha Wolli?" asked Wula excitedly.

"With Bapa Raga. They will all be here soon!"

Moments later, Raga, Wolli, Hamoli, and Lara entered the village.

"Wolli!" Koni shouted.

Wolli ran to his mother.

Waleka limped toward the group, along with his grandchildren.

Wolli led his parents back to Lamura.

"Lenggu Lamura!" Wolli was stunned to see Lamura's condition. "Is your wound dry?" The horse lifted his head, and his eyes seemed to glow. "Lenggu Lamura …" Wolli leaned against the horse's side as Lamura gently licked the salt off his palm.

Koda stood next to Wolli. He had known from the beginning that the horse's wound was very deep. The blood had never totally stopped oozing. The festering, open wound and Lamura's feverish body temperature never improved. The horse was in bad shape. All of them fell silent around Lamura.

"Lamura …" Wolli bowed his head, "you are sick." He lovingly rubbed Lamura's back and took a small bottle from his waist bag. He squirted drop after drop onto Lamura's wound, gently rubbing in the medicine. Wolli vowed to heal Lamura with the herbal mixture he had brought from Lamboya. He felt certain that soon, the wound would dry and heal, and then the fever, too, would soon disappear.

As he doctored Lamura, Wolli thought about what had happened on the Pasola field. He remembered how Lamura had reared up at the exact moment that Ndalo's sharp javelin was flying toward him. The pointed tip of the javelin had flashed as it plunged into Lamura's raised neck. Wolli's last memory was falling to the ground, trying to clear his spinning head, and struggling to get back up to continue the Pasola. Then, darkness.

Trembling with emotion, Wolli embraced his wounded horse. "Lamura, thank you," he whispered tearfully. "I'm sorry for making you hurt and suffer like this."

Lamura's ragged breathing grew quieter and quieter, as Wolli pressed his head against his horse. Koda made room for Raga to hug the shoulders of the young man who shook violently. Wula stood next to Wolli, as Ida and Lara knelt beside Koni. Logo, Uka, and Waleka's other wives watched from a distance.

"You will recover, Lamura," Wula whispered. She still believed in the unusually good nyale harvest this year. Deep down, she also believed that this year's Pasola would also yield good results. Wula begged the Big-eyed and Wide-eared One with all her heart to heal Lamura — and heal the wounds of all those present.

Ndalo would not accede to Wula's request to marry immediately. Everyone gasped when Ama Dula approached the group standing around Lamura with the news.

"Ndalo wants to postpone the wedding?" Raga asked with sparkling eyes. "That means —"

"That means the wedding needs to be postponed!" Ama Dula interrupted. He knew that Wula would be sent home from Ndalo's house immediately, for reasons he did not want to explain.

"Postponed?" Wula asked, as she turned to face Ama Dula.

Ida, Wolli, and Koda stared at the man. No one understood for a moment how Ndalo had given Ama Dula permission to abduct Ida in order to achieve Ndalo's goal of postponing the wedding.

Wula had sensed that. "Postponed." Wula said again. "That means I will be taken back to my home immediately, according to custom!"

"Yes." Ama Dula did not dare not raise his face. "You will be officially returned to your parents' home with a traditional ceremony, just as when you were escorted to Ndalo's house. Immediately. Ndalo couldn't come to return you because of a back pain." Ama Dula kept looking down.

"No!" Wula said sharply. "Bapa Ndalo himself must stand in front of my house, the house without a tall roof. He has to stand in the midst of the elders and the women, just like when I was escorted to his house."

"Wula!" Raga warned.

"Fine." Ama Dula turned and started back toward Ndalo's house. "I'll tell him that even though he's not feeling well, you insist he returns you personally, himself."

The next day, Wula was returned to Waleka's ancestral house according to the appropriate custom. Ama Dula carried Ndalo to the door of Waleka's flat-roofed house. Only a few words were spoken by one of the elders as Wula was returned.

Koni welcomed her daughter with a woven wrap she had taken out of her special chest. Ama Dula quickly carried Ndalo back to his house. The decrepit old man was accompanied by the elders and other caregivers.

After Ndalo and Ama Dula left, the villagers approached, one by one, and circled Lamura with questions and admiration. Among them was Inya Pitu, who came with her baby and other children. Logo and Uka also came. Zoga stood silently among the others.

The wives of Waleka and Ndalo, their children and grandchildren in Ratenggaro, they all knew what pain and sorrow the old horse was suffering. They all knew how the horse owed his recovery to his master's kind-hearted spirit.

Waleka was deeply shaken by the apology he was unable to utter. He placed one hand on Wolli's shoulder, and the other on Lamura. Gratitude flooded his heart. Wula had come home.

Koni stood silently behind her husband.

You will definitely recover, Wolli thought, as Lamura's fever had broken. Aloud, he said, "We'll go to Ratenggaro beach. The sea water will make you heal even faster." Wolli's voice faltered before he continued, "We'll go to Lamboya. There's a smart man there who can remove all the poison from your body." Wolli now wept openly. Raggedly, he promised, "We're going to the Maliti Bondo Ate's Pasola field. Next year, you will be Ndara Halato to accompany Ndara Nyale, the leader on the Pasola field!"

Ndalo watched the gathering of Waleka family from behind the lattice wall of his house. Ama Dula sat silently next to him. He regarded Ndalo as his lord, but he had not succeeded in delivering Wula to fulfill Ndalo's wish. He had done the best he could for Ndalo to take Wula back to her home using the shortest and quickest way.

Meanwhile, Inya Tua spun her yarn with a smile, happy that Ndalo was disappointed with the decision that filled her with joy.

Inya Tua went out to the terrace of her house, leaving Ndalo alone.

"Inya, please help me!" Ndalo called out.

Inya Tua ignored him. She watched Wolli, sitting on Lamura's back, reach down to Wula. Grasping his hand tightly, Wula placed her foot behind Wolli's in the stirrup and swung up into the saddle behind him. Immediately, she leaned forward against his back. Wolli dismounted, then re-mounted behind Wula.

Lara and Koda were waiting on Wangga's back. Both girls sat in the front of their saddles. Wolli and Koda had agreed that, for once, the two girls would be in control.

A group of family members had gathered. Ida stood next to Zoga, her father. Hamoli, Raga, Waleka, and Koni were also there.

Everyone escorted Lamura, Wangga, and their riders to the village gate, as they headed to Lamboya, where they would visit relatives, but, most importantly, obtain the medicine to heal Lamura completely.

The horses galloped along the deserted road toward the gates of Ratenggaro. They rode through the cemetery, which lay silent in its own story. Wula and Wolli, followed by Lara and Koda, passed the Maliti Bondo Ate's Pasola field, which was quietly awaiting next year's Pasola.

After overcoming their problems in Ratenggaro, the young people rode through the parted grasses away from their home village, into a future filled with hope.

GLOSSARY

Alambaleko: Sumba motif

Ambu: grandfather

Bapa: father – also used to address a man who is respected / loved
regardless of age

Bau Nyale: the traditional annual ritual of catching sea worms

Belis: dowry

Binya bakolo: the main gate between gravestones

Binya wawa: a lower gate of a cemetery

Bo Kalo Mata Mbe Leko Roka Tilu: God

Bodho: nyale jerky

Destar: headband

Gha, abbreviation of paghogha: older brother

Hamoli: a gold pendant

Hanggi: cloth wrapped around the waist

Henggul: a triangular headband

Henggul katipia: a gold crown

Inya: mother - also used to address a woman who is respected / loved regardless of age

Inya nyu nyale: Mother of Nyale

Kabani pa ate: very clever and wise man

Kabisu: tribe

Kak: Indonesian word refers to someone older than the speaker

Kakek: Indonesian word for grandfather

Kambu luna: horse stable underneath the stilt house

Katendeng: a special place just for men in the Sumbanese traditional ancestral houses

Kawoking: mantra to call the sea worms

Kayiliking: whinnying noises made by female spectators of Pasola

Koro: a special place just for women in the Sumbanese traditional ancestral houses

Lamba leko: sarong

Lete: altar of the Marupu

Mamuli: earings

Marangga: necklace

Marapu: indigenous religion of the Sumba people

Marapu Rato: the Marapu altar

Ndara Halato: horse and rider team responsible to maintain the spirit of Pasola

Ndara Nyale: horse and rider team functioning as leaders of the annual seaworm harvest and one of the three leaders on the Pasola field

Ndara Wini: horse and rider team representing the fertile soil and abundant crops

Nenek: Indonesian word for grandmother

Nyale: sea worm

Nyale palowor: nyale stew

Opor: chicken cooked with coconut milk

Paghoga: Sumbanese word refers to big brother

Pandaluhari: the water of prayer

Pasola: annual traditional equestrian battle competition

Pitu Ndani Awung: the One on Seven Layers Above God

Praing marapu: heaven

Rato: chairman of the board of elders

Rato marapu: a traditional religious leader

Remba: food storage place to keep food for the man of the household when he is not home

Talu pinja namloro: spawn abundantly

To-paholong: pasola rider

Tom mtuna parona: traditional elder

Uma parona: traditional Sumbanese stilt houses

Yang bermata Besar dan Bertelinga Lebar: the Big-eyed and Wide-eared God

About the Author

Maria Matildis Banda grew up in Flores, East Nusa Tenggara, as the fourth daughter of 12 siblings. The two playgrounds she remembers most are the Kartini Field, in front of the local church, and the park beside the church, which was always filled with flowers. The Bajawa riverbank was a place to wash clothes, bathe, and fetch water, while the surrounding hills were a place to gather firewood with her siblings. Her childhood environment shaped her into a hard worker who is sensitive to and concerned about the environment.

As a child, Banda stuttered. This strengthened her passion for reading and writing, from elementary school through her doctoral education at the Cultural Studies Program, Faculty of Humanities, Udayana University, Denpasar. Since 1986, Banda has been a lecturer in the Indonesian Literature Program, Faculty of Cultural Sciences, at her alma mater.

In 2011, Banda received a scholarship to participate in the Sandwich Program, a three-month research period for doctorate candidates at Leiden Law School, Netherlands, where she studied Indonesian oral tradition and culture.

In 2014, she was invited to present on "Lota Script in Ende Flores" at the International Workshop on Endangered Scripts of Island Southeast Asia at Tokyo University, Japan. Banda has been an adjunct lecturer at FKIP UNDANA Kupang and the FKIP of the University of Flores in Ende, as well as a guest lecturer at the Catholic College of Philosophy (STFK) on the island of Flores.

As an author, Banda has won several short-story writing competitions, with many stories published in various magazines and public dailies.

In 2005, Banda began writing novels related to the local setting of the East Nusa Tenggara islands. *Bulan Patah* (Kanisius, 2021) focuses on a patriarchal culture and reproductive health in Ende, Flores.

Between 2017 and 2021, Banda wrote and self-published, in collaboration with the NTT Provincial Health Office, *Wijaya Kusuma dari Kamar Nomor Tiga,* a novel about maternal and child health in the grip of a patriarchal culture. She supported the self-publication of *Suara Samudra* (2017), a story about whaling in Lamalera, Lembata, Flores. In addition to writing novels with regional socio-cultural settings, Banda also researches and writes papers and journals on literature and oral tradition. Banda has written more than 1,000 *Situation Parody* articles in the daily *Pos Kupang.*

Pasola (Nusa Indah, 2023) is Banda's most recent work. The novel chronicles the lives of the people of Southwest Sumba, who are heavily influenced by the annual celebrations of *Bau Nyale* — the catching of sea worms at dawn — followed by the *Pasola*, an equestrian dexterity competition that involves throwing blunted javelins to unhorse opponents.

Banda is married to Dominikus Minggu Mere, Ph.D. They have five children: Carol Wojtila Petrus Advent Mere, MD; Mauren Tesalonika, MD; Yoseph Sinu; Arnolda Gala; Emerensiana Ere; and a beloved granddaughter, Camilla Matea Mere.

Maria Matildis Banda can be reached at: mbanda574@gmail.com.

ABOUT THE TRANSLATOR

Yuni Utami Asih grew up in Samarinda, East Kalimantan, and is the eldest of four children. Since kindergarten, her father pampered little Yuni with reading materials, such as *Bobo*, a children's magazine, fairy tales, and children's stories. She continued her love of words by reading various genres of books, especially detective and allegorical novels. Apart from reading, she enjoys outdoor activities, such as camping and hiking, in a nearby forest in Pampang village, about twelve miles from her home.

Asih started teaching English in 1999 while working on her bachelor's degree in the English Education Study Program at the Faculty of Teacher Training and Education, Mulawarman University, in Samarinda, Kalimantan Timur. She taught at several schools before becoming a lecturer at her alma mater in 2005.

Her love for teaching began in high school when she volunteered at an informal Al-Quran reading school for children in one of the small mosques in her neighborhood. This evoked her interest in continuing her education as a teacher.

During her doctoral education in English language teaching at the State University of Surabaya, in 2011, she received a Sandwich scholarship from the Indonesian Ministry of Education and Culture to deepen her research in phonology at Leiden University in the Netherlands.

Upon completion of her doctorate, Asih spent most of her time teaching at her alma mater, facilitating several national teacher-training programs, and publishing papers on Applied Linguistics and English teaching.

Pasola is Asih's first literary translation. It is a story with strong cultural elements set in Indonesia's old-society background of the 1950s. These characteristics demanded a translator with high sensitivity in determining the narrative language to make sure it was appropriate to the societal setting. Moreover, maintaining the original nuance and tone of the text required extraordinary bilingual skills.

Asih works and lives with her husband and two children in Samarinda, Kalimantan Timur, Indonesia.

She can be reached via: yuniutamiasih@fkip.unmul.ac.id.

MORE STORYTELLERS FROM DALANG PUBLISHING

Only a Girl
Lian Gouw

Three generations of Chinese women struggle for identity against the political backdrop of the World Depression, World War II, and the Indonesian Revolution. Nanna, the matriarch of the family, strives to preserve the family's traditional Chinese values while her children are eager to assimilate into Dutch colonial society. Carolien, Nanna's youngest daughter, is fixated on the advantages to be gained by adopting a western lifestyle. But when she raises her own daughter Jenny by colonial standards, it puts the girl at a disadvantage in new, independent Indonesia, where Dutch culture is no longer revered. The unique ways in which Nanna, Carolien, and Jenny face their own challenges reveal the complexity of Chinese society in Indonesia between 1930 and 1952.

Price: $22.75
Paperback: 298 pages
ISBN: 978-0-9836273-7-1

My Name is Mata Hari
Remy Sylado
Translated from the Indonesian by Dewi Anggraeni

My Name is Mata Hari tells the story of Margaretha Geertruida Zelle, a young Dutch woman married to an older military officer assigned to the Dutch East Indies. Claiming her mother's Javanese ancestry, she changed her name to Mata Hari, Malay for "eye of the day."

As Mata Hari, she danced on stages across Europe and the Middle East, and took many high-ranking military and government officials as her lovers. Convicted of espionage during World War I, she said at the end of her tumultuous life, "I am a genuine courtesan. And I am a dancer in the true sense."

Price: $22.75
Paperback: 342 pages
ISBN: 978-0-9836273-0-2

Potions and Paper Cranes
Lan Fang
Translated from the Indonesian by Elisabet Titik Murtisari

In Lan Fang's award-winning novel, Sulis is a young woman selling potions in Surabaya's harbor district. She meets Sujono, a day laborer with dreams of becoming a freedom fighter, and whose passion for Matsumi, a geisha called to Java by a Japanese general, is destined to ruin all of them. Each tells the story of their lives during the Japanese occupation of Java and Indonesia's transition from a Dutch colony to an independent republic.

Price: $22.75
Paperback: 252 pages
ISBN: 978-0-9836273-3-3

Kei
Erni Aladjai
Translated from the Indonesian by Nurhayat Indriyatno Mohamed

At the end of Suharto's New Order, the Kei people hold on to their traditions as they flee the violence that divides Muslim from Christian and destroys the villages. Namira, a Muslim girl, works as a volunteer in a refugee camp when she meets Sala, a young Protestant man. Grounded in the islander's belief of "We drink from the same spring and eat from the same land, the land of Kei," the two fall in love amid the chaos that will soon separate them.

Price: $22.75
Paperback: 228 pages
ISBN: 978-0-9836273-6-4

Daughters of Papua
Anindita Siswanto Thayf
Translated from the Indonesian by Stefanny Irawan

Seven-year-old Leksi lives in modern-day Papua with her grandmother Mabel and her mother, Mace. Her companions are Pum, an old dog of unknown ancestry, and Kwee, a pig. Together they look back at the past, as they face an uncertain future. In *Daughters of Papua*, the present is marked by a contentious election, with the gold company that wants to rob Papuans of their heritage the only winner.

Price: $22.75
Paperback: 204 pages
ISBN: 978-0-9836273-9-5

The Red Bekisar
Ahmad Tohari
Translated from the Indonesian by Nurhayat Indriyatno Mohamed

The *bekisar* is a fine crossbreed between jungle fowl and domestic chicken that adorns the houses of the wealthy. Lasi, whose father was a Japanese soldier, fair skinned and beautiful, is such an acquisition for a rich man in Jakarta. She is born in a village where the main source of income is tapping coconut palms for their rich sap, or nira. Her life takes an unexpected turn when she is betrayed by her husband and flees to Jakarta. She meets Mrs. Lanting, procuress of companions for men in high government and social circles, who sells her to the rich Handarbeni. Lasi enjoys her new splendor as a much-desired ornament, but is alarmed when she discovers the marriage is a sham. When she reconnects with Kanjat, a childhood friend now grown into a man, Lasi and Kanjat rediscover their affection for each other. Their bond is the village, its people and traditions. Together they struggle to free Lasi from a net of power, corruption, and deceit.

Price: $22.75
Paperback: 294 pages
ISBN: 978-0-9836273-2-6

Love, Death and Revolution
Mochtar Lubis
Translated from the Indonesian by Stefanny Irawan

During the early days of their nation's revolution, Indonesians were driven by passion and built a future on dreams. In a world still reeling from World War II, Major Sadeli of the Indonesian Army Intelligence travels to Singapore tasked with establishing naval and air routes to Sumatra and Java as well as securing weapons and radio equipment vital to the revolution. His desire for Indonesia to be prosperously independent, and independently prosperous, forces him to choose between personal happiness and commitment to a higher cause.

Price: $22.75
Paperback: 324 pages
ISBN: 978-0-9836273-5-7

Cloves for Kolosia
Hanna Rambe
Translated from the Indonesian by Miagina Amal

Elderly widower Gamati swears to save his family line from extinction when he and his family <u>fall</u> victim to the infamous plunder expeditions of the VOC, the Dutch East India Company. To escape the colonialists' cruelties, he leads his orphaned grandchildren and a small group of fellow villagers to the safety of another, more remote, island north of their current location. The birth of his great-grandson Kolosia during the voyage assures Gamati of his family's ability to sail the Moluccan seas freely for generations to come.

Price: $22.75
Paperback: 350 pages
ISBN: 978-0-9836273-8-8

Blood Moon Over Aceh
Arafat Nur
Translated from the Indonesian by Maya Denisa Saputra

The story is set between 1989 and 2002 in Alue Rambe, an isolated agricultural village south of Lhokseumawe City, in Aceh, Indonesia. Born in 1976, into a farmer's family, Nazir's life becomes a part of Aceh's dark, rebellious history that recounts the injustice the Soeharto government imposed on the Acehnese.

Price: $22.75
Paperback: 354 pages
ISBN: 978-0-9836273-4-0

Dasamuka

Junaedi Setiyono
Translated from the Indonesian by Maya Denisa Saputra

A Scottish academic, journeying to the island of Java in 1811, is quickly drawn into the struggle of the Javanese people as they fight back against colonial powers and their own corrupt aristocracy. Willem Kappers, a Scottish scientist, learns about intrigue in nineteenth century royal Javanese court and witnesses colonialism change powerful kings into puppets of the Dutch and English authorities. Kappers' involvement with an ambitious Javanese nobleman, Dasamuka, gives the reader an intimate glimpse into the struggle of the Javanese commoner against the oppression of the reigning sultan as well as the colonial powers.

Price: $22.75
Paperback: 266 pages

Panji's Quest

Junaedi Setiyono
Translated from the Indonesian by Oni Suryaman

Panji's Quest — a love story — is a part of the only original Indonesian stories that have been widely disseminated and were later combined into the Panji Tales which UNESCO included in their Memory of the World Documentary Series. Panji, crown prince of Janggala and Sekartaji, crown princess of Kadiri, have been engaged since they were youngsters. However, court intrigue which references philosophical teachings of old Javanese traditions, to present critique and advice on religion and leadership separates them at the moment they were to marry. Only after Panji has finished his quest is the couple reunited.

Price: $22.75
Paperback: 277 pages
ISBN: 978-1-7357210-1-9

Footprints / Tapak Tilas
This bilingual compilation of 49 carefully selected stories about Indonesia's colorful — albeit painful — history, rich culture, and diverse population features 44 authors and 18 translators.

The multigenerational authors range from established literary figures to young up-and-comers, fresh on the win of their first regional writing competition. The cast of translators is equally varied. Together, authors and translators offer the reader a wide variety of writing styles.

These narratives take the reader back to Indonesia's colonial times, through the revolution, and to today's independent Indonesia. Given this comprehensive range of material substance, the book satisfies most any reader's interest.

The side-by-side presentation of the bilingual short stories we have gathered on our website over the course of ten years, makes *FOOTPRINTS / TAPAK TILAS* a remarkable resource for aspiring translators, as well as writers.

Price: $32.50
Paperback: 878 pages
Bilingual: Indonesian/ English
ISBN: 978-1-7357210-6-4
E-book ISBN: 978-1-7357210-7-1